# MORTAL GODS

SOREN BECK

For my fiancé, who forever will be my person, alpha reader, editor, and beta reader.

Without you, this work would not have been possible.

# CONTENTS

# FOREWORD

Mortal Gods has been a huge passion project—one I always find myself excited to sit down with, re-read, and expand. A lot of blood, sweat, and tears have been poured into it by quite a few people, all of whom have my deepest respect.

It shocked me when I began, and still does, just how many folks it takes to bring a novel into existence. There are so many friends I relied on for support, reading, and love that I cannot name everyone who truly assisted in the writing process.

The first people I should mention are all my friends who acted as alpha and beta readers and bore the brunt of my rambling rants about lore, the writing process, and self-aggrandizing. In no particular order, I would love to thank Ella, Sam, Nic, Brandon, Dane, and JJ. To those of you who suffered through several chapters of my early drafts—you are saints beyond measure.

Next up on my list are my two editors, Kelsey and Jenny. Both of these wonderful individuals helped immensely by pointing out flaws in my story and hammering my prose into a form I'm willing to share.

Of course, I want to thank my fiancé, Ariel. Her consistent, gentle, and kind critiques helped me learn to accept edits in a safe environment. Not to mention, her support in pushing through to the end of the project is immensely appreciated.

Finally, I want to thank you, reader. No matter how you found this, know that I appreciate your foray into the words of my mind. I hope you enjoy your stay and take a brief leave from the tumultuous world we live in.

# CHAPTER ONE

# THOSE WHO WALK IN THE NIGHT

*NO ONE DEFIES THE will of the gods.*

Candles flickered on the edge of the stage, the light dancing as the music ebbed and flowed through rhythms of song. The silhouetted features of the performer distorted as they flitted against the curtain draped behind her. The dress she was wearing, a dull maroon with a plunging neckline, seemed to sway in a gust affecting only her as she stepped from side to side. Her hair, like threads of curled gold, framed her cherubic face as she sang a somber tune about lovers who were together reluctantly in a language the audience didn't understand.

It was utterly beautiful.

Ilara brushed a strand of dark hair out of her eyes as she watched the show. Scanning the crowd, she sipped her scotch. The taste bit her tongue in a way that felt right. She wouldn't have chosen this bar, The Pearl, if business didn't require it. It was best to keep her sister, the singer, as far from Ilara's work as possible.

Still, it was nice to see that Sophia was doing well. They hadn't spoken in years, and Ilara intended to keep it that way.

She had lost track of the number of songs her sister had sung by the time the bartender, a portly man with a graying goatee, indicated that someone at the other end of the bar had sent her a drink. Ilara hazarded a glance in that direction and saw a wrinkled face grinning back at her. The man gave her a gentle wave, as if he were patting the air. She smiled and waved back, taking the new scotch and walking it over to him.

Finding the stool next to him, she settled into the red velvet cushion, thanking him for the liquor.

"Stiff," he said with a grin. "My kind of drink."

"And expensive." She smirked, sliding it to him.

He grabbed the glass by the top and took a long draft. As he set it back down on the bar, Ilara saw a dusting of white powder fall into the dark liquid. She'd expected this and likely would have missed it if she hadn't been looking for it.

"My kind of drink," he repeated as he pushed it back toward her.

Ilara raised the glass to her mouth, barely parting her lips to feign a sip. The man grinned, and she knew the trap was set.

"I'm surprised you aren't swimming in drinks," he said, his eyes darting over her shoulder and then down to the floor. "I haven't seen you in here before."

"I'm new to Eversburg," Ilara replied with a forced chuckle.

"What's your name?"

"Ilara," she said instinctively. She'd had another one prepared, but it felt wrong in the moment. It wouldn't matter if this man knew her name or not. He won't be alive long enough to remember.

"And you are?" she asked.

"Ilara," he said, stretching out each syllable like he was sampling a fine vintage. "Putnam is the name. What brings you to our fine city?"

*Senator Putnam Plithy*, she thought.

"Oh, I'm from a small town a few days south. My hope was that there would be a lot more to, well, to experience here," she said as her hand found his and ran up the length of his arm. It was thin, but there was a certain strength to the muscles. Enough strength to kill a woman.

His grin widened. "I'm sure there is."

*Take the bait.*

"What kind of experiences were you hoping for?" he asked.

"Well," Ilara said, meeting Putnam's gaze, "meeting a strange man in a bar is certainly a good start."

"And what comes next?" He shifted uncomfortably in his chair.

"That isn't something a lady should say in such a public place," she said, her voice rising in pitch.

His cheeks reddened. "Well, I do have a room rented across the street, if perchance you'd like to tell me about it there?"

"Only if you can show this girl a thing or two."

"My, you certainly are to the point," Putnam growled.

Ilara leaned in, moving her face toward his as if going for a kiss, but brushed past his mouth to whisper in his ear. "We can skip the formalities." She felt him stiffen at her touch.

*By the Pantheon, I thought he'd be smoother than this.*

"Sacred Akara, what are we still doing here, then?" Putnam grabbed her arm and stood quickly, his fingers biting into her skin as he dragged her to the exit.

He offered her his coat as they approached the door. She accepted, reluctantly. The slim-fitting dress she was wearing wasn't suited for the cold of this northern city. She wrinkled her nose at the smell of cloveweed as Putnam draped the fur-lined jacket over her shoulders. Ilara's father had been a chain-smoker as well. She'd always associated the smell with men, and she hated it.

Stepping out into the cold winter air made her glad she'd worn her boots rather than anything with heels and open toes.

A fresh layer of snow covered the ground, crunching gently against the cobblestone. A woman wearing metal plate armor stepped forward as they began walking toward the inn. Putnam waved, and she fell in behind them, following at a close proximity but not so close as to encroach upon them. Ilara hadn't been expecting a bodyguard, though the eyes in the helmet were dull, telling her the woman wasn't Akaran. Likely, she wouldn't be a problem.

Those not Chosen by the gods were never a problem for Ilara.

Inside, the walls of the inn were covered in messy, uneven plaster, which had yellowed from decades of cloveweed smoke. The wooden floors were worn, trodden down by barmaids, travelers, and prostitutes. The place stunk of sex, like shame incarnate.

The establishment was sparsely populated. Most people who stayed here were in the city on business—farmers looking to sell an out-of-season crop or clergy learning their trade. This time of year, it was usually the latter. White robes with gold lace and chains garbed most of the residents making use of the pub, and while their profession was holy, their desires were likely not.

Putnam nodded to several men as he marched toward the stairs on the left. They all knew what the inns on this end of town were used for.

"Ever been to a place like this?" he asked. He didn't bother turning his head to look at Ilara.

"Can't say so," she replied. *More times than I can count, to find men like you.*

She followed Putnam up the narrow steps into a hallway lined with doors. After a few moments, his guard clomped up after them. As they walked the length of the corridor, muffled moans and cries wafted out from several of the occupied rooms.

Putnam stopped at the end of the hall, outside the luxe suite. Ilara knew he came here often enough to know the best room. She'd spent weeks preparing for this moment. Tracing his every movement had been time consuming, but it was going that extra mile that made her the best at what she did.

Desire mounted in her mind. It ate at her. It hadn't yet built to a headache, but it would soon if she didn't get a release.

The senator fumbled the key with a shaky hand. The lock clanked, and the door flew open. He gestured her in, and she glanced down the hallway to see the armored figure standing uncomfortably between two rooms. Ilara relished the privacy.

The décor in the suite was modest by a nobleman's standards—wooden furniture decked out with colored cushions and a bed with fluffier blankets than Ilara could stand. Tapestries that depicted the origins of the seven gods of the Pantheon covered the wall. Most were fraying at the edges, except for the one of Almir—the fallen soldier who'd been slain a hundred years ago to be raised to godhood by his trusted goddess, Akara.

Once the door was closed, Putnam drew Ilara's face to his and gave her several sloppy kisses across her lips and cheeks. The smell of cloveweed was overpowering, and she could barely keep herself from gagging. His hands ran up and down her body as he pushed her into the door, the fur coat falling to the floor.

His hand wrapped around her throat. "Is this what you were looking for, whore?" he asked, pinning her against the wood. He was crushing her trachea, cutting off her breath. His features darkened as he looked at her with utter contempt. The mask fell. He thought he'd caught her in his web.

"Close," she choked out.

"You would enjoy this, you slut. I can't wait to unwrap your corpse." He had a wild expression on his face. "I'm going—"

Ilara didn't let him finish, activating a tract of magic hidden deep in a quiet place of her body. Energy ran up and down her forearms like small pin pricks, and a dagger etched itself into existence line by line, from magic into metal.

The handle took shape in her hand, held close enough for the blade to form inside Putnam's chest, under his ribs and aimed toward his shoulder blades. She ripped it out of him, removing a chunk of his flesh with it. Blood dripped across the floor, seeping into the wooden boards like a vile ooze.

Putnam gasped. He released her, clutching the fresh hole in his body. A second blade formed in Ilara's other hand. She didn't hesitate, plunging it into the bastard's throat. He fell to the floor with a thud and reached out forlornly toward her.

"Senator Putnam Plithy. A man who uses public funds to bed prostitutes, kill them, and fuck their corpses," she said. His eyes widened as his sputtering breaths struggled in his throat. "Surprised I know about your crimes? You were very thorough with your victims—hidden in death pits and alleyways. No one investigates a dead prostitute. But no one can silence the dead. They speak to me, condemning you and your deeds. And I, Plithy, will not be your victim tonight. You will be mine."

Putnam's last breath gurgled from his throat, and Ilara saw him slump down to the ground. She smiled, bathing in the pleasure of a well-placed trap. She drank in the scene before her eyes, a sacrifice to her brutal goddess. A condemned soul sentenced to a life of torment.

The lock clanked behind her. She whipped her head around to see Putnam's guard standing in the door, staring at her with wide eyes. In the light, Ilara could see she was a stocky woman with the symbol of the god Almir—a sword haloed by a rising sun—emblazoned on her chest. She raised her weapon toward Ilara.

"Trabema lucin," she shouted, and a blast of light shot from the point of her sword toward Ilara's head. Ilara dodged the beam, which smacked into the curtains on the far wall, immediately setting them on fire. Daggers were no match against the guard's longer blade. Ilara had no choice but to escape.

She ran a finger from one side of her forehead to the other, brushing some of her hair away as she did. A different tract of magic filled, and she felt the pin pricks run down her entire body as she faded from sight.

The guard remained in the doorway, blocking Ilara's only exit. Time was against her as the room filled with smoke from the burning curtains. It would give her away sooner rather than later. The guard shouted again, and another beam of light launched at Ilara. A quick side step, and another tapestry erupted in flame.

Mustering all her strength, Ilara charged the armored woman. Her shoulder caught the guard in the stomach, the grooves of the plate digging into Ilara's flesh. The two of them fell together, crashing to the ground. Visions of ending the guard's life flashed through Ilara's mind. How many women had she let die while guarding Plithy?

But there was no time. Ilara was satisfied that her target was dead, and she needed to get out—now. As she bolted down the hall, many of the doors opened, and men and women of various ages and states of undress looked toward the source of the commotion. Several doors slammed shut again as the guard began firing more beams toward the Ilara. Her invisibility made her escape inevitable, and the growing panic of the fire gave her a crowd she could slink into.

In the midst of the chaos, a bare-chested woman collided with Ilara. Confusion etched her face, but was soon disregarded as other terrified patrons surged with them.

Once outside the inn, Ilara slipped into the shadows, yet lingered. She hoped that all the patrons had made it out safely and that the water brigade would soon arrive. Scanning the panicked faces around the fire, which had quickly become a spectacle, she searched for the guard, with no luck.

A man was standing in an alleyway across from the inn, silently watching the blaze as he smoked a cigar that had already burned down to a nub. The bartender, Tarin. Ilara dropped her focus on her magic, and her invisibility faded as she approached him.

"Hail to those who walk in the night," she said as she leaned against the wall across from him.

"May the shadows have your back," he replied. "What happened in there, Thorn?"

"Senator Plithy is dead, as per the contract. He had an attentive guard, though. Caught me by surprise."

"A contract you pushed to take," Tarin huffed. "Still was a bit clumsy. Was he a paladin, then?"

"Maybe." Ilara shook her head. "She had the symbol of Almir."

"Don't get many of those around here. There a difference between Akaran and Almiran?"

"The name of their god." Ilara shrugged. "I need to go. We done here?"

"Fine," Tarin replied. "See me tomorrow for your payment."

"I'd never miss it. Lady be with you," she said as she reactivated her spell and disappeared again.

She heard him chuckle as she turned down the alley.

Chapter Two

# DEBTS

The streets of Eversburg were empty of the bustling carriages and pedestrians usually dodging and weaving past each other, trying to get to whatever building they were working in or shipping from. Ilara wore a cha'ak, a face mask that covered her nose and mouth, to mark her as a member of the Gray Syndicate.

Cha'aks were the traditional garb of killers for hire. The simple black pieces of cloth had small runic markings embroidered on the inside that masked the wearer's breath and speech. They had been used by the Aoxians, the scaled people of the south, during the time before Akara ascended the throne of the Pantheon. A cha'ak was not bought; it was earned in blood when an assassin's first target was killed. Ilara had won hers by taking a rival assassin's life years ago. The poor fool had thought she was in another city, working a different contract. At least until her daggers found his throat.

Here in the night, Ilara crossed paths with few aside from the occasional mugger or prostitute evading the night watch. They gave her a wide berth—not that they were prey worth hunting.

Killing was easy for her. Zal'Keratha, the goddess of death , had Chosen Ilara early in life. Not only did this allow Ilara to access stores of the goddess's magic, but Zal'Keratha's cult had trained her on how to end a life. Few could call this gift theirs, and a divine could only ever choose one to bestow it on —unless they were part of the Pantheon of gods. Ilara didn't know how many Chosen the queen of the Pantheon had created. She'd killed a lot of them, though.

Ilara's determined pace brought her to a brick tenement building a dozen stories tall, its walls lined with windows spaced an arm's length apart. Far from the smooth limestone cathedrals and houses that characterized the north end of the city, the structures here were run down and smelled of human waste. Discarded food and the bodies of dead animals lined the streets.

Scanning the building, Ilara noted a number of open windows up to the fourth floor. She scaled the side wall with ease. The holds she relied on were familiar, and as trusty as the day she'd found them. An open brick here, an extended waste pipe there, all giving her the leverage she needed to get to the next one.

She'd barely built up a sweat before arriving at her destination: an unassuming, but closed, window that guarded the thing that was most important to Ilara.

Her sister's blonde hair glistened in the moonlight that shone through the glass. Normally, this sight would have been sufficient, and Ilara would climb back down and be on her way, satisfied in knowing her sister was safe. Tonight, however, she slipped her fingers under the windowpane to slide it open. It thudded against the latch, and Sophia sprang up instantly, a blade in her hands.

Their eyes met. Sophia rolled her green eyes as she reached up to unlatch the window.

"What the fuck, Ilara?" she demanded.

"Is that any way to greet your sister?" Ilara grinned. Wind whipped at her side, amplified by the rows of buildings. She glanced down at Sophia's knife, still held between them. "Mind putting that thing down and letting me in? It's freezing this time of year."

"If you took the stairs like a godsdamned normal person, you wouldn't be so bleeding cold," Sophia replied. Still, she placed the knife on her nightstand and moved for Ilara to climb through.

Ilara did so gracefully, allowing the cold to creep off her, and welcomed the warmth. Sophia lit a candle, placing it beside the knife. Ilara slid the window closed and rested her back against the wood-framed glass.

A pillar of brick covered in runes stood in the center of the one-room tenement, one of the enchanted supports holding up the weight of the building. Halga's Crafter Chosen made incredible structures. Sophia had done a lot with the place. Faded paintings of various music groups hung from the walls, but Ilara only recognized the Masked Twins. The wardrobe, bed, and table were all made of matching maki wood. The apartment would have felt welcoming if not for Sophia's reddening face.

"You come here, in the middle of the bloody night, at my fourth-story window, after seven years of not hearing from you. What the hell is wrong with you? I thought you were dead. Or that you'd left. Or worse." Sophia paced the length of the room as she spoke.

"Your set tonight was beautiful, Soph," Ilara said, hoping to deflect the conversation.

Sophia abruptly stopped her pacing and gave a mock bow. "Thank you. Apologies we had to end early due to the fire across the stree— Wait. That was your doing, wasn't it?"

Ilara nodded. "Not mine exactly, but someone after me. Luckily they missed, or I would be suffering the same fate as the inn. Someone who saw my face while I was working."

"And you came here? Were you followed, too?" Sophia asked.

"I saw no one before coming this way. Not just that—the streets feel different lately. Like everyone is waiting for something."

Sophia hesitated again, her eyes wide with fear. "I know what you mean. There's been talk of revolution at The Pearl. New folk each time, too. Then there's the street preachers, who got overrun with young lads talking with the same fire about killing clergy that they used to use for worshiping the gods. Can you believe that? I don't think anyone could kill a pal if they tried."

"Not even a paladin is invincible, Soph. I'm sure many have died to lizards in that bloody war," Ilara replied.

The war burning in the south wouldn't have gone on for so long if the paladins weren't killable. They were holy warriors of the goddess Akara, who controlled the sun and was the reigning queen of the Pantheon of gods. Her war against Aoxia had seemed never-ending—until she killed Aox, god and creator of the lizard-kin and former king of the Pantheon. Akara had deposed him of the throne a hundred years ago, and was dead set on seeing him and all of his creation perish.

"Since I was seen working tonight, I'll need to leave the city as soon as possible." Ilara's hands fingered the cha'ak around her neck. "I doubt the paladins will come for you, but I had to give you a warning."

Sophia's eyes went to the floor. "I had a feeling it would come sooner or later. Hard to say when they'd use the Sight to track you. Know where the road will take you?"

"South, probably. Closer to the front. I should get lost in the mess of supply lines. Even Ameri's Sight can't untangle that."

"You know who it was? Who saw you?"

"No. An Almiran. Dressed in enough armor to show off being a paladin. And she channeled magic, so she's one of his Chosen."

"Oh." Sophia was silent for a moment.

Ilara hated that she was showing up just to tell her sister that she was leaving. She never left Sophia behind, but they were adults now. No reason for them to get caught up in each other's business.

"Did this Chosen have many tracts?" Sophia asked.

Ilara shrugged. The tracts the gods gave their Chosen from which to channel spells allowed them to store a set amount of their god's energy. Ilara's tracts felt like hollow areas in her body, and activating them drained the magic stored there. The magic for Ilara's creation spell was stored in her forearms, and the invisibility spell in her forehead.

"The Almiran channeled a single spell. I'd wager a fortune that she knows a couple more," Ilara mused.

Sophia's eyes were downcast again, as if she were trying to find the words she needed in the wooden floorboards. Balan, the god of magic and Sophia's patron, hadn't given her any tracts. Ilara knew that her sister could access his power, though she was hazy on how the process worked.

"What does Zal'Keratha think of you leaving?" Sophia asked. "She afraid of a single Almiran?"

"I haven't spoken to her about it yet," Ilara muttered. "She'll figure it out."

"Sounds like you're on the fast track to becoming Forsaken."

Ilara shrugged. She'd tried not to think about it. If she were Forsaken, the goddess would strip Ilara of her magic and withdraw her from the Chosen. Even worse, it would paint a target on Ilara's back for anyone who wanted to gain Zal'Keratha's favor, given what serving her goddess was like.

"I'll figure that out if it comes to it," Ilara said.

"So we're going to run from everything again, rather than sticking around to find out?" Sophia asked.

"Not we," Ilara countered. "You have no reason to get caught up in my business. And it's safe here, more or less."

"Aye, it's that 'more or less' bit that's the problem." Sophia cleared her throat and sat down on the bed next to her sister. "I have my own reasons for getting out of this city. About time it came to that, anyways. Been missing the road a bit too much, I have."

Ilara eyed her suspiciously. "I thought your music was going well? You said once that The Pearl was the perfect place to sing, what with the acoustics and all that."

"Aye, The Pearl is great, but I owe money to some people. All the fancy dresses and broken lutes—they add up, and The Pearl doesn't pay well enough." Sophia wiped a tear from her cheek. "I'm done with it, if we're ready to move on."

"Who's the shark?" Ilara asked, though she already knew. She'd discretely directed Sophia to him when she'd learned her sister was having money problems. The Gray Syndicate was supposed to help the family of its members. They were criminals, but the whole organization worked because they took care of each other.

"Some bloke named Jonas." Sophia sighed. Anger grew in Ilara's chest, and Sophia's face grew concerned. "Don't do what you're thinking," she warned.

"I know the man. I'll take care of it," Ilara replied.

"It's not worth the blood."

Ilara sprang from the bed, smoothing out her cloak and leathers. "Let me do what I'm good at for you, one last time."

"And what happens when you're gone? Do you really think they're going to forget? Or that you can murder everyone with a memory?" Sophia demanded.

"For you, I can try." Ilara propped the window open again. "And you've changed cities for me too many times. Build a life for yourself here, find someone who cares about you. Forget that I exist."

"Like that's possible. If you aren't leaving tonight, which it doesn't sound like you are, stop by one last time. If I'm going to forget you, let me have one final memory of my only sister."

"Aye to that." Ilara nodded. "I have a few errands to take care of in the city before leaving. I'll be back tomorrow night. We can have a drink at The Pearl before I hit the road."

She stepped out through the window, and felt a voice in the back of her head whisper, "*You better be finding the altar tomorrow. It is the only thing that matters.*"

***

The night was cold in comparison to the warmth of her little sister's tenement building. Ilara's cloak caught the warmth of her body and held it close. They were useful fashion, cloaks.

Both the gentry and the peasants preferred them in the winter months, which Eversburg had nearly half a year of. Not only did the thick material hold in the warmth, but it also did well at disguising one's form. With her cloak, Ilara could pass as a noble lady, or hide among the shadows.

Not being able to shake the feeling of being watched, she glanced around as she walked. No one was following her. No one even roamed the street behind her. Emboldened, she marched deeper into the Dusk district.

Eversburg was made up of three districts—Dawn, Dusk, and Noon—watched over by Akara, goddess of the sun, Queen of the Pantheon. Eversburg was her holy city, the northern tip of the vast Akaran Empire. Sophia lived on the edge of the Noon and Dusk districts, barely a block into Dusk. The Noon district was predominately where trade happened, with enough stalls set up in the squares to form a long bazaar during the day. Even during the night, most peddlers of darker wares found their way into Noon to sell their services to those of higher status.

Dusk was the lowest section of the city, both by elevation and station. There resided the factories, servants, beggars, and criminals. Dawn was the district of the clergy, where the white temples of Akara stood as monuments to the goddess. It was home to the Palace of the Solar Dominion, from where Queen Priestess Tezza ruled the Empire.

Ilara knew the streets of Dusk like she knew her blades. Those dark alleys were where she'd spent the last decade of her life. As a foreigner in this city, it had been difficult for her to make a name for herself. Luckily, she was good at what she did. She'd discovered that nearly all crime in Eversburg ran through the Gray Syndicate, and while cracking their shell had been tough, it was a lucrative partnership.

As Ilara descended further into Dusk, she saw the gathered gangs loitering about. They weren't the ones she was looking for, nor would they aid her in her task. The darkness of night gave a certain camaraderie to cretins of all kinds.

Jonas and his gang called an abandoned warehouse their hideout. It leaned against one of the city ramparts, one of the building's walls having deteriorated enough to fall away long ago. The slanting was gentle enough that the warehouse had created a huge lean-to. A fire lit in the center of it caused the shadows of the men inside to dance along its deteriorating brick walls.

Ilara's eyes flitted around the closest side of the building as she determined the best path forward. Sections of brick and mortar had fallen away, leaving archways and jagged makeshift windows that men occasionally poked their heads through.

While she was on good terms with the gang, she didn't want to announce her presence until the right time. It was a wonder what you could learn about people when they didn't know they were being watched.

She ultimately chose the archway that had the fewest windows near it, though the light of the campfire slanted out of it in a way that lit up the area outside—fewer shadows to hide in. She crept closer and peered inside to see roughly ten people milling about and a couple sleeping in burlap sacks near the fire. Boxes piled near her offered Ilara cover to move further in, and she took it.

From her new vantage point, she could see Jonas. He was a middle-aged man with a head of thinning hair and a trimmed goatee. Seated around him were a bald man covered in tattoos and a large, muscular thug she recognized as Bleeder. Their conversations carried, echoing off the warehouse walls such that she couldn't hear them over the cacophony of their own relentless noise.

The sound of clattering bricks on her left side drew Ilara's attention. One of the men guarding the outside wall had fallen over, clearly drunk as he stumbled back to his feet. She settled back, watching the guard patrols and searching out the best path. It had been a while since she'd taken tabs on this gang. Jonas was Ilara's contact into the Syndicate, so she'd worked with him when she first arrived in the city. More often than not, he requested the assassination of rival gang members or minor nobles.

Ilara shifted her weight from foot to foot, the urge to kill Jonas growing substantially. As a distraction, she turned her attention to the crates she was hiding behind. They were stamped with a half circle signifying a rising sun—Akara's holy symbol. Curiosity bloomed in Ilara, and she contemplated what might be in them. Jonas must've raised his sights if he was stealing from the clergy.

Her eyes flitted back to the guards, who had all mostly wandered away from her. Jonas never had a disciplined schedule, and the majority of them would draw back to a corner to play cards. Seizing her opportunity, Ilara stood and walked toward Jonas. She took cover around the piles of bricks as best she could, yet still moved swiftly enough that when she did appear, it was a surprise to Jonas as much as his guards, who rushed toward her as fast as their tired legs could take them.

Jonas held up a hand to stop their advance. "Hail to those who walk in the night," he said. "To what do we owe the pleasure?"

"Shadows keep your back," Ilara returned. She called her daggers into her hands, watching his eyes widen as the blades formed. She pointed one toward him, imagining driving it into his throat. "Business."

"Well, if you've come to kill me, you've sorely missed your chance," Jonas said, gesturing to his goons. They circled Ilara and drew an assortment of weapons, clubs, shivs, and swords.

"I've come to talk," Ilara said, lowering the blade. "I wouldn't be opposed to a quick brawl, though. I could whet my appetite on some piglets."

"I don't think so. We are friends, aren't we?" Jonas asked, gently patting the air. His men took the hint and backed off, lowering their weapons. Ilara dropped her daggers and let them disappear. "So, what business? Looking for work?"

Ilara shook her head. "Doesn't seem like you need the help. I came for Sophia Blackwood."

"The singer?"

"Yes, I understand she is a client of yours. One that you are extorting."

Jonas turned to the bald, tattooed man, and they exchanged some whispered words. "I believe she owes us some gali from a somewhat significant loan. We deal with her in no other capacity." Jonas's expression was stern. He had a good poker face.

Ilara tossed a coin pouch to the ground. Jonas and the men around the fire flinched instinctively.

"That is the last payment," she stated. She was sure that it wasn't enough gali to cover the extent of Sophia's loans, but Jonas was lucky to be getting anything. "You will deal with her no more. She is under my explicit protection and that of the Syndicate. Any of your men lay a finger on her, and they'll learn the wrath of my blades."

"Well enough. We will steer clear of her and send her to you if she comes our way." Jonas paused, cocking his head from side to side. He was pissed. "Sophia did have a Syndicate coin when she approached us. She got it from you, didn't she?"

Ilara nodded. The coins were a way to identify people who'd gained the favor of the Syndicate.

"We're taking a loss on this, then." Jonas frowned. "Might you happen to repay us by doing a job, on the house?"

"Never again. Our businesses are separate, and we shall keep it that way."

Jonas growled, but Ilara turned and passed between two of the men surrounding her. They let her go, and she breathed easy once she was outside the warehouse, grateful for their terror. She didn't know if she could have taken so many opponents at once, and she wasn't keen to find out.

# Chapter Three

# TRIALS

Valette stood in the Tribunal's dark audience hall. A tall knight with dark, swept-back hair stood beside her. His strong jaw was covered in small, prickly hairs, and disappointment clouded his eyes. His armor was outlined with red paint, contrasting the gleam of the clean silver. A red-and-gold tabard bearing a stylized half sun was draped across the front and back of the metal plates. He was her highest superior, Knight Commander Ryn, and the fact he was here denoted how badly she'd fucked up. Valette was certain Senator Plithy's death would be placed squarely on her shoulders.

The night's events ran through her head for the hundredth time. Plithy's lifeless body stared back at her, pleading for the justice she couldn't give him. Not that she hadn't tried. Valette didn't know what the consequences for this failure would be, but had a sinking feeling the gallows were in her future.

The Tribunal was a large hall, almost like a cathedral. In place of pews and a lectern, there was a long table with seats for each of the high priests with two stands for the rank-and-file clergy flanked the desk where Valette's jury would be seated. Towering behind was a throne decorated with ornate gems and carvings. This place was not where justice was decided, but where judgment was cast. All the seats were empty, standing in cold silence as they waited to be filled.

As the sun rose, it filled the room with multicolored light, which filtered through stained-glass windows that ran the length of the hall. Priests and priestesses robed in the gold-and-red vestments of their faith began to file into the room and took their seats in the jury stands. The crowd's low conversings slowly rose to a din as the priests prepared to handle the business of the day.

The members of the high clergy entered next. On their heads sat elaborate headwear that indicated their station within the church. If Valette remembered correctly, the first who entered were head priests, each with bands of gold around their foreheads, then the bishops, their white pointed caps lined with gold and gems. Third came the cardinals, who all wore red caps that were taller than those of the bishops.

Finally, in walked Priestess Tezza, Voice of Akara. Her curly red hair spilled out from beneath a crown so opulent that it cast the sunlight in a myriad of different directions, the reflections glinting red.  Her eyes burned red as well, as if alight with Akara's flames.

With the added sunlight, Valette was able to get a better sense of the carvings on the walls and engravings on the windows. The Tribunal was covered in depictions of the goddess, the reigning queen of the gods for nigh on a century. The artwork was not subtle in reinforcing that dominance. Akara was either depicted as a stern ruler sitting on a throne of sunlight or as the gleaming sun itself. She'd passed to her people the knowledge of farming, industry, and, crucially, empire-building. The clergy did only as she commanded, and she communicated on Aerlia through her Voice, Tezza, highest of Akara's Chosen.

Tezza raised her massive staff, and the room fell into complete silence. The rod was easily twelve feet long and topped with a large ruby the size of Valette's fist. The priestess handed it to one of her armored guards and stood, raising her hands to the crowd of gathered clergy members.

"The blessings of Akara to you all," she said. "I see that you passed through the night without scathe. Our kind mistress ensured that each of you saw the light of a new day. She provides and takes all. Her Eye rises again on Akara's glorious empire. Though in these winter months, it lingers on us less, we know it is only due to the great trust she places upon us. We hope to see it increase in the coming years to cleanse all blasphemers and abominations with the holy light of our Lady. Until then, we shall do our best to do it ourselves."

She motioned with a graceful wave of her hand, and the paladin raised the staff high, then brought it back down. As it cracked against the marble floor, the ruby at the tip began to glow, filling the room with a deep red hue. The eyes of the paladin grew a brighter and brighter red as he focused on the spell, deepening the room into darker shades of red. Tezza took the staff back and raised it even further above her head.

"Behold the light of our Lady! Light of the world, bringer of justice and light, from whose beams our crops grow and our children prosper. May her Eye shine from now until the end of days."

The Tribunal hall erupted in applause. Cheers echoed off the marble walls. As Tezza sat back on the throne, a gleeful look radiated over her face. She pounded the foot of the staff on the floor, and the crowd quieted. Valette knew little of Akaran rituals, but she knew that the highest ranked Chosen was the one who led them. Even in the smallest temples, the Chosen channeled Akara's power. It was odd that Tezza hadn't lit the staff herself.

"Now, what is the case of the morning?" Tezza looked toward Knight Commander Ryn, who tugged on Valette's arm.

The pair walked to the center of the Tribunal room, hundreds of red eyes directed at them, which made Valette's stomach turn. With a quick shake of her arms, her training took over and she stood at attention.

*Best not to think of the circumstances*, she thought.

"Your grace, blessed by the highest of the gods," Ryn said, and bowed. There was a hesitance in the movement. He motioned for Valette to do the same. She complied, feeling the weight of her armor on her back.

"Most urgent business prevails upon us from the passing night. I present this Chosen of Almir, Valette Bilaut. She was guarding Senator Plithy at the time of his assassination."

"I understand." The red glow disappeared as Tezza closed her eyes. "You would pass judgment upon her for failed duties?"

"It is proper. All paladins must have their duties observed by the highest Chosen. It is our way. Bilaut let Plithy's life be taken by a heretic, one who would stand in the way of our goddess. We, Akara's Chosen people, should be the ones to bring this failing before her."

"Quite a statement this would make, don't you think? Passing judgment on a Chosen of Almir, an ally of our queen  and member of the Pantheon, without hesitation or trial. Chosen Bilaut, what do you have to say?" Tezza asked.

This was the only time Valette would be heard, and it would need to count. From Tezza's tone, she felt sure that the punishment for failing her duty in Eversburg would be death—or exile, if Akara was feeling merciful. While Ryn said this trial was proper, the more appropriate action would be to allow Almir to pass judgement on his own Chosen, not Akara. Valette hoped Tezza wasn't so lost she didn't see that.

*"Trust in me. This will be fine. Repeat the command I gave you,"* Almir said in her mind.  His voice was smooth and rich, like a gentle father's.

Valette nodded and took a deep breath. "Neither I nor Almir would question your judgment, Voice of the resplendent Akara. Almir owes his godhood to our queen. However, before you decide, I pray you hear a plea from Almir."

"Do continue." Tezza settled back on her throne. "Know that the court of the queen rules over all fairly. None, however, can defy the will of Akara."

"He proclaims that I am duty bound to bring this heretical Chosen to justice," Valette said. Her tone was authoritative and reverent, though it felt as if she had no control over her mouth. "I have looked upon this murderer's face, and I would see that they face justice for the crime committed. It is an Almiran's way to seek justice and redemption. Allow me to fulfill my calling so that none may suffer death by a heretic."

The words tasted like a lie, bitter and self-serving. Valette did think the murderer should be brought to justice, but not for following a different god.

"Tell the assembly all, Chosen Bilaut. Leave out no detail of your encounter with this heretic. Describe her as best you can," Tezza commanded.

Valette did. She explained the whole of the encounter with the harlot and how she had seduced Senator Plithy. Valette described the sound that had caused her to open the door as well as how the woman had disappeared, causing Valette to set the inn on fire.

Tezza's face darkened at Valette's words. Shadows cast by the light from the red gems in her crown danced around her face. "How many perished from the destruction of this inn?" she asked once Valette had finished her tale.

Ryn cleared his throat. "Three were killed, and a dozen were wounded. Fire brigadiers, almost exclusively."

"A messy predicament," Tezza muttered. She cast her eyes up to a skylight set in the ceiling, as if conversing with the goddess herself, rumored to have a palace set upon the sun.

Valette found herself praying to Almir instinctively. It was as natural to her as thinking. She knew that he, as an ally to Akara, gave them standing to make the request. So many gods had turned against Akara in her war against Aox; she couldn't afford to lose more allies. Still, Valette prayed to Almir for strength and to Akara for understanding.

"We have come to a decision," Tezza announced.

Valette's heart froze. It was now or never.

"The clergy will not vote upon this. Our Lady concurs."

An audible gasp rolled through the assembled priests. In the past, Almir had explained to Valette, Akara had so many Chosen that few spoke with her more than once. Tezza was the exception. Akara spoke with her daily, but only while the Eye remained in the sky, and even that was irregular. That Akara deemed to speak on this meant it was something of great importance.

"The Chosen this Almiran has brought to our attention is an important heretic and must be dealt with forthwith. By all reports, Zal'Keratha's last surviving Chosen lives within our very walls. Though the goddess of death may have less power than in ages passed, she is not one to be underestimated. As punishment for failing to defend Senator Plithy, Chosen Valette shall bring the culprit to the courts. Bring this heretic to justice. Send her to meet her foul goddess. You may not leave this city until the deed is done. Knight Commander Ryn will continue to oversee your duties. Go and make it so."

Valette nodded and turned with Knight Commander Ryn to walk out from Tribunal Hall. As the large oak doors closed behind them, he looked at her with a long frown and motioned for her to follow. She obliged, following him through the Palace of the Solar Dominion at such a speed that she barely had time to appreciate the beauty of the architecture. Large columns lined each hallway, covered in art reliefs and flanked by windows that looked out over the city or the bay, which was covered in a sheet of reflective ice.

Burning wax assaulted Valette's nose as they turned down a corridor. The knight commander's office resided in this windowless hallway, along with the offices of a dozen other military officials. Her eyes strained as they navigated by candlelight.

Ryn opened his door and revealed a quaint, utilitarian room with a simple wooden desk. He sat down behind it and glared at her with bloodshot eyes. "Embarrassing. Pull a line like that again and I'll be hanging you myself. Almir ought not concern himself with Akaran business. Sit down."

"The Voice of your goddess seem to agree with me. The clergy would hang you if they heard you say those words," Valette replied.

"They don't have the manpower," he huffed. The image of Tezza handing off the staff flashed through Valette's mind again. "You'll be on the case, but the paladins are still lead. They handle the investigative work, and you'll keep what peace you can."

"And how shall I be doing that?"

"City watch."

Valette narrowed her mouth into a thin line to keep herself from frowning. Almir needed her to be working this case. She needed to be closer to the paladins than the city watch, who were almost all not Akara's Chosen.

"I don't see what use I'll be, then. Or how I'll be able to fulfill my prerogative," she said, crossing her arms.

"You won't. Follow my orders, and you might still make it out of this city. My paladins are putting up poster cards asking the public for information. On the watch, you'll be the point of contact for anything useful."

Valette frowned. Ryn had climbed to a high position in this city without becoming Chosen. She'd need to determine how that had happened.

"I'd like to conduct interviews with the men when they return from an investigation involving any criminal," Valette said.

"Why?"

"If I'm to connect the dots, I want all the information."

"Aye. You'll be allowed to talk to any paladins who deal with violent crime—if you can pin them down and get them to speak with you," Ryn said with a smile.

It wasn't the same as having free reign of the city, but it would have to do. She'd find the information Ryn didn't want her to.

"Fine. Point me in the direction of my patrol."

"Wonderful, the clerk at the end of the hall will show you the way. You'll start tomorrow. And lose the armor. No guard walks about in full plate."

***

Valette sniffed loudly as she entered the barracks. They had the rank smell of sweaty men who'd forgone one too many baths.

A man with a large wart on the side of his nose handed her a uniform: a stitched gambeson and a small breastplate that might stop a blade, though it looked more likely to crumple under the blow. She donned the two pieces and strode back outside, where her two partners for the day were waiting.

One of the men had so many wrinkles that he might be her grandfather, and the other looked like he'd paid the shoe shiner to clean his face. Valette forced a smile as she walked up to them. It had been a long time since she'd served a man like Ryn.

"Soldiers."

"Morning, ma'am," the young one said. He extended his hand to her. "Gavin, at your service."

Valette gave it a quick shake. "Chosen Bilaut."

The older man regarded her with eyes that seemed to see more than he let on. "Not many Chosen around here without red eyes. Akara not giving those out anymore? Sergeant Otto, ma'am."

"Sergeant," Valette said, shaking his hand as well. "I'm not Akaran. Almir is the god I serve, and he doesn't dole out red eyes."

"Aye, we know the children's rhyme," Otto said with a smile. "Akara's have red eyes that shine, Ameri's have an expanded mind, while Balan's ne'er fail to rhyme."

"Halga's have hands of steel, while Almir's, will that sees ev'ry ordeal," Valette finished. "How does patrol work?"

Otto turned and began walking south. "We have our orders from Captain Samith to patrol the Noon markets. Usually a quiet place, though there have been reports of vandals."

"Never patrolled with a Chosen before, much less an Almiran," Gavin said with a sneer. "What brings you here?"

"In from Chrys," Valette started, pointedly  choosing to ignore the statement. "I thought the larger city might help me forge some connections."

"*You are a terrible liar. Don't stretch the truth*," Almir said.

"I served with the Akaran army for most of my youth. Nearly a decade. The provincialism of Chrys felt wrong after it, so I came here," she added with a shrug.

"Army, eh?" Otto said with a smirk. "Lots of people in Eversburg served. Some find their way to the guard, most don't."

"What happens to those men?" Valette asked.

"Fall through the cracks, most," Gavin said.

"Petty crime," Otto chimed in. "I should know. I was one of them. Paladins arrested me after I robbed a bank strung out on clove. A decade later, I have the chance to help."

"I often forget the war has gone on so long," Valette said.

They walked across the district line from Dawn to Noon. The changes were subtle. Limestone buildings gave way to brick, and the streets were clogged with fewer red robes of the clergy and more dress wear of the merchant class.

"After five decades of veterans showing up in Eversburg, the paladins know a thing or two about rehabilitating a man." Otto grimaced as he ran a hand over a scar that ran from the back of his head to his ear. "Spent my whole youth in the ranks.

That changes your perspective from what your mother taught you."

Valette nodded. "At least you have a chance again at a normal life."

"Aye. Normal." Pain surfaced in Otto's eyes before he changed the subject. "Captain says you were demoted."

Valette calmed the panic that rose in her chest. "Aye. The knight commander thinks I'll be able to perform my investigation more efficiently with my boots on the ground. I'm hoping to chase Zal'Keratha's Chosen," she said.

Otto laughed. "Sounds like the knight commander put you in the wrong place."

"I only tell you to be honest." Valette shrugged.

"Aye. Wouldn't surprise me much. Only Akara's people are treated well in this city. Almirans get the worst of it when it comes down to it," Otto said.

She was about to ask what he meant when Gavin's eyes seemed to catch something. "I, uh, need to check on something," he told them, then jogged across the street.

Otto nodded but caught Valette's shoulder as she moved to follow him. "Let him go. He's not looking after anything for the watch," he said.

"He's acting outside his duties?"

"Oh, I wouldn't say that. Gavin has a dark-haired girl he has yet to call his own. Don't know what they get down to on his morning visits, but he always comes back in a better mood. Makes him much easier to deal with."

Before Valette could respond, her  brow wrinkled when a different man caught her attention. He seemed weighed down by the bags under his eyes. His thin hair wisped up in a style common for the city lords, yet the dirt under his nails spoke of a different station.

"I'm told this is where I can give my information," he said with a grin.

"What have you got?" she asked.

The man relayed what he could, and when he left, both Valette and Otto agreed it would go up the chain.

## Chapter Four

# FRIENDS

Ilara felt an ache through her whole body, almost like a hangover. She'd channeled more the previous night than she had in a long while, and her abilities had started to wane. Sitting up in bed, she massaged her temples with her forefingers. Years ago, she could have done that every night for months. A tract was like a muscle—if it went unused, it atrophied in the same way. It was as if the  tracts themselves shrank.

She got up out of bed and let the blanket fall off her, revealing her armor. She undid the clasps and peeled off the plates. They squelched as they ripped away from her skin, the day-old sweat gluing the leather to her, morphing her into a killer.

Confronting Jonas had been one step too far. It could have waited until today. Worse, her impulse to kill had grown quicker. An offering like Plithy would normally have bought her weeks, but she already felt the pain building behind her eyes. She'd need another one soon.

She shuddered thinking of the consequences killing Jonas would have. He didn't have a contract on him, meaning it would turn all of the Gray Syndicate against her. She would need to choose someone else. Tracking a person worth killing took time, and learning their routines to do so safely took even more. Even Plithy's death had been rushed, causing her to make too many mistakes.

Killing without a contract was looked on poorly in the Syndicate. It would lead to the loss of her station as well as any potential income. Hell, there wasn't a criminal in the Akaran Empire who would hire her if the Syndicate's ties were as thorough as it claimed. She had some gali saved in a trunk in her closet, but it wouldn't be enough to live off for long.

Ilara placed her armaments in the chest at the foot of her bed, then peered out through her curtains. The day had started beautifully, though she couldn't see the sun from her west-facing window. Judging by the heavy foot traffic, it was just before midday. She hadn't slept in as late as she usually did. The cafe across the street was bustling with patrons, and waitresses moved from table to table in hurried obedience.

A man with caramel hair caught her eyes and gave her a hearty wave. He had the light armor of a street guard. "Gavin," Ilara muttered as he walked up to her door. This had increasingly become their morning, or afternoon, routine whenever she roused from bed.

She sighed and threw on the robe that hung off the bedframe. She knew Gavin's intentions. She'd relented once, almost a decade ago, and dealt with the consequences of that decision for months.

He tried so hard, and she turned him down often. He didn't know the truth about her. If he had, Ilara was certain he wouldn't be as interested as he was. All men ran when they found out she could skewer a person with a flick of her wrist.

She was nearly at her front door when he started knocking. His simple figure was framed by the doorway as she opened it.

"Good dawn to you, Ilara," he said, flashing a smile. Hints of stubble poked from his chin where the patches of his beard were starting to grow in. "Well, a dawn to you at any rate. The civilized world has been awake for many hours now, with Akara's Eye nearly reaching its zenith."

Ilara smiled back. He was conventionally attractive, with a head of curls that were a constant victim of helmet hair. He'd been her target once upon a time, but she hadn't been able to bring herself to kill him. She had suspected he only played the part of happy guardsman, turning to nefarious deeds in the evening. How wrong she had been.

"Coming in for a coffee?" It was her usual offer, and she couldn't break it now, even if every bone in her body wanted to leave Eversburg. That paladin was out there somewhere, likely hunting her.

"Yes, please," Gavin replied, pushing past her into the living space. "How was the evening shift?"

"You know how I feel about nobles," she lied as she placed a tea kettle on a circular diagram of runes, then murmured, "Calora Quae."

The runes burst to life, and small flames erupted from them, creating a ring of fire just below a wire rack. Ilara thanked the gods Akara hadn't banished the Chosen of the Crafter from her empire. The stove was a simple construction. A Chosen of Halga could create it in an afternoon if they worked diligently, yet it was only the well-to-do who benefited from the invention. No impoverished person could spare an expense so opulent when a hearth did just fine.

"That nobles aren't worth their weight in gali?" he asked. "Still, they need more guards than the common folk, what with all the murderers and thieves. It's nice to have a good job at least."

"So it is. To answer your question, it was a rather eventful shift, with the fire at that inn half the city away. The lady of the house woke and saw the flames. Poor thing was so worried, she made me sit with her the rest of the evening. I spent it listening to how bandits would break in to ravish her." Ilara dramatically rolled her eyes.

"Was that wishful thinking on her part?"

"Gavin! I though the paladins would have taught you better than that."

Ilara grinned. She did enjoy this part of their relationship. She'd miss it tomorrow when Eversburg was far behind her. He would come knocking at her door to no answer, and likely wouldn't even realize she'd left until a week later.

*Is this what a decade of friendship is worth to you?* Zal'Keratha said in Ilara's mind.

*Gavin is no more than a passing acquaintance.*

Gavin sighed. "Well, I don't blame her for being scared. Times like these make me want to get into guarding nobles. Right tragic that inn was. Word on the street is that they found someone stabbed to death inside. It isn't confirmed, but pals think it's Senator Plithy. There were bloody chunks of him missing. First thought is that the so-called rebellion is behind it."

"Was Plithy the one who was fighting against the bill to toss people in Dusk off the city wall for missing shifts?" Ilara asked.

"Aye, but no. He was fighting for it. Insane proposition. It was a warning, and he knew no one would vote for it. And everyone knows what that inn was used for. Nothing but prostitutes in there from dusk to dawn. Can you believe that? Spending hard-earned public funds at a place like that. No wonder the clergy want to dissolve the Senate. You know, you really should pay more attention to the goings on."

Ilara smiled as she poured the coffee into mugs. "Oh, cut me some slack. I was close."

"Fair enough. We aren't losing much with the likes of him, anyway," Gavin replied. Ilara set the mug in front of him, and he hastily sipped the scalding liquid.

"I won't tell your captain you said that."

She liked paladins as much as she liked cockroaches, but Gavin wasn't so bad. He used what he could to make the neighborhood better. It wasn't his fault he was caught up in a system like this. Not to mention his eyes were absent the red glow of Akara's power, lending him trust in Ilara's mind . He wouldn't advance far in the guard without it, but Gavin didn't seem the type to push for more than he needed.

He put his half-empty mug back on the table with a clunk, and a satisfied expression lit his face. "By the Nine, you make the best coffee this side of Dawn. You could make gali by the bag if you ever wanted to sell it—get out of the hired muscle game and into something safer." He made a contented noise as he went back to sipping the black liquid.

"Feels a touch too domestic for me. I'll keep it in mind if I ever get tired of sleeping in." She raised her mug in mock toast.

"Ilara, I do need you to promise me something." Gavin cleared his throat.

"No, I won't go to Port Miras with you in the spring," she teased.

"Ah, no, not that. More so, if Tezza and the clergy step in on the Senate, there's going to be a proper mess. Lots of folk are saying they're going to get violent. You don't hear the young people shout about it during the day on account of your schedule, but what they say's concerning. They preach revolution on the street like a religion. When it comes, and I know it's a-coming, fleeing the city would be best if you have someplace to go.

"My kin do want me and Theo in Port Miras," he continued. "They have a fancy villa outside the city there. I can't, though. I want to stay in Eversburg as long as I can to keep the peace. Long-winded way to get to it, but I'd like you to take Theo there, if you find it in your heart to."

Ilara froze, mesmerized by the steam floating out of her mug and vanishing into the air above. She did care for the kid. Aerlia would be worse off without someone like him in the world. Still, it was for the best if she could get out of Eversburg today.

"I don't know, Gav. I'm not sure if that's something I can commit to," she said, blushing. "I'd hate for him to wait for me to never show up."

Gavin shook his head. "You of all people wouldn't be one to leave him out to dry while the world burns. Please, Ilara. You're the only one I trust. More importantly, he trusts you."

"Godsdamnit, Gavin. You make it hard for a lady to say no." As much as she cared about Theo,  Gavin was supposed to be responsible enough to deal with this himself. "If it means so much to you, I'll help your son in any way I can."

"Thank you. I knew we'd be able to count on you."

Gavin's smile was so innocent. If Eversburg did start breaking apart, he'd be on the front line with the protestors. He wasn't fool enough not to fight back, but he would absolutely take it easy on them. His hope in humanity would be his downfall.

"Fucking knew you were going to invite me to Port Miras," Ilara said with a grin.

Gavin laughed. "I guess I couldn't help it. Have you been before?"

"In another life. Anything else I should know about the goings on in the city?"

"Same old shit-shoveling out there. We arrested a slew of the so-called Revolution. A buffoon by the name of Desmond. He's harmless, but he was planning on taking over the Akaran Temple. They got him before he marched on it, though. They say he had nearly a hundred fighters and a Chosen with him. A Shyllan." Gavin's expression carried a healthy amount of fear.

Ilara only nodded. Chosen outside the Pantheon were dangerous to Akara. It was their divine duty to carry out their god's will in whatever lands they were called to. And many of the gods wanted Akara dethroned, as few approved of her actions in the past century. The Syndicate employed many Chosen because so many found it difficult to find work that didn't expose them. If this Revolution was recruiting Chosen, it meant it might have more momentum than Ilara had given it credit for.

And one of Shyll's Chosen. Ilara wondered if that was still Katri, or if the god had gotten her killed. Katri had been in Jonas's gang around the same time as Ilara, and they'd often worked contracts together. She'd been one of the few people Ilara liked in that place, if only because Katri could understand how contrived the work was.

Ilara looked back to Gavin and smiled, regaining confidence in the conversation. "Best thing to do is keep our head down and return to our labors." She downed the rest of the coffee.

"Good advice for all of us down here in the grime." He sat forward and slapped his armored thigh, every part of his body squeaking and clanking with the movement. "Ah-welp, best get back to the route before Sarge wonders where I am." He stood and put a kind hand on Ilara's shoulder. "Thank you for the coffee. Enjoy the rest of your off-day."

She walked him out and basked in the glory of the ensuing silence.

Ilara wondered what Gavin would think of her if he'd known her the way Sophia did. Chosen of Zal'Keratha, Mistress of Death and Lady of the Underworld. A dagger phased into existence into the palm of her hand. She flipped it absent-mindedly. Magic came at a price. She'd dedicated her life to serve Zal'Keratha for the ability to protect Sophia. And she'd do it again, even if that meant Gavin would never be able to love her.

*"It will all be different in my new world."*

"He assists the enemy," Ilara grumbled. "He'll die, whether I like it or not."

*"An unfortunate truth for you. None such as he will keep me from the wrath I will bring upon the sun. And you, child, will take her place. There is no better way for you to protect your sister from Akara's godhood."*

Ilara smirked. She wasn't sure what Akara had done to earn Zal'Keratha's ire. It didn't matter. Zal'Keratha stood against Akara, and therefore, so did Ilara.

## Chapter Five

# COMPLIANCE

People clogged the market stalls like salmon during mating season. Sophia loved the pop-up markets in the Dusk district. Busking had been outlawed for as long as she'd lived in Eversburg, as the Akaran clergy believed music in any form was worship to Balan, the god of music. The melody of people living was enough to keep Sophia connected. Their conversations were a raucous noise, like an orchestra tuning before an opera.

Despite all the people, the stalls were almost bare. The merchants grew fewer with each day, selling fewer and fewer goods. The sun beat down on Sophia's head, warming her hair despite the chill of the winter wind nipping at her face.

While browsing, she overheard shouting and, cocking her head slightly, she saw two armored paladins and a merchant in rags.

"I'll ask again," the larger paladin said. "How much to give these radishes to the barracks?"

"Th-th-th-the fair rate is five gali a radish. That is what anyone here would give," the merchant stammered.

"I don't think he's listening. He said it's for the barracks, old man," the second paladin said. He shifted his weight forward so that he was leaning into the merchant's face. "Do you have no respect for the men in uniform? We're the ones keeping the streets clean enough for you to sell your radishes at these extortionate prices."

"I s-s-suppose I could part with them for four," the merchant said. He shrank back, trying his damnedest to get as far from the men as he could without insulting them.

"We'll give you four for the crate." The larger paladin grinned. "And we'll leave you with your greedy little hands."

The merchant hung his head. "A fair price."

Coins were slapped on the table in front of him, and the paladins walked by Sophia with their crate, cackling over the crime they'd committed.

She slowly browsed her way to the merchant. He was staring at his palm, which had four golden gali in it.

"I heard you were selling radishes for ten gali a head," Sophia said with a smile. "That's such a deal, I couldn't resist."

The merchant looked at her, utter confusion on his face. His skin was tanned and wrinkled. Tufts of gray hair stuck out from the cloth wrapped around his head.

"I, uh—" he stammered.

Sophia smiled. "No worries, not much of a haggler myself. I'm sure this pouch will suffice," she said, handing over the gali.

"Thank you, miss." The man bowed as he took the coins from her. "You've paid this man a kindness." He took five radishes and dropped them into a small sack, handing it over the table.

"Think nothing of it. We all have to look out for one another." Sophia turned her back from the merchant, the small bag swung over her shoulder as she walked out of the busy market.

The total of Sophia's purchases would last her the week and, with her generous number of radishes, had cost nearly all the gali she'd earned from The Pearl. She'd need to find other work, though she'd rather sing more nights. Try as she might, she couldn't convince herself that was likely to happen. Customers were dwindling, and others needed the gigs as much as she did. Ilara clearing her debts hadn't changed the price of anything. Sophia would be behind again if she couldn't pay for rent and food.

Five years. It was a quarter of her lifetime, nearly all of her adulthood, spent without Ilara. She wasn't sure whether she should be happy about that or not. Life was so uncomplicated without her sister in it. And Sophia had offered to go with her. She didn't want to, but there was no denying that the tone in the city changed. There were as many red eyes on the street as not.

Are there more Akaran Chosen, or just fewer people?

Sophia walked into the city square and braced herself for the chaos. People were moving to and fro, the sound of their feet like the beats of a hundred chaotic drummers marching out of tune. The square was lined with two- and three-story buildings, and the streets framed a central monument featuring the gods of the Pantheon.

Sophia sat on one of the stone benches surrounding the monument and studied it. It was dominated by a massive statue of Akara. The goddess wore a full set of armor and a helmet with a glass visor, sword raised above her head and wings outstretched. The other six gods of the Pantheon knelt before her.

Sophia hadn't been there long before a young woman in a drab brown tunic got up to stand on the dais with the gods. Her eyes scanned the crowds moving on the streets around her. Soon, a small throng of similarly garbed people moved in around the monument.

"People of Eversburg," the woman shouted. "Feast your eyes on the gods of the age, feeding on the desperation of the people at the whim of a tyrant. Shyll, god of nature, clad in the leaves of betrayal."

A crowd of passersby stopped, caught by the noise and staying for the rhetoric. A portion of them had glowing red eyes. If nothing else, Sophia admired the woman's courage.

"Balan, god of music, wearing the lyre of deceit. Ameri, goddess of knowledge, the one who sees all suffering. Halga, the Crafter, who created the machines of war and oppression. Worst of all, Almir, the so-called god of justice, whom Akara herself called to her side.

"All of them leave Akara unchecked as she torments the people she claims to love. Even more, some send their Chosen to do Akara's bidding, never stopping to think about the power they're giving her."

Several of the people in the crowd were shoving others around them, trying to get to the front row.

"And Akara, the Queen of the Rats, Bringer of Darkness. Insufferable! I—" She halted abruptly as several people joined her on the base of the monument, all holding weapons. A man wearing the same garb as the speaker tackled one of them to the ground.

"Sabira, run!" he yelled.

Too little too late, as Sabira's wrist was grabbed by another one of the men, who was wearing a devilish grin. She screamed as he buried his knife in her stomach. Sabira fell, and Sophia felt panic rise in her throat.

*"Get away, child of song."*

Sophia didn't need further instruction. The crowd erupted into chaos as people wearing tattered clothes struggled against those with red eyes. Screams echoed off the buildings, and the roar of the riot grew to a head. Sophia stumbled by several paladins. They seemed to be coming from everywhere, their swords raised as they charged past her. She couldn't think about anything but fleeing.

She ran to the edge of the square, then down the street. She didn't feel safe until she was standing outside the tenement building she called her home. Her head whipped around, looking up and down the road, and she breathed a sigh of relief. Pain radiated from her head, and she realized she was clutching the bag of radishes with a death grip.

No riots here. No preachers against the gods. If she had been unsure before, she knew now: this city meant death, and her sister would save her from it whether Sophia wanted to or not.

Sophia willed herself to loosen her grip, lest her fingernails draw blood from her palm. As she walked to the front door, a shadow crept out from the alley next door. She froze with her hand on the knob until the figure came into the light. Bleeder.

"Sophia Blackwood." The big man was a head and a half taller than her and muscled, covered in the kind of purple tattoos that were common to the southern tribes, hunters of bison.

"Bleeder." Sophia grinned. "To what do I owe the pleasure?"

"My oath requires me to tell you that you sister is a fool."

Ilara had saved Bleeder's life once when they'd journeyed together. He felt it was worth a life debt. He lived in the apartment above The Pearl, where he worked as a bouncer, and had recommended Sophia for the singing gig. She felt like that paid his debt. He disagreed.

"If that is all, then your oath is worthless."

"You are in danger. Jonas has learned of your relation to your sister, the one he calls Thorn. You must be prepared to fight."

"Figures. We'll be leaving Eversburg before long. Maybe the Empire as a whole, at least for however long we can."

"My oath?" Bleeder asked. "I must follow you."

Sophia shook her head. "I've said it before, and I mean it this time. You're free from it. I have deemed that you have filled the life debt that I am owed , or whatever I have to say. Both Balan and I are satisfied with your service."

Without warning, Bleeder's big arms embraced and squeezed Sophia to the point where she thought her insides were sufficiently crushed.

"Thank you, singer. You are worthy of Balan. I will not forget this. If not for the kindness your and your sister's kindness, I would have bled out on that road so long ago. You could have passed me like so many others."

"Don't thank me," Sophia choked out. "If I remember right, those bandits did a poor job of killing you." She recalled that night all too well. She'd begged Ilara to pause for long enough to rescue the man.

"Then thank the gods," he said, backing away from her. He raised a single hand. "Good luck, Sophia Blackwood."

"Good luck, friend." She held her hand up in return.

Sophia climbed the stairs. Her mind was full of radish recipes she could use to eat the full sack brushing against her back. A stew would work for all of them at once, but she didn't particularly enjoy eating stew many days in a row. It certainly wouldn't keep. Perhaps she could eat them raw. That would ensure they stayed fresh the longest.

Thoughts spiraled through her mind, and soon she was outside her apartment. When she got to her apartment, her jaw dropped, her mouth as agape as the door. She was sure she'd locked it. It swung open, and a woman in plate armor with golden hair emerged. She looked like a paladin but didn't have the glowing eyes of Akara.

"Sophia Blackwood?" The name was a stern question, absent any compassion that Bleeder conveyed.

A bang came from the apartment, which had been left a mess from various people in plate rifling through her possessions. A smash that sounded like wood splintering came from the bedroom. Sophia flinched, hoping it wasn't her lute.

"Yes? What is this about?"

The paladin grabbed Sophia by the wrist. "We need you to come to the palace. We have some questions to ask you about the criminal Thorn."

Images of the prophet who'd been stabbed and killed by the mob flooded Sophia. Her arm went limp in the paladin's hands, and she dropped the bag of radishes. They sprang from the bag and released onto the floor, lost—like her freedom. The paladins would get what they wanted, whether or not she complied.

# Chapter Six

# STEPS FORWARD, STEPS BACK

Every muscle in Valette's back relaxed as she walked through the entrance to the palace. White, iridescent marble pillars flanked each side of the walkway. A lone woman in plain peasant garb was scrubbing one of the nearer ones. The palace had been built in another age, maintained by the people of Eversburg since before Akara assumed control of the Eye.

The entryway to the Solar Dominion was impressive. The ceiling was vaulted like that of a cathedral, and paladins flanked the doorways. Along the ceiling, a dozen arrow slits lined each wall. It was a kill room. Should any invading force make it inside, spells and arrows could be shot down at them, and the furnishings were so sparse that there would be no cover.

Sophia was in front of Valette, manacled between two wide-bodied paladins. A smile crept across Valette's face. Given their last conversation, she hadn't been sure Ryn would grant her access to take the girl in. He did, though he'd made it clear that the captain breathing heavily behind her was the one in charge.

Still, Valette had taken the opportunity to make the arrest. It was fascinating to watch paladins outside of her regiment work. She'd been Chosen when she was young, and she'd rarely strayed from the company of the Almirans and Akarans who'd taken her in—all soldiers. The armed front was like that. It was rare to lose a paladin, so the ones in her company were few, but dear.

These Akarans, however, were brutal. Valette couldn't help but notice the bruises along Sophia's arms where they had grabbed her to shove her forward, laughing whenever she stumbled to the ground. For Valette, walking the length of the city like that had been an exercise in restraint. She wondered, not for the first time, if the Akarans had reason to rule so roughly.

The paladins shoved Sophia toward one of the doors, and a strong hand pulled back on Valette's shoulder. "You'll go no further, lass," the captain said in a nasal voice.

She turned to face the whiskers of his graying mustache. "That is my prisoner, and she's part of my investigation. I'll be questioning her."

"You won't be." The captain's red eyes were firm. "You'll be reporting to Ryn, then returning to your station. His orders were clear—you would come along only to see how we do things around here. You're to leave the rest to us. Go see the Knight Commander, Almiran," he growled. He pushed past Valette, knocking pauldrons with her as he followed the other paladins.

Valette gritted her teeth. She breathed deeply before setting her jaw forward, then took a single step toward the captain's back, gripping the handle of her sword.

It reminded her of the last fort she'd secured against the Aoxians. She was back there in a moment, the red sun setting on the horizon, a multitude of waves below her as she stood high on a turret. Focusing her eyes showed her the truth: a tide of scaled creatures, long of limb and sharp of tooth. They crashed into the village just outside the fortress walls. Her captain's hand on her shoulder insisted there was nothing to be done.

*No. No! I won't go back there.*

Valette relaxed her grip on her blade, and her next step directed her to the opposing door.

Her emotions were getting more difficult to control. While that had been a hard day, she'd had many hard days since, and none of them had affected her nearly as much. And they shouldn't. She had a duty to Almir to make sure they didn't.

As she approached Ryn's office, two paladins exited, with a prisoner between them. He had a scar  running across his forehead. Valette almost didn't recognize him as the man who had finished the morning ritual during her Tribunal. He was thinner now, and his eyes burned more brightly than when Valette had seen him last. His arms hung limply around the two armored guards.

"She speaks to me," he mumbled. "You have to believe—"

"Stuff it, heretic," one of the paladins said. They dragged him past her as he continued to mumble under his breath.

Valette frowned, her eyes following the man. He seemed crazy, but had been fine the day before. He'd been at the top of her list to speak with once she had an opportunity.

Turning back, she gave Ryn's office door a single rap with her knuckles. Then, after waiting a minute, she gave it a second, more resolute, knock. A murmur of hushed whispers sounded from inside.

"Proceed," Ryn finally said.

Valette opened the door and found him seated behind his desk, a white-haired woman standing behind him. She was wearing the red garb of a priestess. Their faces were flushed, and Valette noted that the woman's robes were slightly disheveled.

"You've come to deliver your report," Ryn muttered almost imperceptibly. "Any injuries?"

"None, sir. We have Blackwood in custody. It should only be a matter of time before we can verify the report that her sister is the criminal we're after," Valette said.

Ryn nodded. "It was a good tip. Well done, solider. We'll look forward to the results of her interrogation. You are dismissed." He turned his attention back to one of the papers that littered his desk.

"If I may, sir," Valette started. Ryn's eyes flicked back to her. "I should like to be more involved in Blackwood's interrogation. Almir has instructed me on information gathering, and I should like to put it to use."

"I'll take it under consideration," Ryn said with a flick of his hand. "At this moment, you will not be entrusted with such matters. If you don't recall, trust has been broken. The only way you will build it back is by following orders."

"Yes, sir," Valette said around the stone in her throat. Had she pushed too far?

Ryn grinned. "If you have nothing else, return to your post."

"May I speak freely, sir?" Valette asked. The knot in her throat grew, but it wouldn't recede if she didn't bring her issues forward.

"Speak," Ryn said, picking up a parchment from the stack nearest him, quill in hand. The priestess next to him leveled her eyes at Valette in a commanding stare, but they lacked the shine of Akara's power.

"Frankly, sir, I believe my talents are wasted patrolling the streets. My extensive service has shown me how to deal with foreign adversaries. I should be on the investigation tracking this criminal. Sir," Valette said.

"Oh, should you, now?" Ryn scribbled forcefully on the parchment. "You godsdamned paladins are too cocky. You have no idea how to run a city and deal with a civilian population. Do you know how many years it takes to regain their trust when one of you overpowered lunatics goes and burns down an inn? Too many. You are lucky not to be in my dungeon. Leave. Go back to your position and learn how our system bleeding works. Then, and only then, will I consider sending you back onto my streets unattended, Chosen Bilaut." He slammed the parchment back on his desk and picked another off the pile.

"Sir," Valette replied. The knot in her throat had grown to the size of a dragon egg. Like a defeated dog, she slid out of

Ryn's office. She heard the murmur of whispers start again from behind the door as it closed.

An affair? Or sedition?

"Or neither," she muttered.

Ryn wasn't wrong. There was so much about Eversburg that Valette didn't know, and she wasn't sure how to change that. Her husband, Antony, had said something similar to her before she'd left Chrys.

He had been standing in the kitchen of their home, cleaning the dishes from a meal he'd made. It was something he always did when he was mad. It helped him to have something to do with his hands.

"So you're leaving? You've only been home a few months," he said. The ceramic plates clinked in the bucket of soapy water.

Valette had been away for too many of their years together. Akara had been waging war against the lizard god, Aox, and his children, the Aoxians, since before she'd wrestled control of the Pantheon from him a century before. When the Aoxians attacked the kingdom of Caldor, the goddess had launched a full-fledged attacked on them while unifying the Nine Kings into a single empire. An empire Valette had finally solidified when she'd led Akara's army to Vash'gal'or—a fact her husband would never know.

Almir's knights had been pulled into it when Valette was a child because of their close ties to Akara's paladins.

"Aye," Valette said. "Almir says it won't be for long. A year, or two at worst."

"And what about your sons? They need a mother. Auggie told me the day before you came back that he thought you were dead. That the other kids in the chapel—" Antony choked back a sob. "Gods, I thought you were gone by then, too. It had been five months since your last letter, Valette. Then you show up out of thin air."

"I told you there would be a long debriefing when I got out. You should have known my service was over," she said.

"Aye, so you said. But you won't tell us what that camp was. I was sure Akara's Chosen had killed you. We both know how you were treated those last few years. I mean, by Almir, you barely got leave to have the twins."

"I know. It's not fair to you that I'm being called to this. But I was Chosen when I married you. You knew that my duty to Almir comes before you, Auggie, or Mikel. Not to mention that what Almir told me seems truly dire. I wouldn't trust any of his other Chosen for this. I am the most senior, outside of Halen."

Halen was the leader of the damned order of knights and paladins, and there was no way Almir would call on him for a task like this. No, Valette's father was not one to work outside of his administrative duties.

"I know." Antony slumped over the bucket of dishes. "I do love you because you are so damn motivated. But part of me worries that this is what you won't return from. You were in the war when we met and continued to fight after we were married. I guess I hoped that the birth of your boys would make you realize they are so much more important than all of this. I thought we finally had you back."

"So you'd have Almir Forsake me, then?"

"No, no nothing like that. This politicking with nobles and knights seems out of your wheelhouse. You're a soldier first. I don't want you coming home with a knife in your back after making sure you didn't come back with a sword in your stomach. And then you tell me that you don't want us with you. How dangerous is this?"

Valette shook her head. "It won't be. This is an information-gathering task above all."

"And what are you seeking to discover?" he asked.

She fell silent. Almir had been firm when he told her she couldn't tell Antony, and there wasn't a lie in the world that would be convincing.

"Valette." Antony placed his wet hands on her shoulders. "By the gods, I am your husband. If you don't tell me why this is so urgent that you must leave your family, I can't guarantee there will be a family for you to come back to."

"You wouldn't dare."

"Don't tempt me." His dark eyes were bloodshot, and bags drooped under them.

The two of them were so much older than when they'd met. They'd lost a lot of years to Valette's military career. She hadn't had a choice in that regard. She wished she had one now.

"Almir has seen evidence of Akara's power waning," Valette said. "When he confronted her about it, she didn't take it well. I need to find out why, which means I need to have a meeting with the Voice."

"Truly? The Voice of Akara?"

"Aye. Halen is putting a transfer order through to station me as Almir's representative in Eversburg." Valette didn't tell him that the last of Almir's knights sent to Eversburg had died in a horseback riding incident. She hoped Antony hadn't heard.

"And this will only take a year?" Antony asked. It was customary for Almir's knight to bring their whole family to Eversburg.

"It is not a permanent position. I just have to ask the right questions of the right people. Akara's throne could be in jeopardy. Everything her war has accomplished could fail if she loses it. Anarchy would rule in her stead. Our kids would starve, and Chrys could fall. I have to be sure that isn't the case."

"You think one of the other gods could make a play for it? That would mean Eversburg would be a godsdamned battlefield."

"No different than where I've spent the last decade of my life," Valette said. "If Almir is wrong, then I'll be transferred back here to Chrys. I'll spend the rest of my days as an instructor for new knights and paladins, and we'll have nothing to be worried about ever again."

"You promise me that?" Antony asked.

"I do. I don't want our boys growing up in that city, away from Almir's congregation in Chrys."

"Aye, you'd have a hard time convincing their grandfathers to move to a large city."

Valette laughed. "Oh, aye. They'd complain about the crowd, and how bright it is. 'Too close to the godsdamned sun.'"

Antony nodded. "Are we alright, then?"

Valette grabbed his hand. "You tell me."

# Chapter Seven

# CUTTING TIES

To say Tarin was mad was an understatement, but Ilara knew he'd get over it. They were walking together down the palisade of Noon district. The din of the markets was soft, and many of the merchants were packing up their goods for the day. This was the perfect place to be at sundown. The street ran east and west, so at one end, toward Dusk, was the setting sun, and at the other, toward Dawn, the red hues reflected off the gold domes of the Solar Dominion.

Ilara glanced down at Tarin. The short man had his thick fingers wrapped around the locks of his beard. He mumbled something under his breath.

"Going to have to speak up, brother," Ilara said.

"You are making my life so much more difficult," he groaned. "Jonas is pissed. He told his synd of your evening antics. And he's asking me what your relation to this Blackwood woman is."

Ilara grimaced. A synd was a member's call line in the Gray Syndicate. It was who they got jobs from, requisitioned gear from, and took their problems to. Tarin was Ilara's. It wasn't an issue that Jonas had complained, but it might become one depending on how the synd handled it.

"Jonas was going to be angry no matter what. He was extorting the poor girl who I gave my coin to. It was a small loan. I knew he was a criminal, but he took this too far. All he did was make her life worse. How can I entrust her to a man like that?" Ilara asked.

Tarin sighed. "You directed her to the Syndicate. We aren't known for our compassion."

"We might be criminals, but that doesn't make us leeches." Ilara's hands found the pockets of her cloak, and she pulled it tighter around her.  "Jonas is lucky he didn't find a dagger in his chest."

"You may think so," Tarin whispered back. "Gray does not. And if you take this any further, Jonas is going to retaliate, if he hasn't already."

Ilara shrugged. "Look, it was either a threat or I kill all of them. Which would you have preferred? I still feel like he's mad that I left his little group." She should have killed him when she left. No one would have questioned it if he'd shown up in an alley stabbed in the back. The space behind her eyes throbbed.

Tarin harrumphed and stroked his gray beard. Ilara knew he'd smuggled goods into the city before he was a synd, which was a less bloody path than what she had chosen for herself. Still, it was no less dangerous, and it gave him connections that Ilara wouldn't have otherwise.

She'd met Tarin when she was working with Jonas's gang, and he'd recognized her potential. Once Tarin brought her case to his own synd, he'd taken her under his wing and she'd been able to leave Jonas's gang.

She placed her hand on Tarin's shoulder in what she hoped was a consoling way. "I'm sorry. This is how I handle things. What about my other requests?"

"I know, Ilara. I know. I have a few contacts in Port Miras. There is one synd there, a brutal man. He'll work you for your gali. Could be a good fit, especially if you have trouble here. As far as protection for this Blackwood woman—" He paused. "Still not sure. Why do you care so much what happens to her?"

"Can't say, Tar."

"Trollshit. You know I'll find out one way or another. Out with it—or would you rather I find out from a bum outside her tenement?"

"Gods." There wasn't going to be a way out of this. Tarin was too resourceful. "She's my younger sister. I dragged her halfway across this continent, and I can't rightly uproot her life again because of my own problems. We're adults now, and we have our own lives. It's bad enough she has me for a sister. I'll pay you whatever you need, but she must be safe here."

Tarin grunted in recognition. "I do dumb shit like that for my family too. Don't worry about Jonas. I'll take care of it, no charge, but you better as fuck not leave the guild when you get to Port Miras. As much as you don't like it, there's consequences for what you've done. And my reputation is on the line here. I do have to ask though—I thought you Chosen weren't supposed to have any personal relationships like that? Just you and Sky Mommy."

Ilara laughed. "No, Tarin, no. Only Akara's Chosen have rules like that."

They came upon  the next intersection, where people were crowding around as a royal procession passed in front of them. Pointed red hats stood out above the crowd, a hallmark of high-ranking Akaran priests.

"Bunch of pricks," Tarin muttered.

Ilara cringed. Not all Akarans were Chosen, but most were. The best policy was to treat them all as if they were masters of the light, especially if they shrouded their eyes.

"People starve on the streets every day, and then you have this insanity. How much gali do you think it takes to move Tezza's royal ass from one end of the city to the other?" Tarin continued, uninhibited by the potential danger in front of them. His words carried, and people began edging away from him.

Tarin and Ilara moved closer to the front of the crowd. The cross street was lined with red robes, and many of their wearers were carrying large flag poles. A contingent of paladins, suited in their full battle armor, followed them. Two white-haired horses pulled a carriage decked in red and gold tassels, which was emblazoned with images of the rising sun. A soft red glow emanated from inside, and the curtains were drawn so that viewers could not gaze upon the blessed occupants. Ranks of organized paladins marched behind the carriage, swords held out in front of them, unsheathed and pointed to the skies. Always ready, as vigilant as Akara's Eye.

A chanting came from them, like a low drone of insects. Each rank seemed to be louder than the last and increased in intensity as they marched on. It wasn't until the clergy were in sight that Ilara understood what they were saying.

"Queen Mother, protect us! Usurpers march on your throne. Grant us wisdom in these times of woe."

Their voices layered upon each other. Each member of the clergy shouted in earnest, and their rhythmic chants soon devolved into to barely organized chaos. Unlike the paladins, they weren't in ranks but walked in disorganized throngs. They shouted to the crowd as they marched.

Ilara felt her face blanch, and she felt exposed, unsafe, as if someone had torn away a shield from her in the midst of a great battle. Zal'Keratha's enemies were here, in this street. Despite years of living among them, she never felt fully hidden.

*"They know nothing more than they did yesterday. Stay the course. Find the altar."*

Ilara shook her head. She thought the answer, as if in prayer. *It must wait.*

"Do you suppose the queen priestess wants to be assassinated?" Tarin asked.

Ilara grinned. "What are you offering for such a contract?"

"More gali than it takes to move her royal ass."

"Point taken." She crossed her arms. Tezza had been an offering target once. Ilara had never figured out how to escape after committing the deed.

Once the procession had finished, she and Tarin continued on together. The sun was well below the horizon, bathing the city in the comfort of night, by the time they reached the end of the palisade.

"Thanks for everything, Tar." Ilara hugged her mentor. He might have been the only person toward whom that gesture felt genuine. He'd been there for her more than most, even if it was more out of obligation to the Syndicate than her.

"It's nothing," Tarin told her. "Like I said, I'd do anything for family, and you're the last I got. Don't know if I'll bother finding another to replace you. Make sure you write when you get to the Port. Supposed to be gorgeous this time of year."

"I will, you old gnome. Give me a year and I'll be sick of it. I'll be back as soon as the pals forget me."

"Ha! I'll take that bet. If it's the last time I say it, let the shadows have your back." Tarin raised his hand in a half farewell.

Ilara mimicked the gesture. "Lady guide you."

She had to work to keep the emotion out of her voice. That surprised her. Why did she feel like this was the end of something beautiful? It was godsdamn work. There'd be another Tarin exactly like him in Port Miras.

"*You have attachments. This is not a surprise,*" Zal'Keratha's said like a reassuring mother.

Ilara suspected the goddess didn't know how much it bothered her. There was a privacy she wanted for her thoughts that she hadn't had in a long time.

The walk to Sophia's building was a short one. Glancing up and down the street, Ilara checked for a tail and saw none. The feeling of being vulnerable hadn't left her. She placed her hand on a first-floor windowsill, the first of her many handholds that led to Sophia's apartment.

Ilara smiled. "Suppose I ought to climb the stairs like a normal person."

The apartment staircase was old and made of decrepit wood. Crawling up the outside of the building would have been safer. She mulled over the last conversation she'd had with Sophia.

With the state the city was in, Ilara felt like she had to offer her sister a place in Port Miras. There had been reports of a riot this morning. The place might be crumbling faster than Ilara had anticipated. Paladins might not be enough to keep it together. They were down to obvious shows of force in the street whenever they moved Akara's Voice in the city.

"*The message given: If you don't comply, all these knights and priests will be turned on you. Tools of tyrants. Pathetic,*" Zal'Keratha said again.

When she reached Sophia's place, Ilara's heart jumped into her throat. The door, hanging off its hinges, was stamped at eye level with the holy symbol of Akara in drippy red wax. The handle was missing, with a gaping hole where it had been. Dread filled her chest, and she panicked. She pulled on the door, which fell from its frame, landing with a bang inside the apartment.

When Ilara entered, she saw Sophia's clothes had been tossed everywhere. The kitchenette was filled with broken dishes and shattered pottery, and  broken lutes and flutes littered her bedroom. Feathers lay scattered around her bed, and Ilara's eyes scanned the space frantically, looking for any clues. She saw muddy footprints, and a single parchment on the decimated mattress.

It read:

TO ALL CONCERNED,

SOPHIA BLACKWOOD HAS BEEN ARRESTED BY THE HOLY PALADINS IN SERVICE OF OUR PURE LADY IN ACCORDANCE WITH THE ROYAL DECREES OF QUEEN PRIESTESS TEZZA.

THE ACCUSED WILL STAND TRIAL IN THE ROTATION OF ONE MOON FOR THE CRIME OF AIDING AND ABETTING THE CRIMINAL KNOWN AS THORN. CONTACT YOUR LOCAL PALADIN BARRACKS IF YOU HAVE ANY INFORMATION ON THE WHEREABOUTS OF THIS CRIMINAL.

BY ALL AND WITH ROYAL DECREE,

KNIGHT COMMANDRE RYN

*No. I was so close. I was almost out.*

How had this happened? She had been so careful. The paladins wouldn't have been able to find a link between her activities and Sophia's. They'd spent so many years apart that a single night at The Pearl shouldn't have done it. The only person Ilara had told was Tarin, but there hadn't been enough time since then for all this to happen. Jonas was the only other Syndicate member who could have linked Sophia to Thorn. Had he escalated because of what she'd done last night?

Tarin's warning echoed in her mind again.

It was unbelievable. Blame crowded Ilara's thoughts, and the only person she could point her finger at was herself. She was the one who'd sent Sophia to Jonas. She was the one who hadn't fully been able to cut contact. She was the one who'd threatened Jonas. Tears fell silently down her cheeks. Was Sophia alive? Had her mistakes culminated in her sister's death?

Ilara felt all her motivation seep from her. Nothing mattered.

*"My Chosen. You know she lives."*

Her resolve built for the next moment, and she embraced it. The urge stirred inside her. Revenge would come in spades, and death would come in droves to those who'd committed this injustice, even if that was Akara herself.

No god could keep Ilara's sister from her.

# CHAPTER EIGHT

# INTERROGATION

IN THE BLEARY FOG of sleep, Sophia felt a wall hit her chest. Her clothes sagged away from her, then the chill hit her. She creaked her eyes open. The meager offerings of the cold cell had given her little comfort during the winter night.

Trying to rub her weary eyes, her head was hit with another wall of water. Shocked, she bolted upright and bathed herself in the torchlight. She wrapped her arms around her ribcage, hoping to keep in what little warmth the rags of her nightgown offered.

Two guards were standing outside the bars of the cell, the light behind them rendering them little more than silhouettes. One wore a helmet with a large feather plume that ran from front to back in a line . The other held an empty bucket and was reaching for another. Sophia scrambled back at the realization—not that it stopped the water the guard splashed across her shoulders. Its icy fingers ran down her chest and back.

"It be time, lil Ms. Singer," Plume said. "You've got an appointment with a seer."

"You won't be enjoying it, either." Bucket snickered.

"Back against the wall," Plume ordered.

Sophia shivered uncontrollably as she backed away, using the stones at the back of the cell to prop herself up. Bucket fumbled with a large set of keys and unlocked the door with a heavy clank. It groaned as Plume pushed it open and stepped across the length of the room to Sophia in a single stride. Now uncomfortably close, he roughly directed her wrists into a set of manacles. When he let go of them, Sophia stumbled under the weight, nearly falling back to the ground.

"Follow," Plume ordered, and she did, walking with him out of the cell, with Bucket falling in behind her.

She guessed she'd slept through the night, but it might only have been a few hours. The lack of windows gave her nothing to judge the time by.

The dusty stones were cold beneath her bare feet. One of the clerks had taken all her possessions, leaving only the city dress they'd taken her in, which had soon become a dirtied, muddied version of what it once was.

Packed cells lined the broad dirt-covered walkway. Sophia didn't recognize any of the wide-eyed, thin faces that stared back at her through the bars. The silent terror in their expressions spoke of the agony that had found them in this place. It was only a matter of time before she was one of them.

Panic filled her chest again. There had to be a misunderstanding. Akarans couldn't treat one of Balan's Chosen this way. A certain respect had always been given to Pantheonic gods. Without them lending power to the Pantheon, Akara would have had none.

Plume stopped in front of a large wooden door that was reinforced by several straps of iron. He drew a large key ring off his belt and unlatched it. Bucket shoved Sophia through the doorway, and she found herself on a marble-lined staircase.

Hope surged in her chest. They were taking her somewhere someone could determine this was all a mistake. She climbed the steps eagerly and was greeted by a white hallway lined with tapestries and patterned red-and-gold carpeting. The distant twittering of a flute carried in the air. The corridor was more lavish than the entryway they'd brought her in through.

Sophia decided that she wouldn't be thrown in that gods-forsaken cell again. If her case was heard, she'd make sure it was heard well.

A wisp of blue-green smoke came from the same direction as the music. Her eyes danced along it as she walked toward its source. Ilara had spoken of tracts that her goddess had given her, but Balan had never granted Sophia anything of the sort. But music—there was a magic there that she could reach into. She never got the same spell twice. Music, as disciplined as it was, had a chaos to it. Or at least that was what Sophia thought. She'd never understood what the real variance was. She could reach into a wave of music from the same song with the same instrument and turn her dress blue one night and green the next.

Plume stopped her in front of a set of double doors that stretched all the way up to the ceiling. He gave a pair of commanding knocks that echoed down the empty hallway. Moments later, the doors cracked and swung open smoothly, a gnarled hand grasping the edge from inside.

The guard stepped aside and gave a sharp shove at Sophia's shoulder. She entered the room and found herself staring into the eyes of an ancient-looking woman wearing a blue hood. Her eyes were so scrunched that Sophia wasn't sure if the woman was looking at her or past her to the guards.

The old lady grunted as she motioned for Sophia to take a seat on a padded chaise lounge. A pair of figures, also wearing hoods, closed the doors behind her. Metal grinded on metal in a sharp crack as a bolt slid into place.

The room was lined with overflowing bookcases on either side, and a large stained glass window faced Sophia. The colored shards depicted Ameri, goddess of knowledge and Sight. In this depiction, she wore a coif, her amber locks spilling out of it and down over her shoulders. She held a tome in her hands, and children robed in azure-blue cloaks sat in rapt attention at her feet.

"Calm your shivering, dear," the old woman said. The words came out stiffly, without tone or inflection.

Awareness of her state washed back over Sophia, and her face flushed red. "Apologies," she said, wrapping her arms around her chest. "I had little choice of wardrobe. Are you a Sage?"

The woman nodded.

Ameri's Sages were known for their compassion. In the old stories, they were often the ones to establish orphanages and feed starving villages. Unlike Ameri's Scholars, who were locked in dusty libraries, Sages accomplished the will of their god.

"Sage Anison," the woman said as Sophia took a seat opposite her. The Sage leaned against the arm of the lounge and brushed her hood back in a way Sophia couldn't bring herself to imitate..

Anison was bald, as was common with Ameri's Chosen. Wrinkles as wide as thumbs snaked across her head, interweaving and overlapping one another in a twisting pattern.

"Whose Chosen are you?" Anison demanded.

"Balan's," Sophia answered. There was no use in lying. Sages had ways of drawing information out of a person.

"Some paladins are clamoring to interrogate you. Do you know why?"

"Not entirely."

"But you have some idea. You think there is a valid reason for you to be here." Anison's eyes were fierce, as if she was expecting to get something out of Sophia.

"I only mean that no one has told me," Sophia answered. Her eyes searched the room. The sound of the flute had been cut off, and the space was silent as death.

"There is no music here for you to channel," Anison said. She spoke calmly, so calmly that her words carried little variance in tone or inflection.

Sophia began to understand. Balan had told her once that some of his Chosen could make magic from the melody of spoken words. That was not one of her gifts. Yet this Sage was concerned that she might draw power from her speech.

"You're worried I'd channel here? Balan supports our queen."

"Even so, the Akarans believe you fraternize with a heretic. Is this true?"

"No more true than it has ever been." Sophia stiffened. "Heretical gods outside the Pantheon do not exist in Eversburg. Balan would not condone it."

"You and I both know they do. But we are not speaking about Balan," Anison snapped. "We're speaking about you. Is your sister a heretic or not?"

Sophia felt her confidence deflate. It was always about Ilara. Ilara and her cursed goddess. "Why do you need me for this? Are you unable to See her?" she asked.

The Sage's spine stiffened in response. Sophia had struck a nerve. "I will not discuss with you the gifts Ameri gives her children."

It was enough. Anison didn't have the Sight, Ameri's blessing that allowed her Chosen to see future events. It was rare, but Sophia expected a Sage in Akara's court to have it.

"Tell me of your sister, then. She is the criminal Thorn?"

"Why are you asking me rather than the Akarans?" Sophia said.

"In accordance with the laws of the Pantheon, when a Chosen of one of its gods commits crimes against another god within the Pantheon, a neutral third party acts as a delegate in the dispute. You will tell me what I need to know. Otherwise, you will face the queen's justice with no intermediary. She can be quite unkind to those she deems faithless."

Sage Anison's lips formed a single pale line. Sophia's options were obvious: give up her sister and go free, or remain caged. This wasn't a hearing, it was an interrogation.

"What of Balan?" she asked.

"If you do not cooperate, he will be deemed a heretic and cast from the Pantheon. Another will take his place, as in the past. You ask questions to stall. Answer me, or the Paladins will ask these questions. They will be less accommodating. Akara becomes impatient."

"A-a-aye."

"Then speak."

Stabbing pain erupted from the base of Sophia's skull and dug upward, like a worm consuming her brain. Each throb seemed to eat away at her consciousness, clouding her ability to think. She yelped and fell from the couch. As her hand flew to the back of her neck, she expected the sensation of warm blood but found only cold, clammy skin.

"Wha—?" Sophia writhed as another shockwave of pain blasted her mind.

Anison stood over her wearing a half smile. "As a matter of course, I have become less kind in regard to repetition of questions during my tenure here. Adept Ildan is only so cautious with mind attacks. He is rather ravenous when it comes to gifts from our goddess."

"Aye," Sophia hissed through clenched teeth. Ildan must have taken the hint and eased up his attack, as the pain in her skull faded. The songs didn't tell tales of Sages torturing during their interrogations. "Ask your questions, Sage." She huffed as she pushed herself from the ground. Stars filled the edges of her vision, and it took Sophia a moment to pull herself from the resulting fog.

"Which deity does Thorn champion?" Anison demanded.

Sophia didn't see a way out of answering. If she cooperated, she might be able to weasel away in the dead of night—or at least survive until that was a possibility. Whatever trouble Ilara had gotten herself into was coming to her either way. Sophia didn't want to die for it.

*"Survive. That is all I can ask of you."*

"Zal'Keratha." The word felt like betrayal on Sophia's lips.

"The goddess of death's Chosen. Does she remain in Eversburg?" Anison asked as the sound of the Sophia's answer faded from the room.

"She spoke of leaving. I don't know if she'll change that now." Sophia's eyes widened. Too much detail.

"Why?"

"B-b-because," she stammered. They'll find her. They'll turn her brain to mush. My sister will be gone, and so will any memory of my parents.

She paused and drew a deep breath. Ilara would be fine. Nothing Sophia told these people would change that. Her sister had overcome so many obstacles to get their little family to safety.

"Because I am here."

"And that would concern her?" Anison asked.

"Aye. Ilara doesn't like my life to be compromised."

"Blood of the Martyr. A killer with a conscience." The Sage drew a small black band from the folds of her robes. "Do you know what this is?"

"I'm sure you will tell me."

Anison held it out in front of her and gestured for Sophia to take it. "Put it around your throat, girl," she commanded.

Sophia slipped the band over her head, and it stretched like an oversized tunic.

The Sage gripped her head with both hands. "Ko'matsu dore beni fala fis," she whispered. It was a language that Sophia didn't recognize, much less understand.

Sophia's throat warmed and chilled when the incantation finished. When Anison removed her hands, Sophia ran her fingers over the band. There were no edges to it, as if it had become part of her skin.

"The band cuts the flow of your god's magic. Balan won't speak to you, and you cannot access the magic he's given you," Anison explained.

Sophia's heart fell. Another bar on her cage.

"Try to remove it and you will feel intense pain. Try to access Balan's power and you will feel the same. This is power beyond your understanding. Do not toy with it." Anison stood and walked to the door. "We will contemplate your case and bring it before the Tribunal. You will have a verdict before the end of the month. Expect High Priestess Tezza to drag her feet on making a decision in your case. She does not relish dispensing the Pantheon's justice."

"Aye," Sophia said.

The door screeched open. Plume and Bucket were standing in the doorway, ever dutiful.

"That didn't take as long as the last one," Plume said.

"You may take her. We have all we need. The knight commander will receive my full report," Anison responded.

The two guards flanked Sophia again and escorted her from the room. In the hall, the sound of the flute echoed against the walls as it had before. This time, there was no wave of music.

The richness of the tones was gone, and Sophia couldn't recognize pitch from pitch.

Plume muttered something about missing a torture session. Bucket replied that he was glad it hadn't been necessary. Sophia was too dazed to care.

They marched back the same way they'd come. The dungeon stairs were damp and foreboding, unlike the air of the corridors. It was the tomb Sophia where would go to die.

The men brought her to a cell. A different one, she thought, than the one in which she'd begun this cursed day. A figure was sitting against the back wall, its green eyes flicking over Sophia as if she were a fresh meal. This was the coffin in which her body would rot. The door screeched open, and its occupant stood.

"Brought you fresh meat, Beast." Bucket snickered as he shoved Sophia over the threshold. She couldn't help but stumble down to her knees.

*Everything is over*, she thought. *I've betrayed everything close to me. They'll kill Ilara and Balan, and I'll rot in a cell for the rest of my days. I'll never hear beauty in music again.*

"Fuck off, Larin," Beast said.

Sophia felt warm palms grip her shoulders as the cell door closed with a final thud.

"Hopefully you let this one survive longer than the last," Bucket yelled. He and Plume erupted in raucous laughter. Bootsteps thudded away as they spoke of something Sophia couldn't be bothered to pay attention to.

"Come on, lass," Beast said in an almost motherly tone. "Let's clean you up as well as we can. I'm sure you've had a hard day."

# Chapter Nine

# SACRIFICIAL RITUALS

Valette tapped her finger against her lips, holding her chin as she appraised the market. Shoppers milled around the dwindling stalls, skirting past a paladin in full armor who hadn't moved in hours.

"Getting bored yet?" Otto asked as he appraised her contemplative stance. She wished she'd had her suit of armor on.

"Quite," Valette answered.

The paladin turned and took the hand of a passerby. They started shouting about something. The man she'd grabbed was bone thin and seemed frail. Valette had apprehended three similar market thieves that week. Each one she'd let go with a stern word. These people weren't real criminals. They just wanted to feed their families.

But this paladin seemed about to break this thief's arm off.

Valette pushed off the wall she'd been leaning against, but paused when Otto put his hand on her shoulder. "Not worth it. That pal would chew you to bits," he said matter-of-factly.

"I doubt that sincerely. Someone should say something," she growled. She'd seen enough combat to know that this paladin was green. The only issue would be the ensuing reprisal from Ryn. "You think anyone else could? We're here to keep the peace."

"Walk away," Otto replied. "You fight one of Akara's paladins, you'll end up burned or dead."

"It doesn't seem like we have much of a choice. If we don't do something, she will hurt an innocent," Valette huffed.

Otto stood quickly. "Going for my smoke break. You're coming before you do something stupid."

"I don't smoke, Otto," she said as she pinched and massaged the bridge of her nose

"Do you have much else to do?" His eyes were on the paladin, who'd let the poor man go. "She's taking care of our job for us."

Valette thought about Ryn's last warning. She still didn't understand the dynamics between Akarans and the citizenry. Perhaps she could learn something from Otto. "I suppose not. Some fresh scenery could do me some good."

"My thoughts exactly," Otto said with a smile.

The two of them walked up the street to a small square with a fountain in the middle. The Solar Dominion was only a few blocks to the north. A stone statue of Akara stood just outside the entrance, towering over the tallest pillar of the palace. Her sword extended to the south, casting a foreboding shadow over the city. Her visored helm obscured her eyes, but revealed her stern frown and pointed chin.

The chill of the winter wind blew across Valette's shoulders. The gambeson didn't block it as well as her armor did. It left her feeling exposed.

She huffed as she leaned against the stone railing, and the air began to stink as Otto puffed his cloveweed. Musky and rife with the succor of addiction, the smell always made Valette's nose wrinkle. She turned to Otto, who was already partially through his first joint.

"What're you doing here?" he asked.

"You asked me to come smoke with you." Valette shrugged.

He frowned. "You know what I mean. What are you doing in Eversburg? Almir doesn't send his Chosen here."

She narrowed her eyes at him. "Almir wanted to rectify that. He felt we should have some presence in the capital."

"Trollshit," Otto huffed, then coughed violently as he exhaled a plume of smoke. "You won't be doing that guarding the riffraff in Noon district. Rumor is that you pissed off some clergy in Chrys."

"Almir and Akara," Valette said under her breath. "I don't owe you an explanation, Otto."

"So you're going to mope for another week?" he asked. "Or are you gonna do something?"

Valette felt the fire in her chest. "And what would you suggest?" she snapped.

"Go somewhere else—anywhere else. No one would question you if you left Eversburg quietly. It's what Ryn wants, anyway. Or you can fight him on his trollshit. Anything is better than whoever you've been since we arrested Blackwood."

Walking to one of the limestone buildings, he stamped the burning end of his cloveweed on it, then flicked it away. He sauntered back to the position they'd guarded to let Valette sit with her feelings for a few moments.

Otto's words stung, because she knew it was true. As much as Ryn talked about wanting her to learn the ropes, it felt like he was edging her out. It was like he had a problem that he was hoping would take care of itself. She was done with this game. Whether she understood it or not, if she didn't make a move, she'd lose.

Valette strolled back to her post with renewed confidence. Otto was conversing with a young woman in a red cloak who was leaning against the wall with her leg propped up seductively. The paladin was still standing in the middle of the market with her plated arms hanging awkwardly at her sides. She shifted from one foot to another before turning around and inspecting the people around her. She seemed nervous.

Valette waited until the market had emptied somewhat before approaching. The paladin eyed the knight with suspicion in her glowing red eyes. They were the only part of her Valette could see through the split helm.

"You come too close, guard," she said.

"I am Almiran Chosen Valette. I have a few questions."

The paladin shifted again, clearly uncomfortable. The strain of plate was heavy for those unaccustomed to it. "I've heard of you, Almiran. I've been told not to speak of you. I won't entertain a conversation."

"How long ago were you told to guard this market?"

The woman's eyes flicked to Valette's for a moment before settling back on the crowd around her. "This was my sacred duty, given to me this morning."

"And how long were you Chosen before being given this sacred duty? A day, or a week?" Valette asked.

The paladin seemed to deflate a little, but she put a hand on the hilt of the sword sheathed at her waist.

"You get a sense of these things when you've served for a while. The things people say and how they present themselves," Valette went on. "The outward symbols of how our gods manifest in us. For Akarans, you inherit Akara's gaze. Ameri gives her Scholars her intellect. A Crafter receives the hardness of Halgar's hands. Do you know what Almir gives his Chosen?"

"None have mentioned it. It must be weak," the paladin said.

"Almir was the first paladin. Other Chosen made deals with the gods to gain power, but he was the first to champion his god to the people. He embodied Akara's will on Aerlia," Valette said.

The paladin tightened her grip on her weapon, breathing deeply out of her nostrils. "You have a point?" she asked, taking a step forward. "I can spout facts as well. Akara is one of the few gods who can make many Chosen. The only others who can do so because Akara wills it to be so."

A small circle had formed around them. No one wanted to get near an angry paladin. In that moment, Valette should have felt more vulnerable than she did.

"My point is that Almir grants us enough willpower to be bullheaded. And you need some bullheadedness to go back to your superiors and demand a real assignment. Let guards do the guarding. That's the real test they've given you, not a sacred duty to guard a market. This is beneath your station."

The paladin's eyes flared a bright red. If she was really mad, she would channel a spell at Valette and kill her, or at least try to. Valette was sure she could handle the young Chosen. But instead, she shoved past Valette and sauntered down the aisle. The crowd parted to let her through.

"I have experience being Chosen," Valette called after the paladin. "Come find me if you need real help with that tract she gave you."

With a new spring in her step, she sauntered back to Otto, who had successfully shooed the sultry priestess away. "Looks like you succeeded in giving us more work to do. Find anything useful?" he asked as Valette once again leaned against the wall next to him.

"Maybe," she said.

He pulled out a creased and crumpled map, which he inspected with great care.

"What's with the map?" Valette asked.

"The last woman who came here—you saw her?"

"I can recognize a harlot," Valette said.

"Well, she put a noise complaint out on this building. Said it sounded as if people were gathering after dark and singing." Otto indicated a square on the map near the Solar Dominion.

"Is there a tenement building near there?" The words felt odd coming out of Valette's mouth. As far as she knew, nobody lived in the Dawn district.

"No. She said she was passing by after finishing the Sundown ritual here at the palace. She had a pass. Normally, both gathering after sundown and singing are punishable here in Eversburg."

"Really?" Valette didn't even put in the effort to veil her shock. The people in this city seemed consigned to Akara's odd rules. Or did they stem from the clergy? "We do not have these laws in Chrys."

"Aye." Otto nodded enthusiastically. "I thought you might find it strange. Lived in Chrys myself. For a few years, at least. In fact, her description sounded oddly like an old Almiran chant. Fell to demons, fell to man?" His brow furrowed as if he was searching for a long-forgotten memory.

"Fallen demons," Valette said with a start. She smiled as the memory washed over her. The song told the tales of old mercenaries who'd suffered from physical ailments. Almir had fought with them in his youth, until he was called by Akara.

"Aye, sounds right." Otto seemed to pause a moment in reminiscence himself. "Anyway, we're not going out of our way to investigate it, unless there's more reports. It's your way back, though, since you basically live in the Dominion, no?"

"I do have a room there," Valette said. Chosen of other gods weren't allowed to roam free in the city. Housing them in the Solar Dominion allowed the Akarans to keep tabs on them.

Otto's eyes flicked from Valette back to the map. He handed it back to her. "Might need this to find the place, I suppose."

Valette thanked him, and they went back to watching people come and go among the market stalls.

***

*This is utterly ridiculous*, Valette thought to herself. She'd left her guard post and gone back to the Solar Dominion.

She felt better now that she'd donned her plate armor. It had been crafted by a Halgan back in Chrys. The Chosen of the Crafter were skilled, and there had been a lot of nice improvements made to it that often made the difference in battle. First and foremost, each plate was connected internally with straps and bands that made the whole thing feel lighter. She didn't know how it worked. Protection runes that glowed a soft blue also covered the plate, which allowed her some protection against spells.

The building Otto had pointed out was drab. A sign marked it as a clothier, and robes in Akaran red-and-gold patterns were displayed in the windows as advertisements to passers-by. It would be a good front for any kind of nightly activity. Valette prayed that there truly were Almirans gathering here—it would be idyllic to find a familiar group of believers.

"*You are far too hopeful, dear,*" Almir said.

*Wouldn't you know for a fact if my hopes were well founded?* Valette thought back. She was on edge. The possibility that this was an ambush was just as large as the chance of it being a secret meeting of Almirans.

"*I would, in fact,*" he responded. "*I didn't see the importance in you being around other worshipers. For gods' sake, you've been to war.*"

*So there are worshipers in there?*

Almir's silence said everything he wouldn't. There was a relevance to Almirans being in Eversburg that Valette couldn't put her finger on. Not only was worshipping Almir permitted in the city, but he could be worshiped openly. There was no reason for believers to hide or meet after dark. Yet, she hadn't seen a one since she'd been living in Eversburg.

She huffed. *At the very least, you can't blame my curiosity.*

"*I can't. Your unceasing need to know is why I Chose you. I think about it often.*"

Valette frowned. It wasn't a pleasant memory for her. Almir had Chosen her a lifetime ago, during one of her first campaigns against the Southern folk. Blood—She stopped the thought. It wouldn't think about it now.

The sun rested on the horizon, and a large crowd of people still milled in the square. Certainly it wouldn't draw attention if Valette joined them, though being in full plate, she chose to stand closer to the building than the crowd. She hoped she looked like a paladin keeping the peace.

Akara's statue was easily visible from this angle, stone sword out like a branch reaching too far from a tree. Valette's eyes widened when she noticed three figures standing near the tip of the blade. From this distance, they scarcely looked larger than figurines.

People in the crowd had seen them as well, and many were pointing. Others shaded their eyes from the setting sun. Valette slipped on her helmet, and the world lit up with blue outlines. Heat radiated from the runes on her arms and helmet.

"Aujer," she said, and her vision narrowed on the figures, bringing them into sharper focus. She could make out two Akaran priests in red robes, their eyes shining fiercely. The man between them was dressed in tattered rags, his skin covered in dirt. A dark black band encircled his head and covered his eyes, and tears were streaming down his face. She recognized him. It was the man from her Tribunal, the one who'd lit the staff. His eyes seemed to burn brighter, shining through the blindfold.

The priests said something to him, though Valette couldn't hear what. Then, as the last light of the sun faded beneath the horizon, the priest's hand erupted in flames, the light of the fire dancing across the man's skin. The priests didn't react as they brought their hand to touch their prisoner. His face twisted in pain.

He caught fire moments later. As the priests stepped away from him, he took one step off the tip of the stone sword, plummeting down at a frightening pace.

"Ajure," Valette said again, and her vision widened back to normal. Against the newborn night sky, the man looked like a shooting star straying too close to the world. Valette turned away from him as he disappeared behind a building. The resulting smack resonated across the square.

The crowd cheered, their faces twisting in joy at the man's death before they slowly began dispersing.

*Almir, explain.*

"*Your explanation will be as sufficient as mine own,*" Almir said.

Valette swallowed the horror and did her best to control her thoughts. There had to be a reasonable explanation—there always was.

*Public execution, or a sacrifice to Akara? We're missing some pieces of the puzzle. What was the black band? Why kill him of all people?* Her hand rose absentmindedly to her chin, but was blocked by the metal tip of her helmet.

"*You know the first man to ask,*" Almir said.

Valette nodded. Otto. Intentionally or not, he pointed her in this direction.

She strolled across the square and tried to open the front door of the clothier's store. The knob resisted her turn. Locked. To be sure, she tried the back door as well. If there had been Almirans here, they were long gone now. Valette eyed the large glass windows, contemplating the ramifications of breaking and entering.

Ultimately, she walked away, back to the palace, trying to stomach the thought of other believers. It could wait.

Instead, she contemplated the burning fireball that had fallen to the ground. The fear in the man's eyes when he went up in flames. The terror of having no paths left. She knew what it was like to stare death in the face. For her, it had been the yellow eyes and scaled face of an Aoxian, charging at her with a lance twice her size.

## CHAPTER TEN

# GRAY

ILARA'S THIGHS ACHED AS the night's cold wind nipped at her face. She willed her body lower, as if trying to become one with the sloped rooftop. Below her, a drunken figure stumbled out of a well-lit tavern. Jonas. The thought of driving her daggers into his throat was too tantalizing for her not to grin slightly.

Jonas took a few steps and yelled at the top of his lungs, "The maiden! The maiden!" The first few words of a popular drinking song. He righted himself with the help of two larger, well-armed men and a man with a tattooed head, whom Ilara recognized from the warehouse.

Sophia's arrest had been so sudden. Ilara hadn't realized the paladins were close to her sister. They must have gotten the information from somewhere. She might be taking a leap in thinking it was Jonas, but she'd fucking find out. Not to mention there were those Akaran crates in Jonas's safehouse.

Could be he'd stolen them, but he usually didn't plan heists that grand. Embezzlement was far more likely.

When she'd gone back to the safehouse, everything had been cleared out, and it had taken her the better part of a week to track down his location. Every moment she waited was another moment Sophia rotted in a dungeon.

"I'll get to the bottom of this, Soph," she muttered under her breath.

*"The bottom of what, now?"*

The voice echoed through Ilara's head like her goddess's, but this one was different. This one lacked the power of divinity. It was Markus, Jonas's pet Amerite. She'd known he would crawl out of the woodwork eventually, and she hoped she could kill him far from Jonas.

*"Good plans. But you could just ask,"* he said.

*What are you doing in my godsdamn thoughts,* Markus?

*"Chosen to Chosen, I have to make sure my employer is safe. You look a little threatening crawling across the rooftop."*

Markus's Sight was why Jonas hadn't been surprised by her at the safehouse. He could see future events, with more likely ones being clearer—depending on the actors involved. Markus had also sensed her thoughts. It was common for Ameri's Chosen to have the ability to connect minds, but the Sight was a rare talent. Ilara had never worked out how a low-life criminal like Jonas had been able to entice a Chosen as powerful as Markus.

*Then you know that Jonas sought Death. Death seeks Jonas. He will die tonight.*

The bald man on the street below stopped walking, letting Jonas and the guards pull away from him. That one was Markus, of course. Ilara should have known. All Scholars, regardless of ability and gender, lost their hair eventually. It was more obvious when looking at a bald woman—men of Ameri's Chosen were harder to pick out by their bare heads alone.

*"Aye. I know a lost cause when I've Seen one. Honestly, I didn't think you'd find us so quickly. Don't torture the bloke too terribly. I'll be in the Kittering when your mistress sends you to me."*

*Why? You were so loyal to Jonas for so long.*

*"You'll find out in time,"* Markus replied as his form on the street below dashed down an alleyway.

"You traitorous bastard," Ilara huffed under her breath as she hopped to another rooftop.

Jonas and his lackeys continued on as if nothing was amiss. Ilara continued to creep after them. She made sure to keep out of sight, not that she particularly needed to. Few paid attention to anything above eye level. These guards were no different, so she saw no reason to start using her reserve of invisibility.

Still, they posed a problem. They walked with an alertness lowly gang members didn't, and their gear was spotless. One was carrying a large hammer on his back, and the other had a shield emblazoned with a lion—the crest of a noble family, though not one with which Ilara was familiar. If they were trained muscle, she was sure it would be a difficult confrontation, one she would likely come away with a wound from.

Sophia didn't have time for Ilara to recover from anything serious.

Yet another oddity in this was that they were far on the north end of the Noon district, close to the Dawn district. Not only were the roads and homes better kept here than around Jonas's safehouse in Dusk, but the people would be better put together. Clergy, nobles, wealthy merchants and high-ranking paladins called this area of the city home. It was far more dangerous for someone like Jonas.

Could he be of noble birth? That would be strange, certainly. Many of the gang leaders in the Syndicate were of higher birth than those they led, however, that usually meant they were the children of merchants or travelers. They had enough gali to fund their nefarious deeds, but not enough to be well-off without it.

As the trio turned onto a street lit by enough lanterns to keep the shadows at bay, Ilara descended a pipe running down the side of a building. She considered rushing the men, now no more than a hundred steps away, but brushed away the thought. Open confrontation brought paladins, and paladins brought more danger. For now, she continued to follow at a safe distance, her face obscured by the hood of her cloak and the cha'ak mask.

Finally, they stopped at a free-standing building not unlike Ilara's home, but larger. It was made of brick and stood a full five stories high. Jonas flung the front door open, and distant cheers reached Ilara's ears. He sauntered in and slammed the door closed. His guards stayed on the street, taking position on either side of the stairs to the entrance.

Ducking into an alley, Ilara thumbed her forehead and felt a shroud fall over her form, the supply of magic in her tract diminishing slightly. Within the safety of invisibility, she strode confidently out onto the street, slowing her pace only as she neared the men. She might be invisible, but the crunch of the snow under her feet could still be heard.

She stopped in front of the alley next to the building Jonas had disappeared into. Fogs of breath blew from the mouths of the guards outside, their noses and ears turned red from the harsh cold.

"How long do we have to deal with this wretch?" the one carrying the hammer said. Now that she was closer, Ilara could see that its head was made from some kind of black stone. Its edges were sharp and crooked, like he'd picked it up off the ground and mounted it to the end of a stick. He had a crooked nose and a hint of a mustache on his upper lip.

"As long as the boss says we do," his partner said, then spit on the ground as if in spite. He wore an eyepatch and seemed to be missing as many teeth as he had. A scar ran from the base of his neck to his chin. All likely wounds from battles previously won.

"Boring work. He's a real dumbass, I'll tell you that," the guard with the crooked nose replied. Neither said anything more, and Ilara assumed the was conversation over.

Jonas's synd must have moved him here. Either Tarin had warned him of how much danger he was in, or he wasn't as stupid as these guards thought he was. Tarin had spies everywhere, and likely knew Sophia had been arrested. It wouldn't be a stretch to think Ilara would try to kill Jonas. She'd nearly done it once over a loan. Truthfully, she was surprised Jonas hadn't tried to kill her himself, or sent his goons after her.

*Not going through the front door.* Ilara turned back to the alley. Creeping down it, she found an empty section of wall with enough loose handholds for her to climb. Hopefully one of the windows would be unlatched and the room beyond it empty. She grabbed a brick chipped deep enough for her to slide her fingers in the crack and began pulling herself up, hand over hand.

Ilara peeked in the first window and saw a maid cleaning. The second one revealed a group of men playing cards. The third story seemed empty, save for a lit candle on a table next to a large, cushioned chair.

A multitude of books lined the shelves of the room. Not ideal. There had clearly been an occupant here recently, but Ilara wasn't in a position to seek out a different route. She edged the window up and felt the resistance of the latch.

Silently, she called upon the power in her wrists and summoned forth a long, slender dagger, thin enough to wiggle through the space between the panes. With a practiced hand, she slipped the latch from its hasp and slid the window open. She crawled into the room just as a man entered through the doorway.

"Drop the spell, Chosen," he said, regarding her with eyes that glowed an iridescent blue.

Ilara complied and let the invisibility spell fade, but she created another long dagger to accompany the first.

"You're here for Jonas, I take it?" His footsteps silenced by the carpet, the man approached the chair and picked up a book lying open on the arm. His face bore the burden of his advanced years, yet his movements were spry. He clasped the book shut as he approached her. Ilara backed away from the man, who matched his steps with hers.

"I told the boy he was a fool to anger a Chosen," he continued. "He was confident you wouldn't learn of his ruse until he had guild protections in place. Partially true—I am here, after all."

"And you are?" Ilara tightened her grip on her weapons and lowered her stance. She could spring forward and slit the man's throat, or dive back out the window. Still, she'd come here for information, and he was confirming everything she'd suspected.

"More important than you, Thorn." He narrowed his eyes as he stepped over to the nearest shelf and placed the book into an empty slot. A drinking glass sat next to a bottle of amber liquid in front of the neat rows of spines. He poured a hefty amount into the glass, brought it up to his nose, and swirled it. "Tarin would be disappointed in your course of action. However, I won't stop you—as long as you agree to what I have to say."

"Better start talking, then," Ilara growled.

"There's no doubt Jonas deserves the death you intend to deal him. He betrayed you, a Syndicate member. His time will come. Yet you know this situation could be handled with a little more tact. The synds would decide Jonas's fate. I'm sure Tarin told you the consequences of avoiding Syndicate authority. Did you even go to him when you realized your sister had been taken?"

Ilara kept her expression calm with the help of several deep breaths. This man knew she'd gone to Tarin but didn't know the details of their conversation. Either they'd spoken with Tarin and he'd lied, or they were torturing him.

Something in her wrenched. Ilara wanted to kill this man. Her palms were sweaty, and her head began to ache. Zal'Keratha required tribute.

"Soph was not a member." Ilara sunk further into her defensive stance. "She had an outstanding debt. The synds wouldn't have been sympathetic."

"Based on your previous loyalty, the trial would come to a duel between you and Jonas. We would help you liberate your sister if you were victorious. You are aware of Jonas's martial prowess? No doubt, you would get your justice in that arena," he said with a shrug.

"How can you be so sure?" Ilara scoffed.

The man gave her a dry smile. "Because I organize the Gray Syndicate."

"You're Gray? Why on Aerlia would the head of the Syndicate be guarding a lowlife like Jonas?" she asked incredulously.

"He is my son," Gray said. "He is disappointing, but the truth is the truth. I will not have him lawlessly killed by a criminal posing as a vigilante."

The offer was tempting. Ilara could get out of this without fighting her way to Jonas. And she still hadn't figured out a way to save Sophia yet. Having the full weight of the Syndicate behind her would give her a lot of credit when it came to enlisting help.

"And if I don't believe you?" she asked.

"Then I kill you." Gray's hand rested on his cane, which looked remarkably like the handle of a sword.

*"This is a trap. It was all a trap, idiot girl!"*

Gray slid into a combat stance, drew a rapier from his cane, and flourished it in her direction. The blade was blacker than the night and seemed to pulse like an infected wound. Ilara brought her blades up to parry, but they were knocked from her hands, quickly dissipating.

"You will find I am a well-studied opponent. I know that you rely too heavily on your magic blades—so much so that you carry no physical weapons. First weakness."

As he finished speaking, Ilara lunged toward him, newly formed daggers leading the way, aimed at his throat. He side-stepped her, and the momentum of her lunge carried her to the opposite side of the room. She spun quickly and threw one of the weapons toward his face. Desperation crowded her mind as it sailed past him and dug into the spine of a book.

"A feint into an attack. Creative, but not good enough," Gray said as he directed the point of his rapier toward her. The longer blade was as challenge she'd need to overcome. "Again."

Ilara formed another dagger, using the last of her reserve to make it as long as possible. It came out more like a short, stunted sword. It was still only about half as long as Gray's, but it would have to be enough.

*There is no time for this*, she thought. Anger and frustration burned in her. In the small room, she wouldn't be getting around his defenses, so she'd need to go through them.

Want throbbed between her eyes. The need to kill this man grew, and she imagined his blood spilled freely on the carpet. Gripping her longer blade as tightly as she could, she threw her remaining dagger at Gray's thigh. He brought his rapier down. It hadn't even touched her blade before it seemed to fade and disappear . Unfazed, she lunged again, the longer weapon directed at Gray's chest. With a speed she couldn't comprehend, he stepped back and brought his rapier up to parry. Her sword bounced off his and fell apart in her hand. He stabbed forward, the tip of his dark blade catching her in the shoulder.

Ilara grunted and moved away. Instinctively, she ran her hand over her forehead to activate her invisibility, but she felt no magic flow over her body.

Gray laughed a dry, haughty laugh. "Chosen, you rely much too heavily on the powers of your patron. What escape do you even have without it? Did you even consider you'd be dying here? Your hubris is your true weakness."

Ilara barely registered the footsteps behind her. Darkness crept around the edges of her vision as strong hands grabbed her arms.

"Take her away and tie her down," Gray yelled as they dragged her away.

She could barely hold her head up as she was pulled into the hallway beyond. Sound faded to nothing shortly after her vision went black.

# Chapter Eleven

# BEASTS

"So, music?" Katri, Sophia's cellmate, asked. She stood a full head taller than Sophia, set on a thin frame. Her auburn hair was caked with mud, and she had wild green eyes.

"Aye, music is the preferred way. Balan grants spells certain tones. It can be hard to see the nature of the spell from the sound waves," Sophia said.

"You can see sound? What're some things you've cast?"

It had been days since Sophia had been thrown in the cell. It had taken her that long to speak to Katri. She still wasn't sure how trustworthy the woman they called Beast was.

"Hard to say. Sometimes I do little more than recolor my hair. Other times I can influence a person's emotions and thoughts."

Katri's eyes widened. "You can control someone?"

"Not quite." Sophia huffed. "I can brighten their mood or ruin their day. If it's a particularly powerful wave, I can give them a thought. I've never masterminded someone like a puppet."

Katri breathed a sigh of relief. "Glad I won't be losing my wits about you. Recoloring the hair sounds exciting though. I've always pictured myself as a blonde. So you don't have tracts like other Chosen?"

"Not in the same way. I heard a Crafter once say that when they look at an object, they can see what runes need to be carved in it to make it work. It's sort of like that. Balan lets me see the magic in the world around us, rather than giving it to me to use," Sophia explained.

Katri's brow furrowed.

"Can I ask why the guards called you 'Beast'?" Sophia asked.

It seemed to shock Katri out of whatever thought she was having. "Keep in my good graces and maybe I'll show you some day. I can't rightly do that with this around my wrist, though." She up her hand to show the black band, embedded in her skin like Sophia's.

It surprised Sophia that they had so much time to talk freely. There was an ease to hushing a conversation whenever a guard unlocked the dungeon door. The joy of having someone here with her made the time pass, as if they were an old couple playing cards. A little joy before whatever dark end awaited them.

"What time of year was it when you were thrown down here?" Katri asked.

"Winter. The day was the middle of Trandor, a week past the half-year mark."

"Close to the end of Trandor now, then," Katri mused. She massaged the back of her neck. "Time passes differently here. Slower, I'd say. It's bloody hard to track. I was counting how many times I slept, but—" She trailed off, either bored with the conversation or with something on her mind she couldn't say. There was a certain beauty to the way her mind scattered.

"How long you been in here?" Sophia asked.

"It was autumn." Katri shrugged. "Forgot the day. What did they get you for?"

"Associating with a known criminal." It was all so ridiculous to Sophia. She didn't know what evidence they had, or what would become of her. The Amerites' vague warnings told her nothing. Her mind pulled back to the conversation.

"That's a good excuse," Katri said. "Used to run in that world myself. Too much trouble. Pals called what I did 'illegal revolutionary activity,' which is to say I set fire to their stockades. Think they'd been tailing me for a while, and I gave them an excuse to pick me up."

"You regret that? You've had months of imprisonment, months of your life taken away, for arson."

"What, the stockade? Aye, I do a bit. I could be doing so much if I weren't in here. But they would have found a reason eventually. I was in the resistance, however small it is. I would have been hanged already. Except once they found out I was a Chosen, that slowed down the process a bit."

"Why wouldn't they ha—"

The clank of the key in the door hushed all talking in the dungeon. It was common for the din of conversation to rise a bit while the jailers were away. They made their rounds a few times an hour to do a head count or take prisoners out for work duty. Sophia prayed to Balan they hadn't heard them speaking, and that they wouldn't take Katri that day.

The sound of chainmail clinked through the door, and a conversation between the guards echoed off the walls. Sophia turned away from the bars so that she didn't have to look at the men. Judging from the number of bootsteps, there were more than the two that normally patrolled the cells.

"And this is our dungeon," one man announced, silencing all the others. "Seeing you're all transfers from the city watch, this is where all the saps you arrest go—at least all the ones that have done crimes against the clergy."

"Seems a bit full," a second man said in a dulcet tone. A younger man who was working his way through the force, then. "Aren't they supposed to clear out after their sentencing?"

"No," the first man said. "Most of these ones are all Chosen. And no, not Chosen of Akara—they get what's coming to them. Bloody traitors. Chosen of other gods don't get executed until the Tribunal makes a ruling. Akara herself has to rule on them. Usually they're sentenced to rot here until they die. Now, lock our prisoner in this cell."

The clank of a latch and screech of a cell door sounded. There was a quiet shuffle as the new prisoner was pushed in. Sophia risked peeking over her shoulder to see a man with messy dark hair and tan skin lying on his side in the cell across from hers.

"Get out of here, you lot," the first guard shouted again.

The retinue shuffled from the dungeon, and the door clicked shut again. Slowly, the conversations between the prisoners rose to the same level as before the guards entered.

Katri rolled her eyes and settled back into the corner of the cell. "Looks like they found some new gents to torture us with."

Sophia leaned against the metal bars, facing the area both of them used to defecate in. She'd thought she'd get used to the stink of human feces. She'd thought wrong. "What is all this about not killing us, anyway?" she wondered.

"Did Balan not teach you anything about being Chosen?" Katri asked. "Or are you just new to it?"

"I've been Chosen for most of my life, thank you."

"Don't come at me for stating facts. Balan should've told you, it's one of the basics. When a god makes a bond with a Chosen, they give some of their power to them. That doesn't get reclaimed until the Chosen dies or the god Forsakes them. You know about that, right?"

"Aye, I know what a Forsaken is. A Chosen becomes a husk of themselves when a god draws their power from them. I've heard it only happens when a Chosen infuriates their god."

There were tales of Crafters forgetting how to work a chisel or a lathe. Sophia supposed it must feel similar to the way she felt now. Her hand flitted to the band at her throat, and a sting bit at her finger.

Katri nodded. "Thing is, it can't be reversed, so most divines won't do it unless there's something wrong with the Chosen. Not like we can tell them anything with these fucking bands around our necks. Balan might have taken his power away by now if he knew you were stuck in here."

Sophia let her fingers rest on either side of the band. If this was the only thing keeping her from Balan, then she needed it off. "Is there really no way to take this o—"

She pinched her fingers around the band. As she did, stabbing pain radiated up and down her throat as if someone had driven a knife into it. Then it started to burn her neck and her hand as the band became hotter than fire. Sophia's vision blacked out, and she felt her side hit the hard dungeon floor.

When she opened her eyes, Katri's thin face was contorted into a concerned expression. "That was mighty stupid," she said. "You alright?"

"I—I don't know," Sophia stammered. A fresh burn welted up on her hand.

"It'll calm down in a day or so. We've all tried it a time or two. Except my last cell mate. He went mad from his connection to Halga being severed. Tried to take off the band and didn't stop until he killed himself. Being cut off from our gods does that to a Chosen. " Katri fell quiet for a moment. Silence descended on them until her eyes met Sophia's again. Sophia felt the concern in them.

"Don't do that again," Katri said sternly.

"Aye." Sophia wondered if Katri said that to all her cell mates. "So, what do we do now?" She sat up, wincing as her neck burned. From what Katri had told her, it sounded like they were going to be down here a long time.

"Work assignments will start for you tomorrow," Katri said, with a wave of her hand. "You seem the gentler type, so you'll get an easy one."

"What do you have?" Sophia asked.

Katri turned her head to the side, toward the back wall. "Nothing now except listening to the howl of the outside world. Tried to escape during my last assignment." Either it was a trick of the light, or her face had turned a visible shade of red. "Should've bloody made it too," she growled.

Sophia nodded and did her best to clear her throat. She wouldn't be here in the mud and shit if it weren't for Ilara. Without her, Sophia would still be free, likely back in their home of Vash'gal'or. Or she might have been dead. It would be preferable to this. The dungeon felt like a purgatory. People came here to die. It was just a matter of time for her as well.

***

Sophia stood in the massive library. Scholars wearing shawls and coifs meandered by her as she was held awkwardly between two guards, who weren't Plume and Bucket. The familiar faces would have been reassuring.

A man with a black beard with streaks of white was peering at a gigantic book sitting between him and Sophia. It hid half his face as he perused a page that was as large as a seat cushion. He hummed a slow tune that she, sadly, couldn't recognize.

Her eyes wandered to the rows of shelves. They were packed to the brim with manuscripts and scrolls. Scholars shuffled in between them as they lugged hefty tomes from place to place. They were a flurry of blues and whites as their robes shuffled along the dusty floor.

Sophia assumed this was Ameri's Grand Library, which was nestled in the Palace of the Solar Dominion. Ameri, being a god on the Pantheon, had her fate tied to Akara's. Knowledge brought a power that Akara would hold on to. How better to control them than to put the largest collection of knowledge within the goddess's reach?

"We do have work for her," Blackbeard said at last. "Balanites are typically trained. You can read, can't you, girl?"

"Aye," Sophia said. She sounded meek even to her own ear.

"Good. Note that your mind will be erased at the end of each session. The Librarian has need of a new Reader," he said.

"Uh, if I can ask, how much of my mind will be erased?"

Pain cascaded through Sophia as one of the guards rammed the pommel of his sword into her side. She gasped and fell to one knee.

"Don't speak unless spoken to," he commanded.

"No, it's alright," the Scholar said. "A reasonable question. The Librarian will only erase from the moment you entered their office to when you leave. Their hand is particularly gentle. Do you have any other questions?"

"No," Sophia said through tears.

"Very good. Follow me, lass," he said. She did so, and the guards clomped with heavy boots behind her. "We have great need of literate servants," the Scholar said over his shoulder as he walked between shelves. "The Librarian is blind. Losing their sight was part of their sacrifice to Ameri. We do not let that prevent the completion of our duties.

"You will find that they research some very important topics that are of interest to our divines. If the Librarian appreciates your work, you'll be expected just after dawn to midafternoon, when they retire from their duties."

Shelves of books passed Sophia in a wash of colors and textures. The Scholar led her to an oak door in a far corner of the library. It was nestled between two bookshelves, and she might have missed it if he hadn't stopped there.

"Understand that the Librarian is a very powerful Chosen. If you take any hostile action against them, you will quickly find your brain a puddle on the floor." The Scholar paused, waiting for Sophia to respond.

"Aye, I understand," she said.

"Fantastic." He gave her a terse smile. "You may open this door. Do not open the next one until you have this one fully closed. My good man," he said, turning his attention to the guards. "A Scholar will see her returned to her cell once her duties are complete."

"Very well," one of them said. "See that she's returned before the morning count." They clomped off as quickly as they'd come.

The Scholar turned back to Sophia with the same polite smile. "I am Scholar Terrick. Should you need anything, find me at the front desk. You have access to Ameri's Library during your duties. Do not keep the Librarian waiting."

Sophia nodded and turned the knob on the door to reveal an identical door beyond it. She stepped through and closed the first one behind her, the light extinguishing with it. Fumbling about in the dark, she found the next knob after flailing her arms around a little. Upon turning it, she revealed a small room containing a single ornate lantern. It hung above piles of books stacked up to her stomach.

"*You have finally come,*" an unfamiliar voice echoed in her mind.

A suit of armor stood in the room, bright white tendrils of light connecting the various pieces together. They converged in a cluster where the breastplate should have been. It had been removed to make room for something about the size of a small dog to rest there, tendrils coiled around it. Sophia approached slowly, stopping immediately when the thing came into view.

There—pulsing, pink, and held up by the tentacles of light that coiled and writhed around it—was a large brain.

It took a step back. The brain seemed able to manipulate the armor, as it had moved the arms and legs. The creature, the Librarian, took another step, and the brain seemed to sway slightly between the tendrils. Sophia recoiled instinctively, back pressed against the closed door.

*"This form disturbs you,"* it said. *"My body is a blessing of Ameri. Servant of Balan, pick up a book from the stack to your right. The Chronicles of the Ruin of Athenor should be the one to look for. Be quick about it, and do not try my patience."*

Sophia froze. Should she do what this thing said or let it melt her mind? Perhaps it had only brought her here to crush her skull. Why else would it need those large, gauntleted fists? That seemed to be the quickest way to suicide, if she wanted one.

But she couldn't. At the very least, she could relish in having something to do. And if the Librarian's research was so important to Akara, perhaps she might learn something.

She bent down and ran her hands over the spines until she found the requested tome. Retrieving it required shifting the stack around and removing half the books. She steadied her breathing as she held it in her shaking hands.

"*I'm glad you came to your senses. Bring the book to the light. Read the second paragraph on page 503.*"

# Chapter Twelve

# DISCOVERIES

Valette tried not to let her eyes glaze over as she listened to the young merchant in front of her, who was complaining that a paladin had stolen his goods. In the case of paladins, all she could do was make note of it and send a report to Ryn when she returned to the Solar Dominion.

She couldn't get the image of that Amerite falling to his death out of her head. There had been a formality to the event that bothered her. Akara executing another god's Chosen was not out of the ordinary, but that was an odd method.

Finally, the merchant was done with his story. Valette pushed off from the wall as he walked off. Otto had left an hour ago. She turned down one of the aisles of market stalls to ensure her presence was seen, though she hoped there would be no more incidents.

Snow crunched under her feet as she strode with her hand on her sword. She could see the top of Gavin's shield across the market stalls. He was laughing as he talked to one of the merchants. The man was good at this. He made people feel safe.

As Valette glanced back, she saw the dim-eyed paladin walking up the aisle toward her. Their eyes locked.

"Chosen Bilaut," the pal said as she drew near.

"And you are?" Valette asked.

"Maer Valdronis." She pulled up her faceplate. She was young, with greasy, dark locks that fell out of her helmet and down around her faintly glowing red eyes. Valette recognized the prim armor of the Chosen she'd seen in the market some days before.

"You guessed correctly that my trial was to decide for myself that guarding a market was beneath me. My commander expected me to take the entire day to realize that. I want to know what else you know."

"I think we can help each other. Information for information," Valette said.

"Depends." Maer crossed her arms. "What do you want to know?"

"Walk with me." Valette turned and sauntered off. Maer, thankfully, followed. "I saw a man die a few days back. It was curious to me. Never seen a man executed like that." She guided them to the edge of the market, where they could be seen but not noticed or overheard.

"You're speaking of the Sundown ceremony?" Maer asked, pulling at the tunic beneath her breastplate as if to vent the hot air building up beneath it. Even in the winter, the layers of armor and padding provided enough insulation to be of discomfort to the wearer. Gods, Valette missed wearing her armor.

"Aye," she said, folding her arms across her unarmored chest. "Can you tell me what that is?"

"Really? Gods, children know this. An offering to Akara. We give her a sacrifice most days now, though it used to be once a year when I was a girl. Usually they are Chosen who have wronged the Pantheon."

Valette nodded, disbelieving the paladin. She thought she would have heard of such a practice among her troops, or at least an insistence to adhere to it. Maer's expression was unreadable. It was as if they were discussing the weather instead of the death of a man.

"They do not do this ceremony where you come from?" Maer asked.

"We do not," Valette said. "Tell me, there was a band covering his eyes."

Maer gasped. "He was a Chosen of Akara. That is something that rarely happens. Usually they are Amerites and Halgans."

"Is that all the band signifies?"

"I know not. We are told to ignore the Chosen who have these bands. They are no threat," Maer said off-handedly.

"But why?" Valette asked. What could be so disarming about the black bands?

"I've told you what I know."

Valette nodded as they neared a cleared market stall. She placed her elbow on the open table. Her open palm offered Maer the game.

"An arm contest?" Maer asked.

"Aye. You cannot channel yet, correct?"

Maer blanched, proving Valette correct. It was common for young Chosen to struggle with their first tracts. Valette knew Akaran paladins who didn't receive a spell from their goddess for years.

"I do not understand how these contests of arms will teach me to channel my tract," Maer said, confirming that she did have one.

"The tract is like a muscle," Valette said as she stood from the table. "You have to flex it like you're in a contest. The more practiced you are, the easier it is." She flexed the tract in her left arm and created a small translucent shield. A ring of white light surrounding an inner ring of runes marked the space it would block.

"A contest with whom?" Maer asked, as if she hadn't noticed Valette's shield.

"In your case, Akara. It is her power you're trying to leverage. She should give you her power freely, but if you're on poor terms with her, she may make it harder for you. And try praying to her every now and again. Even if you don't think she's listening, a god always is. They like to be talked to," Valette said.

Maer's eyes widened for a moment. "I should get back to work, and likely so should you."

"Aye to that," Valette said as she dismissed her shield. "If only they'd give me actual work."

"Have you taken the Syl?" Maer asked.

"What is a Syl?"

Maer shifted uncomfortably as she moved to leave. "Something the Voice does with Chosen outside our faith. Ask her about it, or one of the clergy. I can't really say more than that."

"I'll look into it, then," Valette said as Maer moved to walk from the market square.

She frowned. Otto might know what the paladin was talking about, but he was still absent. Gavin would be able to handle the square on his own. Probably.

It was time to be done with this. Valette wasn't confident, but she was mostly certain there was a connection between Maer being unable to channel and the Sundown ceremony. When a Chosen died, their essence was committed back to their god. Since Ameri had many Chosen, that essence was going back to the Pantheon. Or it was going back to where Akara ruled. Was the goddess hoarding it?

Nonchalantly, Valette patrolled back to the Solar Dominion. It felt wrong, as if she were a toddler disobeying the orders of her parents. Once there, she flew through the hallways of the building. The clergy she passed seemed wholly unbothered by her presence. She figured she'd find the answers to her questions in Ameri's Grand Library.

She stopped dead in her tracks as she opened the door to the last hallway. Framed in the doorway was the form of High Priestess Tezza, Voice of Akara. Her face brightened when she saw Valette, and her curls bounced as she did. Flanking her were a half dozen paladins wearing red-plated armor with gold trim. Their faces were hidden by the visors of their helms, yet their red eyes shone with intensity.

"Chosen Bilaut," Tezza said. "I was hoping to converse with you. I haven't seen you since the Tribunal. How goes your search for the Zal'Kerathan?"

Dead in the water, Valette thought.

"Voice," she said with a slight bow. "Akara deems to grace me with your presence this day."

"Posh, you give me pleasantries I dare not deserve. Walk with me while the day is bright and the Eye shines upon us," Tezza said. She turned and marched down the hallway past Valette, who followed, knowing this was the same thing she'd done to Maer.

"Very well, your grace," Valette said. The royal guard fell in around them, marching close to her sword arm. Should she try to pull her weapon on Tezza, they'd have her disarmed in a twist of her wrist. If nothing else, these paladins were dedicated.

"Chosen Bilaut," Tezza started. Her face was red, as if what she was about to bring forward was embarrassing.

*Gods, she's about to ask about my progress. What do I tell her? That Knight Commander Ryn is blocking me? She'll have me locked up in a dungeon if I blame my superior. I ought to be able to handle this Zal'Kerathan on my own. I just need the space to work.*

"The knight commander informed me of the way you brought in the Balanite. I must say that I was very impressed by his description. It's not often Ryn says anything positive about anyone. You should consider that a victory," Tezza continued.

"I appreciate your noticing of my act, your grace," Valette said, turning slightly red herself.

"One matter did come to my attention, however." Tezza cocked her head to the side as if annoyed. "It seems to me that no one had bothered to give you an overview of etiquette for a Chosen within the Solar Dominion."

"I apologize if I've offended you," Valette said.

"Gods, no!" Tezza laughed. "I'm never offended by such frivolous things. But I wanted to make you aware of a ritual we practice here in the palace. A Chosen has a right to the Syl once, and I'd hate for you to miss your chance. Are you aware of it?"

"I—I have only heard rumors, your grace," Valette stammered.

"Well, it is a private ritual between myself and Chosen of gods within the Pantheon. Few are aware. Most use it as a time to make their case outside the Tribunal. Leave it to Ryn to omit such an important detail. I'm certain we can clean up whatever mess was made here. If you have any questions about it, I leave you in the capable hands of our Scholars." Tezza motioned to a pair of large oak doors in the hallway ahead of them.

"Is that the Library of Ameri?" Valette asked.

"Indeed."

The doors were so unassuming that she might've walked right by them. There were no markings on the large stone walls to indicate where they led.

"This is where I must leave you, unfortunately. I am a busy woman outside of my time allotted for the Syl. Again, ask your questions of my Scholars, and I'm sure you will find what you're looking for." Tezza turned, her eyes gliding up Valette's frame as if they were rolling across ice, then she continued on with her retinue, marching by Valette as if she weren't there.

Did the leader of the Akaran Temple just look at my— Valette stopped the thought before she'd completed it. Had Tezza known this was where Valette was going? It seemed too coincidental for a woman like Tezza to have led her here. Valette shook her head and reached for the door handle. Perhaps this Syl was exactly what she needed to find out what she needed.

The scale of the library awed her. The vaulted ceilings were upheld by massive pillars almost entirely obscured by bookshelves. Many blue-robed men and women scurried from place to place, arms laden with books as they organized. Valette passed a row of tables where a dozen scribes were sitting, each writing in one book while they read another. Thousands of volumes must have rested on these shelves, cared for by dozens of Ameri's Chosen.

Unsure where to begin, Valette stood in the center of the massive room, slack-jawed.

"Paladin. You have questions."

She turned to see a brown-skinned man with a clean-shaven face. His blue hood hid the majority of his features.

"It's that obvious I don't belong, isn't it?"

"No Scholar carries a blade," the man said. "We need no metal to defend our space."

"Understood." Valette cleared her throat. "Would you be one to answer my questions?"

"Aye. That is why my goddess brought us to one another." He smiled. "I am Markus."

"Markus. Have you served in the library long?"

"I've never served in the library, milady. Yet Ameri said I could answer your questions, and so here I am. The Scholars that serve this library only answer to Akara. They would be of no help to you."

"I see. I should see it as fortunate that Ameri's Sight is so fortuitous."

"Truly."

"Do you know the questions I will ask?" Valette wondered if there was a point at all to this interaction. Ameri and a select few of her Chosen had the ability to see the future. If

Markus was here, Ameri must see the interaction as beneficial to her—and possibly Akara.

"I know the questions you ask are heretical, or I would not be here. For the sanctity of the timeline, you must ask them," Markus answered. He motioned to a nearby table. Once they were both seated, he rested his chin in his palm.

"I witnessed an execution yesterday. I have reason to believe it was a Chosen of Akara," Valette said.

"Is that your question?" Markus asked.

"Did he belong to Akara?"

"He did."

"Why was he killed?"

"He gained too much power. There were those within the palace who wanted to see him killed. So it was done ," Markus answered. His voice was cold and calculating, like it didn't bother him that a man's life had been taken with such disregard.

"Why not Forsake the man?" Valette asked.

"Akara did not will for this one to die."

"So someone within the Solar Dominion is working against Akara, then?"

"Yes. Akara's many Chosen deign to work against her. Some believe they may succeed where Almir failed—to ascend to Akara's godhood," Markus responded.

Valette didn't like his implication. "Almir was never to succeed Akara. That idea is ridiculous."

"Ridiculous because it might be true? You should ask your god what he thinks of that," Markus said.

"No mortal has ever succeeded a living god," Valette responded.

"Not that you know. You have more questions?"

"In my time in Eversburg, I've seen one Akaran channel. Why no others?"

"Why do the leaves fall in autumn or flowers bloom in spring?" Markus asked.

"Such riddles do not answer me."

"Quite astute of you." He rubbed his chin. "This is not an answer I can give, other than to say that what you've observed is merely the way of things. More detail may lead you to find what happens to objects that fall."

Valette sat back in her chair. This was the second threat this man had levied against her. Next time, he might not stop at just a warning. "I believe I understand," she said.

Markus nodded, putting his hands on the table. "Ameri said you would have other questions. You may ask me without retribution. Any other Scholar could not answer this request."

"Aye. My last question: Akara has tasked me to seek out the Chosen who killed Senator Plithy. What do you know of her?"

Valette would do more than that. Few wrongdoers escaped her, and she would make sure this one didn't either.

"Zal'Keratha's only Chosen. A well-tempered assassin. She remains in the city, though you will not find her as you are."

Valette nodded. Zal'Keratha had lost many of her Chosen in killing Akara's paladins in Akara's War of Ascendency. Since the goddess of death left the Pantheon a century ago, she'd been able create no more than one at any given time.

"You can assist me in finding her?" Valette asked. Whatever else happened, she knew that she'd need to dispense justice to this Chosen. It was Almir's way. Not to mention, completing this task would give her the freedom to continue the investigation that truly mattered.

"I can," Markus said with a smile. "That service, however, will cost you."

"What do you need?"

"Ameri would seek to forge an alliance with Almir. She recognizes that no kingdom lasts to the end of an age." He grinned again.

"Almir and Ameri have an alliance through the Pantheon," Valette said.

"And that alliance will be maintained through whatever changes shall be brought about?"

"*Aye*," Almir said.

"Almir agrees," Valette said. "His word is as binding as that of his forefathers before him and all that come after."

Markus nodded, no doubt recognizing the words of an Almiran contract. "Very well. You will find the Zal'Kerathan in an abandoned Crafter's guild in Dusk. Tell your knight commander that Ameri tipped you to it. He'll let you free to investigate."

He stood and left Valette at a table in a forgotten part of the library. She could have sworn they'd been sitting at one just off the main floor, yet right in front of her was a bookshelf, and her back was to a quiet corner. Her hand rested on a book.

"*Scholars. They play with your mind. He might not even have been here,*" Almir said. His form appeared in a chair next to Valette. He was wearing a simple helm that obscured his face, and a white tabard covered his chest plate. Embroidered on it was a fist haloed by the sun.

Valette knew from experience that she was the only one who could see him.

*Ameri aligns with your cause,* she thought. *What did Markus mean about your succession to Akara?*

"*Truly? Of all the man said, that is what you ask of me?*"

*Truly. He implied something very different than what the Chyriddion teaches, Valette thought. Give me the no-trollshit version and I'll reconsider asking you to Forsake me. I gave my life to you so that the world would be made clear, yet the more I learn, the murkier these waters get.*

*"Very well. You know the battle in which I gave my life for Akara?" Almir asked.*

*The battle of Endoshar.*

*"Akara was fated to die that day. Zal'Keratha had her by the throat, bound only by the ancient law that prevents gods from killing gods. As the armies of Death and Light collided, I paused. Over the scrape of lizard claws and clang of Akaran steel, I heard my goddess weeping. Seeing her tears fall through a sky full of clouds of black, I tore through her enemies like a wolf through a chicken coop. Yet she commanded more of me. She demanded I kill Zal'Keratha before Death's Chosen could kill her.*

*"I couldn't bring myself to it. My honor could not be stained with the blood of a god. Instead, I found Death's Chosen and fought him in a duel. It was a duel beyond any I have ever ex-perienced, until a my enemy's spear tore through my chest. I was certain my death loomed. I still remember his face nearly a cen-tury later. The skin was stretched thin on his skull, revealing the shape of the bone underneath. Zal'Keratha's thousand-year-old Chosen.*

*"Still, I had something in me that he did not. Empowered by something higher than my goddess, I rushed him, breaking my*

bones and spilling my blood until his throat was in my hands, just as his unjust goddess held Akara's. I overcame him in a moment, and his neck snapped like a thick twig.

"This act allowed my goddess to strike back, casting the wicked Zal'Keratha back to her domain. Yet, my fortitude released from me, the blood pooling in my armor finally caught up to me, and I fell that day. A light enveloped my soul as I left my body. I knew it to be the hands of the holy Akara, ready to guide my faithful soul to the promised afterlife. I expected to be absorbed into her, so that I might find peace after years of war.

"Yet I continued to exist. I knew that I had a power few others had. The power to create and destroy filled my being from end to end. I no longer felt the connection to Akara that I once had. That was when I knew that my light was greater than hers. I was to succeed her. She, however, survived the ordeal and claimed victory over Aox, becoming queen of the Pantheon.

"She came to me later, explaining that we can rule as mother and son. Queen and Prince of the Light. She would show me how to rule mortals with divine retribution.

"I knew then that I was a different god than she was. I saw her every flaw with honest eyes and knew I could not rule as her subservient. I would be her equal. Akara raged and cast me from the heavens. It was some decades before she agreed and gave me a place on her Pantheon."

Valette was silent as the musk of old books grounded her in reality. Almir had spoken earnestly, not like a god did to his children, but like a brother spoke to a sister.

*You refused to tell me when I left Chrys, but I have to know now. What do you think is causing this lack of Akaran power?* Valette asked.

Almir's reply was slow to come but when it did, zeal filled Valette's mind.

*"It must be the Zal'Kerathan. That wicked goddess never truly died and has returned to destroy my Lady of Light. It is imperative that you find this Chosen and kill her before more damage can be done."*

Valette nodded. It was the answer she'd expected, but she couldn't shake the feeling that she was missing something important. She stood, only to remember her arm was draped over a book, likely placed there by Markus.

"The Benefits of the Syl ," she read aloud. She flipped it opened absentmindedly. All blood drained from her face when she realized what a Syl entailed.

"Gods, she was checking me out," she muttered under her breath.

# CHAPTER THIRTEEN

# BLOOD

ILARA MOVED HER WRISTS back and forth, rope biting into her flesh as she slowly worked at her bonds. Blood ran down her fingers and dripped onto the wooden floor. Grimacing, she tugged on her wrist, and pain shot up her arm. Worse, the added slickness did nothing to help her free herself. Her legs were, of course, also bound to the legs of the chair.

Adding to it was the constant throb of her head. Zal'Keratha needed an offering, and she had to give it soon.

She was sitting in a dark room, or at least she thought it was dark. A cloth was wrapped around her eyes, and there was a fabric band around her neck. Attempting to access any of her tracts caused the band to slowly and painfully heat. She assumed it was some type of magic-blocking device. So, no daggers to slice herself free. She'd woken up here some hours ago and didn't know how long it would be until Gray and his cronies were back.

*What are they going to do to me?* A sudden fear filled her. Ilara had never been tortured before. Or might they do something worse? The Syndicate had access to something that could block her goddess's magic—who knows what else they had.

"You rely too much on your magic." The words Gray had spoken reminded her of the weakness he'd used to defeat her. His blade, which had radiated darkness, terrified her. Her daggers had been so easily deflected by it.

Deflected, or destroyed? If she'd carried a normal sword, would she have been able to kill him? She wouldn't make that mistake again—if she ever escaped this room.

A cold dread crept over Ilara's skin. Goosebumps rose on her arms, as if the space had suddenly become a freezer. The familiar presence made her anxious. Zal'Keratha coming here would only mean trouble for her.

"Coming to gloat over your failed Chosen?" she asked the empty space.

*"I'm merely intrigued by what you're doing here,"* the goddess said. *"Killing Jonas does not save your sister. Or find my altar."*

"I don't think you even need it." The chill in the air intensified. "And the cathartic release of seeing that scumbag die might do me some good. I've put up with his shit for too long. Been having a hell of a week. Figured I could treat myself."

"*Did you think of the trouble that might cause?*" Zal'Keratha spat. "*His death barely makes a difference. Your former employer would hunt you down.*"

Ilara's arms went limp as she felt the chill of the goddess's fingers run up her cheek to remove the blindfold. In front of her stood a woman who oozed darkness. Her thin frame was more like a silhouette or shadow. Massive, curled horns extended from her forehead, running parallel to the floor. Zal'Keratha had pale blue skin, purple eyes, and was wearing a beige corset over a thin, flowing dress.

She relaxed down onto a stool in front Ilara. Her stare was as icy as her presence. Ilara couldn't maintain eye contact. She felt the disappointment in her mistress's eyes.

"*It has been far too long since we spoke candidly. You've lost sight of why we came here.*"

"How could I forget? You remind me so often," Ilara retorted.

"*Then you've been foolish. Sophia is a weakness. Your feelings toward her cloud your judgment.*" Zal'Keratha paused, eyes clenching shut. "*What have you learned of the altar?*"

"In truth, little. Ameri's Scholars have horded all knowledge of it into their library in the Solar Dominion. I'm also confident that is where they are holding Sophia. There is nowhere else."

Zal'Keratha bristled. "*This is significant, but not five years' worth of investment. What do you need to breach the palace?*"

"A selak of Aoxians would be helpful. There will be an opening in a few weeks' time. How many of the lizards do you know near Eversburg?" Ilara asked.

Zal'Keratha put her hand on Ilara's cheek, and her eyes grew distant. She tried to focus on anything that wasn't the burning pain in her wrists. The goddess stood up and paced the room, her footsteps silently gliding over the floor. Her hand came to rest on a spinning wheel with a needle sticking from it, the point glistening in the moonlight.

"*It would not be the end of Aerlia if the disgraced lizard god ascends back to the throne, should he use this opportunity against us. While my vigilance has waned in his exile, I know he is in Eversburg. Go speak with Aox once you finish here.*" Zal'Keratha fixed her gaze back to Ilara. "*Do not, however, think to underestimate the Aoxians. None will work harder to regain power than those who once knew it. Find that altar soon, or you shall be among those who know what it's like to lose it.*"

"Might you know where these Aoxians are?" Ilara asked.

"*You're resourceful. Find them.*"

She nodded as best she could in her restraints. "I'm still killing Jonas."

A slight chuckle came from her goddess. "*If I could purge my pettiness from you, I would do so in a heartbeat. Well, an offering does need to be made, at any rate. Our time runs short, so I will assist you, lest you bloody your wrists more.*"

Ilara gritted her teeth. She wanted to kill Jonas for what he did to Sophia, but wouldn't if not for the pain her goddess's offering required. Before Ilara had time to comment, the darkness around Zal'Keratha deepened, and the atmosphere around her thinned. Her chilling presence dissipated a moment later, creeping away from her like a crack of ice over a pond.

The tension around Ilara's wrists and ankles broke a moment later, and the choker fell from her neck. Relishing her regained freedom, she picked up the black cloth. It was colorless, but that was the wrong description. It was almost as if reality stopped where the band began and started again where it ended. There was an eeriness to it that reminded Ilara of Gray's blade.

*What do you know of this material?* Ilara prayed to Zal'Keratha.

No answer.

Her mouth tightened to a line. It wasn't uncommon for her goddess to fall silent or ignore her. She did, however, generally answer Ilara's questions.

Sighing, Ilara tucked the broken band in the pocket of her tunic. Spinning around the room, she saw it was cluttered with random hefty objects, all five feet away from the chair she'd been tied to, which appeared to be bolted to the floor. A spinning wheel, large wardrobe, and a potter's lathe lined the walls.

"A Crafter's paradise," she muttered. This building might have been a Crafter's guild before the Syndicate took over. It wasn't uncommon for them to buy up random buildings across Eversburg for working their operations.

Investigating further, Ilara found her cloak and cha'ak in the wardrobe. She donned both immediately, savoring the slight protection. The cloak wouldn't stop a blade, however. Absent her armor, she'd have to be careful in escaping this building, in killing Jonas. If he was even here.

Ilara turned her mind inward and checked her store of magic. Both tracts were full of Zal'Keratha's power, ready to be used. She ran a finger across her forehead and felt the chill as invisibility enveloped her body. Her killing urge welled within her, and the need to exact her vengeance grew to the point where it overwhelmed her. She tried meekly to quell it, but failed as she reached the door, which was, mercifully, unlocked. Swinging it open, she saw two guards stationed outside. Both looked up as the door moved, seemingly on its own. One of the men approached, noticing the empty chair through Ilara's invisibility.

"The prisoner—" He ended the statement with a gurgle as a freshly created dagger landed in his neck. Swiftly, Ilara strode forward and drove another dagger down into the second guard's collar bone. She immediately lengthened the blade so that it pierced the man's heart. He fell down with a thud, gripping the wound.

Both men had swords sheathed at their sides, which Ilara relieved them of, buckling them to either side of her hips. The blades wouldn't be invisible, and the extra weight would slow her slightly, but she appreciated that they weren't magical. If Gray were here, she'd have a shot at actually fighting him.

She kicked the door open, the hallway before her full of thugs dressed in black. Ilara brandished her blades as they all turned to her and pulled their weapons from their sides.

The closest rushed her, his rusty mace scraping the ceiling. She threw a dagger at him. It buried itself in his eye socket. While his momentum took him past her, she recognized his trajectory would take him to the floor. She pulled the dagger out and held in front of her, forming another in her free hand.

The rest of the thugs would fall easily, but this was about sending a message to the Syndicate that she would not be fucked with.

As the next man stepped forward, he drew a set of curved daggers, assuming a defensive stance, waiting for her to move and make a mistake. Her own blades became a flurry around her invisible form. The thug's eyes darted from side to side, and he managed to dodge some of the strikes, but he was moving slowly in the cramped hallway. Ilara nicked his thighs, and he fell to the floor. With force, she drove the blades into the man's temples.

Her next opponent attacked over the fallen thug. A fist clad in brass knuckles drove toward Ilara's face. She stepped back, and the hook swung through where she'd been. The next swing was wild, the man trying to guess where her body was based on the sword belt. Ilara dove into the hole in his defense and stabbed both blades into his back, hitting the kidney and liver. As she withdrew them, blood spattered over her chest.

With the guards all dead, she went to work, slicing their bodies to make the scene something that the Gray Syndicate would never forget. The blood of the men mixed with her own as the wounds on her wrists opened again. She paid it no mind, just moved her cloak out of the way to keep the sticky liquid from coating the clothing.

Her bloody work finished, Ilara approached the staircase. It was set into the wall, carved into the stone that made up this corner of the building. Her invisibility faded as she ascended. The blood on her chest and arms made it practically worthless anyway.

Ilara wouldn't need it. She wanted Jonas to see his death coming.

***

The climb made Ilara's legs burn. She steeled herself.

The top of the staircase opened into a simple-looking foyer with a green rug that hugged the sides of the room. Two men stood beside a door adorned with silver decals depicting the hands of the Crafter, cupped side by side with their palms up. They drew their weapons, a large black stone hammer and a sword and rune-covered shield, which were made of the same black metal as Gray's rapier. These were the guards who'd escorted Jonas from the bar.

"Traitor," the man gripping the hammer growled.

"No chance I can convince you otherwise, then?" Ilara asked as she drew her stolen blades.

In response, the man stepped forward and swung the hammer toward her. She narrowly avoided it, yet she could feel its hungry presence as it swung past her, as if it were reaching out, longing to feed on her. A wave of exhaustion hit her, and she stumbled back.

Grinning, the man hefted his weapon up for another swing. "Soul Eater will have another Chosen. Your soul will be consumed." He brought it down again. Ilara risked parrying it from its path. Her blade held as she knocked it away, smoke suddenly spilling from the head of the hammer.

The smoke seemed to dive into Ilara's sword, turning it as black as the stone of the hammer's head. Wasting no time, she swiped her other blade into her attacker's stomach. Intestines spilled out, and he fell backward, the giant hammer thudding onto the rug, resting there as his blood soaked into the floor.

The second man held his shield in front of him, black smoke pouring from it as he chanted an incantation. The shield flashed, and a burning ember shot toward Ilara. She side-stepped, but the smell of burnt flesh filled the room as the flame hit the dying guard. He screamed, and fire began to lick at his leg.

Seizing the opportunity, Ilara lunged at the remaining man, who expertly parried the blows from her iron blade with his shield. The smoke formed tendrils again and wrapped around her sword as it made contact with the wood. With a force she hadn't been expecting, it ripped the weapon from Ilara's hands, knocking it to the floor.

Backing up, she held the remaining blade in front of her. With her free hand, she formed a dagger and threw it at the man's head. With insane reflexes, he moved the shield to block it, but it was dispelled by the tendrils of smoke. He started chanting again, and Ilara rushed him, not wanting whatever spell it was to go off.

Too late. The sword he was holding began to glow a faint blue. He brought it forward, launching a flurry of ice shards toward Ilara. As they engulfed the room, they bit and dug into her skin. It felt like the sting of hundreds of angry bees. She fought through the pain as she took excruciating step after excruciating step forward.

When she got close, she swung her blade with as much strength as she could muster at the man's knee, cleaving flesh and bone. Screaming, he fell to the ground. Smoky tendrils jumped from his shield to Ilara's remaining blade, knocking her onto her back.

Her vision went black for a second, but she was on her feet a moment later. The guard was holding his bleeding leg, sword and shield at his side and both her blades in front of him. Anger filled his eyes as he panted large mouthfuls of breath. The black stone hammer lay at Ilara's feet.

"Whose Chosen are you?" she asked as she bent down to pick up the weapon. It was heavy in her hands, the weight of it sinking her feet into the carpet.

"A lesser god," the man gasped. "You wouldn't know her."

"Try me. You know as well as I that there's honor to fighting Chosen," Ilara said, taking an exhausted step toward the man. "I'll have to venerate your goddess."

"Beni, goddess of the sands. I am her Chosen, Benin."

Ilara nodded. Some Chosen of lesser gods gave their lives, their names, to the ones they served.

"Shall I commend your soul to her?" she asked, now standing over Benin. The hammer seemed to yearn for him, though no smoke was seething from the stone.

"If you would prefer. I could not stop you now," Benin answered. "But, please, do not use that hammer to do it."

"Tell me of these weapons you use," Ilara said.

"Gray gave them to us. They hunger for Chosen blood, as you can now feel. It counters Chosen magics, but it is as if it consumes them. That stone used to be half the size."

"Thank you," Ilara said, raising the hammer over her head. If this man had used the thing against other Chosen, she would show him no mercy.

"No, no, no, n—" Benin stammered, until the hammer came down on his head. His skull exploded into a thousand pieces.

Ilara took a step back, leaving the hammer on his neck as she took her blades. Her supplies of magic were extinguished, so she'd need to rely on physical weapons.

"Beni, be honored at the just death of your Chosen. I commend your essence back to you that you may Choose another," Ilara said.

She turned to the door and tested the handle. Remarkably, it was unlocked, and she pushed it in. The room beyond was well lit, and filled from wall-to-wall with luxurious furniture. Jonas was sitting on the bed, hands folded over his fine clothing.

"Daddy leave you to handle me this time?" Ilara mused, strolling across the lavish bedroom.

Jonas whimpered as he stood from the bed, drawing a thin rapier that he held out shakily. Ilara easily knocked it to the side, fully exposing his frail torso.

"I don't know what you thought you were doing, reporting my sister to the paladins, taking me to the Syndicate. Maybe it was wounded pride at having been bested by a woman. Maybe it was greed, or some combination of the two. I will tell you this, Jonas. Of all the contracts I've had over the years, supplied by you or otherwise, the one head I wanted above all others was yours," she spat.

"I thought we had mutual respect," Jonas murmured, dropping his blade to the floor.

"Respect? You sent me to kill prostitutes and drug lords. People you felt had wronged you over the slightest petty offense. Men and women who were trying to support their families. No, Jonas, I know scum when I see it. And scum does not deserve respect."

Ilara brought her blade down and unceremoniously cut his throat. Jonas gasped for air as blood ran down his neck onto the chest of the silk tunic he wore.

He fell to his knees before her, and she took a handful of his hair and turned his face to hers. "Know that you will be made an example of what happens when you fuck with me and my family. Hope in your last moment that your sacrifice will deter Gray, or you'll be seeing him in my Lady's realm with you."

Ilara held Jonas there until he was pale and drained of life. Finally, the throbbing in her head ceded. Zal'Keratha had been satisfied. She let go and let his corpse slump to one side.

Walking from the room, she found Benin's corpse shrunken and limp. The hammer was coated in his blood, its grooves and crevices filled with it. Picking it up, the blood soaked in until the stone was completely dry.

"Isn't that interesting," Ilara muttered.

# Chapter Fourteen

# MEMORIES

"It came about at the time when Regent  Ti'un visited Eversburg in the 544th year of Akara's blessed divinity, when the sundering of relations with the Aoxian kingdoms began," Sophia said. The words marched from her mouth in a toneless, rhythmic pattern.

"*A century before the war of the Pantheon. Very curious,*" the Librarian's voice echoed in Sophia's head. The sensation of having someone in her mind other than herself or Balan was unnerving.

"We are all told that the tensions started when the Aoxians invaded Caldor," she said.

"*Caldor started the war, this is true. But it always seemed convenient to me.*"

"And you're doing this research for Akara?"

*"The why does not concern you, Musical One. Keep reading,"* the Librarian said. Ripples passed over the disembodied brain as if the thought itself riled it up.

Sophia pushed down the urge to vomit. The smell of chemicals permanently filled  the Librarian's room, and she was often in here for whole mornings and afternoons at a time. Just long enough to get used to it before leaving again.

She shook her head and found the place where she'd stopped reading. "While Ti'un resided in Eversburg to learn of the Akaran priesthood, he presided over the death of a young sword-priest, whom Ti'un claimed was a Chosen of Zal'Keratha, not Akara. After the funeral, Ti'un and his accomplices absconded with the young man's body. Ti'un and his entourage were apprehended on the road back to Aoxia. Since no body was found, it is believed that Ti'un feasted upon it to gain the powers of the Chosen."

*"Very curious. And highly irregular. Most irregular, indeed."*

"What is this sword-priest?" Sophia asked. "That seems odd."

*"It isn't,"* the Librarian said. *"Sword-priests were ancestors to paladins. This all occurred before Almir arose as the first paladin."*

"But they obviously existed before—they just didn't call them paladins," Sophia said.

*"Perhaps no one had thought of the term? Though that isn't irregular."*

"And we're looking for something most irregular?" Sophia asked.

*"Is there more to this account?"* the Librarian demanded.

"No, that is the last. The next account appears to be another chronicle of Akaran priests traveling from the Kingdom of Chrys."

*"Useless."* The Librarian's armor shifted as they started pacing around the room. Sophia made herself small by the stack of books that she'd made from the Librarian's requests.

*"Do you know what an Aoxian Regent is, Chosen Sophia?"* the Librarian asked.

"They are similar to the kings the Northern Kingdoms had before the Empire, correct?"

*"Yes and no."* The Librarian lifted their hand. *"You see, the rulers of Aoxian cities are called Regents because it is a reflection of their belief that Aox, their god, still rules them on this mortal plane. Any power they have is a gift from Aox, which they will return when their station is complete.*

*"The implications of this are that Aoxian Regents are very particular in how they use this power. The fact that one of them came here is most interesting. Have you studied Aoxian religious practices?"*

Sophia didn't think it mattered how she responded. "I learned a funeral rite once, for a friend."

She leaned back in her chair as the Librarian prepared what she was sure to be a lengthy response. It became easier to read their emotions the more time she spent with them. She was certain they enjoyed having someone around to explain things to.

*"Very good. Then you know that there are Aoxian societal worship centers on Aox, but that each Aoxian chooses another god or goddess to be the center of their household worship—a sort of protector god. As far as we know, the practice began during Aox's reign on the Pantheon, prior to Akara's godhood. The fact that any Aoxian traveled here means that they were interested in adding Akara to their list of deities."*

"Or that some already had," Sophia said.

*"Likely so."* The Librarian appeared to nod their brain—head—in approval. *"Even more interesting was that all Aoxians were forbidden from having Zal'Keratha as their household goddess."*

"Odd. Were they afraid of her?" Sophia asked.

*"No, no, nothing of the sort. They had an utmost respect for death. So much so that they believed that no single person should inquire anything of the goddess themselves."*

"An interesting fact." Sophia was unsure where this was going.

"*You do not see,*" the Librarian continued. "*How did that funeral rite of yours go? Specifically, the last verse.*"

Sophia said searched her memory. "Roughly translated, 'Lost in the sea of mortal woes, we see your holy vessel back to Mother, burned by fire of holy dragons created by our Creator and Father.'"

"*Recall, then, this account of this Regent feasting upon the corpse of the fallen. Do you not find it odd that an Aoxian would come here and eat the corpse of a Zal'Kerathan?*"

"Because their custom is to burn their dead?" Sophia asked. "But I have always wondered about that bit about the Mother. Which mother are they referring to?"

The Librarian began swaying excitedly. "*This is a highly contentious question according to the Aoxian priesthood.*"

"And you love contentious questions." Sophia smiled.

"*That I do. Shall I continue?*"

"I don't know if that pertains to your research question."

"*My research question pertains only to Aoxians. I shall contin-ue that however I wish. You are right, however, that it does not contribute to my line of thought. I shall put it simply, to fulfill your curiosity.*

*"The Aoxians fall into two sides on these issues. Some believe that 'Mother' in that line refers to Aerlia, since Aoxians were created from Aox's will and the soil of the world on which we stand. Others believe that the Aoxians are being commended back to their goddess Mother."*

"Zal'Keratha?" Sophia asked. "There are Aoxians that believe they are the product of a union between Aox and Zal'Keratha?"

*"Aye."* The Librarian sounded almost sounded giddy. *"I'm glad that you also find this topic fascinating. Ruminate upon it this evening, and we will discuss it further tomorrow. I'll have Ameri's priests pull books off the shelf concerning Aoxian religion. It is a wonder, as it is so different."*

"Different from worshiping a singular god through actions they would approve of?"

*"Precisely. Aoxians live their lives for themselves, and from that, Aox is worshiped. I will look forward to your return tomorrow. You … are a good Reader, Chosen Sophia. I appreciate that you are willing to follow this line of logic with me."*

Sophia walked to the door, her hand hovering over the knob before she turned back to the Librarian. The question in her mind ate at the back of her brain, itching like an incessant worm. She'd be better off not asking, but a part of her had to know.

"The Scholars said you would erase my memory. Is there any reason why you haven't done that?"

*"Oh, was I supposed to? And have you gawk at my appearance every day before going to work? No, that wouldn't do. We deal with sensitive documents, it is sure, but there is truly nothing here that your remembrance of would deter my Lady's plans or the integrity of Akara. Besides, I think life is lived through memories. Even a convict deserves to keep hers intact,"* the Librarian intoned, but they were growing more and more passionate with each word, sounding almost feminine.

*"Do you have any further questions that I might satisfy before your rest?"*

"So many," Sophia said, feeling the rush of honesty flush her cheeks. How did you come to be the way you are? Who were you before it? Sophia didn't know what to ask first.

*"Those are not questions I can answer, dear."*

Her eyes widened as she realized the Librarian had heard what she'd been thinking. She bowed her goodbye, and, with a shaky hand, opened the door.

As always, the same old Scholar was standing outside, with the same grim expression on his face. Wordlessly, he motioned for Sophia to follow him from the library back to her cell.

It wasn't a short walk, and Sophia dreaded it as it began. Unfortunately, it was all too similar to every interaction she had with her sister.

Years before they'd come to Eversburg, the two of them had been holed up in a small town—Sophia couldn't remember the name—while Ilara was still training to be Zal'Keratha's blade. Sophia had spent what felt like days in the inn where they were staying, wishing that Ilara would come back to end her loneliness. When she was around, she was so distant that Sophia felt even more alone. Ilara would look at her like she was disgusted to be related to her.

Now, Sophia passed by a tapestry depicting Balan in several dramatic poses. His big bushy beard was made of thread, and he strummed lutes of yarn. She couldn't suppress her smile. She did enjoy seeing it each day. Like with this walk, she'd also had good moments with Ilara.

Such as the night Sophia purchased ale for the first time. It had been in that same sleepy inn made of brick and plaster, where smells of lilac and honey filled the rooms. The cook was a mean-spirited man, but the barmaids had been kind to Sophia. They'd at least allowed her to play her lute in the common area.

One day when Sophia came down for the evening, Ilara was already in the bar, brooding over a cup of quickly cooling tea.

Sophia sat down across from her, dull rags hanging off both sisters like ghosts.

"What?" Ilara grumbled.

Sophia looked across the busy room. It was filled with the farmers who worked the surrounding land, who were in various states of drunkenness with their field hands.

"Is this a festival night?" Sophia asked.

Ilara grunted in affirmation. "Young Harvest, they call it. First harvest of the season."

Sophia frowned. "We must have had something like it when we were kids."

"You think you want to remember, but you don't."

"Can't you say anything about Mom and Dad? You knew them, didn't you?" Sophia asked.

"I did."

"Out with it, then."

Ilara hesitated before continuing. "I can't. You should be glad you can't remember them."

"No. I won't be glad until I remember them. Who are you to keep them from me?" Sophia asked.

"I will say nothing of it." Ilara tightened her grip on her clay mug. "Trust your older sister—this is for the best."

"Gods," Sophia said with a huff. "You are not the one who gets to tell me what I want or not." She stood with a dramatic flourish.

"And where are you going?" Ilara asked.

"To get drunk enough to remember!"

"You can't buy alcohol," Ilara shouted back.

"I made enough gali from busking today for an entire night of ale. And it's my godsdamned nineteenth. You should be able to remember your own sister's birthday, since you're so bloody good at remembering."

Ilara caught Sophia's wrist as she turned. There was a strength in the grip that surprised Sophia.

"I don't care if it's your sixteenth or thirtieth. Be careful. That shit is dangerous," Ilara warned.

Sophia tore her hand from her sister's grip and stomped toward the bar. Sanandra, the dark-skinned barmaid with black, curly hair, was pouring drinks for a particularly rowdy customer.

"Sophia," she said with a big smile. "It's your first Young Harvest. You've got to go check out how the town is decked out."

"I saw some of the setup earlier. I'm looking more for the celebration now." Sophia tried to sound as cool as she could.

"Well, what can I get you, darling?" Sanandra had a goofy grin on her face. She was only a few years older than Sophia, but she seemed to have so much more experience. Sophia often felt she had to fake any kind of confidence.

Her small bag of coins came down on the counter with a slight clang. "How much of the lilac ale does this get me?" she asked. "I've been dying to try it."

Sanandra took the pouch and propped it open with two fingers. "Enough to kill a horse," she exclaimed. "You've got several gold gali in there. Must've been some wealthy passersby today."

"Just more than usual," Sophia responded.

Sanandra took one of the gold pieces out and handed the pouch back to Sophia. "This'll be more than enough for now. If you and your sister drink more than a gali worth, you can come back to the bar."

Sophia had been planning to drink alone, or with any lass she could chase down. The thought of drinking with her cold sore of a sister put a damper on her plans.

Sanandra disappeared back into the kitchen, her curves dancing in front of Sophia's eyes like a welcome relief. She returned with a pitcher as tall as Sophia's forearm and as wide as her face, placing it and two mugs on the bar. Sophia took the handle, hefted the pitcher shakily, and splashed some of the pink liquid into one of the cups. Sanandra caught it before she'd poured more than a mouthful.

"Rule of the bar: no drinking alone. Take it back to your sister. Never seen that one as down as she looks right now. She could use the company. Need help with it back to your table, dear?"

"No, no," Sophia said with a courteous smile. "I think I can handle it."

She grabbed the large tankard, the muscles in her arm burning. Walking the pitcher back to Ilara, Sophia slammed it on the table. Cold ale splashed onto her arm and soaked into the grain of the wood.

"What's all this?" Ilara asked. "Do you think I'm joining you?"

"Sanandra wouldn't let me drink alone. She insisted you help me finish this." With both hands, Sophia lifted the pitcher and poured some of the ale into both mugs, splashing more of it over the table. The beer had a subtle pink color, and filled the air with a sweet, spring-like aroma. She smiled at the gentle reminder of warmer, lazier days.

"Come on," Sophia said with a deep breath. "We've been staying here for months, and neither of us have tried the ale they're famous for. Give it a sip. If you hate it, we can find something better to do with it."

"Fine." Ilara picked up the cup. Pinkish foam rolled down the side as she brought it to her lips, sipping gingerly. She immediately burst into a fit of coughs that lasted several seconds.

"Gods, was it that bad?" Sophia asked.

Ilara finished coughing and rolled back up to her sitting posture. "I think I breathed in the foam," she said. Both women laughed. She took another, longer sip, and her expression soured. "I'm not sure I'll be able to finish that."

"Oh, you're making this sound appealing," Sophia said sarcastically.

"Try it." Ilara grinned. "You'll like it better than I do."

Sophia took a sip from her own mug. The initial taste was sour as a lemon, but as the liquid settled on her tongue, warm, floral flavors flooded her taste buds.

"Aye, I do like that." She smiled. "It is does bite a bit too much for you, doesn't it?"

Ilara nodded as she sipped again. "You're right. I can help you finish this pitcher. I'm sorry we haven't spent time together recently. And I'm sorry if I've been a bitch."

Sophia met Ilara's eyes and found a sincerity that hadn't been there before. "It's fine. We've both changed so much in the last few years. But you're my only link to our parents. It's hard when you don't let me in."

Ilara nodded, then took a long gulp of her ale. Her face contorted in pain, and Sophia couldn't help but laugh.

"You really don't have to drink it if you don't like it."

"No. This is exposure training now. And you're right. I should tell you about Mom. Father wasn't worth mentioning then, but Mom—Well, unlike this ale, Mom was sweet."

"How?" Sophia asked as she finished the mug of beer. Pouring another was easier than the first had been—it felt as if there was new strength in her arms that hadn't been there before.

Ilara stroked her chin. "Whenever she did chores, or had to do something she didn't want to do, she'd always say, 'Nothing to it but to do it.' And she'd tell you that right now."

"What on Aerlia are you talking about?" Sophia asked.

"Come on." Ilara rolled her eyes. "I've seen the way you look at that barmaid—Sanandra. Didn't know you had a type, but I'm not surprised."

Sophia felt warmth flush her cheeks, and she knew it wasn't the alcohol. "I—"

"Can't deny it," Ilara said with a shrug. "Means I'm right."

"Wait. No, h-h-hold your dragons," Sophia stammered, then let out a big sigh. "Guess I shouldn't be surprised, given your training."

"Aye." Ilara grinned again.

"Tell me something else about Mom," Sophia said.

They sat there, talking into the early morning, well past when Sophia had finished the last of the lilac ale. She drank in everything Ilara had to say about their mother.

She'd worn dresses of all colors, tended to the flower gardens like it was her duty. She'd liked to make soup when the autumn chilled the woods. She had a laugh that could light up a room and a steady hand from years of sewing and knitting. Sophia felt she had a good idea of the type of woman her mother was.

Still, nothing had been able to save her in the end.

Ilara had never budged on her resolve not to tell her sister how their parents died, and now, Sophia didn't know if she'd ever find out.

She was jolted out of her memory by a rough shove from the guard behind her. She shifted her eyes from the tapestry to his sad, tired eyes, so much like her sister's. A deep breath steadied her as she turned back to her path.

# Chapter Fifteen

# RANK

Valette shifted uncomfortably in her armor. She hadn't worn the heavy metal plates for more than her training hour in the last week and could feel the atrophy of her muscles. A Scholar, a thin woman with wispy white hair that didn't cover her scalp, was giving her report to Valette in a bored, monotonous voice. They were standing in a hallway that had been deemed the "hallway of death" by every other investigator.

Blood covered the walls, and each of the corpses littering the floor had multiple stab wounds in seemingly random places. They had been killed as efficiently as possible, vital organs or large life-giving arteries pierced through the folds of their armor. Brutally efficient. Yet it seemed the killer had come back to create post-humous stab wounds.

"I believe the men were killed within moments of each other. The culprit must have moved with incredible speed," the Scholar said.

"Unnaturally fast. They must have been Chosen," Valette mused as she put her hand to the chin of her helmet.

Ryn had commanded she come here and investigate after she told him Markus had said the Zal'Kerathan would be here. A small group of paladins confirmed that a crime had been committed, and Ryn tasked it to her after several larger groups of paladins had gone over the scene. He likely agreed that their assassin was behind this.

Still, Valette didn't think Zal'Kerathans were known for such quick kills. More often, they stalked their prey for weeks before pouncing, armed with the knowledge of their foe's habits.

"Aye, lady," the Scholar intoned. She seemed unperturbed despite the nature of the scene. "Would you like to speak to one of the dead? I could wake one so that you might query him."

"Wake him?" Valette asked. The Scholar was here to assist the investigation, but Valette hadn't been briefed on what exactly the Chosen of Ameri could do.

"Bring his mind back for a few moments. Would you like to query this one?" The Scholar motioned to a corpse resting awkwardly against the nearest wall, his neck cocked unnaturally to one side.

"Aye." Valette nodded, wondering what kind of dark god Ameri truly was. "Wake him, then."

The Scholar lowered her hand and rested it on the man's forehead. A slight blue light flowed into him, sending a sickly glow through his skin. His eyes flicked open and darted from the Scholar to Valette.

"Gods, two Chosen. What hell did I wake up in that you're my tormentors? Did we get the bitch? Guessing not, if there's a paladin here," he huffed. Light flowed across his lips as if it were the air he breathed.

"We do not have long before the spell fades," the Scholar said. "Be quick about your questions, Almiran."

"Who is it that killed you?" Valette asked.

"Invisible Chosen. Thorn is what they called her. Won't be calling her that now." The man laughed a bit. It came through his damned lips as little more than an increased exhale of light.

The Chosen at the inn had been able to become invisible too. Valette heart raced. Markus's tip was good. He could track Thorn.

"Why was she killing you and your men?" Valette asked.

The man scoffed. "Some shit she had with Jonas, the bloke upstairs. Fucking prick."

"You weren't with this man, Jonas?"

"Not truly." He cocked his head back, or tried to. "His gang was killed by—" The man stopped as if frozen.

Valette cast a worried glance at the Scholar, who continued to hold the spell. The man started up again a moment later, unperturbed by the hiccup in his speech.

"We were just here as additional protection. Thorn was tied up and stripped of magic, so she shouldn't have been a problem," he continued.

"What was that?" Valette asked the Scholar.

"A break in his memory. The mind after death is fickle." She gasped as if she was having trouble breathing. Her brow furrowed. "Continue your questioning."

Valette turned back to the man. The glow of blue light under his skin had faded significantly. "What do you mean by 'stripped of magic'?" she asked.

"Can't cast nothing," the man replied, as if it were obvious.

Valette's frown deepened as she considered her next question. "How did you capture Thorn?"

"We had something she wanted." The man grinned. "That aforementioned prick." The light in his skin faded on his last word, and he slumped over again.

"The spell ended," the Scholar said with a shrug. "Ameri has deemed it so."

"His lapse in memory—could that knowledge have been purged from his mind?"

"If it is possible, it is unknown magic to me."

Valette nodded but turned to the other corpses in the hallway. "How many times can you cast that spell?"

"As many times as you need. Such is the duty of the Scholar."

One by one, they went through the fallen men, and Valette probed their memories. None held knowledge of who'd killed Jonas's gang or captured Thorn. It seemed too convenient. Finally, Valette and the Scholar climbed the stairs. Several more bodies lay on the upper landing, and Valette glanced to the Scholar, who stood there dutifully.

"There are no more remaining to query," she said, answering Valette's question before it was asked. "Knight Commander Ryn waits for you in the next room."

"You might have mentioned that sooner." Valette took off her helmet and fixed her hair. "I forgot to ask, what is your name?"

"Yila," the Scholar said.

"Can you provide me services outside this crime scene?"

"Indeed, I can. The knight commander made it clear that I would be your Scholar in the coming months."

"That also might have been ideal to know beforehand. Do you know a Scholar called Markus?" Valette asked.

"The name is new to me. There are many of our order, though, as Ameri exercises her use of the Pantheon's power," Yila said.

"Can you look into him? I think he might have something to do with all this."

"Aye. I will report to you at the palace with any information I can gather." Yila gave a salute before leaving the room.

Valette took only a moment more before opening the doors before her, which were carved with Halga's open palms. Inside, she found Ryn standing over one final corpse. He was looking down at the dead man with a bemused expression.

"Sir," Valette said, flourishing a salute.

His attention pulled to her, and he glanced briefly up and down her armored form. "Chosen Bilaut," he grumbled. "About time. Did Yila assist you with the investigation, or do I need to reprimand her?"

"We interrogated the corpses in the hallway, sir."

Ryn's gaze slowly returned to the body at his feet. "Learn anything valuable?"

"Nothing we didn't know already, though I believe some information has been purged from their memories."

"You believe that is possible?"

"Each corpse was missing the name of who captured Thorn," Valette said. "The deaths were efficient, though disguised to look like they had been killed more recklessly. Each confirmed that they believed they'd been fighting Thorn, though the individual was invisible. She may not know Scholars can interrogate the dead."

"A well-guarded secret. If Thorn is this Zal'Kerathan you seek, then she likely believes that death is too sacred for a soul to cross back from the other side. You sound almost impressed by that bloodbath."

"Almir disdains those who kill for pleasure, sir."

"Dusk district scum. No big loss of life. Do you know who this is?" Ryn asked as he kicked the leg of the corpse.

"Jonas," Valette said, echoing what each of the dead men had told her. Her eyes settled on the mutilated body at Ryn's feet. His head sat at an awkward angle atop a skillfully slit neck, and blood had run down to intermix with the matted curls on his chest . Then she fully recognized this man, with his fluffed-up hair and sparkling eyes. "He's the one who tipped us off to Sophia Blackwood."

"Aye. Seems if Thorn killed him, that would make her a Blackwood. I doubt she would go to the trouble if he'd lied about Sophia being her sister."

"That puts us in a winning position, sir," Valette said.

"How did you reach that conclusion?"

"We have something Thorn wants. Bait the trap well, and Thorn will be ours."

"And the last Zal'Kerathan will be killed," Almir said.

Ryn met her eyes. "Coincidentally, I agree. Jonas's information was good."

"Do we know anything about the Blackwood family, sir?"

"Likely not. The Amerites in the library may have something in the records, though. Go back to your desk and write up a report, then gather your things. I want you on the streets tracking this criminal down. You're the only one who saw her face. I trust you will be the first to recognize her." Ryn extended his hand to Valette. "Take my sigil."

"Yes, sir." She took the small silver coin he offered, which had Akara's face stamped in profile on one side and the letters "K.C.R" on the other.

"Do not disappoint me, again," Ryn warned. "While your first mistake merely cost Plithy his life, this will cost us the crown. Make no mistake—I will be watching your movements."

Valette nodded. "Sir, if I may, I have an idea about how to draw Thorn into the trap."

"Speak it."

"I'd like the dungeon to release Sophia into my custody. With Yila and another, I could determine when Thorn would strike. It would give us significantly more control to set the stage."

"Very well. I appreciate the thought. Make it so. Use the sigil I gave you to compel any paladin to aid you. Carrying it gives you the rank of lieutenant. Consider it a reward for learning the information desk as well as you have," Ryn said, then went back to regarding Jonas's corpse.

A figure approached from the edge of the room, a woman wearing a blue cloak and red scarf. This was the same woman who'd been in Ryn's office just after Plithy's murder.

"My lord, is it time?" she asked.

"Indeed. Chosen Bilaut, leave us. I meant what I said about not disappointing me."

Valette walked from the room, floating a prayer to Almir, not for the first time, asking why she had to be in this godsforsaken city.

"This is the most important quest in the world. We can go nowhere else," Almir said. He seemed on the point of rage, an emotion Valette had never heard in him before.

She picked her way back out of the building and into the busy afternoon crowds. In all the years they'd served together, she'd never known him to get upset. Even during her upbringing, he had been inflexible and strong. The stoic philosopher and mighty knight. When he asked her to come to Eversburg, he'd practically begged her in a way unbecoming of a god.

Valette had obliged, and she wasn't sure why. She had a nice home in Chrys, close to Almir's temple, where she worked just like her fathers before her—and, she hoped, her children after her. She missed them most of all. Her darling boys, growing up without her. Being away from them broke her heart. Still, it was all the more reason to finish this investigation as quickly as possible.

Which was why it was so frustrating that this city had so many rules. Nowhere else in the Empire would she be regulated as a Chosen of Almir. If she'd worshiped Zal'Keratha or Ytria, it would be understandable. Those gods were actively working against Akara, but Almir was literally her ally—nay, the closest thing a god could have to a child. He'd ascended through Akara. He'd fought and died for her cause.

Still, the sigil would make Valette's life much easier. The rank might force some of the Akaran paladins to make way for her.

Passing through the Noon district reminded her of the things she loved about this city—the feeling of people bustling from place to place and businesses packed with people. Even Akaran street preachers raised her spirits, reminding her that there were plain folk in the Akaran Empire, above the goddess's war and divine grudges.

As she passed into Dawn, a guard started waving his arms to flag her down. His armor was new enough that the metal reflected the sun. "My Lady," he said as he approached. "I need to see your city pass when you cross districts."

"Got to be fucking with me," she grumbled. They always stopped her, without fail. She reached down into the pouch at her waist and handed over the slip of paper she'd had since arriving in the city. It was badly faded and creased, but it they wouldn't renew it.

The guard opened the parchment and looked it over. Valette crossed her arms over her chest as the his brow furrowed. He was taking longer than every other guard she'd shown it to.

"One moment," he said, holding his hand up as he returned to the side of the walkway.

Valette followed him to a small hut that butted up against a building. Another guard was huddling inside, likely to keep out of the cold. Valette saw a glint of red in his eyes. Of course the paladin was waiting in the warm hut while the recruit did the real work.

After several excruciating moments, the guard came back out. "I'm going to need to escort you back to the palace for Tribunal, my lady," he said.

"Really? For what exactly?"

"Several parts of your city pass are illegible. The Tribunal will have to verify with the clerk's office that you are able to move about freely." He gave her a soft smile. "It should only take a few days."

"Bleeding hells," Valette muttered as she reached back into her pouch. She stiffened at the scraping of metal as the guard unsheathed his sword.

"Please withdraw your hand from the bag," he said sternly.

Valette did so, holding the sigil the knight commander had given her. The silver glinted in the sun. "Do you know what this is?" she demanded.

"A sigil," the guard answered dutifully. His sword arm eased, but he made no move to return his weapon to its sheath.

"Yes, and which sigil is this?"

"A royal sigil."

"Aye, you're not a total dunce. Knight Commander Ryn gave this to me not an hour ago. Should I spend the rest of my week at a Tribunal, do you think the knight commander would be pleased?" Valette could feel the tension in the air rise around her.

"No, my lady,"

"Good. If we're on the same parchment, may I go?"

"One moment, lady," the guard said, quickly spinning on his heel.

The young man retreated into the shack. Inside, his hands waved about wildly while he had a conversation with the older paladin. Valette tapped her foot. If she was going to play the upset Chosen, she'd do it well. She'd wanted to do this for a week, but finally, with Ryn's sigil, she felt she might not face blowback as hard as she would have otherwise. It was time to test a theory she'd been mulling over since the Tribunal after Plithy died. Tezza had passed her staff to another paladin to light. She hadn't lit it with her own magic.

Both men left the hut and approached her. Valette let her hand rest on the pommel of her sword. The paladin slipped on his helmet, his gray beard sticking out awkwardly and his eyes burning fiercely. "Almir, eh?" His breath reeked of alcohol. "Young god, that one."

"Gods, I hope you have a point," Valette said, hoping to push his emotions .

"Thing is," the paladin said, looking down his nose at her, "your Almir likes to pretend he's so much higher than the rest of us because he stands for 'justice.' I'd say the rest of the gods were enforcing his justice well before he came along. My family worshiped Akara for her justice for ten generations before he ascended.

"Fact being, the other gods worked for their godhood. Almir just had it handed to him like a bastard. How does it feel to be the Chosen of a bastard god?"

"Listen—" Valette started, but the paladin's fist collided with her cheek, filling her mouth with the taste of iron. Black filled her vision, and the next thing she felt was the wet snow against her cheek, contrasting with the warmth of the pain.

Spitting blood, she looked back at the paladin, whose eyes were red with hate. "Does the goddess stay your hand?" she spat.

The paladin raised his fist again, and Valette braced herself, priming her shield spell. The man chanted a series of words under his breath. Valette expected to feel the amber-red light of Akara that was used to smite. It would likely burn her to death. She prayed her shield would be enough, but that horrid light was legendary for burning through metal and flesh.

Yet it never came.

"The disgrace of lost combat is your Tribunal for today," the paladin said as he turned from her.

Valette sat in the snow, dumbfounded. Warmth filled her chest as she called on Almir's magic. Her hand brightened, surrounded by an aura of white light. She held it to her face, and she felt the bone heal moments later, cracking back into place. Lucky for her, a broken jaw was the worst of it. The man had a hell of a hook, but he hadn't had the magic to back it up.

After a few minutes, she stood up creakily, completely aware of how stupid she would have looked if she'd been wrong.

# Chapter Sixteen

# FATE

A haze of cloveweed smoke settled over the bar, sitting like mist on a bog. Lantern light reflected in odd directions through the purple fog. Ilara had watched Markus pound ales through the afternoon and into the evening.

Now, she shifted her cha'ak uncomfortably as several men eyed her across the room. The Kittering sat deep in the Dusk district and acted as a recruitment building for the Syndicate. Most here didn't know her from the average patron, but there was always a chance she would run to Gray. She'd deal with that if it became an issue.

She glanced toward the black stone hammer, which shone in the lantern light next to her wooden chair. She hadn't been able to leave it; something about it bothered her. Gray had more of those weapons, like the black rapier he'd stabbed her with. It had drained something from her. Had it been blood? Life? Magic? Her mind flitted back to the way the hammer had sucked the blood from Benin's corpse, and she shuddered. She didn't understand these things, and she needed to if she was going to encounter more of them. The hammer would hopefully help.

But that was a problem for later.

Markus still hadn't noticed her in his drunken stupor. The goddesses Ameri and Akara were close allies. The Scholar's goddess had aided Akara in usurping Aox, despite the fact that they both sat on his Pantheon. Ameri's Great Library even resided within Akara's palace. It begged the question why a Chosen of Ameri would help Zal'Keratha. Ilara hoped the Amerite knew something she didn't.

Swirling the glass of untouched scotch in front of her, Ilara tried to convince herself this wasn't a massive risk. Markus chugged another beer, the shine of his bald head reflecting the lanterns as well as the stone of the hammer. A drinking song started among some the drunks at the other end of the tavern. Their lighthearted ditty stumbled through the air like an inebriated dancer in a crowded hall.

On a normal night, Ilara would've enjoyed this atmosphere. Tonight, she was terrified one of the patrons would shank her in the side for betraying the Syndicate. Not as terrified as she was of Markus, though. They'd never been close when they worked in Jonas's gang. When a group had access to multiple

Chosen, they were often paired up for jobs. She and Katri, another born and bred killer, had often been sent to kill targets together. Not so with Markus. Jonas had always kept his talents close to him.

Yet Markus had been there when Ilara needed him most. She owed him a significant debt.

She raised her glass, pulling down her cha'ak to down the burning amber liquid in one gulp. Standing, she gathered the large maul, the weight of it pulling down her shoulder. She sat down next to Markus, making the smallest of sounds as the stool creaked.

"Shadows have your back," she said.

He started, then settled back into his seat. "About bloody time you came over. Wasn't sure I'd go another round." He belched loudly. "Least that's what the Sight told me."

"Why not come talk to me if it was inevitable?"

"Because I don't want to do this. I already had to purge the memories of the dead before those Akarans showed up. And I shouldn't have to tell you that nothing in the Sight is final. Ameri's orders, though—those are," he huffed.

"Feeling's mutual," Ilara muttered. She glanced around the bar. No one was paying them any mind. Still, it irked her, sitting in this place of her enemy. "Fancy somewhere quieter to chat?"

"Aye," Markus said.

The two stood, and Ilara placed a handful of gali on the counter. They wandered out into the cold night and found themselves in a nearby alley. Moonlight shone in it, making it a poor hideout for any other criminal. It stunk of waste and the fresh smell of rotten food.

"What do you know?" Ilara asked.

"Death seeks the altar," Markus grunted.

"You don't need to be so dramatic. Zal'Keratha's domain is death, but this"—she motioned around her—"is death. This city, the whole Empire, oozes suffering from its every tenet. My lady wants to stop it, to bring life back to the world." Ilara wanted to believe those words.

Markus cocked his head. "Now I'm not the one being dramatic. I'm not sure the Mistress of Death fights for life."

"You would think that," Ilara grunted. "Akara has been queen for a century, and what has it gotten but war and death camps? You were here for the roundups?"

Markus's eyes shot to the ground. "I was in Nox at the time, but there are rumors." He meant the ones about the Aoxians who lived in Eversburg, who'd flocked here expecting wealth and success, being killed en masse. They'd lived here for generations.

"Folks were told that the lizards were to be taken to be with their own people. None of them are alive anymore, and Zal'Keratha was the one who passed every soul to the other side. To see the pain of mothers watching their children butchered, dead souls who couldn't understand why their lives were taken from them. Your Sight doesn't show you such things?"

"The Sight does not show me such events, only futures I can change," Markus replied.

"Such as the death of Jonas?" Ilara mused.

"Aye, that." Markus's face flushed red. "I tried to convince him to save himself, but he was too stubborn to abandon course. I knew only that turning Sophia into the paladins would cause his demise."

"It must be a blessing and a curse to see how fate moves against you."

Markus shrugged. "I find my way to flow with the tide of fate. I do as my goddess instructs me."

"And why does Ameri want us to work together? You know Zal'Keratha's motivations. What of your goddess's?"

"Do you question your goddess like this? I don't know, nor do I care to. Ameri's Sight spans farther than mine, and she sees this to her benefit. I'm sure Zal'Keratha feels the same—that's why we're here," Markus said as if it were obvious.

Ilara paused. Betrayal was common when dealing with gods and criminals. She knew Markus well enough to know that he would betray her as quickly as he'd betrayed Jonas if his goddess ordered it. She'd have to confirm with Zal'Keratha whether she felt sure that Ameri was a worthy ally.

"Let's be clear," she said, hoping to sound definite. "My goal is to save my sister and find information on the altar. What are you getting from this?"

Markus ran a hand over his smooth head and let out a long breath. "I was told to assist you, and that's what I aim to do."

Ilara nodded. "I can work with that. Both my aims lie within the Solar Dominion, so that's where I'm headed."

"The bleeding palace?" Markus crossed his arms and leaned back against the alley wall. The movement was intentionally disarming. Ilara kept her hand clenched around the maul at her side. "What's the plan?" he added.

"A week from now is Solar Day which presents an opportunity."

It was the anniversary of Akara's declaration of war on Aox, marking her victory on all the Northern Kingdoms. It was celebrated all through the Empire, but nowhere as regally as in Eversburg.

"You mean with the paladins parading through the city?" Markus asked.

Ilara nodded again. The celebration always started with a parade of paladins from the South Gate to the Solar Dominion in a mock recreation of the day the Akaran army conquered Eversburg. There was no one in the Akaran Empire who hadn't been conquered by Akara.

"They'll be away from the Solar Dominion. If we can find a Chosen to teleport us into the palace, we could infiltrate the library and save Sophia all at once."

"That could be messy," Markus muttered. He closed his eyes, and his lids twitched. Black, stenciled tattoos of eyes appeared on his head, covering every inch of his scalp. The ink was splotched, as if they'd always been there. The pupils darted from side to side as Markus's head moved. "You use Aoxian magic. It does not go well. The Aoxians betray you. You're captured shortly after freeing your sister. She escapes—you do not."

Ilara smiled as she walked to the front of the alley. "Good thing we have a week to change that outcome."

She paused, watching the man's face contort back to normal. Swinging the maul onto her shoulder, she stared into the city streets. It was a still night, the only sounds in the air wafting from the tavern near them. Few travelers were willing to venture into the cold, and snow was slowly dancing from the sky.

"I, ah, do need a place to sleep," Ilara said, turning red. "I lived in Syndicate housing, and they are likely watching it."

"You are a dangerous ally. I have a place you can stay." The eye tattoos on Markus's head slowly closed, disappearing as they did. "Walk with me."

***

Markus's apartment was disturbingly close to Sophia's tenement building, though farther into the Dusk district. A man was screaming outside, and dogs barked on the streets below. Ilara drew a certain amount of safety from knowing that everyone had their own problems to deal with. It meant they'd be less focused on her.

She was sitting uncomfortably on a pile of blankets that gave off a musky man smell. For the next week, it would serve as her bed, and she did not look forward to trying to sleep on it.

Grunting in relief, she pulled her leather armor off, letting the tunic below fall freely. No longer having the restriction around her ribs was freeing. She suspected they may have been broken, but there wasn't time to see a healer.

Markus teetered into the room from the adjacent kitchen, balancing a tray holding a green teapot and mugs. Ilara was worried the man would topple.

"That weapon. Why do you have it?" he asked as he sat the tea set down on a low wooden table.

"Gray captured me with a weapon similar to it. Do you know anything about it?"

Markus carefully filled the cups and extended one to Ilara. "No. But there's something off about it. I didn't see many like it in my time in the guild. I know little about such power. You took it from Benin?"

Ilara took a sip of the tea. The taste and scent of lemons overwhelmed her, and she couldn't help but scowl. Markus was lying, but it wouldn't do to call him out on it. He'd double down and refuse to give her anything else. Best to tease out what information she could.

"Aye, it's on my list to investigate tomorrow. Hopefully I won't have to kill many to learn what I need. If Gray has more of these weapons, we need to know how to fight them."

"Aye," Markus said as he sipped from his own cup. "I never asked when we worked together—do you enjoy killing?"

Ilara nodded. He was redirecting the conversation. "At times. It's necessary. There are evil people in the world that deserve death more than life. They'll keep fucking things up if they live. Jonas is a good example. I relish killing people like that."

"What of paladins? There are plenty to spare in this city, and they are sworn against Zal'Keratha."

"Paladins are difficult. I tried to kill one once, a street guard. I tailed him for weeks only to abandon the idea when I saw him save a homeless man against a group of thugs. Some of his actions were questionable, but he was following orders. Would I be making the world better with that man's death?" Ilara mused. "I do my best to vet my kills as much as I can to ensure they deserve what's coming to them."

"You sound like a shit assassin."

Ilara shook her head. "Aye? Zal'Keratha never wanted me to be one, yet she gave me the skills for it."

"What else do her Chosen do? I've never heard of a Zal'Kerathan Soothsayer or Scholar. The only stories I hear are of assassins who bring down kingdoms," Markus said.

"Truth be told, I've only met one other of her other Chosen, the one before me, and he spoke of performing rites for the faithful when there were more of us. Or helping those the dead have left behind through communing. I've never seen that, though. Just the death."

Markus cleared his throat, and the two sat in silence for several minutes. Ilara let her tea sit on the table as she massaged her muscles, while Markus occasionally brought his cup to his lips.

The apartment was well furnished. Bookcases lined the walls, most with titles in a language Ilara couldn't read. A large oil lantern sat on a small table  near her, casting flickering light around the room.

"What would you do if you weren't here killing people?" Markus asked.

Ilara blinked slowly at the ridiculousness of the question. There wasn't anything but saving Sophia. "Find a quiet hamlet in a warmer place and live off the garden, I suppose. You?"

"Sounds peaceful," he said with a grin. "I'd run a library or a bookstore. Anything to pull me out of the Sight every now and then."

"Why is that so important to you?"

"The Sight is like worship, but in a way that eddies my soul. Lighting up my mind with magic to see a million solutions to the world's problems."

"What is your solution for Eversburg?" Ilara asked.

"That's a big question. It starts with a lot of death. You know, bring her to justice," Markus said.

"I don't think I need to ask who to kill to bring down a monarchy."

He laughed. "You're right. Akara's death seems like a necessary one. But the people she is exploiting need to understand why, or they'll find a different goddess. A different oppressor."

"You think that's likely?"

Markus nodded. "I've seen it. The protests and street callers are increasing. Pals are always quick to shut it down—kill the people involved and jail the Chosen they find. That's no longer enough to quell them."

Ilara tilted her head. "You  know of anything that kills a goddess?"

"Only the gods know—Ameri hasn't provided that information. Who knows what chaos the death of a god would bring? Or that Zal'Keratha commanded her death?"

"Zal'Keratha commanded Akara's altar. That, or I am Forsaken," Ilara said.

"A fate worse than death for a Chosen. She would see you ascended to Akara's plane. It is the only thing an altar does."

"I know."

"This means you have to kill her."

"I know."

"And take her place." Markus's face was hard. He might have been well-studied in what an altar did, but he was mistaken about what Zal'Keratha would do with it. Or at least what she claimed she would do with it.

"Not sure if I'm looking forward to that part."

# Chapter Seventeen

# TARHA

Moist air filled Sophia's lungs as screams filled her ears.

A woman with a black band covering her eyes cried out as she tried to channel. "Akara, hear my pleas! Let me see your light again," she screeched as a metal-clad paladin pulled her behind him down the hallway. She was the fifth prisoner in as many days to be hauled from the dungeon. The woman wailed as her flesh sizzled, and her muscles tensed as she tried to channel again.

Sophia didn't know where they went when they were dragged away, but they never came back. Other prisoners whispered of sacrifices, but Sophia wasn't sure Akara's clergy would stoop to that. Then again, she'd never had a handle on what was in vogue with Akara's clergy.

Trying not to think about it, she focused on what the Librarian had told her earlier that day. They'd been on another tangent, looking up food preferences in the Aoxian kingdoms.

They liked to tell Sophia that they were researching merely to assist in the war effort. Sophia felt like there was something more to their words. Their passion was knowledge, but they treated the Aoxians like they were special, almost more elevated. It was as if the lizard kin were closer to the gods.

Maybe there was truth to it. Aoxians were the only creatures on Aerlia to have a god whose creator still gave commands. Creator gods were a thing of myth. They'd long since departed Aerlia, and their names had failed to be documented, at least according to the Librarian.

Sophia started as Katri's lanky form was shoved into view of their cell. Plume unlatched the door, and Katri growled as she sauntered inside and sat across from Sophia. She reeked of sewer. The guards threw several buckets of water on her before sending her back to the dungeon, but it never rid her of the smell.

"How was it today?" Sophia asked once the guards were out of earshot. Unclogging the palace sewers was Katri's workload. It had been assigned just a day after Sophia got her own. Katri blamed it on her failed escape attempt, but seeing the ripple of muscles beneath her skin, Sophia knew that her cellmate would always be assigned manual labor.

"Shitty." Katri grinned, brushing some of her red hair out of her eyes. Sophia blushed as she met Katri's wild gaze. "Certainly can't be as cushy as the Library of Ameri. What did they have you doing in there?"

"Just moving some books. Nothing grand," Sophia said.

She didn't want to tell Katri the truth about how little work she did. The Librarian had asked her read to them again today out of several textbooks. Not to mention, Sophia didn't want word to get out that the Librarian wasn't wiping her memory. Keeping all the ones she had seemed important.

"Lucky you. I'm sure they keep the books warmer than the sewers," Katri huffed.

Sophia nodded. "You never did mention where you were from."

"You never asked," Katri teased.

"Aye, I didn't."

"The Forest of Tarha." Katri rubbed the back of her neck. "That was where I was born."

"A Tarian? I didn't think there were any of you left." Sophia regretted the words as she said them. No one wanted to be reminded that they'd been the first people assimilated into Akara's Empire.

"I haven't met one of my kin since I was a girl," Katri said.

"Why Eversburg?" Sophia asked, hoping to change the conversation.

"My god demanded I come here. Both of us wanted to find Tarians, but all we found were dissidents. People who wanted to hurt Akara as bad as we did."

"If you're Tarian, then your god must be S—"

"Don't say his name. It's bad enough I can't speak with him. We don't need to talk of him," Katri growled. She turned her head and wiped an eye with the back of her hand.

Instinctively, Sophia stood and walked to Katri's side of the cell. She stiffened as Sophia sat next to her.

"I know how you feel," Sophia said, a little louder than a whisper. *What am I saying? She just said she didn't want to talk about this.*

Sophia took a deep breath, stilling the doubts, then blundered on. "I didn't know my kin. Ilara, my sister, she says that they aren't worth remembering. Aside from my mom. And Balan's absence weighs heavy on me, too. Not only do I not have him—every sound that once would have been musical to me sounds dull in comparison to what it was. There's a richness in the tones of everyday life that I can't hear. It hurts. Especially when I know there are new sounds that I want to hear."

"What on Aerlia could there possibly be that's worth hearing in a cell?" Katri asked.

"You'd be surprised." Sophia grinned. "The tapping of the water is a lovely rhythm, and with the shuffling of boots for a melody, it can create a tapestry. Not to mention, certain voices are quite pleasant when you really listen to them." She blushed again and turned away from Katri.

Warmth enveloped Sophia's hand as Katri gripped it. She blushed as deeply as Sophia. "Thank you. It warms me to know that you feel this way. Gently, though, I can tell ye that I can't hope. This place is death, and it isn't likely either of us will see freedom again, much less hear our gods again."

"I know. It's hard for me not to hope," Sophia said sheepishly. She felt stupid, like she was a girl who'd been rebuffed by her crush. Desperately, she wanted to retreat back to her side of the cell.

"How can you be so hopeful when we hear the screams of condemned Chosen dragged to their deaths? Akara will crush it out of you eventually. Whether it's taking away everyone you love or when you're staring your execution in the face. She'll take it like a sadistic offering."

"Oh, gods," Sophia muttered, pulling her legs to her. She buried her face in her knees as she fought back tears. "How did we get here?"

"None like I know," Katri said.

"Tell me about Tarha." Sophia wanted to hear the stories about it. Mostly, she didn't want to be alone with her thoughts.

"The forest was beautiful," Katri began, the hint of a smile flitting across her face. "Tarha Forest. The towering Maka-maka with bark like iron made for fine homes. We built high into the treetops, trusting one another that our well-crafted homes wouldn't fall from the trees. My mama saw to the upkeep. She was better with her hands than most, and she knew by instinct the way to plant a tigi pole to keep a platform off the ground.

"My da spun leaves. The sounds he could make out of two Maka-maka leaves was beautiful. You would have appreciated the stories he could tell. Leaf spinners passed our history down from ancient days, days when we knew our Creator gods. When none were deemed Chosen to fight for their god's honor on Aerlia."

"That sounds like a different time."

"Aye. It does. We were happy then, I believe. Our god cared for us and protected us."

"Who would you have been, if you had been able to stay with them?"

"A hunter, likely. I practically was at the end."

"How does that work?"

"It was a long process that started when I was young. I prepared to join the kal—the hunting teams. I was always good with a bow, so I prepared for my kal'da: my first hunt, undertaken alone. There was much studying of my potential prey, and learning to craft the weapons of the hunt. When I was ready, I set out alone. On my way down the lift, I heard howls and knew my calling was to hunt a great wolf. In bringing back this predator, I would declare myself the kaldina of the woods."

"Wolves were the strongest predators in the Tarha? I've never seen a one bring down a fendeer."

"Great wolves were not the wolves you have here in the north, which are starved and small. Wolves in Tarha grew to be taller than a grown man, with claws sharp enough for them to pierce Maka-maka bark. I pursued a wolf pack through the whole of Tarha, followed tracks, confirmed their kills, and listened to their howls. I saw her in the evening during a week of hunting. She stood atop a tall hill, and she seemed as tall as a mountain, with fur like autumn leaves.

"It took nearly a month before I had the shot. Late one evening, the pack was resting in their den, and that great majestic wolf was standing in the mouth of a cave like she was the guardian of a sacred treasure. The pack leader, in all her ferocious majesty, stood vulnerable.

"It was only then that I began to question myself. To take such a great life from this world would deprive the wolves of a mother. A provider. In that moment, I heard Shyll in my ear, that great god of the forest. He said, 'Do not fear taking this aged wolf from her kin. It will give room for others to grow. Her time is passed. Take her to your people to show your strength.'

"Still unsteady, I took the shot, letting my bow string slip my timid fingers. I pierced through her side, deep enough to hit one of her organs, yet I knew I hadn't struck her heart. She bounded toward my hidden position. She'd not let me go without a proper fight. I prayed to Shyll as I launched another arrow. In a flurry, I drew the talka swords at my side—massive curved blades. Just in time, I held one up to defend myself from tooth and claw. Hours, we fought. I was on the defensive the whole time. I darted up trees, fled into ravines, and each place she followed me. It wasn't until I circled back to the cave that I saw the blood from my first arrow. I knew she had lost much of it and would fall soon.

"I turned and met her in combat. A warrior ought to die fighting, not chasing. I met her claw with my blade, and we fought until the small hours of the morning. In the end, she fell due to the first injury I gave her. It was all I could do to wear out her spirit.

"I ate of her flesh that day. The heart is what we must eat, the strongest organ that keeps all for their entire lives. Steady, unwavering. We believe you must eat your kal'da to gain their strength, and I would need the strength of this one.

"I knew then I would be Chosen of Shyll, though he did not accept me until much later. On my way back to my village, I skirted the edge of the forest and saw smoke plumes on the horizon. I returned a hero, with the largest kal'da since Queen Valti, who hunted the sould of Aerlia. Yet my success was marked with despair. The village elders knew trouble was coming when I told of the smoke. It was an army, and the leaves spoke that they wouldn't pass us by.

"Sure enough, Akara demanded acquiescence—that we would chop down our woods and build her a great city. We defied her, and she turned on us.

"My da was the reason we survived so long. He'd spin a leaf to keep the whole village distracted for hours during the long days."

"The long days?" Sophia asked.

"Aye, long days. You must not have been far south. When Akara turns her war on a people, her Eye rests upon them relentlessly. For many months, we never saw night. The heat of the sun made the Maka-makas dry. They withered and became brittle. Eventually, they caught fire. We couldn't stay in our tree homes any longer. The Akaran army was set up at the bottom of our lifts. We were their prey that day—no way to fight back, and we couldn't flee. It was into Akaran spears or into Akara's fire."

"How did you survive?" Sophia asked.

"Shyll saved me. When I rode down the lift, I prayed to him that I would be like the great wolf of whose flesh I'd partaken to save my pack. When we landed and the spears and arrows flew to us, I became something new. A spirit took root in me, and I fought like I never had before. Tooth and claw were mine to wield, and many Akarans died that day before they fled from our forest.

"The fires had done the damage that Akara needed them to. Her Eye continued to burn above us, and the forest died in flame. Her army kept us in until the last ember died."

Katri sat still, tears staining her cheeks as they rolled freely down her face, mixing with the dirt and grime on her skin.

"I'm sorry," Sophia said. She was at a loss for words. Still, there was one thing she might offer. "I'd—May I write your story into a song? I can't sing it, but I'm certain poetry can capture the beauty of your people."

"You may try." Katri chuckled half-heartedly. "And if you finish it before our souls leave this place, then I'd be glad to hear it. The leaf spinners would love to sing it when we enter the Chasm of Souls."

Sophia stood and stretched, the bones in her spine popping and cracking as she twisted in the lone cell. Anxiety bounced in her chest like an unwanted fly. Did she truly want Katri, or was it the closeness of circumstance, a convenient distraction to rid her mind of her impending death? Of waking alone in the darkness and mud to slave for a brain too large for a head.

The dungeon door at the end of the hallway screeched open, and a flurry of boots marched toward them. A group of guards stood in front of Sophia and Katri's cell, one of them in particular eying Sophia. She was well armored for a paladin, but her hair was pulled back into a tight braid. Sophia recognized the woman as the one who'd seized her from her apartment.

"You're Sophia Blackwood, then?" the guard asked.

"Aye," Sophia said, surprised this woman didn't recognize her.

"Valette Bilaut," the guard said. "You're going to tell me everything you know about your sister."

# Chapter Eighteen

# GRIM FUTURES

The interrogation was exhausting. Valette was sitting across from Sophia, who was now in a multicolored dress. It was much more dignified for her station as a Chosen of a Pantheon god. This was no heretic who deserved the muck and grime.

The singer was thinner than she had been several weeks ago. Father Halen would have called Sophia poor bait for a rabbit. She now wore a black band fastened tightly around her neck, almost as if it was fused with her skin. She'd shied away when Valette tried to remove it. Valette had been a fool to think that the Akaran Empire would take care of this poor woman the way they should have. And there were more in the dungeon that Valette couldn't save.

Sophia had answered Valette's questions as faithfully as she could. She gave no signs of being untruthful or putting up resistance. Either she was an excellent liar, or resigned to her fate. Still, she hadn't given up any weaknesses that Ilara might have, aside from Sophia herself.

Valette found Ilara's name interesting. In the tongue of the old kingdoms, a dead language, it meant rose.

The old kings would give their betrothed a rose freshly picked from gardens they'd grown by hand. The new queen would dry the roses, then burn them on their wedding night as a sacrifice to Zal'Keratha, a plea that a child made from love wouldn't to be taken by death before birth.

Before they burned the roses, it was customary for them to clip the thorns from the stems. Queens then fashioned the thorns into bracelets that could be worn over their knuckles. If their husbands abused them or their children, the queen would slash the man over his cheek. When the wound scarred, all would know the shameful act he had committed. Valette wondered if Ilara had known all this before she'd chosen the name Thorn when she turned assassin. Was her intent to leave Akara with a scar to let Aerlia know her shame?

Valette stood from the table. Yila was sitting awkwardly at a desk in the corner of the room, her eyes closed and brow furrowed.

Maer was leaning against the door, plate-covered arms crossed as her red eyes followed Valette around the space. "I thought Ryn assigned you to street duty," she said. Her eyes flicked from Valette to Sophia, as if worried that the prisoner would pick up the tension from their conversation. "What happens when he learns you've spent the better part of the day interrogating a dead end?"

It had been difficult for Valette to convince Maer to join her. Thankfully, Ryn's sigil gave her authority to increase Maer's pay enough that she'd been tempted to join them, and a promotion from cadet to sergeant had sealed the deal. Valette was sure Maer was throwing the title around and would have her own set of cronies soon. She hoped she would have concluded her investigation by then.

"Ryn released the prisoner into my custody. He'd understand that I know what I'm doing. As you should," Valette countered. "Yila, how goes the investigation into this unknown Scholar?"

"He is elusive." Yila spoke with her eyes closed. A third, tattooed eye had opened in the center of her forehead. It darted around erratically, as if seeing invisible shapes and forms. "The Sight has been tampered with. There are paths of my future that have been stained by another's influence."

"How is that possible?" Valette asked. She knew little about the Scholars' Sight, but she'd thought that the future was always set. What would happen would happen, no matter what she did to change it.

"Each choice has a possibility. When one path is chosen, others are invalidated. Each path affects another path, and each action of every person affects another, usually in small ways," Yila answered.

"And there are small choices that affect your path drastically?" Valette asked.

"Aye. Think of it as if you were foreseeing a visit to a fruit stand to buy an apple, but then there are no apples left because someone bought them all an hour before you arrived," Yila explained.

"Or someone poisoned the apple tree," Valette mused.

"Precisely. If another Seer is working against us, it could close certain paths of action."

Valette nodded. She knew Markus could see future events, and that Ryn was colluding with an Amerite. Either of them could be working this chaos.

"At the moment," Yila continued, "I see my death frequently. Such an event is a disturbing inconvenience when seeing one's future."

"Your death?" Valette asked.

"Correct. It seems the path we've chosen is quite a deadly one."

"And when did that change for you?"

"When I was assigned to your charge. I've seen all our deaths equally," Yila responded, and opened her eyes, letting the tattoo on her forehead close. It slowly dissipated, as if sinking into her skin.

"Fucking great," Valette said. This Seer had been working against her for a while, then. Maybe since Plithy's death. They either hadn't seen ahead enough with the Sight to prevent Yila from aiding Valette, or it simply wouldn't matter.

"I'm sorry to involve both of you. You are free to leave," Valette said, and moved to a window behind the chair Sophia was chained to. It afforded a spectacular view of the giant stone blade of the statue of Akara. From this angle, it seemed to hover over the whole of the city, as if Akara herself were prepared to decide its fate.

"I am bound by the contract that binds Ameri to Akara. Akara has decided my fate through Ryn's decision. There is nothing I can do about that," Yila said.

"Ryn is not Akara's Chosen."

"He is knight commander, appointed by the Voice," Yila replied.

"Fine. Tell me about the deaths," Valette said.

Yila blushed deeply. Speaking about the Sight was typically forbidden, but Akara's contract required Scholars to inform the paladin they were contracted to.

"The Zal'Kerathan attacks the palace on Solar Day. In most instances, all of us perish victoriously. The enemy is taken into custody as we die, or it requires our sacrifice to kill her," Yila said.

"And the Scholar?"

"Not in any version of these events."

"What of Akara's paladins? Do they not respond to the intruder?" Valette asked.

"They do not, Chosen. In some variations, they arrive as we are attacked, but they do not assist in the combat, fearing for their own lives," Yila said.

Valette paced the room, her heavy footfalls ringing off the walls. Sophia flinched with each step.

"And what if we petition Ryn for more paladins in this room on Solar Day?" Valette asked.

Yila frowned at the request but closed her eyes. The third eye on her forehead opened again.

It would be a huge ask of him. Most paladins were required to march the streets of Eversburg on Solar Day. The parade required solar rays to focus from Eversburg's southernmost gate and run up the city to the Palace of Solar Dominion. It created a beam strong enough to be seen from Rildor, the icy continent to the north. In a way, it was Akara's way of promising them that her light extended everywhere. Needless to say, the spectacle required most of the city's paladins.

Yila's frowned deepened. "Should you convince Ryn this is a good idea, he slays both the Zal'Kerathan and you. It is unclear to me if that is intentional until he levels his blade at your fallen corpse and remarks that you serve an 'upstart' god," she said.

Maer's eyes narrowed on Valette.

"Maybe. I find it hard to believe that Ryn turns against us so drastically. If so, I'm surprised he gave me as much reign as this. Do you know if he has allied a Scholar of his own?" Valette asked.

"He is not a paladin. Only paladins are ever contracted a Scholar." Yila shrugged. "If you think Ryn is the one creating these dead-end paths, then I should think he has allies we do not know about."

"Maybe," Valette repeated. She sat roughly back into the chair across from Sophia. The woman seemed to shrink back into the wood. Valette gestured toward her, then put her hand to her lips. "What do you think of all this?"

"I, uh, me?" Sophia asked.

"Aye. Seems I've asked you all I can about your sister, and the only weakness I see in her is you. You see that Akara's paladins work against me. That means you are doomed as well. Surely, you could weigh in," Valette said.

"You can't be serious," Maer scoffed.

"I am." Valette shot an icy stare at the young paladin. "Do not forget who has rank in this situation. I've served Almir and Akara much longer than you. You may have a rank now, but I have status that only a divine can give."

"Aye, Chosen Bilaut," Maer growled.

Valette settled back and looked at Sophia. "Speak, singer. What do you think of our situation?"

"I think I was doomed in the dungeon, and I'm just as doomed here. The parable of the corpse knights comes to mind," Sophia said timidly. Too timidly for the event she was referencing.

It was one of Almir's parables about knights whose lives served as examples for the rest in the Chyriddion, Almir's holy book. In this particular tale, a group of Almirans had held off a horde of reincarnated corpses. Their stated goal was to cut the head off the necromancers, yet each time the horde drew near, the Almiran knights would fall back to a different defensive position. This let the necromancers reanimate more corpse walkers. In reality, all they accomplished was to buy time for Akara's army to make a hasty retreat. The Almirans were cut down in a heroic defense of a town that was consumed by the necromancers' madness. They'd known they were nothing more than walking corpse knights when they mounted their defense.

Valette had studied the event intensely during her studies at Almir's temple. Many Scholars speculated that the Almirans would have succeeded if they'd abandoned their defensive positions in front of the town. Many would have been spared if they'd turned away from the lives they were protecting and fought their enemy directly. Almir's message was that it was better to move decisively than fall to defensive positions.

Was Sophia trying to lead Valette's mind along this path? Or was this the correct course of action? Maybe it was time to face her enemy directly.

"An interesting premise," Valette muttered, then turned back to Yila. "What happens if we turn Sophia over to Ilara?"

Again, Yila closed her eyes and explored the option. Valette waited nervously, the option weighing on her mind. If this was the correct path, she be giving up all rapport she'd built in the last few weeks. Not that it would matter with Ryn turning against her.

When Yila opened her eyes, there was a brightness to them that seemed almost hopeful. "I believe this will keep us from our deaths. It is the one path I've seen where we survive, although there will be some hard choices despite that," she said.

"Naturally," Valette said. Her neck and shoulders ached. It was as if she'd been carrying a great weight that her body was only now acknowledging. It made sense. This was the only option their Seer adversary wouldn't think likely. It went against everything Valette was made of to let Thorn win. "What kinds of choices do you mean?"

"None of us will be welcome in this palace," Yila said gravely, folding her hands in her lap. She stared at Maer, her eyes seeming to drill a hole in the young woman's skull. "My goddess condones my actions. I would not be Forsaken. You should both decide if that is worth it for you."

Valette met Maer's eyes, and they nodded to one another. Maer opened the door and exited the room, and Valette followed. "Hey," she said as Maer began walking quickly down the hallway. She jogged to match the determined pace of the younger paladin. "What are you going to do?"

"Decide what this is worth," Maer grunted. She continued on, leaving Valette behind.

Stunned by her bluntness, Valette she suddenly regretted asking Maer to join them. More people meant more liability. More liability meant a higher chance of failure.

"Yet, more skills and blades mean a higher chance of success. Have you considered the Syl? We could use a guarantee from Tezza that she won't interfere," Almir said.

I shouldn't have trusted Maer. She has only known Akara. She's never had to defend the innocent.

"You were giving the young woman a chance. There is no harm in that."

And how would Tezza be any different?

"Trust in me. I believe she will," Almir replied.

Valette remembered Tezza's words about the Syl. Fine. I will trust you. I will consider the Syl again, she said, then turned to Sophia's room.

Valette didn't like the prospect of being with Tezza in that way, and she'd need to do more looking into what was involved. Her initial research seemed to indicate that the Chosen and the head of the Eversburg Temple had to lie together on a cushioned altar. It felt wrong, but the importance of a guarantee of paladins against Ryn couldn't be understated. As Valette slid the lock of Sophia's room closed, she decided against it. She wouldn't compromise her ideals. There had to be a way around this.

Locking Yila and Sophia away seemed right. The singer was harmless, Valette could feel that even without the band around her neck. She wouldn't harm the Seer. In addition, Valette had instructed Yila to guard Sophia, but that was more because she worried for the Seer's safety. There was something deeply wrong about this palace, especially if it were even a possibility that Ryn would bring paladins against them.

As Valette was in the midst of these thoughts, Markus appeared in the hallway, as if stepping out from behind an invisible curtain. "Chosen Bilaut," he said, lowering his hood to expose his bald head.

"Markus. You are a curious man. The tip you gave us on the Zal'Kerathan was good," Valette said. Yet you could be the Scholar working against me.

"I know," he growled. "I see you were too late to capture her. A pity. I am surprised you let her slip through your fingers."

"It gave me the leverage needed to move forward," Valette retorted.

"Tomorrow. She will be in the square of champions in the late afternoon. You know the place?"

"Indeed," Valette said. It was one of the locations Plithy had visited religiously before he died. Before Ilara killed him. "Are you trying to draw me out into the open?"

"Capture her there, or you will find death in this palace. Bring the girl, Yila. She will be essential to your survival."

"Markus, I don't know who to trust."

"You can trust me," he said.

"How do I know that?"

"If our first meeting wasn't enough to guarantee your trust, I don't know what will." He stepped back behind the invisible curtain.

Valette pursed her lips, not certain how to view the interaction. She returned to Sophia's room. Yila was going to have more calculations to do in the Sight. They needed to learn something useful, and fast. Valette had to decide whether to set the trap or follow Markus's advice. Looking at Yila, whose eyes were closed and deep in the Sight, she decided to trust her gut and set the trap.

# Chapter Nineteen

# BROKEN BONDS

A multitude of colors swirled around Ilara in the well-lit café. The place was packed with people, all holding mugs of dark brown liquid and conversing with each other. It was loud, but she found the calm within her, the black coffee in her cup giving her that stillness. Conversing with the thoughts inside her mind was easy—there was much to think about. Zal'Keratha had been quiet over the last few days since the death of Jonas. Ilara prayed he was a suitable offering.

The hammer she'd taken from the dead Chosen rested against the outer wall next to her, covered well enough by her cloak. It had seemed a lighter burden to carry today, and the stone on top almost seemed smaller. Did she need to feed it blood? Could such a thing die? Benin had been clear that it grew in his time with it. Markus had shied away from any question she'd had about it, stating that there was an evil to the weapon he couldn't define. Ilara wasn't so sure.

She was halfway through her coffee when Gavin sauntered into the café. He was wearing a plain red tunic with the emblem of his house, a stag with two sets of antlers protruding from its head. Ilara believed the people of the north called them yelags, though she'd never seen one herself.

Gavin's head whipped to the left and right, sending his dirty-blonde hair into a flurry. "Ilara!" he exclaimed as his eyes landed on her. He rushed over and slid into the chair across from her. "I came as soon as I got your message. That courier was in a hell of a hurry. What's going on? I tried to check in on you yesterday, and your place looked like a yelag had torn it to bits."

"Aye, they probably did go through the place," Ilara said, taking another sip of her coffee. She didn't want Gavin to worry, but she wasn't sure how to approach this conversation. He needed to know she was fine, and she needed to rely on him. If there was a chance of changing Markus's prediction for Solar Day, she needed to use every asset she had.

"Who? Who would do something about that? Where on Aerlia have you been?" Gavin asked again.

"Staying with a friend. My sister was taken by paladins. I've been trying to get her out of the palace, but—she's Chosen. There's a lot I can't say here." Ilara flicked her eyes across the café. It had been part of the intention in meeting here. She didn't want to tell Gavin everything.

"Oh. Oh, gods. Outside the Pantheon?" he asked. It was a reasonable assumption. A Chosen of a god outside the Pantheon would be arrested on sight.

"No. I wouldn't risk having her in Eversburg if she was. She's a Balanite. Gods, this shouldn't have happened. But I do need your help with it, Gav." Ilara met his eyes for the first time. They had a depth she couldn't know, and they were filled with sorrow.

"What can I do?" Gavin asked, sitting upright in his chair.

"I need you to go to the palace and ask around. They won't let me get close since I'm not Akaran clergy or a paladin. Find out where they have her and what they've done to her. I need to know that I still have time to fight this." Ilara sat back in her seat.

"What in the hells are you going to do?"

"I'm going to get her out," Ilara said. *And raid the library for any information on Akara's altar.*

Gavin's jaw went slack. "You can't be serious. There's no legal recourse once Tezza has ruled on something like this."

"I didn't say anything about legal recourse," Ilara growled. *What am I thinking? Gavin's as much a paladin as anyone could be without being Chosen.*

Her mind flashed to the night they met—a dark evening when lust had conquered the heart and darkness consumed them. Ilara had thought they had a bond, but knew it couldn't last. She didn't live a life that could sustain a family. The next time she saw Gavin, he didn't remember her, she'd made sure of it.

"A-aye," Gavin said. His gaze grew distant, as if he was trying to digest her words. When he looked at her again, his eyes were harder. "I'll get you what you need to know. Tell me about her."

"Sophia Blackwood. Chosen of Balan. Blonde of hair. Twenty-seven years. Until she was taken, she worked The Pearl. She was taken from her tenement building in Dusk," Ilara said.

"That's a rough place. What did the arrest note say?"

"That she was associated with a criminal known as Thorn."

"You know who that is?" Gavin asked.

"Aye. Very well."

Their eyes met again, and his eyes widened slightly. Fuck. Why did I say that? Gavin was dull, but not dull enough not to put together the pieces.

"How do you know a criminal like that?" he asked.

Ilara's heart broke, and she couldn't bring herself to lie to him again. "I told you. There are things I can't tell you," she said.

Sudden realization spread across his face. "Was everything a lie, then?"

"Not everything, Gav." She took his hand. When she felt his spine stiffen, she regretted it. "That night we shared to—"

"Thorn has ties to the Syn—"

"I know."

"Do you know how dangerous they are? Nobles killed in their homes. Inns burned down. Why—"

"For gali, Gav," Ilara hissed. "It worked for so long I forgot the danger. I'm not going to let Sophia pay for my mistakes."

"Fine," he said. "I won't judge your choices. It might look suspicious if I go looking for this sister of yours, though. What's your plan on getting her out?"

"Still working out the kinks in it. I'll have to move soon, but what you tell me will help me gauge how much time I have."

Gavin hung his head. His tunic ruffled up, as did his hair. When he straightened again, he crossed his arms over his chest, covering the house emblem. "If I do this, I need a guarantee that you will defend Theo as this is going down. The Sy— Your employer is planning something in this city. You will do everything you can to guard him."

"Done. I can't guarantee he'll be safe, but he will be as guarded as I can make him." Ilara didn't mention that she'd parted with the Syndicate already—she needed Gavin's intel.

"Furthermore, if something is to happen to me, you will take Theo to Port Miras—or wherever you deem safest—and watch over him until he's grown."

"Gav, you want me to adopt your son?" Ilara asked.

"Only if I die. If you're willing to go to this length to protect your sister, you would be good enough for my son. And we really don't have anyone else."

Ilara nodded, but Gavin didn't know everything. He didn't know she was Chosen, and he didn't know what she'd need to do in this city before the this was over.

"Consider it done. Hopefully it doesn't come to that." *It is right that the boy would come back to me.*

"Good," Gavin said, the smile returning to his face. "I know why you lied to me. And I know this bond we have is weak, but I want to grow it if we both make it to the other side."

"I do, too," Ilara  said with a smile. "Bonds grow stronger with time. And I know we'll have it."

"Me too."

She didn't know why she felt a warm feeling in her chest. These moments weren't for people like her.

"I have a dream sometimes," Gavin said suddenly. "That I knew you before. It's hazy, but it's persistent."

Ilara's eyes widened. He couldn't know. "What do you mean before?"

"Before we met. You know, I can't remember what Theo's mother looks like, either. She flits in and out of my memory, like a bubble in a pot just before it boils. Some days she's so clear, and other days she's like a woman without a face. The dream always ends the same way, the one I have about you. I come home, and a bald man is waiting for me with a baby in his hands. I don't know how, but I know the child is mine, even though I know I've never had a kid."

"That's a weird dream, Gav." She knew the spell was breaking. He would be furious if he ever found out.

"Aye, weird."

***

Waves of people moved around Ilara like a river of flesh. It was Ridesday. While it was still the middle of the week, the city was gearing up for a week of feast days, and merchants were banned during the celebration. Akara wouldn't let any business detract from her worship. In the Dawn district, there was enough food for most families there to buy to excess. Folk in the Noon district would fare worse. Those in Dusk would starve.

Dark clouds blocked the rays of the setting sun, and it was nearly as dark as night almost an hour early. Guards held torches above their heads as lamplighters scrambled to ignite the evening lamps to illuminate the streets for the few hours until curfew.

Tarin was standing on a street corner a block away from Ilara. He hadn't noticed her. He was a creature of habit, and she was well versed in his routine. He'd just finished his dinner at the Rose Gold Tavern, a place he went every Ridesday, where he'd rented a room. He was strolling Dawn until it was time for the prostitutes to come out in the Noon district.

Ilara moved as he moved, staying far enough away to avoid detection, and waited for her moment. Normally, she'd walk right up to him and make her presence known. She was sure that the mess of Syndicate bodies she'd left would have made any member call on the support network.

Tarin walked up to a street vendor and started making conversation. She couldn't hear him but was sure it wasn't important. Beggars, paladins, nobles, clergy, shopkeepers—he would talk to anyone even half-prepared to listen to his ramblings.

It was only a moment before he started moving again. He turned down a dark alley shortly after. The hairs on Ilara's arms stood on end as she moved to the mouth of the alley. She rested the head of her maul on the cobblestone.

"Gods, why did you have to be so heavy," she muttered as she considered her options. Climbing over the buildings was out of the question—it would take too long, and she'd lose him. Going around the block would also take more time than she was willing to spend. She could wait him out if he was setting a trap, but if he wasn't, she'd lose him as he walked out the other side. Her only option was to storm through, potentially into Tarin's trap.

As she picked her maul back off the ground, pain shot through her palm. Reflexively, she let go, and the wooden handle clanged to the ground. The stone warped as if made of liquid. Roiling and changing, it formed itself into a blade, then seemed to harden. Ilara didn't find any wounds on her hands.

"A spear I can work with," she muttered as she bent down and retrieved it, marveling at the shine of the black spearhead. It seemed lighter in addition to the change in shape.

She took a step into the dark alley, and the shadows seemed scatter away from her.

"You're shit at tailing."

Ilara smiled, half-glad he'd caught on to her. It would feel a lot better to tear the answers from his throat.

"I have questions," she responded. "I hope you'll be good enough to answer them. For family."

"You were family before you betrayed the Syndicate. Even if you thought what you did was for family, Gray doesn't take kindly to betrayal. I told you not to hurt Jonas," Tarin spat.

"I don't care about Gray." Ilara shuffled farther into the alley. "I thought our bond ran deeper than the guild."

The shadows seemed to follow her, leaving her in the most lit section of the passageway. She gripped her spear with both hands. Feet shuffled around her, the shadows unable to hide the sounds of unsheathing weapons. She expected she was surrounded by thugs—more than five. They had a Chosen of Ytria, god of darkness, who could manipulate the dark. It couldn't harm Ilara, but being unable to see the likely armed thugs around her would make defending herself all the more difficult.

"Our bond existed because of the Syndicate. What could have possibly made you think your actions wouldn't change that? We took care of you, Thorn. When you were at your lowest, we cared for you. When you had no home, we housed you. You shit all of it away when you killed Jonas."

A sword flashed from the shadows. Ilara parried with the staff of the spear. Spinning away, she knocked the blade from one side as another struck from the dark. They were uncoordinated. This group had been put together quickly, and hadn't had time to sync with the Ytrian's movements.

Ilara spun again, sweeping the spear around the outer edge of the circle, and felt a satisfying vibration along it when she hit flesh. A body dropped, and there was shouting she couldn't discern. The shadows all moved at once, and a jagged corner of them seemed to lunge toward her.

She sidestepped and felt steel bite into her arm. Grimacing, she formed a dagger in her hand. She flung it into the darkness and heard the soft sound of it hitting flesh. Grinning, she evaded several other weapons swinging from the darkness. Then she lunged and thrust her spear forward, knowing precisely where the concealed Chosen's throat would be.

The man cried out, and the shadows dispersed, falling back to their corners and crevices. She'd missed his throat, but the blade had found his chest, piercing through his chainmail. He was older, lines creasing his thin face. Ilara suddenly had the urge to drive the spear in farther. She drew it back and let the man fall to the ground. The urge relented.

Turning, she found herself surrounded by four thugs holding a variety of weapons. A cloaked man lay on the ground, clutching his leg where Ilara had struck him. Tarin was standing just beyond them, arms crossed as he watched the group.

A woman holding a staff lunged at Ilara, while someone shuffled forward behind her. Ilara lunged forward as well, dodging the woman and hearing a blunt weapon slam into the ground behind her. Turning quickly, she drove her spear into the woman's side. As she pulled it out, blood drained into the crevices of the metal.

There were still three more thugs, but none of them stood between her and Tarin. He turned to run, but Ilara was on him in a moment. She tripped him with her spear. Drawing her leg up, she stomped as hard as she could on his calf. She knew she'd been successful when she heard the bones break. Tarin cried out, and heavy footsteps sounded as the remaining thugs broke their circle and gave chase. Ilara turned and brought her spear into a defensive position.

She became a flurry of parries and strikes as she worked to turn the Syndicate fighters against themselves. The tight quarters gave her an advantage, as only two could attack at a time, both from the same side. Her blade found the leg of one, then his neck as he fell to the ground. The next found his liver pierced, and the last was stabbed through the heart. All three fell to the ground within minutes.

Ilara stalked forward. The Chosen of Ytria breathed heavily as he leaned against a building. "Traitor! You will be Forsaken for us—"

Ilara drove her weapon through his mouth and into the wall behind him. He slackened into it, hanging from the spear that had killed him.

Tarin tried to crawl to the other end of the alley. He made it five feet in the time it took Ilara to finish off Ytria's Chosen. She left the spear in the man's throat, letting it drink his blood as its earned reward.

"I thought Gray wouldn't abide cockroaches living in his house," Ilara muttered as she marched back to Tarin. Calling on her creation magic, she made a dagger in her left palm. Clutching a fistful of his cloak, she dragged him to his feet, holding the blade to his neck.

"Wha—ack—do you want?" he gasped as her fingers dug into his neck.

"Black metal weapons. What are they?" She lessened her grip so he could answer.

"Let me go, and I'll tell you," he choked out between large gulps of air.

Ilara dropped her hand and dug the dagger into his neck. "Speak."

"Gray got them from the Akarans, along with black bands. We don't know how they're made," Tarin said.

Ilara remembered the crates she'd seen in Jonas's camp the night she resolved Sophia's debt. "Explain what they do. The bands and the weapons. Leave out no details," she growled.

"Block a Chosen's abilities. In the short term, at least. Long term, it alters them in a way that we don't understand," Tarin said.

"Alters?"

"A form of madness. Due to the lost connection to the gods or . . . something else."

"Describe it."

"They take on a whole other personality, like they've lost themselves and another has found them. I don't know anything other than that." Tears streamed down his cheeks. "Please, please don't ask more."

"Why does Gray need them?" Ilara asked, driving the knife into his flesh deep enough to draw blood.

Tarin whimpered before he could compose himself to answer. "I-I don't— Oh, gods. I don't know. Something big is happening. And soon. Gray was holding the weapons for someone. We were paid well in advance for them, but he never said who," he said through sobs. "Fuck. I've said too much. Kill me. The Syndicate will do far worse for what I've told you."

"Where can I find these weapons?" Ilara demanded.

"They—they move too much. The ones at Jonas's hideout have already been moved. Only Gray knows where they all are."

Ilara dropped Tarin. He slid roughly to the ground, his broken femur unable to support his weight. She kneeled down and leveled her eyes at him. "Any final words before you meet my mistress?"

"I hope the paladins kill you and desecrate your corpse, traitor. Your sister will rot in their dungeon," Tarin said between his tears.

With a flash of steel, Ilara committed his soul to Zal'Keratha. She told herself she hadn't delighted in his death before turning to retrieve her spear.

# CHAPTER TWENTY

# ILLOGIC

SOPHIA WAS NOW ACCOMPANIED by Valette instead of her regulars on her visits to the Librarian. The Scholars wouldn't allow a paladin—let alone an Almiran one—into the room, but she stood dutifully outside, sword drawn as her metal boots sank into the plush carpet. The Librarian didn't seem bothered by this development. It didn't matter to their research whether Sophia was accompanied by a jailer or a paladin.

On this particular day, they were having Sophia read a dense text on the throne of Caldor, the kingdom first attacked by Aoxians, an event which had sparked Akara's rise to queen. Sophia was a hundred pages into the daily activities of king who-the-bloody-hell-cares in year completely-not-relevant. She finished the sentence she was reading, then set the book down on the desk. The Librarian shifted uncomfortably on their cot, a sorry excuse for a bed. In a way, they seemed as much a prisoner as she was.

"*Sophia? Why have you stopped? Need I mention that I could have any of the literate prisoners read to me? It would be a bother. I do so envy your voice,*" they said.

"No. I just need a minute." Sophia rubbed her shoulders and neck in slow circular movements. Her neck tightened when she was stressed, and it gave her a headache.

"*Would it help you to speak of it?*" the Librarian asked.

"Maybe. I've told that damnable paladin everything I can think of. Wouldn't hurt to tell another soul."

"*I've never considered it proper to call an Almiran a paladin. Akarans are paladins. Almirans are more akin to the holy warriors of the past. I assume this has to do with your sister, the Zal'Kerathan?*"

"You know about that?" Sophia asked, fully ignoring the comments on paladins.

"*Naturally. Ameri knows all things, though she deigns to tell us so little of them. As her librarian, I know more than most. When I heard of your capture, I demanded you become my Reader. Balanites make excellent Readers.*" The Librarian bounced excitedly.

"Aye. What truly bothers me is that this Chosen Bilaut seems intent on using me as bait to bring my sister in," Sophia said.

The Librarian started, as if taken aback. They violently rattled their meager bed as they did so. *"This distresses you?"*

Sophia nodded. "Aye, it does. I don't want my sister to be killed because of me."

*"But your sister is a heretic. This is what must be done. You would see Akara's people besieged by false ideas?"*

"I fear that soon I will be branded a heretic, if I haven't been already. And that anyone who doesn't worship Akara will be, too. Slowly but surely, each god in the Pantheon and without will be branded heretical, their Chosen cast into shame."

*"Akara stands by her allies,"* the Librarian said. *"Logic dictates that so long as her allies remain loyal, they will remain strong."*

"What of Shyll then? A Pantheonic god who was cast down as a heretic," Sophia asked.

*"Shyll refused to give his forests to Akara for the war effort. And so the cycle began for him."* The Librarian shrugged one of their large metallic shoulders, a movement that stressed the tendrils against the plates of their armor. *"I do not believe Ameri or Balan will make the same choices."*

"I suppose not, but my sister deserves not to be exiled for the actions of her goddess."

*"She worships Zal'Keratha, a heretical god.. Akara is clear on what must be done with such creatures. The correct choice for her would be to become Forsaken,"* the Librarian said firmly.

"That would stop the paladins? You truly believe that? And what of the rest of her life? Should we exact judgment on but one aspect of it? She would be denied the ability to convert if Akara judged her actions for what they were," Sophia said.

*"Indeed. As I see this disturbs you enough that it will impede our studies, we will dedicate the rest of our session to determining the moral ethics of the Akaran Empire. Perhaps, maybe you might be able to convince your sister to lay down her blade and see peace. To choose the life giver rather than the life taker. Such a history lesson is indeed required. If we cannot convince you, I fear the worst."*

"I feel that I have not seen how Akara could be so merciful. Her paladins are a torment on the citizens of Eversburg and her empire. My sister and I saw it from Vash'gal'or to Chrys to Caldor. Now I'm imprisoned despite being allied with one of the Pantheon's gods. What do you see in Akara that I do not? How can you trust her?" Sophia asked. She was aware of the heresy in the questions which meant trouble, but there wasn't much more trouble she could get in, frankly.

The Librarian took small careful steps as they wandered around the room, holding their metal arms in front of them to ensure they didn't run into walls. It was something they did whenever they became overly bothered. They said it was to get the blood flowing, of which Sophia was almost certain they had none.

*"You must be aware of the old stories of the creatures of darkness that roamed our lands? They murdered indiscriminately. Akara was instrumental in destroying them through the strength of her power. We know this through various means.*

*"My mind turns to the Scholar Sutireme, who determined in the tenth year of Akara's reign that her Eye was fully omniscient and omnipresent. Through rigorous testing, he was able to find that Akara knew most, if not all, goings on upon the surface of Aerlia, with the exception of actions completed at night. It was Sutireme's studies, also, that found that our Great Queen has influence over the Eye.*

*"In ages past, Scholars assumed that the Eye, which we at that time called the 'Star,' was orbited by Aerlia over the course of a calendar year of fifteen months. It was presumed that the Star was so much more massive than Aerlia that Aerlia was drawn around it in a slightly elliptical pattern, as were the other colored lights of the sky, which we named Juno, Elho, and Chrysta. These*

were named after three of the four nations of the world at the time.

"The largest kingdom of that time was called Aer. It was where the ancient Scholars called home, so they named their planet after it. They write extensively of creatures of darkness, which they called Qel'm. The Chosen of those ancients were called upon to defeat Qel'm whenever they threatened civilization.

"You know each god has an altar at which a Chosen was created in a time of need. When a Chosen was called, they made a sacrifice on their god's altar and took on all the power of the divine. Their power would burn bright for a moment, sometimes for an hour and other times for months, before the Chosen from the ordeal died. They could not contain that amount of power, you see. It was enough to drive back the Qel'm, though it never destroyed them entirely.

"Until, that is, when Akara assumed the role of the goddess of light. The previous divine of light's name was lost to the ages, yet it is presumed they were satisfied with suffering as the status quo. Akara decided that enough was enough and altered the pattern of the Star so that more light would shine upon Aerlia. The Qel'm, after all, being made of darkness, despised the light. She also created the first permanent Chosen, lengthening their life and granting them significantly less power. The other gods *followed suit, but only because Akara threatened to bring her Eye to burn the creatures from Aerlia. These two changes were presumably what led to the vanquishing of the Qel'm.*

*"It is because of this that Akara must remain at the head of the Pantheon. The threat of her power keeps the other gods in line. So, whosoever she deems heretic will be so. She alone stands between us and utter darkness."*

The Librarian settled back onto their cot, seemingly satisfied with the explanation.

Sophia's mind reeled. She'd never heard any of this before. "What does all of this have to do with the heresy of my sister?" she asked.

*"You have yet to understand. The Eye is tantamount because it is Akara's power. From it, she sees all and the paths of all. She knows who should be saved and who is a heretic. I believe she sees that your sister would always be a heretic. Or perhaps not. Akara did not see fit to truly antagonize her until she ordered your arrest. Perhaps she didn't order it, but malignant forces from within the Solar Dominion did. I cannot know."*

"Why not? Are you saying the Eye of Akara is stronger than the Sight?"

*"I'm a historian, not a political analyst. There are other Schol-ars who specialize in that. Mayhap you should ask them when not impeding my research."*

"I thought you were Ameri's foremost Scholar?" Sophia said.

"*That I am.*"

"And I didn't think Akara had access to the Sight. That's Ameri's domain. How can Akara know the paths of all if she doesn't have the Sight?"

"*I do not know, child. It will be a dire day when the gods deign to tell us their machinations. They exist to protect us from threats we cannot comprehend. Should they give all the details, it would mean their time among us was coming to a close.*"

"How do you know that?"

"*It is a logical deduction from the ancient texts. To explain it would require months or years of research. Even then, it still might be incomprehensible to you. Though if you are questioning . . . perhaps the Empire has fallen farther than I thought in the last several decades.*" The Librarian hesitated, then started as if they'd just realized Sophia was still in the room. "*Are there any other questions that trouble you, or can we return to our research?*"

"I have many questions." Sophia could feel the leash tighten on her freedom. "None that would detract from us today."

The Librarian was such a mystery that she couldn't help but probe their mind every now and then. In another life, she'd like to think she could've been a Scholar. There was an ease to these conversations that she enjoyed. Research was like uncovering bits of stories that had been lost to time.

They returned to the dry tome again, and for the next several hours, Sophia read about the comings and goings of this place called Caldor. Before this, she'd never heard of it, but the Librarian insisted that it was vitally important. Lately, the majority of their research concerned this lost kingdom.

When Sophia was done for the day, she departed the small room, the Librarian barely giving her a farewell. She emerged to find Valette still standing outside the door, looking as aware as she had been six hours prior.

"You didn't leave this spot, did you?" Sophia asked.

"I did not. Your safety is my priority," the paladin replied.

Sophia nodded but didn't respond. She felt at that moment as if she were viewing her life through the bottom of a glass. Nothing felt right. The Librarian had rambled for nearly a half hour about Akara's will on Aerlia. It didn't make any sense. What were these creatures called Qel'm? There was more the Librarian could teach her, and Sophia needed to stick to their side to learn it.

She felt her throat close in fear. *Fuck, I need a distraction.* "Who were you before you became an Almiran?" she asked.

"Hard to say. Both my fathers served in Almir's temple. I was assisting rituals before I learned to talk," Valette responded.

"You might say Almir is in your blood."

"Aye. They brought me up for it, and I'm grateful." Valette smiled as if a pleasant memory had just crossed her mind.

"Must have been something, growing up in a family like that. All the parishioners must've been happy to have you." Sophia was grateful Valette was more talkative than Bucket or Plume. She'd never even learned their proper names.

"It was an interesting place to grow up. I would go from playing with my friends on the lawn to getting a lecture from Father Jesti about an Almiran parable. There was a lot of pressure on me to join Almir's clergy."

"Yet I don't see you here in robes," Sophia said.

"Aye. The pressure was so great that I ran away to the army." Valette laughed. "Father Mikan and Father Halen—my family—didn't see that one coming. Even so, Almir found me, and I've been in his service since."

"How did that happen? An impending battle that had your nerves up, or did you do it to save a comrade?" Sophia loved stories of Chosen finding their divine. There was always a hint of the spectacular to it, perhaps because Chosen tended to embellish for clout.

Valette's face blanched, and there was a hiccup in her step. She soon recovered, moving back into the beat in a moment. "I—do not speak of it," she said.

"Apologies for asking." Sophia returned her attention to the hallway walls.

"What is it like to wear your collar?" Valette asked.

"It is lonely. I've been Balan's Chosen for as long I can remember. Not having him is like missing a limb, probably similar to how you are with Almir. Not to mention the fact that the sounds around me feel wrong, like there's water in my ears whenever I hear music."

"I'm sorry. If there was a way to remove it, we would. Maer and Yila assure me that would be too dangerous."

Sophia shrugged. "I'm a Balanite. There is little I could do to affect you." It was a bit of a stretch to say that, but it was for the most part true. When she reached into a wave of music, she wasn't sure what she would get. "The spells I weave are beautiful, though. I'll have to show you, if we both survive my sister. If I survive this collar."

"You seem stronger than most," Valette said. "I'm sure you will."

"I—I don't know. There's something about this thing that's changing me. It was subtle at first, but there's something different about me now, I think. It's, well . . . I'm not sure I have the words for it."

"Again, I'm sorry there's no alternative." Valette's face blanched again. "I couldn't imagine being away from Almir that long. I should think it would change me too."

"It isn't your fault, Chosen Bilaut. I should blame you for what has happened to me, but I can't for some reason. You elevated me from the dungeon the Akarans held me in," Sophia said. "Yet, dress me in fine clothes and give me a fine bed to rest in, and I'm still a prisoner. That I shall hold against you, I suppose."

Valette was kind, Sophia thought, in her own way. There might be a way to make use of her new situation, as much as she hated to think it. If Ilara didn't show up, Sophia might be able to weasel her way to more freedom.

"We are all doing the will of our gods in our own way." Valette unlocked the door to Sophia's new cell and began ushering her in.

Maer was standing in the center of the room, her sword covered in blood. Yila lay before her, the Scholar's blood soaking into the wooden floor planks, a fresh hole in her robes.

Maer's eyes leveled at Sophia, a wicked grin spreading across her face. "The time of judgment has come, Balanite. Akara has seen fit to relinquish the power in your soul to the realm of the gods," she hissed as she drew her blade up. Yila's blood ran down the length of it and dampened the hilt.

Sophia braced herself to meet Zal'Keratha. That was the only thing left for her now.

She shut her eyes tight as she heard the scraping sound of Valette drawing her own blade. They'd conspired against her, the fancy robes and warm room all a ruse to get everything they could about Ilara. And yet, Valette's metal body pushed passed her, knocking Sophia to the ground. The clang of blades rang above her, and Sophia unclenched her eyes to see Chosen Bi-laut, her armor etched with runes made of sky, meeting Maer's sword with fierceness.

She was a warrior like none Sophia had ever seen.

"You'll not take her, red-eyed demon," Valette growled.

# CHAPTER TWENTY-ONE

# THE NEW VOICE

"YOU'LL NOT TAKE HER, red-eyed demon," Valette growled. Her sword crossed Maer's in the air above Sophia, an angry intensity seeming to spark between the two as steel slid against steel. Valette hoped Sophia would have the wherewithal to move away as quickly as she could.

"The Lady of Light has decreed her death," Maer hissed. "She speaks to me. She told me that I am to ascend to Tezza's place as her Voice. I will be high priestess. I will show the world Akara's truth."

Maer drew back her blade and swung it forward in a disciplined slash. Most of her weight was behind the thrust. Valette deflected it to one side, causing the young paladin to stumble forward. Using the opening, she drew back her fist and slammed it into Maer's face. She relished in the feeling of the cartilage of Maer's nose breaking. Maer fell to ground, whipping her head back to look at Valette, red eyes glowing brighter than the blood streaming from her nose.

"You are a fool," Valette said. "Akara is playing your faith, using you as a tool in her games. You've no tracts. I do, and unlike poor Yila, I have the combat experience to back it up. How do you think this is going to go?"

While she didn't know Maer's fighting stances well, if there was any way she could prevent the young woman's bloodshed, she would try her best to. At this point, Valette didn't care if this was Akara's or Almir's will. She wouldn't stand aside while Maer murdered Sophia before her.

Maer regained her footing in a moment, bringing her blade back in a defensive stance. Her eyes narrowed, and Valette could see the hate in them, so well disguised until this moment.

"That you would even ask me to work with lesser Chosen shows how little you know of Akara's dominance. Ameri has half the power Akara does. Almir even less. You're all so weak. You cannot stand against the might of the holy Akaran Empire," Maer yelled.

She broke from her stance and launched another swing at Valette. She'd learned from her previous mistake and, when Valette parried, drew back again and angled another slash at Valette exposed leg. The runes on Valette's armor glowed brighter as she tapped into her fighting spirit—the spell given to her by Almir to quicken her movements. She parried the strike, but only barely, as she'd only used the spell to quicken her arms rather than letting it flow free.

Maer was faster. As their volleying dragged on, Valette wasn't able to deflect all the strikes, and her armor took several glancing blows on the pauldrons and arms. She tapped into the reserve of Almir's magic in her chest, where the fighting spirit tract lay. Her muscles loosened, and she felt the weight of the metal plates lessen as she grew stronger.

As she blocked Maer's next strike, Valette's quickened reflexes allowed her an opportunity the younger woman should have been able to counter. In a flash, Valette's blade shot forward. An unholy screech grated against her ears as her blade slammed into Maer's breastplate. Maer stumbled back, revealing a large crack in her armor, running down from her neck and ending above her heart, where Valette had struck.

Valette drew her sword back, angling it across her chest to prevent as many lines of attack as she could. "Surrender now, and we can call this a misunderstanding," she growled. "You'll face consequences for Yila's death, but you won't be dismissed from the paladins. We never have to speak of this again."

It was her final offer—one she knew Maer wouldn't accept. Still, she had to ask, as the thought of painting the walls with the girl's blood gave her no pleasure. Valette didn't know where Maer had gotten the idea that Sophia and Yila needed to die. She desperately hoped it wasn't from Akara.

Maer sank lower into her stance. "I will never surrender to an Almiran."

"Prove it."

The two warriors stood, motionless save for their panting breaths, for many moments. Their muscles tensed and tightened as each moment ticked by. The anticipation in the air was palpable as they eyed each other up.

Maer might not be able to channel, but Valette saw the hints of formal sword training in her poses. She was young yet, so she tended to trust in the power behind the strike rather than form, but her movements were fluid, like she'd practiced them for the better part of her life. She wouldn't be an easy opponent, and Valette would need to rely on Almir's spells more than she would against someone her own age.

*Best put this pup to bed quick, then*, she thought.

She was the first to move. Letting go of her blade with one hand, she stabbed toward the cracked breastplate. Maer knocked the sword away, not seeing that the true attack was coming from Valette's free hand.

A small opaque barrier etched with white runes formed in Valette's open palm as she made the strike—a magic shield smaller than Almir ever intended it, but capable of blocking waves of dragon fire if need be. The spell had never been intended to be offensive. Valette drove it into Maer's face, cracking more bones.

Discipline drove her. Maer recovered quickly, stepping back and putting her sword between herself and Valette. Dismissing her shield, Valette returned to her two-handed grip and prepared for the counterattack that came a moment later.

Maer lunged forward with such speed that Valette struggled to parry before the sword slammed into her greaves. Pain shot through her legs. Her armor hadn't given way, but she would have a nasty bruise. Valette tried to backstep, hoping to conserve her fighting spirit, but Maer grabbed Valette's helmet by the face mask and ripped it from her head.

*Gods, I put it on so fast I forgot the strap.*

*"Use everything,"* Almir said to her.

Valette tapped the well in her chest again and drew her fist back. She drove it hard into Maer's chest, expanding the crack there. Maer flew backward and slammed into the stone wall, her sword clattering to the other side of the room.

Valette raised her weapon and brought it down toward the young paladin's grinning face. The last of her fighting spirit ran dry as Maer drew a dagger whose metal was black as night. The smaller blade parried Valette's sword and repelled it like a magnetic opposite. The force twisted the weapon from Valette's hand, then Maer's boot found her chest, launching her away.

Valette slammed to the ground, her armor suddenly heavier than it had ever been. Almir's spirit always drained her when she used all of it. She'd need a moment to regain her strength. It didn't make sense, however. The tract had still been half-full when Maer pulled the dagger.

Maer wouldn't let recovery be an option as she hovered over Valette with that dark weapon. This would likely be her end. It wasn't the first time Valette had faced death, so fear was absent from her mind. A simple emptiness encroached on her thoughts, knowing that these would be the last ones she ever had. Maer brought the dagger down, and it found a gap in Valette's armor, piercing the space between her arm plate and breastplate. Valette gasped in pain as blood trickled down the metal.

"Say your prayers to your fool god, Chosen Bil—" Maer's voice cut off midscream, and she dropped to one knee.

Valette glanced back to see Sophia holding a blade, which was now lodged in the back of Maer's leg. Immediately, the poor woman backed away from the weapon, both hands going to her mouth like she was going to puke.

"I'll kill you, Balanite!" Maer howled, turning slightly to see Sophia's cowering form.

"Trabema lucin," Valette yelled as she brought her hand up. Light enveloped it, becoming scorching hot, and a beam shot from her palm through the crack in Maer's breastplate. It pierced the metal and the paladin it protected, shooting out the back of the woman's torso. The light in Maer's eyes faded a moment later, when her heart stopped. She slumped forward into a lifeless heap atop Valette.

Tears streamed down Sophia's face as she looked to Valette. Valette pushed Maer's body off her and held her hand to the gash on her leg. Light sprang forth to heal the wound as a multitude of heavy bootsteps clomped down the hallway toward them.

She needed a solid plan to deal with this mess.

***

Valette sat awkwardly in the too-plush sitting room. To her, everything felt awkward without her armor on. In place of it, she was wearing a black robe with red trim along the cuffs and hem. Glass windows ran the length of the walls in front of her and behind her. She saw the blue of the ocean lap against the ice that had frozen in the harbor outside. Sunlight danced on it like pixies through a forest of icy trees.

Tapestries hung at each end of the room. Valette had glanced at them when she entered and seen they depicted moments of Akara's life and godhood. Her ascension was likely among them. Akaran's loved to tell that tale.

Akara had been a physician once. She'd tended to the needs of her people with poultices and surgeries. When her village was raided by marauders, she did not hesitate to take up her husband's sword and armor to defend it. She was struck down in the attack. All gods died in their ascension stories, according to Almir. The god of light saw the strength of Akara's soul and took her into her tutelage, grooming her to rule as he did.

Valette wasn't sure what her fate would be but knew she'd done right by Almir.

"Syl," she muttered under her breath. It had been the first word she'd spoken to the paladins at the scene of Maer's death. If what she'd read could be believed, this was her right as Chosen of Almir. It might be the only way to influence the Tribunal she was sure was coming.

The first thing the Akarans had done was strip Valette of her armor and weapons. Then, they'd taken her report of events. It looked like she'd killed Maer, a budding paladin of Akara. She was frank and detailed, leaving out that Maer had proclaimed that she was the new Voice of Akara.

Sophia had been taken from the room, Valette assumed to an interrogation chamber or the dungeons. She didn't know which was worse. Valette was manacled next. The shackles were hefty, as if weighted with something other than iron, likely to keep her from running. A Scholar had then come and interrogated the corpses of Yila and Maer. Both supported the story she'd given.

Each person who walked in seemed to be eyeing Valette with something akin to respect brought on by fear. All of them gave her a wide berth. When she sat forward to mend her bruises with Almir's magic, a dozen swords were drawn on her. They sheathed them when they realized what she was doing. Healing magics were common in the Empire, although Almirans almost never used them.

In this waiting room, Valette took stock of her injuries. Her shoulder wasn't fully healed, though the wound had closed. She'd have another dozen bruises from where Maer's sword had landed but hadn't penetrated the armor. Valette was perhaps less proficient with her blade than she liked to admit. She relied too heavily on Almir's magics.

After the dead had been attended to, Valette had received another stern lecture from Knight Commander Ryn. His face had turned several shades darker than the last time, making his mustache look like a black island in a sea of red flames.

He blamed her for failing to control her underlings. It was why he'd initially kept her in the in the guard and, likely, she'd never see another investigation for as long as she remained in Eversburg. Valette could only repeat to him the request she'd made to the paladins.

If Ilara wasn't caught, Valette would likely never see outside the walls of this city again. It wasn't the fate she'd envisioned during her first Tribunal hearing. The next one would be worse. Valette was certain that, unless Ilara was brought in, she would hang. She didn't think she'd be caught in the middle for the rest of her life—stuck at a desk, unable to affect the cause of her punishment.

Deep breaths. It won't come to that.

Almir would protect her as he always did. She'd see her kids again. She'd laugh and play with them in the fields that surrounded the temple in Chrys. She'd see another harvest festival. Eversburg would not be her prison.

"For now, this Syl is my salvation," Valette said aloud.

"*You do not know if this ancient ritual will save you,*" Almir said.

"I have to try. It will get me time alone with Tezza. Time to plead my case."

"*I am surprised Akara has not declared you a heretic as well. She is so quick to call gods heretics,*" Almir snarled.

"Was there another?" Valette asked.

*"It came from her moments ago. She is furious and has declared Balan a heretical god after the attack today. She blames that Balanite Chosen for Maer's death."*

"Sophia."

*"Aye. They will likely sacrifice her on the morrow, since her god can no longer give her the protections of the Pantheon,"* Almir said.

"Tomorrow. Solar Day. That girl's sister is her only salvation now."

*"And you still intend to kill the Zal'Kerathan. The Balanite has no salvation."*

"I suppose you are correct. We assume that the Syl will be enough to redeem me."

*"I hope you speak well, Valette. You are not often called on to be persuasive,"* Almir said.

"Yila said we were doomed if we didn't try something extraordinary. I don't think our enemies would consider that I would call upon our right to have this ritual. It is outside the choices I would make under normal circumstance," Valette said.

*"Indeed. I find this practice to be quite barbaric. It is too akin to the time before Akara called her Chosen on this world.*

*There was much chaos in those times. We became a much more civilized people after Akara became goddess."*

"Did we?"

The door at the other end of the room quietly clicked open. Tezza, still shining a dull red from the morning ritual, smiled at Valette. She was wearing a thin maroon dress that fell to her ankles yet left her pale breasts exposed through the garment, and her curled red hair fell to her shoulders, unrestrained by band or clip.

"Syl, Chosen Bilaut," she said. "Remove your robe and follow me."

Valette rose and let the garment fall from her shoulders, standing naked before High Priestess Tezza, Voice of Akara.

# Chapter Twenty-Two

# Aoxians

Ilara and Markus stood over a sewer grate. They'd cleared the snow from the top of it, and Ilara contemplated how she would lift it up. Tomorrow was Solar Day, and they desperately needed this to work.

"You're sure this is the place?" she asked as she slipped her fingers between the bars.

"Aye. Not like your goddess gave me much to go on. They are here, biding their time. Hate stirs their hearts. I need not remind you that I've seen there are many ways this could go poorly," Markus said.

"But this is the way that guarantees our success, correct?"

Markus was silent for a few moments before he responded. "It is best, aye."

"Then this is what we do." Ilara spotted the forged hand-holds and pulled up on the grate. With a creaky protestation, the cool metal released from the ground, and she found herself climbing down a ladder into the stink of the sewer.

Darkness engulfed them both as they descended, Ilara stumbling forward and pulling an unlit torch from the wall. Street guards would take one whenever they needed to patrol the tunnels or clean them of ne'er-do-wells. She fumbled with a piece of flint to illuminate the dank passageway.

Markus stepped down from the ladder, covering his nose with his sleeve. "We shall make quick progress. I will tell you when it is your time to speak. Do not mistranslate," he said.

"My Aoxian is still quite good," Ilara told him.

"I have seen differing outcomes." Markus groaned and motioned for her to follow.

The sewers were a maze of tunnels. Ilara lost track of her mental map, which meant she'd need to trust Markus. She'd given him this task assuming that it was impossible. Zal'Keratha had only mentioned offhand that Aoxians still lived in the city. Ilara knew of several individual ones, but none that were organized.

Her mistress had been silent since the night Ilara was captured by Gray. Ilara knew that Zal'Keratha tended to many divine issues regarding the realm of death, but she was usually never absent this long. And she certainly always spoke with

Ilara before an important day like the one soon approaching, if only to bless or curse the event.

Ilara reached out with her mind, seeking prayer in the silence. *Bless our efforts, Mistress. If all goes well, we will forward your designs on Aerlia.*

It was rare that she would commit to the act of prayer, preferring to wait for Zal'Keratha to initiate the conversation. Still, there was no answer. As Ilara drew a deep breath, she reached her mind out again and felt a kind of resistance, as if it the goddess didn't want to be found.

She gripped the staff of her weapon tighter. The spear felt right in her hands, even if it bothered Markus. Truth be told, Ilara felt better about using it knowing that it annoyed him.

"Speak out now, Ilara," Markus hissed.

"Gra'atzia pa'u," she shouted in the Aoxian tongue. *We come seeking council.* She spoke the language confidently but lacked the facial structure to make it sound natural.

A hiss echoed down the hallway like a hundred buzzing wasps. "Vetz kau la?" It was as much a demand as a question. *What do you seek?*

Ilara was sure the wrong answer would earn her a crossbow bolt between the eyes. She couldn't see the creatures, but knew of their deadly efficiency.

"To see the glory of a new Aoxia," she shouted back. She heard the gravelly chortles that marked an Aoxian chuckle. It was odd for someone not of Aox to say those words.

"Come forward so that we may see you," they shouted back.

Ilara ushered Markus toward them, and they soon saw two creatures standing by the entrance to the next tunnel. They were on their hind legs, taller and with limbs longer than those of their Akaran counterparts. They were covered in glittering scales of different colors, one primarily red and the other blue with streaks of gold. From atop their long necks, they peered down at Ilara with their billiard-ball-sized eyes.

Both lizards gripped crossbows and had long-bladed scimitars on their hips—likely too heavy for Ilara to hold with a single hand. They managed a fighting style called yu'ina, which involved many dancelike movements with the unwieldy weapons.

Markus had found the Aoxians, indeed. Ilara began to wonder whether this had truly been a good decision.

"What do you wish to accomplish here, Akaran?" the red-scaled guard asked in the Akaran tongue. He licked his sharp teeth as he did.

"Been here awhile, have you? To master their language is impressive," Ilara responded. This Aoxian had likely survived the riots and camps. He'd seen as much death as she had.

"I need to see your master, Blessed One. Zal'Keratha has a proposition he will want to hear."

"Silver tongue on this one," the blue-scaled Aoxian said as he looked to his compatriot. "Come with me. A Chosen knows a Chosen. Understand that one wrong move will see you becoming our dinner of the eve."

Ilara nodded and stepped ahead of Markus, letting him fall behind as she kept pace with the larger lizard.

Small tents lined the next hallway. They were decorated with the icons of Aoxian household gods—blessings written in the curling script of the Aoxian language. The encampment here was small, but it was undoubtedly well lived in. How long had they been here, lurking under the capital of their most hated enemy, the goddess who had thrown their own god from the heavens?

They had hardly walked a hundred paces before Ilara laid eyes on it. In a part of the sewer where a dozen tunnels made an intersection was a small collection of refuse, cobbled together to make small throne. Upon it sat a lizard with vermilion scales and violet streaks on his neck and arms. He wore a crown that extended a faux cobra hood down either side of his neck.

Ilara had never seen this lizard, but his tale was told across all of Aerlia. This was Aox, outcast god of the Aoxians and former king of the Pantheon.

"Who approaches the last living Creator god?" the lizard snarled.

"Your grace," she said with a bow.

"Chosen Ilara of Zal'Keratha," Aox said slowly and melodically. "It has been long since a Zal'Kerathan graced my court. I was beginning to think she'd forgotten me."

"She'd never forget you, sire," Ilara said carefully. Zal'Keratha didn't speak of Aox much, but Ilara sensed a tenderness between the two that she couldn't begin to broach. "Your location is never far from my mistress's sight. She bid me call upon you for aid."

The god's countenance changed from pleased to furious in an instant. "Aid? She has not spoken to me in decades, yet feels able to call upon me for aid? Frankly, I have more self-respect than that."

Markus stiffened next to Ilara. If the stories could be trusted, anger easily clouded Aox's judgment, and too much would lead him to command the large lizards against them. Ilara didn't like her odds of fighting her way out of the encampment. The Sight had told Markus that was a possibility, albeit a remote one. Aoxians were formidable opponents, and those Aox had for his honor guard were likely some of the best.

"But," Aox said, sitting back on his throne. His long arms rested on a armrests made of bone . "You've gone to the trouble of seeking me out. Explain yourselves. Why should I not kill a Zal'Kerathan who has brought an Amerite into my encampment?"

"Your grace," Ilara said. Aox expected reverence, and she would give it to achieve her ends. "Ameri has grown tired of Akara's rule. She sends her Chosen to help in the necessary regicide. For that, I have need to infiltrate the Solar Dominion on the morrow . I need the exemplary help of you and your children to do so. Zal'Keratha means to call upon the favor you owe her."

"Favor? I should think saving me from my plight would be the least she could do for how close we once were to one another. Restoring a god fallen from the heavens is not a mere favor. It is justice. Centuries have passed, and I still feel her icy hand calming the fire beneath my scales. And now, she asks me to sacrifice the lives of my children for her Chosen. Of all the arrogance."

Aox's mouth kept moving as if he were chewing on a length of meat. His face grew contemplative. "Yet, what is a lover who does naught for the other half? A sorry excuse I have been, cowering in these sewers. It is time I struck out and do something. I ought to do so without grievance. Sacrifices must be made in the name of love. If there was any chance of regaining the affection that blossomed between us in those times of my rising sun, I would sacrifice anything.

"Still. I must know, what does Zal'Keratha wish to gain by assaulting our enemy's palace? I know she does not believe that one such as you could kill one of the divine."

Ilara cleared her throat. " Ameri's Scholars know the location of Akara's altar. Markus believes that one called the Librarian will know where it is and how to use it. It is the first step of Zal'Keratha's plot," she said. "There is also one of Balan's Chosen who has been arrested unjustly. I wish to see her freed."

"A lover?" Aox asked.

"A sister."

"I see. What would one not sacrifice for family? Likely more than what one would give the gods. My Chosen will be privy to this information that your Amerite derives from this Librarian?" Aox stood and walked over to Ilara and Markus. The god emanated a wrathful aura of fear  and confidence.

"Aye," Ilara said without hesitation.

The god stood over her, and she had to remind herself that he could end her with a thought. While cast from the heavens, Aox still retained his divine power.

"Tell me your plan in detail," the lizard said. "I will agree only once I've heard all of it."

***

"You're sure you trust them?" Markus asked.

He and Ilara were sitting in an Aoxian tent, far from the earshot of the lizard folk, in a realm of virtual privacy. As much privacy as one could have behind a sheet of cloth. Their accommodation was a mere lean-to propped against the sewer wall, which didn't provide enough isolation to cut the stench of rotting sewage. Two fur mats made of several small gray pelts lay on the ground. Ilara couldn't decide if they were rat or cat pelts. Not that it mattered—they wouldn't be here long.

She sat cross-legged with her spear balanced on her knees, the mats only slightly cushioning the stone. A calm feeling washed over her, as it did before any true battle. It was the sense that, as death approached, it wouldn't be as bad as living.

"I'm sure we can't," Ilara replied.

"Indeed. I've gone over every way this goes wrong after our discussion with Aox. There are as many, if not more, ways that we can die. So, why are we still here?" Markus asked.

Aox had heard their plan. He'd agreed it would be the best way to attack the Solar Dominion. And he'd agreed Solar Day was the most opportune time. Before committing, he said he wanted to spend time with his people.

They had asked him for much. The Aoxians had likely been in these sewers for years, based on the wear on the tents. And there was a lived-in feeling here that only came over a camp when it had been in place for a while: Patrols left on a routine schedule. A pot on the fire was constantly boiling over the fire. Soldiers went to bed with other soldiers with a sort of familiarity.

"Have you been to war?" Ilara asked.

Markus perked up, the eye tattoos on his scalp fading as he met her gaze. Ilara couldn't deny that the Sight was useful, but he seemed to use it like a lonely girl used a fortune teller.

"No. It is a desperate time when Scholars go to war, especially against other Scholars, as we will tomorrow. It is a nasty business," he said.

Ilara nodded her head. "I can't imagine there being so many Chosen of one god that they fight each other. I've never been to war either, but I know a war camp when I see one. Useful training grounds for an assassin to practice prowling."

She could see Aox through the tent flaps. He was surrounded by a large accoutrement of warriors. They wore headdresses woven with large teal, red, and green feathers—tail feathers from the cha'an, a common ritual bird in Aoxia. Ilara touched her cha'ak. It was made of the skin of a cha'an.

The god ignited a large fire between them, breathing flames from his jaws. It was no wonder that a creature such as this had created the dragons that roamed the skies.

"You found many targets in war camps?" Markus's question jolted her from her thoughts.

"Aye. And a lot of incentive not to be caught. Prisoners taken in camp are never treated well." Ilara shuddered, remembering her first cold night in an Akaran prison camp. "My master thought it would be the only place to learn."

"Why can't we trust them?" Markus asked, returning to his initial line of inquiry.

The scaled mass of Aoxians were now bobbing up and down rhythmically as they all chanted—a low melodic chant, one without any meaning but for the rhythm.

"Something Zal'Keratha once said to me: 'None will work harder to regain power than those who once knew it.' As much as Aox waxes poetic about sacrificing for love, there is as much stake for him in this game. I can't guarantee he wouldn't sacrifice my mistress for another chance at his throne."

"And you still want to go through with this?" Markus asked.

Ilara locked eyes with him. "Aye. I prefer an ally when I know what their motivations are. I can see their betrayals before they happen."

The Aoxians erupted into screeches of glee, babbling frantically as Aox held one of them over his head. The lizard was limp, arms dangling to each side as blood poured from between the scales on their chest. It rained down on Aox's crowned head.

"Barbarians," Markus muttered.

"You're wrong," Ilara said. "It may look blasphemous, but we do equally ridiculous rituals in the presence of our gods. They are living the life their god gave them. It inspires them to desire something higher from their lives."

"And what does the sacrifice think of that?"

"I'm sure she knew what she got herself into."

"And you're saying that's a just act to impress a vengeful deity?"

Ilara raised her brows. " Who's to say that any of the gods are truly just? I'm saying that those people are not barbarians."

Aox turned and threw the sacrifice on the fire. She writhed one final time before going limp in the flames. Akarans told horror stories about Aoxians walking through fire and surviving.

"You should be excited about this, Markus," she said, turning to him.

"Why's that?" he asked.

"That ritual means that the Aoxians are preparing war."

Their chant grew louder. It had become a single word now: Grani'as. It was a word that meant many things—war, death, kill, battle. An Aoxian war cry. Ilara held Markus's gaze until he understood.

"They are going to help us?" he said.

"Aye. Go back to the Sight and tell me when you have a path that keeps us both from dying." Ilara stood from the uncomfortable fur mat. "I have another meeting to attend to this evening."

# Chapter Twenty-Three

# A New Bond

Amber light filled the space beyond the well-decorated waiting area. Valette found it unnerving. The room Tezza had led her to was round, with a wide round cushion lifted up on a dais that stood at chest height. It was so large that it left Tezza and Valette only a few feet to walk around it.

A relief was carved into the curved wall. The depictions were crude, both in their content and their artistry. Valette was only familiar with half of the acts that the people depicted were participating in. There was no waste of space, such that one person blended into the next, creating the impression of a never-ending orgy.

Tezza turned, her red eyes meeting Valette's, then darting down her figure for an instant. Her curls fell attractively around her face. A smile crossed it slowly, like a burdened hiker over a great mountain range.

"This relief was carved when the temple was first built. Do you know who they were?" Tezza asked.

"Ancient people, as far as I understand it," Valette said.

"Correct in its vagueness." Tezza leaned against the wall. "They were pagans by all accounts, yet they existed before gods lived in this world, before creatures made of darkness tormented us all. Is it right to call peoples who did not know our gods pagans?"

"And yet these people were the first to practice—"

"The Syl, yes. We give honor to them by continuing to give our bodies to one another. History, in all its imperfection, led us to Akara." Tezza's eyes wandered across the relief. "There is much to be learned from them. They designed this practice for good reason."

"And what was that?" Valette asked.

"Sex is a powerful motivator. Bonds are created in moments of pleasure. When the ancients practiced it, they allowed foreign dignitaries to partake in the fruit of the temple. In those days, it was little more than a brothel with priestesses who specialized in those activities." Tezza's face took on a contemplative expression as she ran a hand across one of the legs carved into the relief.

"Now, we allow any Chosen outside of Akara's to lie with our high priestess. Within or outside the Pantheon, Akara accepts the offering. Passion to temper the soul." Her voice was little more than a whisper, calm and low. "It surprised me that you wanted to participate in the Syl, particularly given the ordeals you have gone through as of late. Have you been with a woman before?"

Valette felt her face redden. "No, Your Grace. Truth be told, I've—I've not been with a partner aside from my husband, Antony." Why was she saying this? She only needed Tezza alone, away from the paladins.

"It is easier—dare I say, more enjoyable—than with men." Tezza smirked. "We will have to make good use of the altar so that I can show you the full range of my techniques. I am well practiced. You are in good hands here."

Her fingers slid  up Valette's cheek. They were soft and warm, like a pastry on a comforting winter's morning. Valette almost let go of the fire that raged within her. She could let her worry fade away and spend a night not thinking of the coming tempest. A brief respite before the storm.

As Tezza's fingers traced her neck, Valette couldn't help but grab her hand. The high priestess's eyes widened, and a smile lit up her face again.

What would Antony think about this? They'd made a vow that they would only have each other until time forgot their names. He'd done nothing against Valette, forever being a loyal husband. He didn't deserve a wife who traveled away and fucked other people. And not just anyone—Akara's Voice.

Before Valette had her thoughts sorted, Tezza's face shot forward. Her tongue found Valette's, and Valette's chest tightened like a knot straining against a great wind. It was an eager, hungry kiss. One that needed the other like water in a desert. Valette fought the urge to grab for Tezza's body and squeeze her waist into her own.

Stepping back, she broke the embrace surprisingly easily. Hurt washed over the high priestess's face for a moment before she quickly composed herself.

"Before we do this," Valette said, "you must know what I have discovered. Your paladins will not tell y—"

"Is this politics, Chosen Bilaut?" Tezza asked.

"One could call it that."

"Then I will not hear it until after the passion. And the pleasure."

For a moment, Valette considered walking away. Her bond with this woman could not be worth betraying her bond with her husband. Despite the increasing number of enemies Valette had in the palace, no potential safety could be worth more than the bond between her and Antony. She couldn't break his trust.

As Tezza leaned into Valette again, her lips finding her neck, Valette could only see Maer's crazed eyes. Yila's blood coated her blade, freshly spilled over the floor of Sophia's room. Valette gave in and pulled Tezza close, feeling tightness grip her chest. Lust and anxiety mixed in her as the two stumbled onto the cushioned altar. Valette pulled back in a swift motion as Tezza dropped the skirt from her waist to the floor.

The high priestess was good at what she did. The harder Valette tried to ignore it, the more she enjoyed herself, but she couldn't find true release. She didn't know if it was because Tezza was a woman or because of Maer's death on her conscience, or because all of this felt wrong. Tezza was persistent, and Valette felt the final tug of pleasure. Even then, the tightness in her chest didn't subside. Tezza did not seem to have the same issue.

Tezza rested against Valette now, her head on the Chosen's chest. Her slight frame was sidled up against Valette's bulkier body. Years of heavy-armor training had toned Valette's muscles, but she'd always been larger than the average woman. Perhaps if she'd known her parentage, she'd know which of them was to blame. Still, Tezza wasn't only small, but frail, with thin arms and bones visible through her skin.

The cushion on the altar felt like a cloud solidified and stuffed into a mattress. It shifted easily with them, conforming to their curves, accentuating each movement. Valette couldn't get the images of Tezza's body out of her head, as if they'd gone through a dance of pleasure.

She found herself blushing again. She couldn't be into this, could she? She remembered admiring the women who'd ridden into Chrys sporting the armor of the Akaran Empire. It hadn't been anything more than a girl looking up to the people who did what she wanted to do. Had it?

No, of course not. Antony was more important. The bond we made through Almir stands taller.

"Now, you had something to tell me?" Tezza asked.

"Aye. I will say that this is not pillow talk in the slightest." It has to be said. She must know what I know.

"You'll get no other opportunity. The Syl is a Chosen's right a single time, though I wish it could be more. Make use of it. Convince me that Almir requires a higher place in the Pantheon," Tezza whispered. "That is why you're here, after all."

Valette grimaced. "No, your Majesty. That would be impossible for you to accomplish."

Tezza's hand froze, and her eyes widened. "Care for your words."

"Do you know about the paladin I killed this night?" Valette asked.

"You did what?" There was no accusation in Tezza's words. In fact, they had a breeze of comfort to them, as if here, in a lover's embrace, nothing mattered aside from the two of them and their breaths breezing onto each other's cheeks.

"A paladin named Maer, one I'd intended to take under my wing, claimed that she could do something impossible," Valette said.

Tezza's cheeks turned redder than her hair. "Maer was young. She—she was my niece. Before I got swept up in the politics of the clergy, I cared for her. A decade ago, we were inseparable."

"She said that she heard Akara speaking to her."

"Then it was good of you to put to death such a heretic, Chosen Bilaut." Tezza's breathing became heavy and fast.

"High Priestess," Valette said. Her brow furrowed as she searched for the right words. "You've not channeled for years by some accounts. If the paladins don't doubt Akara speaks to you yet, after word about Maer gets out, they will. When the next one Akara calls comes, they will cause more to doubt you. Your position as Akara's Voice is tenuous."

"You know not of what you speak, Almiran." Tezza was no longer whispering. She hauled herself up and awkwardly took a seat several feet away from Valette, facing the other direction.

Blankets were scrunched up around her, and she ran her hands along the side of her head, pulling her curls back.

Valette slowly sat up and moved toward her, running her fingers up the skin of Tezza's back. "You need allies in Eversburg," she whispered into Tezza's ear. Tezza slowly leaned back, resting her back against Valette's chest. Valette wrapped her arms around the smaller woman. "If it is true that you are no longer the Voice, then you must lean in to new alliances."

"I have many," Tezza whispered.

"You need allies who know your secret."

"Of those, I have one."

"You need godly allies."

"Aye. Are you implying Almir would ally himself with a failed Voice?"

Valette nodded. "All he requests is that you tell us your tale, and the might of Almir will fight for your throne," she cooed.

"I'm not sure you understand, Chosen Bilaut."

"Call me Valette," she whispered back, squeezing Tezza in her embrace. It still felt wrong to hold her this way, but she could fake it.

"I will—Valette. Where to begin this sad tale?"

"At the start."

Tezza seemed to take a moment to consider before speaking. "My transition to the Voice was bloodless. Unlike my predecessors, who slaughtered Aoxians by the hundreds to gain Akara's favor, I tended to the fallen. This was when I was a cleric serving in Akara's army. I never took up a sword, but my words healed men a thousand times over. Do you know the Path of Pu'tal?"

Valette nodded. "I've marched through it, a small pass between the Teva Mountains and Rainy Forest. It's barely wide enough for two armored paladins to walk abreast. When I heard you'd held that pass against a thousand lizards, I was astonished."

"Most of the stories embellish it. The truth is simpler. We learned that a legion of Aoxians were planning to strike deep into Akara's new lands—lands we had recently taken from them. I had ten paladins and a company of clerics. All of us were Chosen, but those were the days when Akara's power was starting to wane."

"It has been dimming for that long?"

"In truth, yes. Only in recent years has it been noticeable to outsiders, though even then, we knew we couldn't rely on any large spells to deal with such a force. We rigged several traps along the pass, but we still needed to kill a large number of them. So, we lined up with two clerics for each paladin. As the Aoxians crashed into us, we did our best to heal their wounds as they took them."

"A priest's gambit. A powerful tactic, if you can keep the clerics protected to focus solely on healing," Valette mused. "With the way the Aoxians would have to line up to fight you, it might have worked."

"Aye. We knew it was risky, but it was the only idea I could come up with. And it did work. By her Eye, it worked—for a time. Until Brother Merrick died. Aoxians are crafty, and they saw our strategy quickly. Writhing beasts they are. They jumped our lines in massive leaps, surrounding us on all sides. One by one they killed our clerics, until I alone remained."

Valette knew this. This kind of gambit had worked very well when Akara began uniting the Nine Kingdoms of man. Cracks showed in the strategy when applied against the lizards. More often than not, if it was used, it would be with many more troops than had been at Tezza's disposal.

"Then I heard her speak to me, a sound only heaven could make. Pure bliss poured into my ears, and I felt insurmountable power flow through me. It was like I was too full, and her power poured from my veins—I couldn't contain it. The wounds of my comrades weren't only healed, but light burst from them, piercing our enemies. They suffered so many causalities that they ran. As Akara's power drained from me, I tried my best to channel it into my fallen clerics. Brother Merrick was the only one to stand from the grave."

Valette was stunned. "You brought him back from death? Why haven't I ever heard of this?"

Tezza's face darkened. "Leaving this world takes its toll. Merrick couldn't maintain his life. He lost faith soon after and fell on a sword. He claimed we were committing atrocities against Aoxians as well as our fellow Akarans."

"I've seen enough war to wonder about that myself," Valette said.

"He did more than wonder. It ate him alive." Tezza swallowed hard. "I promised I'd never forget him. Now I think I was made to forget, in some ways. After he came back, Merrick had a unique understanding of the ways of our world. The ways of our gods. He kept saying, 'What of the children? What shall we leave our children?'"

"Not so odd, perhaps." Valette's mind drifted to her own boys. What would her legacy leave them? A mother who was absent, holding the most powerful woman in the world in her arms?

"In truth, I agreed. What world would we leave them? When I came back to Eversburg, it was different. The previous Voice was already in bonds. He was sacrificed at the end of Akara's blade, a ritual that was started in my absence by the very Voice who died by it. I spoke with Akara once a week. She would fill my tracts and instruct me on new laws to bring to the citizens. In the last year, they became quite cruel: banning music, establishing curfews, increasing sacrificial executions. Then she demanded I hunt down and capture each Chosen in the city, barring her own."

Valette couldn't help but stiffen.

Tezza squeezed one of her arms reassuringly. "Worry not. I—I simply couldn't. These were gods that we called allies. How could we put their Chosen in front of our blades? That week, I spoke not a word of it to the Senate, fully intent on arguing the point with Akara. When she found out I hadn't proceeded, she was furious. She reminded me that I could easily be replaced. The last time she ever spoke to me, she accused me of heresy.

"I struck out on my own after that, putting on an act that I was still the Voice. In honor of Brother Merrick, I crafted my own law. Instead of hunting down the Chosen, I established an orphanage for children of the slain."

"A place I've never seen," Valette said.

"You wouldn't. The week I opened it, Akara called another as Voice, and he led a group of paladins in and murdered all the children."

"Oh, gods."

"I began gathering allies that day, though I've never been quite so bold. You know one of them quite well."

"Oh?"

"Aye. Knight Commander Ryn has been invaluable. He helped me quash the rebellious Voice as well any others Akara called. Each we could put down without notice, killing many in their sleep or in the early stages of their calling. I wondered how long we had. She continues to call Chosen, but as you saw with Maer, she gives them almost no power. Whenever one began to gain it, we'd know that they were hearing her Voice. She has been predictable—or she was."

Valette couldn't help but droop slightly. In her mind, Maer's dead face stared back at her. Akara had given her enough power to rend Valette's plans for the Zal'Kerathan. There had to be something missing, though. Akara wouldn't have gone to such lengths to save the plans of her enemy.

"What does Ryn get out of helping you?" Valette asked.

"He told me once that it is for the stability of the government. I do not doubt his sincerity. He wants to see the people of the Empire flourish under the strength we can provide."

"Well, then it sounds like you don't need me. Ryn has you taken care of."

Tezza sat forward, turning to face Valette, smile edging at the sides of her mouth. "I wouldn't say that, Chosen Bi-lau—Valette. If Almir knew of our plight, he could learn the truth about Akara. Why is she so intent on killing other Chosen?"

"I don't foll—" Valette started to say, before Tezza's mouth collided with her own into a kiss that lengthened into several moments. Valette couldn't help but let her hand drift into Tezza's hair, the soft strands tickling her skin.

When Tezza drew back, her smile extended to her eyes. "Valette, you are the key to the puzzle. We've known for a long while that Akara's power is fading. But you—you could learn the truth of it all. Gods, I'm so glad I didn't execute you like Ryn told me to."

"Aye."

Tezza's face hardened as she leaned into Valette again, the weight of her body knocking Valette back to the altar. "I mention it because we are safe in this room. My paladin guards are loyal to me. Each has resisted Akara's Voice. In fact, they believe it not to be the Voice at all, but the speech of a demon. Even so, they wouldn't allow Ryn to interrupt a Syl, and he knows that. And I'm sure he wants your head for Maer's death. It is convenient."

"So what do we do?" Valette asked.

"I have a plan. Akara can be resisted, but she must be waited out. I'm sure we can organize a force against her. We can retake this city for ourselves. We may not be bonded by the hip, but we are by the heart," Tezza mused.

Valette entwined her fingers with Tezza's. "Your plan may test the strength of our newfound bond. I don't know if I can get this city to where it needs to be."

"I trust this bond," Tezza said, nuzzling her head onto Valette's chest again. "I trust you. They say no one defies the will of the gods, but I believe that the strongest of us must."

Humming in agreement, Valette wasn't sure that she truly did.

# Chapter Twenty-Four

# SEVERED

Sophia's chains felt heavier than ever before. Heavier than they had any right to be. They weighed her down, and a rope tied around her head acted as a gag. The paladins had taken everything from her before marching her back to the dungeon. Mostly everything. They hadn't fully searched the folds of her dress, where she'd stowed the knife. She still couldn't feel Balan. His continued absence made her even more anxious, the black band around her neck burning with the stain of her guilt.

Paladins surrounded her, their bright armor glinting in the torchlight. Several feet away, two of them were arguing over what to do with her. Executing her on the spot was an option. The man making a case against it was dull eyed and at least a decade older than Sophia. His black hair was swept back and well trimmed. He held himself like Akara's Chosen, but his eyes showed he clearly wasn't. What would they do with someone who'd aided in the death of an aspiring paladin?

*You didn't have a choice. It was kill or be killed,* Sophia told herself again. Even if it seemed like it was leaning toward kill and still get killed. She didn't know what she'd expected to happen. Ever since she stabbed Maer, the paladins had kept her in as many chains as they could. She'd fulfilled the unspoken prophecy. She was now what they'd always known she was. A heretic. An evil paladin-killing wretch.

And as much as she hoped otherwise, she knew Valette would be in the cell next to her. She was supposed to save me. She was the just one.

Yet Valette hadn't jumped to Sophia's defense. She'd seemed as rattled as Sophia had been. But that didn't make sense either. Paladins were killing machines. They weren't supposed to be surprised by death—not like Sophia was. She recalled how easy it had been to cut into Maer's flesh. How much blood had streamed from the wound—that evil, pulsing liquid flowing into the dark knife like it was drinking it. She stifled the urge to vomit.

Hunger struck her next. Thirst was its companion. When was the last time she'd had a full meal? What would she do to sate her stomach? Betray her sister? Betray her god? Create lies about the Librarian? Even that seemed far-fetched to her.

"I'm glad the thought of betraying me is still repulsive to you," the Librarian said.

Sophia's head was swimming from exhaustion. Had that been real, or was she hallucinating? She'd never heard the Librarian outside of their little room.

"*And yet I could always hear you,*" they said again.

What? Panic filled Sophia's chest. Someone could hear her innermost thoughts? The curses she'd leveled at the Akarans? What was she to do?

"*Hold. We'll talk more momentarily. Do not give up hope yet. Many events have occurred since we last spoke.*"

Sophia felt that was obvious given her current situation.

Heavy footsteps approached—she couldn't count how many. More than a pair, less than a dozen. More paladins coming to gawk at a failed Chosen, soon to be executed for treason for betraying the queen.

"This is her, eh?" Sophia recognized Plume's voice. Fucking asshole. "Still doesn't look like she could float a tune." The guard ran his finger along her throat as he said it. Sophia's bonds kept her from pulling away.

"Aye," said a man she didn't recognize.

Sophia arched her neck to see the newcomer, who was squat, with caramel hair and kind eyes. He was the kind of man who made a girl comfortable before trying to bed her. It took all kinds to keep her imprisoned like this.

"What is her crime, sir?" another of the guards asked. Not Plume or Bucket, but one she didn't recognize.

"Assisted in the killing of a paladin. One of the new ones. Turned out to be a heretic," Plume replied.

The older man Sophia didn't know breathed deeply, then spit heavily on the ground in front of Sophia. "The paladin or the girl?"

"Both."

"If the girl killed a heretic, then shouldn't she be lauded?" Bucket asked. Sophia knew no paladin would stand for a Balanite killing an Akaran, no matter how much of a heretic they were.

"We will leave her here until we can determine how to give her life to Akara," the older man said, then shifted uneasily. "Without weapons, she's harmless as long as the collar remains around her throat. Are you joining the fools around me to question that decision?"

"No, Knight Commander," Plume replied.

Sophia's eyes widened in realization. Valette had spoken of this man with a mix of reverence and fear. He wasn't known for kindness.

"Good. And good for you, little singer," Plume said as he stepped forward and ran his hand over the back of her head. Sophia stifled another urge to vomit. "The knight commander decided to be gracious and grant you leniency. He said you could spend your last night with your favorite cellmate."

Beast! Katri! Relief washed over Sophia as she realized her final moments on Aerlia might be spent with a woman she could call her friend.

"Get on the other side of her and grab her by the elbows. Pull 'em back as soon as I have her manacles unlatched," Plume said.

One of the newcomers did just that. When Plume unlocked the latch, he pulled her upright. There was a little to-do over undoing her chains, but eventually she was shoved back into her familiar cell. Her arms slapped against the cold stone, sending a jolt of pain through them.

"There you go, Beast! We got your dinner back for you. Eat her up before we take her to her execution in the morning," Plume said with a short, curt laugh that sounded more like a dog's bark than a sound a man made. He and the newcomer stalked back out of the dungeon with the rest of their entourage.

Knight Commander Ryn lingered, eyeing Sophia hungrily. She'd seen that look in men before and feared the outcome would be worse than with the last man to touch her. She'd been able to defend herself then.

Eventually, and undramatically, he stalked from the dungeon, and Sophia let her eyes rest on Katri again. After a week of being away from her, she was glad to see a familiar face. She didn't think about what the guard had said. Still, she knew it was coming.

Katri's green eyes met hers, and Sophia glanced away awkwardly. "So, I heard you killed a paladin?" Katri asked. "That's more than I did when I got out."

Sophia couldn't help herself. She threw her arms around Katri's neck and grinned as her friend's warm arms wrapped around her waist. Tears flooded down her face, clearing it of grime.

"I didn't kill her," Sophia said as she sobbed into Katri's shoulder.

Katri placed a comforting hand on her back. "Don't move too quickly. Your muscles are stiff from standing in the same place for so long. What do you mean you didn't kill her?"

Suddenly conscious of what she'd done, Sophia backed out of the embrace. Her face was warm, and both women looked at each other in shock.

"I—I mean that I didn't kill her. Just stabbed her in the leg. An Almiran killed her."

"And where is this Almiran?" Katri asked.

"I'm not sure. She disappeared after the Akarans showed up. She was murmuring something about a sell? A still?"

"A Syl?"

"Maybe."

"That is odd."

"What is it?" Sophia asked.

"Not really important. Well, maybe not." Katri's face turned red, but she proceeded to explain the ritual to Sophia in detail.

"Gods. Valette didn't seem the type to do something like that." Sophia shivered. She preferred intimacy to be in private with whomever she decided to share it with. She couldn't imagine doing so in a ritual.

"Honestly, it all sounds fake to me, though you may want to brace yourself for the idea." Katri's eyes darted back to the door of their cell. She ran her fingers along the metal bars.

"Why?" Sophia asked.

"I heard some of the priests speaking earlier, the way women do when they have a good deal of drama. When I finally caught what they were saying, I heard that Balan was removed from the Pantheon. One of the clerics had a bloody vision, or however they determine that."

"What?" Sophia let her mind whirl around the idea. Balan would lose a lot of power. Music would lose power.

*"Don't think like that,"* the Librarian said. *"I have been For-saken. Ameri moves. I should have trusted your heresy. We do not have time to dally. All will be explained on the morrow. Rest. Then free the Beast. Use the blade."*

Sophia's hands wrapped around the piece of metal in her dress. She pulled out the black knife, still coated with Maer's and Valette's blood.

Katri's limbs stiffened. "Who let you have that?"

"Not sure. I grabbed it, and the pals never took it from me. I think I have a friend looking out for me—a friend that can alter their perceptions. Hold still," Sophia said, raising the dagger.

*Tell me what to do.*

*"On the morrow. Before your sister arrives. She will bring an Amerite war,"* the Librarian said.

*I thought you didn't have the Sight? Not only that, but you are Forsaken?*

*"I do not, but we do have some here with the gift. Ameri is withholding vital information from our Seers. We know that the Zal'Kerathan is coming with a Seer in tow. He will be the doom of us all, unless you escape your binds."*

Sophia nodded, not entirely sure what to make of that infor-mation. She looked into Katri's iridescent eyes. They almost seemed to glow in the torchlight in the same way an Akaran's did. As if there was a fire in them.

"This knife is the key, I think," Sophia said. "There is a power to it that I don't understand, but it must be the way."

"The way to what? The key to what?" Katri asked.

"Look, when I was with that Chosen Bilaut, a Scholar said that my sister was going to try to free me tomorrow, on Solar Day. I have a feeling that this dagger will make that possible. Give me your wrist."

Katri extended her hand. The black band was burned into her wrist, faded like an old tattoo. As Sophia brought the dagger toward the band, it appeared to lift, unknitting itself from Katri's skin.

"Brace yourself," Sophia warned as she slipped the knife under the band. Katri winced as Sophia pulled it away.

"*Not yet, this is too soon!*"

Sophia didn't care. This had to be done. Freedom could not wait.

The band severed and fell to the floor.

# Chapter Twenty-Five

# UNRAVELING

"You're going to die, Ilara," Gavin said.

Ilara nodded absently. Gavin's son, Theo, was snoring on her chest.

She tussled the boy's black hair. "I could say the same for both of you. Markus hasn't told me what exactly is going to happen tomorrow, but it will be enough to draw most paladins away from the Solar Dominion."

"And what do you reckon I should do?" Gavin asked.

"Get out tonight. Take Theo and as much gali as you can. Flee through the Dusk district gates."

He shook his head. "No. I'm certain that whatever comes tomorrow, we'll be safer inside the city walls. What is the worst that could truly happen?"

"The last time I thought that, thousands of Aoxians in the city perished," Ilara said.

"Aye, but the paladins won't kill us like that. I'm a city guardsman! There will be no Night of Black Knives for us."

"When folk have lost sense, no title will matter."

"It must be those bloody terrorists. The Revolution. I heard they raided a barracks yesterday. If that's so, and they have the manpower, they're going to revolt. If they do and succeed, I have to be here for everyone who survives. They won't get the countryside under control for weeks, but the capital should still be stable." Gavin shrugged. "I'm sorry, we can't just leave our home because it is uncertain how the future will fall."

Ilara didn't want to tell him that if he worked for their enemy, this Revolution would probably hang him as a symbol—if he survived. Things might be even worse than what he'd described. The majority of Akara's paladins were still far to the south, fighting a war in Aoxia.

"Did you find out anything about where they're holding Sophia?" Ilara asked.

"Aye," Gavin said as he slouched against the table. His shoulders folded in on themselves as the muscles in his back bunched up under his tunic. "You aren't going to bloody like it. She was in the hands of an Almiran until last night, likely for extended torture. The woman sounds like a menace. Former lieutenant in the thirteenth legion. That's the one Akara sends everyone to die in. But she survived—spent her whole deployment there. She likely faced some of the worst battles the Aoxians could throw at her. No one survives that without becoming a hardass."

Ilara nodded as Theo struggled to get up, pushing his hands painfully into her collar bones, and made eye contact with Ilara. "Why aren't both of you sleeping?"

Ilara's own eyes looked back at her as he spoke. The boy had eight years and was everything she wished she could be. Innocent, naïve to the ways of the world, yet he was bright. Gavin had done well in raising him.

"Grown-ups get to stay up late," she said.

"Grown-ups always talk about wanting to sleep," Theo grumbled.

"So why don't you go to bed?"

"You haven't come over in weeks. And you haven't told me what happened to your hands. You always have the best stories."

He was referring to the marks on Ilara's wrists. She winced at the thought, knowing she couldn't tell him that they were rope burns from being tied to a chair.

"I've told you all I can," Gavin said as he stood to shoo the boy to bed. They disappeared into a room further in the house.

Gavin had said that Sophia was being held in a dungeon. An Almiran had taken an interest in her for a few days before she was returned, likely the same woman who had been guarding Senator Plithy. It began to dawn on Ilara that she'd been the catalyst that led the paladins to Sophia. Jonas hadn't helped, but he hadn't been the cause.

Ilara had handled the interaction with Jonas poorly. There could have been a better way. And she'd been so slow to get Sophia out of the Solar Dominion that she should rightly be dead.

By the time Gavin emerged from the back room, tears were streaming down her face. "Ilara, are you okay?" he asked.

"No," she whimpered. Gavin moved closer, and she wrapped her arms around him.

A frown flickered across his face. "Do you want to talk about it?"

*My sister is locked in a dungeon and it's entirely my fault,* Ilara thought.

"I don't," she said as she wiped her cheeks. "I'm sorry. It's not fair for me to dump all my problems on you. Thank you for the information on Sophia."

"Ilara, don't do this. It isn't your fault she was arrested—"

"You know that it is," Ilara said. "She's my lightforsaken sister! I have to do everything I can to save her."

"Not if it means you'll perish."

"Especially then. Soph would do the same for me if our positions were reversed. If she dies, it means everything was for nothing."

"What does that even mean?" Gavin asked.

Ilara opened her mouth to reply, but the words didn't come. She felt tension on the bond between her and Gavin. The only way to slacken it would be to explain, and she couldn't bring herself to.

"Nothing. Only that I would do anything for her." Ilara moved toward the front door.

Gavin shook his head. "You've gone on and on about me taking Theo out to the countryside, but you should take him. It would be a horror to him if we both died."

"That makes no sense, Gav. You're his father. I'm nothing to him."

"You are if you want to be, and you know that. He can't survive without a m— Well, without you, anyway."

She let the silence hang between them. Something about him was coming undone. Gavin was starting to unravel. All her plans were falling apart. First Sophia. Now this.

"Ilara, can we at least talk about what's between us?" he asked.

"What is there to say, Gav?"

"What even are we to each other?"

"I don't know," Ilara said.

"What do you bloody mean, you don't know?"

"I didn't expect to care for anyone. Right now, I have to live my life like I don't."

"I—I—Fine." Gavin's expression hardened, and Ilara walked out his door.

Her feelings around him were complicated, and she had neither the time nor energy to deal with those emotions now.

The night before the Solar Day celebration was quiet after the several days Ilara had spent in the noisy Aoxian camp. She was happy to have had them, but the training had been arduous.

There was no one around. No sex workers roaming or guards proclaiming that the streets were safe. It was if, on this silent winter evening, Eversburg knew there would be an eventful morrow. The city urged all to rest, as there might be no chance for it in the coming days, weeks, or months. Rest for the last time, safe in bed.

"*Ilara*!" Zal'Keratha said, so loudly that it felt like a dull spike had been shoved in the back of her head, and a migraine spider webbed across the base of her skull. "*My Chosen*!"

*Yes, Mistress?* Ilara prayed back once she'd gathered herself.

*"You have not responded in days. What has occurred with the plan?"* the goddess asked.

*We are set to move. I've secured the assistance of an Amerite, and Aox lent a selak for my aid.*

The powerful Aoxians, organized in a selak, were Aoxia's most elite fighters. They'd learned powerful magical abilities that complemented their flowing fighting style.

*"An Amerite? One with the Sight?"*

*Aye. One of Jonas's men defected just before I attacked him. He foresaw the outcome.*

Ilara took the time to update Zal'Keratha on all the events since they'd last spoken just before Jonas's death, including her acquiring—and successfully using—the black metal spear.

*"I trust little,"* Zal'Keratha answered. *"I shall trust your judgment on the Amerite. I remember him well. He seemed devoted to his goddess's movements. Ameri works in strange ways, but I believe she does tire under Akara's yoke."*

*Do you think Ameri will take the Pantheon?*

*"Perhaps. It is not likely. Ameri understands its power but sees more in knowledge. Still, she is an unknown. But not as unknown as this strange weapon of yours. I forbid you to take it to the Solar Dominion,"* Zal'Keratha said.

*My Lady,* Ilara started, unsure where to begin. It was strange to try to negotiate with a being of such power. Her mind raced to the crates in Jonas's camp and Tarin's admission that Akara's paladins were storing them. *Our enemies will have these blades that nullify magic*, she told Zal'Keratha. *If I do not take one myself, I will be walking to my death.*

"*My power will guide you, child. Trust in me,*" the goddess answered. "*There is no concession here. You will not take it.*"

Ilara shook off the sting of being called a child. *Very well, Mistress. Need you anything else of me this eve?*

"*No. Make sure you have news of the altar for me when we next speak.*"

Ilara felt Zal'Keratha 's icy presence leave her mind again. The pain at the back of her head faded slowly, and she looked up at the stars. They shone far away, out of the reach of all in this world, mortal or divine. Ilara wondered, not for the first time, what lay in that dark, misty void. Did the people on those worlds toil as she did? Was there no place she could flee to that was safe from danger? Was there no place she could guarantee she was safe? Or Sophia? Or Gavin?

Or Theo?

***

The warmth of the sewers was a welcome relief given the chill of the evening. Organized soldiers were also a welcome distraction from the chaos of Ilara's feelings for Gavin.

Markus was sitting cross-legged in their makeshift tent. Aoxian drums beat loudly in the common area outside. How the lizards hadn't been discovered in these tunnels was beyond Ilara, yet the clothing and tools painted a picture. Bits of armor covered their scales—pauldrons that didn't quite fit their shoulders, breastplates cut in half and worn low on their torsos, swords as long as their arms that were smelted in a clean line through the center. They also had small metal helmets, which they used for bowls.

Plate armor, however slight, was offensive to Aoxians. Their scales, hard as metal, were sufficient to block the blow of blades and arrows. Growing up, Ilara had heard that only an Akaran could kill a lizard on the battlefield. It was necessary for Akara's armies to march south onto their land, or the Aoxian threat would never be quelled.

When Ilara learned to kill, she'd learned to kill Aoxians, which was almost the same as killing knights wearing armor. There were weak spots along their neck and thighs, where their scales were thinner and weaker. Their fighting stance blocked those areas. When they trained, they became more disciplined about keeping those areas blocked from attack. Catch one unawares, and it was easier to kill them.

"Gavin is unraveling," Ilara said.

"Unraveling?" Markus asked. The eyes tattooed on his head ceased their chaotic movements to fix her with their cold, unblinking stare.

"He's asking questions about the spell you cast on him. He's remembering things that you said he never would."

"I told you the spell was permanent. He should dismiss the memories as a bad dream."

"He isn't doing that, though. I don't need to have him asking questions about false memories right n—"

An Aoxian with golden scales brushed the curtains of their tent aside and entered. He waited with his arms held in front of him, fingers interlaced and claws covered as a sign that he came in peace. Ilara waved him forward, and Markus opened his eyes and glanced from her to the lizard with a bored expression.

"Honored Chosen of Death," the Aoxian said with a slight bow. He spoke slowly, head bobbing from syllable to syllable as if to a gentle melody. "I am Chek'Va. I am told that you will be with my selak for the assault. My warriors are already impressed with your technique."

"Thank you, honored child of Aox," Ilara said, raising her hands in front of her, mimicking his gesture with her palms pressed together. "You come from Tonid's house?"

"I see my father's scales represent me. You are learned of my house's deeds?" Chek'Va asked. His blank expression indicated this was rote to him.

"Indeed. Fear of Master Tonid's success in the Akaran wars follow Akarans wherever they go. Your honored lord was correct to elevate such a man to a noble of high renown," Ilara replied.

She'd heard that Tonid had defended an Aoxian swamp village against an entire Akaran legion. Accounts varied as to whether or not there had been Akaran Chosen in that legion, or if they'd merely been foot soldiers. Ilara did not think that diminished Tonid's actions. Great tales came from great deeds.

"This pleases me. You must know that those in a selak trained by the successor of his seed will be formidable warriors," Chek'Va said, his long lips turning upward in satisfaction.

"I have seen as much. I would trust no other warriors in the coming battle."

"You will not be assisting in the combat," Chek'Va replied. "You will be cham'do."

Ilara lowered her eyes to the gold-scaled lizard. She knew the position, reserved for the important, implied they were too frail for combat. "I would not take such dishonor. I would best be employed as han'do due to my mistress's gifts," she replied.

It was the position of scout and flank attacker in the selak and would put her within enemy lines.

Her eyes flitted back to Markus, who looked at her knowingly. He'd foreseen this conversation and had instructed on her on how it needed to go. They needed to use all their resources to succeed, even with the majority of the paladins absent from the palace for the Solar Day celebration.

"And should you die, Zal'Kerathan? Are we expected to bend the knee to this Amerite?" Chek'Va asked, not realizing Markus understood his language. It was as intended. The Aoxians needed to vent their frustrations before they would submit to any plan Ilara or Markus concocted.

"Ridiculous. We both know that you and your selak will betray us as soon as we are through the portal," Ilara said as she leveled her gaze at Chek'Va. His eyes widened slightly, and his claws tightened. She could tell he had the urge to pull his long, curved scimitar on her.

"You speak foolishness. How dare you accuse me and my selak of such dishonor?" he growled.

"I have an Amerite. We have seen the outcome of these battles. I know you seek to betray me, and yet I am still here," Ilara said.

"Do you support Aox's claim to the Pantheon?"

"No."

"Explain." It was but a syllable in the Aoxian tongue: ga. Pronounced as Chek'Va said it, it indicated a challenge. If he didn't accept her response, he might unclench his claws.

"The Aoxians in this sewer have never assaulted the Solar Dominion," Ilara started, pressing her palms together harder. "Aox has never blessed an assault. He does now, so you believe that this is enough for you to overcome the Akarans. This is incorrect, just as I know my mistress's blessing is insufficient.

"An alliance with Zal'Keratha is, ultimately, in Aox's best interest. He recognizes that Zal'Keratha will grant him a place on the Pantheon, which means more power and a future for you and your people. He recognizes that if things continue as they are, your people will die out. Even now, the great dragons of the world have been killed. The Aoxians are the remaining members of Aox's creations. He would accept exile over your death. He would accept service over kingship, if it means you all survive."

Chek'Va's scales seemed to glow intensely for several moments before he unclenched his jaw to speak. "What do you propose, Chosen of Death?"

Ilara glanced back at Markus, who had closed his eyes again. The tattoos popped back onto his head, one at a time. They were past the crux of the interaction, and he was gaining more insight on the battle.

"Even with us all fighting, most of the selak will die. All but the three in this room. When we get in, we'll need to battle together to establish our foothold. Then, we will split the selak—half will go to the Great Library of Ameri with Markus, and half to the dungeons with me. Those in the library will discover the secrets of the altar. Those in the dungeon will rescue as many Chosen as we can."

"Why rescue these Chosen?" Chek'Va asked.

"More allies. Akara has angered many gods in recent months. The more Crafters, Scholars, and Bards we find, the more likely that Akara's Pantheon will turn against her as Ameri has."

"I see," Chek'Va growled. He eased, and his muscles relaxed, releasing the tension in the tent. "I will choose which warriors go where?"

"Aye. You are selaka," Ilara said.

He was indeed leader of the selak. Ilara couldn't overrule him on the field of battle. If he decided he didn't have the warriors for their plan, after the initial charge, he could change paths. Markus had assured Ilara that he wouldn't.

"Good." Chek'Va grinned, showing many of his pointed teeth.

# Chapter Twenty-Six

# SOLAR DAY

THE SUN ILLUMINATED THE western wall of the circular chamber. Shadows played on the carvings locked in a constant state of pleasure. Tezza had long since left. Valette had felt the high priestess get out of the too-large bed, but she couldn't find the energy to rise.

Sleep hadn't found her so easily since she was thirteen, before she served. It couldn't have been anything more than the comfort of the bed, could it?

She scooted to the edge of the mattress and found her armor and clothing stacked in a neat pile with a piece of parchment lying on top. "Trust in our bond" was scrawled on it in still-wet ink.

Valette sought out the tub she'd used the previous night. In an anterior room that was lined with clear windows, it stood like a dutiful servant. From it, she had a bird's-eye view of the city. A line of paladins were walking south from the

Solar Dominion, their armor glinting in the morning light of Akara's Eye. They would march from outside the city back to the palace in a recreation of when the first army of paladins had conquered Eversburg. It had been Akara's first act as queen of the Pantheon. From Valette's vantage point, they disappeared behind the statue of Akara that waited at the Solar Dominion to welcome the paladins back home.

As Valette studied the statue, she noticed a line of people on Akara's Sword, little more than shadowed dots. Her eyes widened. There would be executions today? On Solar Day? While she had learned much from the evening, this seemed like a prime opportunity to gain more information.

She cleaned herself quickly and donned her armor in what she felt had to be record time. One thing the stories often omitted was how long it took to put on armor such as this. Every plate had a strap that needed fastening, and if she rushed, a loose piece could slide and expose her skin.

A sword rested near the exit. It wasn't the one she'd fought Maer with—that blade was now full of nicks and cracks and would need reforging. This was a fresh one, with a large blue jewel lain in the pommel. Valette unsheathed it to reveal a flash of steel, crafted to perfection. She confirmed its sharpness by cutting a lock of her hair. She pulled on her helmet, bathing the world in blue hues as the magic ticked on, and was out the door a moment later.

***

Sophia was prepared when the guards came to take them. The Librarian had informed her of the coming execution. Almost all of the Chosen in the dungeon would be killed on this day.

The window to escape was going to be small, and she had given up hope that Ilara would be there to save them. She met Katri's eyes again. There was something else there, an energy Sophia couldn't place.

"Are you ready?" she whispered.

"Aye," Katri replied, a smile flitting across her face. "At the very least, we'll be taking a few of these bastards with us."

Sophia nodded. She heard the clank of the dungeon's lock a few moments later, and she felt her heart sink. Was she prepared for this?

The shuffling of feet echoed around them as the Chosen were taken from their cells. Sophia's pulse raced. A warm hand gripped her shoulder, and Katri's green eyes met hers.

As Plume and Bucket stepped up to their cell, the guards gazed into the cage with blank stares. Sophia hoped they wouldn't notice that the band around her throat had fallen away. As the key turned in the lock, she gripped the

hilt of the dagger hidden under her robe and sang. The words
enveloped her, the waves of sound gripping at her skin like a
long-lost lover.

Beneath the moonlit waters, a tale unfolds,
Of a siren's song, so pure and bold.
In a cage of whispers, where echoes go,
Of a hidden key to a secret glade.

A lighthouse gleams, beckons bright.
Her voice, a compass in the night,
Breaks free from chains that
Bind. Her enchanting song,
Ties unwind.

The glimmering key, bathed in silver light,
Unlocked the cage in the night.
In the cage of whispers, where echoes go,
She yearned for freedom,
A sailor's blade.

Among the stars, she found her place,
The cosmic dance, and endless chase.
Whispers of the wind, tales unfold,
The key in his hand, the story foretold.

As Sophia sang, she rejoiced in the vibration of the air. A rainbow of jittering colors swept from the words, surrounding her with potential spells. She reached into the strand and grasped one. It rocketed from her and into the minds of Bucket and Plume. Their expressions turned downward for a moment, all deep frowns and angry eyes, and they reached for their blades. Sophia could feel their emotions shift, as though they were connected.

With a turn of her hand, she directed their minds to wander to their worst fears. It was odd that the spell would do that, but she felt it could work in the moment.

The two guards froze. Unable to parse reality from fiction, they were drawn into the song. Terror overcame them, and Plume dropped the keys on the floor as they both bolted from the dungeon.

Sophia and Katri stumbled outside. They were alone, as all the rest of the prisoners had been filed out before them. Sophia met her friend's gaze again, expecting gratitude, but saw something else.

"Let's get the hells out of here before you do that to me," Katri said.

***

Ilara was standing with a group of roughly fifty Aoxian warriors. Large-feathered headdresses adorned their scalps, and long sleeves of plumage covered the scimitars at their waists. Several held magical flames in their hands, using the light to assist one of their comrades in fixing his garments.

Against Zal'Keratha's wishes, Ilara shouldered the dark metal spear that she'd taken from the Syndicate. She felt it touch her mind, recognizing the cold caress that blocked Zal'Keratha from speaking with her. There was no other answer to the weapons she knew the Akarans had. She wouldn't die from something she could see coming. Not to mention that Sophia would have no chance if she did.

Markus shifted uneasily next to her, the hood of his cloak pulled low over his brow. His brown eyes scanned the room, darting from lizard to lizard as they finished their preparations.

"The portal will open soon, Markus. How are you feeling?" Ilara asked.

"I find it impressive that the Empire ever won a battle against such creatures," he said. "The grace, the power balled up in them."

"Because of their magic?" Ilara asked.

Aoxians were closer to Aox than any of the gods who'd created the other races were to their Chosen. As a result, each Aoxian had a speck of Aox's power, allowing them some magical prowess. A Chosen of any god was stronger than any individual Aoxian, but they were formidable when several came together.

"Aye. Akara's Chosen must have been powerful, indeed. It is a shame that Akara destroyed Ameri's library in Caldor. Many records of Aoxian magics were lost," Markus said.

"Are you jealous that Aoxians made magic a study?" Ilara asked.

"How could I not be? To think of the innovation that could be achieved if they used it to improve their culture."

"Instead of for war?"

"Aye. There are tomes dedicated to Aoxia's great innovators. They were using magic to water crops and improve their cities before Aox was cast from the Pantheon. They never used their abilities to subjugate others. Perhaps that is why their god fell."

"Perhaps, though I do not know the history well enough to know if Aoxians used their magic for war. They seem fairly adept at it."

Markus mumbled something under his breath. His forehead furrowed and his eyes closed, the edge of a tattoo opening between his brows.

Chek'Va took up a post near Ilara. "Waiting is always the worst part," he said in the Aoxian tongue.

"Aye. I'd give a finger for them to open our portal now," she replied.

"With enough impatience, you'll soil the feeling of battle," Chek'Va said. "How does a Zal'Kerathan feel about the likelihood of meeting your mistress in person?"

"Death is merely the beginning of my service."

"Spoken like a true believer." Chek'Va chortled, the Aoxian version of a laugh. "Are worshipers of your goddess as zealous for the end as Akara's tales imply?"

"While our Lady teaches Death is the beginning, it is truly an end. We have but one life on Aerlia, and she teaches us to make the most of it before embarking our true purpose—serving in our Death."

"So you are to enjoy the vacation on Aerlia before the master calls you to the fields?"

"Not quite. For most of us, our time on Aerlia is a chance to love and gain skill. Once Death calls us, we go to finish our Mother's house so that all may benefit."

"And for you? Are you not part of most?"

"I have already laid the foundation. I know not if Death will be easier or harder, but I know there will be fewer blades held to my neck."

Ilara raised her cha'ak to cover her nose and mouth, indicating to Chek'Va that the conversation was over, as she couldn't speak through the material. The Aoxians in front of her fell to their knees. Green feathers adorned their heads, denoting them as shaman s. In Aoxian magics, they were no more than sacrifices.

The shamans started an unintelligible chant, growing louder and louder. A spark of blue light erupted above their heads, darting through the air and then dying out. They chanted louder, and more sparks flew about erratically. A wispy, smoky substance seemed to flow from the shamans to where the sparks were flying. One of them stood, their head feathers more ornate and longer than those of their fellows. They screamed, and the sparks began to follow the movements of their arms, which they were rhythmically moving in a circular pattern.

As the sparks multiplied, the chanting intensified to words Ilara understood: "Aoxia will come for her enemies. Aoxia will attack Akara. Aoxians will slaughter or be slaughtered."

More and more sparks jumped through the air, joining the others, until they created a circle. The shaman strode forward, screaming again with hands outstretched as the sparks jumped toward them. For a moment, Ilara saw the entirety of the long bones of an Aoxian skeleton before it was fully disintegrated.

A wall of blue energy remained where the shaman had been, feeding on the magic in the creature's flesh.

Aox strode in front of the newly formed portal, the azure glow caressing his back, throwing his silhouette onto the squad of warriors.

"My kin!" He raised his hands toward the ceiling. "After a hundred years of exile, the fruits of our labor come to yield. For years, we fought to find purchase in the city of Akara, whose ambition deposed us of our position. We lost many of our selak and will lose more by the end. Each was a noble soul whose loss caused me to weep.

"We forge on for our people, and we forge a future where we are oppressed no longer. Go, my children! Go forth and claim the future that is your birthright. Give our clutch, our children, the future you were promised by your ancestors."

The selak screamed and surged forward as one. Their disgraced god stepped from their path, and they dove into the blue energy, disappearing to the other side.

Aox locked eyes with Ilara. "Do not disappoint me, Zal'Keratha," he snarled.

Ilara nodded as she and Markus stepped into the portal. It was cool, like diving into an ice bath. When Ilara emerged, she came face-to-face with carnage.

***

Valette stood at the base of the statue. Prisoners were lined up next to its legs, all of whom wore bands around their heads, which she recognized would block power from Ameri. The line snaked in through a doorway in the statue's heel that must lead to a set of stairs, and out of the shoulder along the sword. Men and women in blue robes guarded the prisoners. This included several palace guards as a show of force. There were no paladins as far as Valette could see.

She approached the nearest guard, and he looked at her with bored eyes. His helmet had a massive stupid plume coming out of the top of it.

"What is going on here?" Valette asked.

The guard looked from her face to her armor and the Almiran holy symbol on her chest, then back to her face. He shrugged and scratched his eye with the back of his wrist. "Clearing out the dungeon," he said, as if it were obvious.

"Why are we doing that? Has Tezza seen all these Chosen in a Tribunal?" Valette asked.

"How should I know that? The palace Amerites said it would be good to offer Akara sacrifices on Solar Day."

Valette flinched as one of the sacrifices hit the stone, emitting a sickening squelch. She looked from the fallen man to the tip of the sword. Tezza was likely at the other end of the city, leading the paladins in their march back to the palace. Valette shook her head and decided then that enough was enough.

Who are these Amerites to decide what to do with Akaran prisoners?

She pushed her way past the line and found a spiral staircase in the leg of the statue, barely wide enough for two people to walk abreast. She shouldered her way through, and as she took a step onto Akara's stone blade, she saw the truth for what it was.

There, on the tip of the sword, stood Knight Commander Ryn with his back to her. His hand was on the bald head of an Amerite prisoner. There was a Scholar standing next to him with her arms outstretched. Ryn stepped back and kicked, knocking the prisoner forward and off the tip of the sword, then turned and faced Valette, his eyes glowing amber with Akara's power.

Valette drew her blade and marched forward. Ryn drew his own blade, and the Scholar put her hand to her forehead. Ryn reached out and touched her forearm, saying something that Valette couldn't hear.

"Chosen Bilaut," he shouted, pointing his sword at her. "I must ask you to stop there, or I will have to release Scholar Theyda upon you. Her power over another's mind is not one you will survive encountering."

Valette stopped, her feet feeling heavy on the stone. She wondered how many the statue could hold. Halga's Crafters were skilled, but she didn't know if it could stand the weight of two armored paladins and a dozen Amerites without breaking and crashing to the street below.

"What are you doing here, Knight Commander?" she shouted back across the twenty feet still between them. Several of the Amerite prisoners looked at her incredulously, as if they were surprised she wasn't in alignment with Ryn.

"Akara speaks to me now, Almiran. You and the whore Tezza will pay for the evil you've wrought," Ryn said as he took a step toward Valette. He was in armor with plates painted the color of blood. The blade he held out was made from a black metal Valette had never seen before. She was sure it had something to do with the black bands the prisoners wore.

"I am her Voice, and my first act will be to sacrifice all of you heretics to my glorious goddess. The light will purge you." He took several steps closer, but stopped outside Valette's reach.

She settled back into a defensive stance. He was right, though. She wouldn't be able to kill him with the Scholar behind him.

***

"*Good, Sophia, good,*" the Librarian encouraged as they moved deeper into the Solar Dominion. They were adamant that Sophia and Katri couldn't walk out the front of the palace, which Sophia agreed with, quite frankly. Even on Solar Day, she was certain there would be at least one paladin milling about.

The path that the Librarian was leading them on was suspiciously familiar. As they passed the tapestry of Balan, she recognized it as the route to the Library of Ameri. There was a certain kind of comfort that the familiarity brought, despite how quickly Sophia's heart was racing.

When they rounded the last corner, they saw a massive Aoxian standing at the other end of the hall. His scales were spattered with blood, and he lifted his curled lip in a snarl. He disappeared back down the corridor from whence he'd come. Sophia had never seen such a beast before, and he lived up to the stories—defined muscles powerful enough to crush a man's head, and claws long enough to disembowel him.

"What in the bloody void was that?" Katri hissed as they sprinted forward. "There aren't supposed to be any Aoxians in Eversburg."

They arrived at the massive oak doors that indicated the library, and Sophia paused to catch her breath. Katri did the same, resting her palms on her knees. Even hunched over, she towered over Sophia.

"Are you sure you trust them?" Katri asked. "Did that Librarian warn you there'd be bloody Aoxians in the Solar Dominion?"

"No, but I trust them. We're going to need allies if Aox thinks he can bring down Akara's Empire. Hopefully the Librarian is one of them." The Librarian had been one of the few people to show Sophia respect, ask her opinions, and they hadn't erased her memory, as much as the Amerites had promised her they would.

"I hope you're right. I would hate to throw my newfound freedom away."

Sophia threw the massive doors open to find the library empty. Books were piled in the center, and most of the shelves had been cleared. She panicked but retraced her steps to the Librarian's room, to which the doors were propped open. The Librarian was standing just inside, surrounded by Scholars, all of whom had their hoods down and bald heads exposed. Each was different, and some had thick veins running around their heads, which reminded Sophia of the folds of the Librarian's brain. They seemed mournful.

One of them rushed to Sophia. She recognized him as the Scholar who'd introduced her to the Librarian. "Good," he said. "You've shed your bonds. Come quickly, the first step is complete." He ushered her and Katri forward.

"I don't understand. What is going on? Why are they out in the open?" Sophia asked.

"*They know, as we all do, that our time has come.*"

"What do you mean?"

"*One of us with the Sight saw the future that Ameri desired,*" the Librarian said. "*We told her we couldn't be a part of her plans, that it was to the detriment of Aerlia and we would oppose her designs. She, in turn, has Forsaken us. You, Sophia Blackwood, are integral to opposing Ameri and Akara. We will do all we can to protect you. I'm sorry I did not trust your idea of Akara.*"

"How do you speak with me if Ameri has taken all your power from you?" Sophia asked.

"*Ameri and I are one and the same. I've been her Chosen for nearly a century. One does not live so long dependent on magic without having enough reserved to succeed in mutiny. I, however, must conserve it. This shall be the last time we speak, Balanite.*"

"What did you see? What are Ameri's plans?" Katri asked.

"You shouldn't have to give your life for me," Sophia said. The Librarian remained silent.

She tried to turn, but the Scholar stood in her way. "We must hide—singer, Beast," he said to the pair. "Quickly! They will be here in moments."

***

Ilara stepped onto the stone floor in the Solar Dominion and winced at the gruesome display. Men and women around the exit of the portal were bleeding out and slowly dying. They were all in similar fine clothing and seemed to be of a varying ages and sexes. Their blood covered lavish wooden desks, and papers were strewn around the floor.

Markus stepped through as the portal closed. He immediately began retching.

"Chek'Va!" Ilara shouted over the din of the Aoxians slaughtering the defenseless.

The gold-scaled lizard killed a man cowering for his life, then turned to her. "You have a command?"

"You're going with me to the dungeons. There will be powerful Chosen on that path. Kill them, not the bloody servants. Get a group together to send with Markus," she said.

Chek'Va nodded, then shouted to the rest of the selak in Aoxian. Ilara couldn't parse everything that was said, but they began to corral the remaining people into a corner. Chek'Va shouted more orders, and a group of Aoxians formed around Markus.

"I will see you on the other side of this, Zal'Kerathan," he growled, and made his way from the room and down the hall.

Ilara did the same, running in the opposite direction, followed by Chek'Va and his half of the selak. The palace halls were mostly empty, and she had to wonder at the scale of the place. She'd never penetrated its defenses before. She'd drawn up plans when she'd considered a contract on Tezza, but she'd always thought it would be more easily done in her carriage.

As much as she hated what the Solar Dominion stood for, she couldn't help but marvel at the marble hallways, covered in tapestries and carpet. There were centuries of history told here; it would almost be a shame to burn it down.

They turned a corner and were confronted by a group of palace guards. The red eyes of a single paladin glowered at Ilara from behind their shoddy line. He was a hulking behemoth of a man, plate stretched over his muscles, and he was holding a flail with a large ball at the end of a chain.

He shouted words of encouragement at the line of guards. They were wearing significantly less armor than him—little more than breastplates and pauldrons, which were decorated with a large amount of golden ornamentation. They scrambled to block Ilara and the selak, their holding spears out, tips sharp and ready for the Aoxians to run into them.

Chek'Va shouted for the Aoxians to halt. They did so, each lizard nearly running into the back of the one in front of them. He pulled his long scimitar from its scabbard, metal grinding against the sheath like a bow against a violin. Then he held his free hand out, palm to the line of Akarans. The Aoxians beside him did the same. In a moment, their hands were alight, flames dancing in their outstretched hands, conjured with the powers of their god's magic. They lobbed balls of fire toward the guards.

The Akarans' tunics began to burn beneath their fancy armor. The line broke a second later as each soldier tried to put out the flames. Chek'Va gave the command to charge, and the Aoxians were on them in a moment. Ilara jogged behind them, mouth agape at their efficiency. Chek'Va hadn't been lying when he said he trusted his selak with his life.

As the lines met, the paladin shot forward, smashing an Aoxian's head with his large mace. The creature fell to the ground instantly, and Chek'Va let out a bloodthirsty scream. Immediately, he met the paladin in combat, blade crossing the chain of the flail. They separated and clashed back toward each other.

Ilara sensed an opportunity and snuck behind the large paladin, slipping into invisibility, the chill rushing over her body. She waited. Chek'Va fought skillfully, but the brute strength of the bulky paladin was proving to be his downfall. Ilara smirked as, on Chek'Va's next swing, the man parried again and wrapped the length of the lizard's blade with the chain of the flail. With a flick of the wrist, he disarmed Chek'Va.

Ilara readied her spear, but as she went for the kill, the paladin lined up another attack. He swung, but Chek'Va caught the chain of the flail in one claw and stabbed his other claws into the eye slits of his opponent's helmet. The paladin screamed in pain, dropping the flail, and the lizard drew his hand back, ripping free the eyes of the Akaran, then swiped his throat.

Ilara let her invisibility drop, making eye contact with Chek'Va as she did. "Effective," she said, and he gave her a smirk.

The next moment, they were moving again—after ensuring that the palace guards were all dead. Despite how well they'd routed their enemy, one Aoxian had died in the skirmish. They couldn't afford a fight with many more paladins, as there were only ten more members of this half of the selak.

They arrived at the dungeon without further incident. They encountered more palace guards, but all fled. Ilara recognized the dungeon's entrance from what Markus had told her about the damp descent of stairs and the door. She pushed her way through, finding it unlocked. An empty prison stared back at them.

Her grip tightened on her weapon. Markus hadn't mentioned this possibility. Had he lied or been negligent? She'd find out at the tip of her spear.

***

"Explain this," Valette demanded as she gestured to the line of Amerites behind her. They cowered away from her, defenseless with the bands on their heads.

Ryn smiled as he held his blade out, his eyes newly shining with the amber light of Akara's power. "Sacrifices for my resplendent goddess, who has finally deigned to bless me with her power. After years of service, I am her Chosen. I am her Voice. She demands their power be returned to the Pantheon."

"And what of Tezza?" Valette asked. The high priestess had spoken of how Ryn had assisted in killing those Akara called to the Voice. It was clear to her now why he'd aided her.

"The former Voice? She will go the way of all the others who block my path. An executioner's axe ought to be sufficient," Ryn growled.

Valette clenched her free hand, and a circle of light expanded over her left arm, deflecting Ryn's strike. The shield was covered in runes similar to those on her armor and weighed slightly more than a feather. She'd channeled most of that tract to make the shield as close to the length of her body as she could, unlike the one she'd used to smash Maer's face.

"Almir's famous shield. A shame he never gave you his blade," Ryn said mockingly.

"You'll find that steel is more than sufficient for your death," Valette hissed.

Ryn brought his hand forward. She hadn't seen the runes emblazoned on it until it was nearly too late. Red light erupted from his palm, and Valette barely had time to bring her shield forward to deflect the blast. The beam ricocheted off her shield and into the street, carving a line of char into a building below. A crack formed on the shield at the area of impact.

Akara's smite? This shield should not have blocked something like that.

"His power are new still. I can't guarantee the shield will hold next time," Almir replied. "Best dismiss it and hope we can refill the tract before he fires again."

Valette let the shield dissipate. She felt Almir filling the tract almost immediately, like a bucket dunked in a stream. Ryn lowered his blade as well, revealing the woman in red behind him. She pushed another Scholar from the tip of Akara's stone sword.

"So this is what you chose over loyalty?" Valette asked. She needed to stall Ryn. She needed to find out more about this woman.

Ryn barked out a laugh. "I've done nothing but benefit from the will of a traitor. I knew for years that Akara's hand would fall to me soon enough. I gave her years of my life. Years of toil for her to realize the stability I could bring to her empire. Together, we will crush all."

"So it's you and one of Ameri's clergy against the rest? Have you been planning this coup since the beginning?"

"Aye." Ryn grinned. "That's the best part. Without Theyda's help, there would be no machination. She relays her Sight to me. We have endeavored for years to return Ameri's power to the Pantheon so that she and Akara might crush the other gods. They are the only two who might tip the scales, allowing us to finally drive the Aoxian menace from our lands and kill all gods outside the Pantheon."

Kill the gods? With the Amerite? Was she the mastermind behind this? Valette needed to get by Ryn and threaten her—Theyda, he had called her. Ryn blocked the path forward, and Valette wasn't lithe enough to slip by him, not with all her armor. She took several steps back, and he matched her, giving her a new opportunity.

Ryn lunged forward, too late. Valette tapped the spell and sidestepped his strike, pulling her arm back to form the shield and driving it into his face as she had with Maer.

Ryn stumbled back, and Valette raised her sword, pointing it toward Theyda. "Trabema lucin!" she shouted.

A beam of white light shot from the tip of her blade and punched into the Scholar's red robes, causing her to fall to her knees. Valette shouted the spell command several more times and saw the light pierce Theyda's chest. Soon, Ryn regained his stance and blocked her sight of the Scholar. Valette couldn't tell how many times she'd hit the Amerite, but she knew it would be enough.

The stone beneath Valette and Ryn shook violently, as if threatening to move on its own. Both fighters lost their balance. Valette's metal boots slid from the statue's blade as she flailed her arms wildly. Dropping her weapon, her gauntleted fist caught the edge of the marble sword before she plummeted to her death. The empowered suit helped her clamp on tighter than she could have without it. On the horizon, she saw a cloud of smoke rising above the buildings far to the south.

Near where Tezza and the march of paladins are.

"Their Revolution has begun, which means you've lost," an unfamiliar woman said in her mind. "You may have struck me, but such a blow could never kill.

Valette's temples exploded with pain, as if a giant were pinching the sides of her head. The sky above her darkened as Ryn hovered above her, his sword poised to strike her hand.

"You are too late, Almiran. Your pitiful god is part of the old way—one of the last gods on Aerlia to ascend to godhood. From now on and forever, there will only be Akara."

He brought his sword toward Valette, and she let go before the blow connected. Without thinking, she brought Almir's shield between her and the ground.

Then, she prayed until she made impact.

***

Sophia hadn't noticed how cold the Librarian's room was before. She sat while Katri paced like a wounded wolf. They'd been led here and told that it would likely be the safest place for them. Few knew of these rooms, and even fewer knew the complicated combination needed to unlock the door. Thankfully, it opened easily from the inside, so they could wait until the commotion died down. The Scholars continued to dodge their questions about Ameri's intent.

"We are further from freedom," Katri growled.

"How are you not focused on staying alive?" Sophia asked.

"Death is no longer in our fate."

"What?"

"Today is Solar Day. When I was with the Resistance, we had plans for this day. If they are successful, they will liberate the Solar Dominion," Katri said.

"How do you know they'll be successful? Or merciful to two Chosen?"

"I don't. We should, at least, be able to escape in the battle. We won't escape from this room, however."

"You heard the Scholars as well as I. Ameri schemes, which could only mean that she has a ploy for Akara's throne. Aoxia is attacking the palace, too," Sophia said.

"Aye. It seems the gods are predictable. Shyll warned me that they all would try to kill each other eventually. I guess I hoped it would be outside my lifetime," Katri said.

The door to the room screeched, and Katri growled. Sophia huddled back into the opposite corner.

Gods, how did I get into this? I just want to survive. I just want to sing. I want peace for once in my short godsdamned life.

When the door opened, the Librarian shuffled in, the light of the beams connecting their armor shining off the stone walls of the small room. Katri visibly relaxed, then resumed pacing.

"Apologies, I should have warned you that I would be coming. The other Scholars—former Scholars—requested that I sequester myself as well. They will do their best to keep us from harm. My knowledge is too vast to lose, I fear. We can hear the Aoxians outside the door. They'll be in within minutes," the Librarian said to Sophia.

"What knowledge do the Aoxians want?" she asked.

"Not the Aoxians. They are led by an Amerite. They demand the knowledge we refused Ameri: the location of Akara's Altar and how to activate it."

"I don't understand," Sophia said.

"*You wouldn't. I shall pass the knowledge to you, just in case I— Well, at least from here, you won't be able to have the information taken from you. Lead in the walls blocks mind reading.*"

"What if we don't want your knowledge?" Katri hissed, confirming Sophia's suspicion that the Librarian was talking to them both.

A loud crash and screaming erupted from the library. Sophia's blood froze.

The Librarian wilted slightly. "*Fine, I shall pass it only to Sophia.*"

Visions flew through Sophia's mind. The tallest tower of the Solar Dominion, walls decorated with naked statues, a stone table covered in runes. Two Chosen lay upon it, stabbed through the chest. Sophia recognized the horns of an Ytrian and the red eyes of an Akaran. Their blood ran onto the table and pooled in a central well, where another stood. A moment later, they were gone in a flash of red light.

*"You know now how to see the queen of the gods. Make sure she perishes. I care not if it is you or that sister of yours who takes her place,"* the Librarian growled.

Sophia opened her mouth to ask, again, what had changed, when the cracking of wood sounded from the library, then many sounds of metal on flesh. The Scholars outside, now Forsaken, had few methods of defending themselves. The noises built on themselves until Sophia couldn't differentiate between them, melding into a terrible symphony. Horrified, she saw the streams of sound waves flowing through the door. Timidly, she reached out and touched them.

*"Don't, child,"* Balan said. It had been so long since Sophia had heard him that she nearly mistook his voice for the Librarian's. He sounded frightened. Or hurt. *"You will not like the spell that comes from battle."*

Sophia dropped her hands and stuffed them in the folds of her dress. She still had the black metal dagger tucked in there. If Balan's music couldn't save her, it might.

*Will it be worse that those unarmed Scholars being massacred?* she thought back.

Her chest started to ache at the loss of life. Balan didn't answer, and the chaos from the other room slowly died down. Sophia's breath caught in her throat as the door creaked open again. Katri growled, but the Librarian held up their hand.

A man in a tattered blue cloak stepped through, a single tattooed eye open on his forehead. He made eye contact with Sophia and Katri before his gaze settled on the Librarian. A large Aoxian walked in as well. Their eyes had been gouged out, and their scales were pale, as if they'd been drained of all their color.

"Ameri's Librarian. It is good to see you are still standing," the man said.

"*Markus,*" the Librarian's voice rumbled through Sophia's mind.

Markus must have received the message as well, as he smirked. "Ameri hasn't fully cut you off, has she? She knows there is more information you must pass to me," he said.

"*What have you done to this Aoxian?*" the Librarian demanded.

"A simple spell—one denied us by the Akarans. You'll find nothing remaining of their primitive thoughts. They are now extensions of my mind," Markus said. "Tell me of the altar."

"*I'll speak of no such thing,*" the Librarian hissed.

Markus closed his eyes and fell silent for a few moments. The eye on his head darted around chaotically. Sophia felt a vile presence in her mind, as if there was an intruder she could barely feel.

Markus clapped his hands together, and a satisfied expression crossed his face. "It seems you've already given what I need to this singer. The vision in her mind is hazy, but I should be able to torture it from her, one blast at a time. Marvelous. I won't be needing you at all, Librarian."

He made a slight motion, and the Aoxian stepped forward. It brought its long, jagged weapon into a brutal arc. The Librarian deflected the blow with the arm of their armor. A clang rang out in the small room.

"*Markus. She is using you. You'll be nothing once she is queen. Ameri makes sure that her Chosen do not rise to her power, lest they pose a threat to her.*"

The next strike severed the tendril of the Librarian's arm, metal plate clanking against the stone floor.

"I doubt that very much. I wouldn't ever let myself become what you have. You've let your desire for knowledge ruin you. Ameri controlled you easily."

*"I'll do what I can to buy you a moment of peace. Run, Sophia."*

The lizard drew back its wicked weapon again, light from the tendrils holding the Librarian together flashing across the steel. When it swung the blade, it connected with the Librarian's exposed brain, slicing through their center. A bright light flashed through the room. Markus and the Librarian were no longer there when it cleared.

The Aoxian shook its head, then looked to Sophia and Katri. It stood, weapon in hand, without mercy in its eyes.

***

Ilara and Chek'Va stood in front of the massive library entrance. Blood stained the carpet outside, and the doors were splintered apart, as if the selak had broken them down. The emaciated bodies of Amerites lay in front of them, chopped to bits. Four dull-scaled Aoxians were standing next to the carnage, shoulders and head slumped as if they were being held up by string.

"This is wrong," Chek'Va said. He stepped forward, and the four Aoxians bolted upright, blades held awkwardly.

"I feel that these are no longer your kin," Ilara said as she gripped her black metal spear firmly with both hands.

"Whatever has them desecrates the dead," Chek'Va said.

The other Aoxians of the selak stepped forward, and more of the dead Aoxians emerged from the crowded bookcases. Ilara counted most of the other half of the selak.

The closest one looked at her with empty eye sockets and almost seemed to grin. She had no time to contemplate it before it lunged at the selak, letting out a half-formed war cry. The rest moved at the same time, Aoxian fighting Aoxian. Ilara tracked the action as she faded from view, magic trickling over her body.

The only one who didn't rush forward was Chek'Va. He stood awkwardly by the entrance to the library, holding his weapon limply at his side. "This is wrong," he muttered. "These are ancient magics that control my people. We have been betrayed."

A figure stepped out from behind a bookcase, his eyes awash with fear.

"Markus," Ilara shouted, letting her invisibility fade. "What in the gods has happened?"

His expression shifted from terror to a cunning smile. "Maledensus," he hissed, sneering at Ilara.

Inky black lines snaked from his outstretched fingers into her chest. She felt the air escape from her lungs and fell back, stumbling to the ground. Chek'Va turned and rushed Markus. The Amerite cackled loudly, and his form slowly dissipated, as if his body were little more than fog.

Darkness edged Ilara's vision as she met Chek'Va's wide eyes.

***

Sophia braced herself as the dead Aoxian took an uncertain step toward her. The creature seemed to have forgotten how to walk, though it had swung a blade confidently a moment ago. It was as if Markus's absence made it lose strength. Katri was standing between the Sophia and the Aoxian, arms raised. Sophia knew they'd die here, despite the Librarian's assurances.

Fighting had started back up in the main room of the library. The snarls of Aoxians rose, and the wave of sounds flooded through the door again, surrounding the two women. Sophia contemplated reaching into the wave again to see whatever spell Balan had warned her against. Surely it couldn't be as bad as his warning. There was no way they'd survive this without it. She was sure a small spell wouldn't be as bad as the end of an Aoxian blade.

Katri snarled loudly, and hair seemed to grow from her skin. Bones snapped as her arms and snout lengthened. Her fingers morphed into several-inch-long claws, and she lunged toward the Aoxian. The Beast.

Taken aback by the attack, the slow-moving Aoxian tried to react, but Katri's claws were in its chest before it could bring the blade to bear. She ripped through it like a clerk tearing apart bad paperwork. The Aoxian's torso separated from its legs, then its arms, then its head. The wild-eyed wolf looked back at Sophia before she rushed out the door. Tentatively, Sophia followed, unsure what she was walking into.

Katri crawled up the bookcase that faced the wall and disappeared over the top. Sophia rushed around the corner and down a long aisle between two shelves, trying to track Katri's lupine form. When Sophia emerged back into the main entrance of the library, she saw Aoxians fighting Markus's hive minions.

The Aoxians were losing.

Only two of them remained against a half dozen of Markus's creatures. They had their backs to the library entrance, and one was bent over a prone form.

Ilara.

Katri came down on one of the eyeless creatures as the last standing Aoxian was cut down by two of the others. She finished mauling one and took another by surprise, ripping it to pieces as easily as the first.

Without thinking, Sophia rushed through the opening her wolflike friend had given her. She met her sister's eyes and felt the panic in them. Words bubbled up her throat, and she struggled to say them as they all fought to come out first.

Ilara said something to the Aoxian in his own tongue. He nodded and grabbed Sophia's arm. He began chanting forcefully in the snarls of the Aoxian language. Ilara limply raised her arm, and Sophia took it.

"Ilara," she was finally able to say as she grasped her sister's hand. Ilara held her back, albeit weakly.

Blue sparks formed into rings around them. Sophia glanced back and saw the former Aoxians fleeing Katri's claws. The wolf turned and enveloped the small group in a massive embrace, the blue rings of energy malleable enough for her to pass through them. Sophia felt her feet lift off the ground, and she began to turn slowly with Ilara, Katri, and the Aoxian.

The blue rings had turned to walls of solid azure energy. Sophia's stomach fell as she felt herself move a massive distance. She'd read of Aoxian teleportation magics but had never dreamed she'd be able to experience it. Once the azure walls fell away, they were standing in a darkened alley, bleakly lit by torchlight.

# CHAPTER TWENTY-SEVEN

# HER SWORD

VALETTE WOKE IN DARKNESS. Her hands were bound behind her back, and she was kneeling on a hard surface. She could feel the steel of her armor pushing back against her; it was how she had remained upright while she was unconscious. Her trusty plates still encased her arms, legs, and torso, but her helmet was gone. A felt band covered her eyes. Her armor was inert, and she couldn't move it no matter how much she struggled, though the empowerment runes should have been enough to rip through whatever bonds restrained her.

She grunted softly as she tried to shift. Her body was sore. It was a wonder she'd survived her fall from the statue of Akara.

"Valette?"

"Aye," she responded, her heart racing.

"Akara's Eye! I-I-I hoped it wasn't you." The woman spoke with a rasp, as if she'd been yelling. It took Valette more time than it should have to recognize her voice.

"Tezza?"

"Aye, it is I," she whimpered.

"I guess I was too late to warn you, then. I thought Ryn was going to kill me," Valette said.

"We may find it unfortunate that he didn't," Tezza told her.

"What happened to the parade? What was that explosion? That is the last thing I remember."

"Peasants attacked us. They were armed with these awful black weapons that cut through our paladins' armor like it wasn't there. One of them, a dark-skinned man, threw iron balls into our rank—those were the explosions you speak of."

"I've never heard of such a thing," Valette said.

"It was as if the fires of Akara visited Aerlia. I know not whether it is the machination of a Crafter. I escaped with some of my honor guard, all of whom were killed by Ryn. I tried to tell him what happened, but he wouldn't hear it."

"Aye, he is Akara's Voice."

"Indeed," Tezza said. "He used me in a way I couldn't fathom. I thought I could trust him because he wasn't Chosen."

Valette didn't have time to ask what she meant by that. She heard the creak of doors opening, and a flurry of boots on stone echoed in the room.

Sudden brightness filled Valette's vision as Ryn removed her blindfold. His red eyes bored into her. She was in the Tribunal hall, Tezza shifting uncomfortably next to her. Dozens of men and women in red-and-gold armor crowded the stands. Each held their helmet in the crook of their arm, letting the bright intensity of their glowing eyes shine onto the two women. She and Tezza weren't the prisoners here, Valette realized. They were the judged. The sword hadn't connected with their necks yet, but it soon would.

A large glass circle hung above them. It was concave and directed toward the setting sun.

Tezza made a movement. Ryn's eyes darted toward her.

"Knight Co—" she started, and his gauntleted hand smacked into the side of her face, knocking her to the ground as the deafening sound of metal cracking bone resounded in the hall.

"Treacherous witch!" he said, blood dripping from his fist.

The paladins in the stands watched Tezza squirm. She was sobbing loudly, crawling away from the knight commander.

Valette struggled against the inert confines of her armor. Glancing down, she saw a black-hilted dagger protruding from her breastplate. It wasn't in deep enough to fully pierce it, but it seemed firmly lodged in the metal. Was it blocking the magic of her armor?

Both the rebels and the paladins are using these cursed things.

She thought back to the dagger Maer had used against her. She'd hit Valette with it once, which caused an unnatural emptiness in her tracts, as if it had drained them. It had to be related to the black collar Sophia had worn.

"This woman," Ryn shouted again as he placed a boot on Tezza's back and pinned her to the floor.

Tezza shot a look at Valette. Her hazel eyes were fraught with worry.

"She lied to all of us! Akara has Chosen me and made me her Voice, my years of service rewarded with the highest position among you. I've led each of you every day in enforcing the law in our divine city—a law I thought came from Akara, yet only came from the bitch's mouth."

The previously silent paladins erupted into a thunder of shouts and hisses. Ryn grinned as he looked from Valette to Tezza.

He held a hand up, and the paladins fell silent. The light of the setting sun hit the glass disc that hung above them, which channeled it into a slim beam. It fell several feet to the side of Ryn. A paladin with short blonde hair that shone like woven gold stepped forward, carrying a six-foot-tall staff with a red gem at the top. Valette recognized it from her first Tribunal.

Ryn grasped it and lifted his boot from Tezza's back. She gasped, forcing air back into her lungs.

"These two heretics have defied our queen. Both will face punishment. Tezza, traitor to her own Chosen, then Valette, Chosen of a bastard god," Ryn yelled.

The golden-haired paladin grabbed Tezza by the shoulders and brought her up to her knees, the ray of sunlight shining next to her head.

"As my first decree as Voice of the greatest goddess on Aerlia—" Ryn paused as cheers erupted around him again. He turned the staff and held it so that the gem was just above Tezza's head. Tears streamed down her face as she was illuminated by its glow.

He held his hand up again, and the cheers dampened only slightly. He raised his voice to carry over them all. "—I will place this heretic's body into the service of our queen eternally. Then, we shall show this Almiran what we think of Chosen of lesser gods. We will cleanse them from our city. From our empire!"

He lowered the gem into the beam of light. The ray turned from an orange to a deep red as it refracted onto Tezza's forehead. It held there for a moment, then broke into squirming tendrils that traced paths down her face. They wriggled and writhed across her cheeks, searching every pore of her skin.

Tezza screamed, and the coils poured into her mouth, more forming from the ray on her head. They dug into her skin, and blood ran down her face. She convulsed, and red mist curled around her as the light forced itself into her body. She struggled as she was lifted into the air, her feet kicking out wildly until her heel collided with the dagger in Valette's chest and pushed it farther into her breastplate.

Ryn didn't seem to notice, eyes fully on Tezza. Valette squirmed her hands and arms into the chest of the armor. The arms of the suit remained extended behind her, bound to whatever magics the dagger applied to it.

Unlike most, her suit had been constructed so that straps and metal bindings held it together when it was assembled. A single strap, if pulled from the inside of the waist, would pop the breastplate open. It was that strap that Valette now held with one trembling hand. She needed the right opportunity.

Tezza hovered ten feet off the ground, no longer beholden to the beam from the staff. The rest of the tendrils of light raced down her throat and through the openings in her flesh. Her hair hovered around her head, and her eyes opened and revealed shining red light. When she smiled, her mouth was filled with that same cursed glow. Paladins stymied gasps as they lowered their heads, most choosing to kneel.

"You have the pleasure of working with our goddess's champion," Tezza said, her voice warped and layered, as if a dozen people were talking at once. "My name is Al-Kaise, but you may formally address me as Akara's Sword."

Her hand, now controlled by this Al-Kaise, came forward and gestured to the paladins gathered in the Tribunal hall. "Are you my guard? My knights? Are you prepared for the gifts I might bestow upon you?"

Several of the paladins shared worried looks. Still, one stepped forward, the blonde man who'd held Tezza for this cursed ritual. "We accept your decree as Akara's Sword. Lead us to victory over the heretics that swarm our city," he yelled back, and the paladins around him shouted a singular word of agreement.

Al-Kaise smiled again. She extended her arms, and dozens of arcs of amber light shot from her extended fingers and drove themselves into the foreheads of the gathered paladins. A sharp crack of bone sounded through the hall as each man had their  head pierced. Ryn and Valette were the only ones spared from this act.

"Akara's power flows from me to you. Feel it and tremble. Soon, we will hunt our enemy—and purge them from our world," Al-Kaise said.

The paladins began to convulse in the same way Tez-za had a few minutes ago. Valette decided at that moment that she'd seen more than enough and pulled the strap in her armor. The front of her breastplate flung open, and she fell forward. Pulling herself from the shell, her eyes met Ryn's frightened eyes for a moment. She yanked the black metal dagger from the front of her armor and hurled it at Al-Kaise, hoping that it would stem Akara's power as it had Halga's and Almir's. The dagger caught in Al-Kaise's shoulder and caused her to falter.

Not waiting to see the result of her attack, Valette turned and rushed toward the side of the room. On the way, she liberated one of the convulsing paladins of their sword, glad that it was of a similar size and weight to the one that she'd lost. With another two steps, she reached the wall of stained glass, yet she didn't slow her momentum.

Valette jumped. Clenching her fist, she formed Almir's shield. Typically, she would need to taper the magic in the tract so that she could control the size of it. Now, she didn't. Valette flushed the tract of magic and let the shield grow and fully envelop her, creating a bubble of golden light.

Tendrils of Al-Kaise's magic light smashed into the back of the bubble, sending Valette into the full-length stained glass windows. She crashed through them, colored shards falling around her, and dove toward Aerlia's surface. Valette knew that the Tribunal hall was in one of the spires of the Solar Dominion, but she'd survived a higher fall than this. The change in position seemed an improvement to the room she'd just been in.

The shield held around her, just beyond her outstretched limbs. This meant that when it made impact, she would slam into it just as if she'd hit the ground herself. She had only moments to figure out her survival.

Her tracts had been full, she realized. She'd spent everything in the shield tract, so she wouldn't be able to adjust the shield, aside from dispelling it. There was one trick she thought might work, but she'd never had the opportunity to try it. She tapped her fighting spirit and felt her body strengthen. The ground raced toward her, faster now. She was falling toward a small slab of stone at the side of the Solar Dominion that looked like a dais for an unbuilt statue.

Valette sucked in her breath and tucked her legs and arms into as tight a ball as she could, so that they would take the impact. Just before the shield bubble smacked into the ground, she tapped her reserve of healing magic. She let it wash over her body, but focused it on her limbs.

The shield hit the stone, and Valette collided with the bottom of it less than a second later. The bones in her arms and legs cracked painfully, blowing into dozens of pieces. Almir's healing began to work instantly. She gasped as the fragments slowly mended back together. After a few minutes, she found everything was moving as it should, but her legs felt numb when she stood.

"Sunlight, why did I ever bother with a suit of armor," she wondered aloud as she took up the blade she'd stolen from the paladin.

"*My power is limited in a way that steel is not*," Almir spoke back to her.

"I'm going to have to live without it," Valette grunted as she dispelled Almir's shield.

There was no one on the palace grounds, but when she looked up, she saw Tezza's head leaning out the shattered window high above. Valette shivered as her gaze met the solid red orbs of light that looked back at her.

"That thing is not Tezza, and I need to adjust," she muttered, then turned her attention back to Almir. "What is Akara planning?"

"*That creature, Al-Kaise, accused me of heresy and banished me from the Pantheon. Already I can feel the power slipping from me. I will have to Forsake Chosen to keep giving you power. A shame, but I will reclaim them if I'm ever able to. If what Al-Kaise said is true, thousands of Chosen across the Empire will be slaughtered. All the rest will be enslaved. You are the only one in a position to stop it.*"

"If only Father Halen were here," Valette huffed. He was much better equipped than she to deal with this, having been Chosen a decade longer.

She turned to the gates and was off the palace grounds a moment later, the tall walls and towers behind her. Night had fallen on the city during her short journey, but fires to the south caught her eye. The riot that accosted Tezza was still burning.

Valette didn't have a plan as she approached the Dawn district. A massive line of Akaran soldiers holding torches were standing on the district border with their backs to her. They held their shields in front of them and their spears extended. Archers were standing behind them, pulling their bows back and releasing arrows tipped with fire into the southern parts of the city. Farther down the block, the rebels were preparing themselves for a charge. Corpses littered the street between, indicating this was not their initial attempt.

"And so a revolution begins. It seems that Akara's people have decided enough is enough," Valette muttered.

"*And that Akara had to take extreme steps in response. This goes against everything we decided in the beginning—to rule with justice. This, in addition to Aoxians attacking the palace, must terrify her,*" Almir replied.

"Aoxians attacked the palace?"

Almir relayed all he could, indicating that the attack had been focused on the Library of Ameri, and Almir wasn't sure who'd repelled them.

"But the Zal'Kerathan was with them?" Valette asked. She lingered near the line of soldiers. They didn't notice her as she paced along the street.

"*Indeed,*" Almir replied.

"Our enemies rally against us. Where do we go from here?"

"*You recall the parable of the generous knight?*"

"A man named Hegthor, one of your first Chosen. He rooted evil from his enemy's lands and gave his spoils as alms to the poor in those lands. I don't understand how that relates," Valette said.

"*At the time, we didn't know who the true evil was. When he revealed himself, we killed him. We only thought of them as lands at the time. We weren't aware that the one ruling them was perpetuating the injustice we were fighting. We killed many innocents before we realized the truth. Perhaps we still didn't know.*"

"You believe that evil is Akara? That Zal'Keratha is righteous?"

One of the men on the line shouted, and the soldiers gripped their spears and shields tightly. Valette recognized they were preparing a charge.

*"Aye, and she may have been here since the beginning. This means the Zal'Kerathan must be reevaluated. Seek out this Chosen. See what use she would be to us now,"* Almir said.

"She murdered a man under my care. I must see to her execution."

The rebels smashed into the army of soldiers. They buckled back, but there were no breaks in the line. Their hands worked furiously as they thrust spears into the rebel forces.

*"Actions often do not fall into right or wrong. With what we've seen, it may be that the Zal'Kerathan is as committed to justice as we are. Find her, so that we may make a true determination."*

"You yourself said that murder can never be abided."

*"And yet I armed you with the tools to kill when needed,"* Almir answered, his temper flaring. A moment later, he seemed to calm. *"I cannot be angry with you for obeying my commands. You grew among my most faithful. Do as I say now, please. And know that your fathers taught you well."*

"I will. I miss them deeply," Valette said.

The soldiers began pushing forward. If they weren't careful, their lines could break on a countercharge. She didn't want to stay and find out, lest she be labeled as a member of the Akaran forces.

*"I know, as I know you miss your own children. You worry that your actions here dishonor them. I assure you they do not. It will not be long before you go to see them. Our work in the city is nearly finished. I warn you, these last days will be all the more trying."*

Valette nodded and began making her way toward a nearby alley when a familiar face stepped from the fog. His aged visage looked wrong beneath the steel of a guard's helmet.

"Otto, what are you doing here?" she asked.

"I ought to ask you that, Chosen Bilaut. As well as where your armor walked itself off to," he said. A pained smirk graced his face accentuating his wrinkles.

"Things have become complicated."

"No longer welcome in the Solar Dominion, are we?" he asked.

Valette froze. Of course she shouldn't have risked coming so close to their front with the rebels. If Ryn was here, he'd already given them the order to kill Chosen on sight.

Otto's eyes widened in recognition, and this time, the smile that graced his face was more genuine. "Worry not, lass. I have a place for you. We both walk in Almir's light."

# CHAPTER TWENTY-EIGHT

# THE DOCTOR

SOPHIA MASSAGED HER NECK for what felt like the hundredth time since they'd left the library. The Aoxian's portal had taken them to a darkened alley, hours later than it should have been. As far as she knew, she and Katri had escaped the dungeon sometime during the morning, and it seemed now that night was fast approaching.

Ilara groaned as she hung between Katri and Sophia, arms draped over their shoulders. She'd passed out just after the portal closed. Sophia had panicked until she found her sister's pulse and, even now, Ilara's chest seemed to heave violently with each breath. When Sophia removed Ilara's armor, she had seen a patch on her chest that looked like black moss. Katri learned from the Aoxian that a Scholar had hit Ilara with a spell of some kind—he didn't know what.

*Ilara is going to be fine*, Sophia told herself again. So long as they got to wherever this Aoxian was leading them.

The gold-scaled lizard turned down another one of the winding alleyways toward a doctor Sophia had never heard of. Katri had recognized the name in Aoxian and relayed the information. She'd assured Sophia that they were trustworthy, but it didn't help Sophia's confidence that the Aoxian was limping badly. Katri, despite the blood that had matted the fur of her lupine body, bore no sign of injury once she'd transformed back into her human form.

Sophia tried to swallow, and her throat scratched against itself. The ache in her throat and stomach hit her all at once as the thrill of escaping the Solar Dominion subsided. The lack of food and water was catching up with her, not to mention that her muscles ached fiercely.

"Only a little further," Balan said to her, as if that was enough to coach her on.

Sophia nodded, grateful that she could hear him as well as the song that flowed around her. The city was alive with noise and seemed to thrum beneath her feet, yet the waves of music she saw were all tinted red—the spell that Balan had warned her against. Whatever was happening here, it reeked with the sound of violence.

After what felt like miles of walking, Chek'Va leaned against an alley corner and gestured toward a metal door with a closed slit at eye level. It was clear that he lacked the strength to open it. Looking closer, Sophia saw there was no handle on the outside. It reminded her of the secret lairs she'd imagined villains had in fairy tales.

"Can you hold her?" Katri asked. Her breath smelled like lavender.

It took Sophia a moment to realize she was talking to her. "Aye. Be quick," she grunted as Katri shifted Ilara's full weight onto her. Sophia leaned over and slammed her free hand onto the alley wall to keep herself and her sister from hitting the ground.

Katri eyed her, but strode up to the door. Using both hands, she produced a complicated series of knocks. Sophia recognized the rhythm as one of the tunes written by the Masked Twins, an Aoxian musical duo. They'd been chased from the Akaran Empire a decade ago.

Several moments later, the slit creaked open to reveal a pair of yellow serpentine eyes. "Name and condition," their owner growled in the Akaran tongue.

"Katri. I'm here with Thorn, sister of Thorn, and an Aoxian."

"Chek'Va," the golden lizard growled.

"We're all in various stages of ill. Chek'Va has multiple under-scale wounds, and Thorn's been cursed. The sister is doing the best of all of us," Katri gasped.

*Ilara's been cursed?* Sophia's thoughts spiraled. She didn't know much about that kind of magic, but it was an ailment one never truly recovered from. According to the stories, a curse sapped one's energy until there was none left. It could be battled back, but it was never truly healed. Such a wound reshaped the way people lived.

"Thorn?" another voice behind the door said hurriedly. Unlike the first, this one was higher pitched and enunciated so well that it sounded almost regal in comparison.

The door screeched open to reveal a stocky black-scaled Aoxian sitting on a stool. Overtaking him, a taller lizard rushed to Ilara and Sophia. His red scales were streaked with gold, and he had a long spiked tail. He easily stood three feet taller than the women, yet handled himself with a delicate grace.

"Quickly, now," he said.

Sophia all but fell forward before Katri caught Ilara's other arm. She helped the sisters over the threshold and into a clean, well-lit room with a large rune-covered table in the center. It hovered over the floor, powered by magics that Sophia couldn't pretend to understand. Chek'Va followed and assisted the women in lifting Ilara onto the table, which shifted slightly beneath her weight.

The red-scaled lizard pushed Sophia out of the way. He used a long claw to cut Ilara's tunic down the center, revealing the whole of the black mark. It was fuzzy and had spokes like a star, and it pulsed over the left side of Ilara's chest. Several of the points reached around the side of her ribcage. It was still growing, the arms of the star lengthening as if it were consuming her.

The lizard turned back to Sophia and stretched out his claw. "Mal'Evir, at your service, ma'am." He gave a slight bow as she took his claw in a brief handshake. "You must be the sister, as I recognize these other two. Thorn has told me so much about you and your gift. She will be okay, but she will need my treatment and a good deal of rest."

Sophia's eyebrows furrowed. "I-I-I don't understand. Who are you? How do you know my sister?"

"Oh, did they not tell you? I am a physician," he muttered, as if it were obvious. He busied himself with inspecting the table. After he'd touched several characters, it began to glow a dull red.

"But you're an Aoxian? And this looks like no treatment I've seen before," Sophia said.

"Yes, yes, yes. And if you'd heard of this treatment, you'd no doubt be administering it. I resided in Eversburg long before your people and mine started their political spat. When it began, going elsewhere was not an option. Certainly not Aoxia. This is my home. Or did you mean to ask how I survived the paladins corralling each and every one of my kin and executing them? I have talents, and there are those who appreciate them. The Gray, specifically, are my benefactors. Not that it appears to matter anymore."

Sophia's eyes widened.

"City has to have her pleasure," Katri said dryly.

Sophia knew Gray organized crime in Eversburg, and she'd certainly had her own run-ins with them—with Jonas, of all people. Yet she'd never surmised they were who Ilara worked for. She felt like a fool for not concluding that sooner.

"Ever-long in Eversburg," Mal'Evir retorted.

He went back to applying a green salve to her sister's chest. He gave several directions in Aoxian to the black-scaled lizard, who left the room and returned with several humans dressed in the familiar dark garments of attending physicians. They immediately began dressing Chek'Va's wounds. Amid the flurry of activity, a clay cup was stuffed in Sophia's hands. It appeared to contain water.

"Both Thorn and I worked with Gray for a long time," Katri said. "I left, and I hoped she would as well. The people

Jonas made her kill were well beneath her. Honestly, I never thought I'd see her again."

Ilara knew Jonas. The letter Sophia had received recommending her to him hadn't been coincidental after all. The underworld hadn't known Sophia needed money. Ilara had. A sickening feeling rose up in Sophia's stomach. What else had her sister lied about? She'd rescued Sophia from the Solar Dominion, but how had she known to look in the library? Why had she contracted Aoxians to do it?

A pit formed in Sophia's stomach. "I knew she killed, but I never bothered to ask for whom. It never mattered to me before whether it was drug smugglers or the Akaran army. I guess it shouldn't matter now. You know El— I mean, Thorn?" she asked Katri.

"Aye. We were in that bloody gang together. Basically partners. If I'd known she was your sister, I would have told you to stop your fretting. Thorn's saved my life more times than I can count."

"If I could have some quiet, please. This is a delicate ritual," Mal'Evir said, touching part of the runic etchings on the table.

It creaked as it changed from stone to emerald, a slightly darker green than the salve smeared across Ilara's chest. The curse mark began to sizzle, and smelled like cooked meat. Ilara gasped as her skin turned a shade pinker. The black moss began to throb faster.

"Zel ver ka'an do hai cais," Mal'Evir recanted. He placed his open claw upon Ilara's forehead.

Steam rose from her chest and flowed into a bracelet on Mal'Evir's arm. He spoke more, but Sophia couldn't make it out, her eyes transfixed by her sister's pained face.

Finally, the doctor withdrew his hand, and the emerald glow lessened for a moment, then deepened again. The sizzling sound ceased, and Ilara's eyes popped open. She gasped large mouthfuls of air, her chest heaving as her hand came to her forehead. "Almir and Akara, Mal! What bloody happened?" she asked.

"I'll explain in a moment. Don't move. The procedure is still underway," Mal'Evir said as he placed an open claw on Ilara's collar bone. He removed a stone bracelet around his wrist and placed it in a small cutout around the center of the curse. Emerald mist still flowed from her chest to the bracelet. "You took a powerful curse. If I didn't know better, I would have said it looked like it came from a divine. These three dragged you in here, so thank them for your life before you pay me."

Ilara's eyes flicked from Chek'Va to Katri before landing on Sophia. She smiled before frowning. "We're all alive? Thank the gods—at least Markus didn't lie about that. Good to see you, Soph."

Sophia nodded. With all the thoughts that whirled about her head, she wasn't entirely sure what to say. She didn't have words for them at this moment.

"Chek'Va says that you brought this with you," Katri said, placing a spear of black metal along the wall next to Ilara. "Seems like it might be a powerful weapon."

"Aye," Ilara said as she glanced back at it. Not only was the end made of that black metal, but it appeared to be creeping down the pole as well, as if it were trying to strengthen the weaker wood. "That has already saved my hide more than once. I guess it can't do anything against Scholar curses. How the hells did you end up in the Dominion, Kat?"

"That's a hell of a question to ask me after the last time we saw each other," Katri said.

"Ah, you know how the Syndicate is. They would have skinned me alive if I talked to a former member. I can't count the number of contracts for you I turned down. Though I guess we're both in that boat now," Ilara said.

"Aye? And how'd you cut that tie?" Katri's arms hovered out to her sides like they had the first time she transformed into her lupine form.

"I killed the cunt, Jonas," Ilara said with a smirk.

Katri paused, as if unable to comprehend the statement. "Bloody hells. Probably shouldn't have brought you here, then."

"Aye. No sense in hiding it, though. Mal probably already knows," Ilara responded.

Sophia tensed as she realized their situation. Mal'Evir hovered near the bulkier Aoxian, who had a large sword strapped to his back. His gaze was on the door that they all had stumbled through, as if he weren't following the conversation.

"I am aware of the sins of the woman on my table. I am, however, a doctor first and a Syndicate member second. I will have to send the bill for this procedure to your synd. However, it can wait until after your recovery," Mal'Evir said.

Ilara nodded curtly, and her face turned white. The curse sizzled on her chest again, and the emerald light darkened. She sucked in a sharp breath, then her eyes flitted closed.

"She'll be like that for a while," Mal'Evir explained. "Every time the treatment kicks in, it will render her unconscious, then wake her once complete. The curse is draining her energy, trying to cling to life. While I'm at it, I ought to mention that this ailment of hers will take several days before dissipating. She'll need uninterrupted bed rest. Not to mention, if we're to keep her from meeting her Dark Lady, we'll need her to remain on the table until morning. Can I trust you to remain here with her? We've had an influx of new patients that I must attend to."

Sophia nodded, gripping her still-untouched cup. One of the aids placed a chair next to Ilara, and Sophia took a seat. "Since the rest of us aren't with the Syndicate, do we owe you anything for the visit?" she asked.

Mal'Evir nodded, then looked at Ilara. "We'll discuss that when your sister wakes. I, of course, must mention that curses are tricky. I can't promise she won't live with the effects for the rest of her days, even after we've quelled it. Now, what happened to you?"

"Paladin. They— Ah!" She gasped as Mal'Evir placed a claw on her shoulder, using one of his long nails to pull her skin tight around her neck, where the band had burned her.

"A band that blocked your divine powers, I assume? Which god do you serve?"

"B-B-Balan," Sophia stammered, suddenly nervous from the amount of attention his green eyes were giving her. Katri's relaxed posture seemed to tell her she could trust the tall lizard.

"Akarans attacking bards now? The situation must be dire for them. Balan has been kind to me, though not all Aoxians feel the same. It looks like you have a few remaining fibers in that burn of yours, which could affect your ability to channel.

They really should caution you when they put these godsforsaken death traps on. Channel too much and it could have killed you."

"I warned her. Can you do anything about it?" Katri asked.

"Hold still. This will be painful," Mal'Evir warned as he rubbed two of his claws together. He directed them, pinched together, at her neck and started gently brushing against the burn.

The sensation was like being brushed by a cactus. Sophia clutched the arms of her chair and closed her eyes. Her chest tightened, and each breath came harder than the last. Tears formed in the corners of her eyes, and she couldn't hold them back.

After several minutes of excruciating pain, Mal'Evir patted her knee. When she opened her eyes, the room was awash in streams of music that hadn't been there before, as if he'd unclogged a blockage in the flow of magic and it was all exploding out of her senses at once.

"That is wonderful," Sophia gasped.

"Always is." Mal'Evir smiled, and Sophia detected more than a hint of satisfaction in it. "You're all more than welcome to stay in the clinic for as long as you need. We have room enough for the lot of you. But you must take your medicine." He clapped the cup of water back into Sophia's hand.

"I thought this was just water," she said.

"Well. It is."

# Chapter Twenty-Nine

# Licking Wounds

Red and black dots peppered the backs of Ilara's eyelids. They darted around erratically, creating complex patterns. She felt her body lift from Mal'Evir's runic table. She imagined it to be a gurney, one that glided on felt pads across the clean limestone floors of the clinic. She couldn't recount the number of times she'd been in the clinic, and she had a solid mental map of it now. Not that it mattered—she didn't have the strength to lift a finger.

A part of her still couldn't believe that Markus had betrayed her. She'd trusted him too much. It wasn't a mistake she'd make again.

Weightlessness engulfed her as her body was lifted and placed, somewhat roughly, on another mattress. The sensation was irritating. She could sense the environment around her with no feasible way to interact with it. Like she was aware she was asleep. Was this what death felt like?

Not long after she'd been moved, the red and black dots morphed and transformed, and soon a plane of red stretched out before her. They coalesced above her into a huge red sun that hung low over the new horizon. The world around her seemed to breathe color, as if annoyed that it was caught in the amber light.

The dirt below Ilara, still reddish, had a hue of darkness, as if mixed with black sand. A cool breeze lapped her face. Then a gust hit her and kicked up the sand around her, which buffeted her like a flurry.

Ilara was standing on a massive dune, looking out over an empty valley. Jagged edges jutted out of the sand, like once solid structures that had been eroded by centuries of being exposed to the elements. The dune beneath her feet shifted and set her down on a stone floor. She soon found herself atop a large rectangular tower, looking out over crumbled buildings.

She blinked, and when she opened her eyes, Zal'Keratha was standing before her, holding her side in pain. The goddess's dress flowed in the breeze around them. Blood stained her blue-gray hands and arms and streaked her lips. One of her massive horns glinted in the red sunlight, revealing a crack that ran from its base. Her dress had a new tear across the stomach, revealing a massive burn.

Zal'Keratha looked at Ilara  with hunger. "You know where the altar is?" she demanded.

"I don't. We were betrayed by Ameri. We made it out alive to serve another day," Ilara said, feeling a pit in her stomach.

"I am aware of Ameri's treason. I recognized her ploy after we spoke, though I was unable to warn you," Zal'Keratha said, her eyes narrowing.

"What happened to you?" Ilara asked. She hoped the misdirection would distract the goddess. She had brought her spear to the assault, the thing Zal'Keratha had commanded her not to do. Ilara didn't want to argue the point now.

"I sought Aox. Ameri commanded her Chosen to murder the Aoxians, to murder god. I barely stopped them."

"Is she dead, then?" Ilara asked.

"No." The response was cold and remorseful. "She escaped. Her Sight foresaw me. I turned the battle against her, however. The blood on my hands is mortal blood. They have been escorted to my realm." A tear formed in her eye and ran down her face, dropping to the desert below them.

"Aox will be a steadfast ally now that you saved his life. This place is new—where is it?" Ilara asked.

"New to you, perhaps. It is an old world far from Aerlia and any other place you've ever seen. It orbits a star unfamiliar to your skies, a place I've not been to in eons. No power rules this land since long ago, yet it has great value to me. My home. A place I must go to lick my wounds and prepare for the coming battle. A place where Ameri's Sight cannot see."

Ilara tried to picture the empty wasteland covered in a sprawling civilization of people who looked like the horned goddess. "It might have been beautiful once. What happened?"

"My people were vast. We had gods of our own who protected us, and we had technology of which you can only dream. Yet we peered into the void above us and were not prepared for it. There are powers that prey on life lurking in the darkness between worlds. My people made noise enough for them to find us, and our gods could not save us from the hunger that burned beyond. They all perished. My people. Our gods. "

Ilara nodded. "I would have liked to have seen it when it lived."

"It is a future we endeavor to prevent for your world," Zal'Keratha said weakly.

"Are we in danger now?"

"More than you know. The screams of the slaughtered Chosen sing to these entities. Should Akara continue with her plans, the beasts will be upon Aerlia before we can prepare."

"Does Akara really want that? What could we possibly do?" Ilara asked.

"Akara and Ameri never believed these creatures existed. That they were horror stories told by the gods before us to scare us into cooperating. Fools both. Aox believes we are doomed to the void already. He created his people on Aerlia so that you might be able to defend yourselves. You can see how that has worked—Akara has slain the mighty dragons. The rest of us craft our Chosen into champions capable of killing them when the time comes."

"How do you know that will work?"

Zal'Keratha considered the barren earth they stood on, seemingly weighing her response. "We do not, in truth. It requires time to build such creatures, perhaps longer than we have. The Pantheon was created to protect the peoples of Aerlia until the Chosen are ready. I and six other gods poured our energy into that great weapon for nearly a century before Akara stole it from us. She uses our power to create her army of Chosen. It was never sustainable, as we can now merely manifest ourselves as ghosts in your world. We are but a shade of our former glory."

"How is the Pantheon a weapon? I thought it was merely the combined power of the gods."

Zal'Keratha hummed thoughtfully. "It is more than that. Should you take Akara's mantle, I will explain then."

"You once said that when you reached the altar you would enact judgment on Akara. What did you mean by that?"

"If you are asking if I'd kill her, know that I cannot. Her soul would be like a beacon to the void, and Aerlia would be a doomed world. There is a prison for gods who defy their sacred duty. It is there I would put her."

"How many gods are there?" Ilara asked.

"On Aerlia? Less than a hundred. I couldn't name all the lesser deities. In this universe, there are thousands for whom the void hungers," Zal'Keratha told her.

"And, once this is all done, once you have Akara's altar, you would become queen?"

"Yes. That is what must be done. I doubt I will be the one to do so—the one who reigns must rally the gods to fight the threat of the stars. Akara neglects her duty to this day. My plan to overthrow her is a simple one, but you must be the one to carry it out. It hinges on Ameri's Chosen having found the altar already. Find him and defeat him. This is your task."

As the foreign sun set, Zal'Keratha dissipated, and so did the world around her. When Ilara opened her eyes, she was staring at the bottom of a rotten bunk. The room she was in held two sets of bunkbeds, four beds total. At Ilara's foot was an uneven stone wall on which hung a painting of Aox. The paint was cracked, and much of the color had left it.

Aox's faded purple-streaked scales were a pale representation of the god who'd sat on a throne at the top of the massive pyramids of Aoxia. Sadness panged Ilara when she thought about how he'd tried to save them.

Sophia sat on the bottom bunk across from Ilara. She was absentmindedly plucking the strings of an old, weather-beaten lute. Ilara recognized the lazy tune; it was a melody Sophia had often sung when they were teenagers, about life and love with a boy in the guard. Sophia adored songs of unrequited love, and many tavern owners paid for her performances with room and board. Soldiers loved that particular song enough to be distracted from their pockets being picked clean.

Sophia was different now. There was a deep frown on her face, and Ilara couldn't overlook the scarred burn on her neck. Her hair was frizzy and dirty, and her hands looked like they'd seen their share of blood. Still, nothing could reduce the beauty of her face, and Ilara hoped they wouldn't add more scars by the time they left Eversburg.

That was the thing she realized in that quiet room before Sophia noticed she was awake. They had to leave this place together, the sooner the better. Zal'Keratha wouldn't appreciate it if they didn't find the altar first, which meant they needed to get into the Solar Dominion again, as quickly as possible. Sophia needed to agree, though. No more would Ilara go behind her back.

"Welcome back to reality," Sophia said, snapping Ilara from her meditations.

Ilara glanced at the lute. "What crevice did you pull that antique out of?" She tried to sit up. Stars raced into her vision, and she fell back to the thin mattress.

"It's one of Mal'Evir's. His study is littered with artifacts. I also saw a memory bowl, though he wouldn't let me near it. Are you feeling better?" Sophia asked, though her attention was still partially on the music coming from the instrument.

"Aye, probably still need a few days." Ilara pulled up the collar of her tunic. There was a well-defined star pattern of new skin where the curse had grown. It would scar nicely. "How are you feeling?" she asked Sophia.

"Certainly better out here. Thank you for bringing our Aoxian friend. Katri and I would have died in the library." Sophia set the lute aside and crossed her arms.

"It's the least I could do considering I got you in there."

"Aye," Sophia said with an eye roll. "You did quite a bit. I fully blame Akara, though. She declared war on Balan, and I'm the one who bore the brunt of that action. What have you been up to while I was locked away?"

Ilara brought her sister up to speed on how Markus and the Aoxians had assisted in attacking the Solar Dominion. "What are you going to do about Akara?" she asked after she finished.

"I talked with Balan about it. He doesn't want to challenge the queen of the gods. He says we don't have the power." Sophia went quiet for a moment, as if trying to muster the courage to speak. "I want them to pay for what they did to us. To Katri. To you. To the Librarian. To me." She spoke quietly, but Ilara heard the determination and anger in her voice.

"Good." Ilara smiled. She would take everything she could from her sister's new resolve. The gods knew she would need a helper in the coming days. "Zal'Keratha demands I continue the onslaught. We'll need to get back to the Solar Dominion, and I have a lot I need you to do."

Sophia scoffed. "Well, I am glad you're feeling well enough to boss me around."

"Chek'Va and Katri, too. We have to contend with Markus's Sight to get to Akara. I have a plan, but it's a long shot. Where are the other two?" Ilara asked.

"Katri went out to scout the city. There are riots that aided our escape. Chek'Va went to find Aox," Sophia said. A trill echoed softly from the lute as she started plucking it again.

"Zal'Keratha mentioned Aox was safe, but she seemed to have taken some wounds in the process."

"One thing I don't understand. What does Ameri benefit from betraying both Zal'Keratha and Akara? Seems like she'll be fighting a two-sided war."

"Ameri wants the throne and doesn't care who she pisses off to get it. She'll have her Chosen defend her when she ascends, and she thinks her Sight is stronger from the Pantheon's power. Has Balan truly not chosen a side? Even after your torture?" Ilara asked.

"He hasn't. He doesn't understand why he needs to. He's the god of music, not war, and he would prefer peace. He views my imprisonment as inconvenient, but he believes Akara will come to her senses. I don't have to agree with him." Sophia shrugged. "So long as he gives me leave to participate, I'll not be Forsaken."

"Part of me wants to leave and let Zal'Keratha win her bloody throne by herself," Ilara muttered.

"You would be Forsaken for such an act. No power. Everything you've worked for would be gone, and we'd have to deal with a furious goddess. What would you do?"

"I'm still skilled with a blade," Ilara said. "Any mercenary company would be glad to have me. Or I could serve as a lord's palace guard across the sea in Nox, far away from Akara and her wretched empire. I don't think both of us will leave this city alive. I nearly died rescuing you."

"You'd be hunted by anyone trying to gain Zal'Keratha's favor. Forsaken never get to just disappear. And you wouldn't have been able to free me without Zal'Keratha or Aox. Is that not worth keeping your end of the bargain?" Sophia asked.

Ilara shook her head. "There wouldn't have needed to be a rescue if I didn't serve Zal'Keratha. We could live our lives in peace. But, it's not really a question. I have to continue serving her."

Sophia shook her head. "Don't lie to me, Ilara. Ever since we were kids, you had to be the center of Aerlia. If we left now, that guilt would kill you, knowing that you could have changed the world. Not to mention, look at the people here. You would let them perish under the boot of Akaran paladins? I won't stop you if it's the choice you need to make, but I think it's the wrong one."

Ilara nodded. There was an injustice in this city, and it needed to be righted. There wasn't any reason that Ilara, or Sophia, needed to be the one to do it, aside from the fact that they could. Did Zal'Keratha have the right to the Pantheon's power? Ilara didn't know, and she had the feeling that the goddess was keeping something from her—something more important than void beasts. Her eyes flicked to the black metal spear, resting against the side of the bunk.

"Well." Ilara winced. Her chest flared with pain as she pulled herself up. "As I said, I'll need some assistance from you. There are some ideas I need to put into action."

"I don't leave Eversburg until you do," Sophia told her.

"Good. First thing, there's a boy at the south end of Noon that I need you to check on."

# CHAPTER THIRTY

# THE RITE

VALETTE FOLLOWED OTTO AS he led her away from the carnage quickly unfolding on the main street. He assured her that he wouldn't be missed; they'd lost so many that he would be assumed to be among the dead. Valette couldn't help but think about what would happen when Al-Kaise got to the revolutionaries. There was great power in her, a goddess's power, that the soldiers and paladins couldn't emulate.

"I forgot you were a combat veteran," Valette said.

"Not that it matters," Otto huffed, pausing at a corner to inspect the street sign. He was breathing heavily. "Turns out those poor peasants that we weren't supposed to be worried about have some weapons that cut through paladin armor as if it's nothing. There are so many dead that they're putting anyone they can in steel wrapping and throwing a shoddy weapon in their hand. Us guard weren't excluded. Truthfully, those rebels will be at the Solar Dominion before the day is out."

He turned down a street headed south, Valette striding beside him. The air of the city was calm, and she noticed that the windows of the buildings around her were boarded up tight. It was as if the residents were preparing to weather a storm rather than a war. It had been the same way in Vash'gal'or all those years ago. No one had bothered to leave their homes, as if a battle were merely an inconvenience rather than something to be feared.

"How did you know I'd need help?" Valette asked as Otto strolled confidently down the middle of the street.

"When you first arrived in the city, our valiant knight, Almir, came to me in a dream and assured me that I would be integral to his plans in the future. So I remained vigilant to Akara's plans and how I might help you see them. I didn't imagine I'd be hands-on like this."

"So, you directed me to see the sacrifice of the Akaran that defied Tezza," Valette said.

"Truth. I did not want to let the Akarans on to our trail. There were other ideas I tried to lead you to that bore no fruit." They approached a rather unassuming shop that had sign that read "Knightly Tailors" handing in the window. "We have arrived," Otto said as he popped open a green door and ushered her into the faint candlelight.

An ornate desk sat in the dark foyer with a closed door on either side of it. A cloaked figure sat behind it, a veil covering their face and robes hiding their form. Only their pale hands, folded neatly in front of them, peeked out from under their billowing sleeves. In many Almiran temples, this figure was represented by a statue, but here it was clearly a living person.

"Guide," Valette said with a smile.

The role of a guide at an Almiran temple was to present an unbiased choice to returning parishioners and newcomers. There were only ever two options: chapel worship or meditation rooms. The selection wasn't the point. The guide created a barrier between the temple and the outside world to force the worshiper to make a choice. If one's heart wasn't prepared, it was ideal to choose meditation before surrendering oneself to Almir's worship.

The decor here perfectly mimicked the foyer of the Almiran temple in Chrys, with white-and-black curtains hanging from the walls. That familiar sense of home washed over Valette.

"Light and Grace be upon you," the guide said. As Valette and Otto became visible in the low light, Valette saw the fingers of their exposed hands stiffen. "I-I-I mean, Chosen."

Guides were meant to speak androgynously, but the flustered person in front of them spoke with subtle hints of a woman's voice.

"Thank you, guide of our ever-gracious Redeemer," Valette replied.

"Um, how can the chapel assist you, Chosen? And priest?" the guide said.

Valette almost laughed at the ridiculousness of being called a priest before she remembered she wasn't the only one in the room. "You're a priest, Otto?" she asked.

"Indeed. I apologize for not making my station known to you sooner. We'll need use of the chapel, dear," he said to the guide, who nodded and gestured toward the door to her right.

Valette nodded and followed Otto through it. A humble sanctuary greeted them, beckoning them to sit in their pews and pray at its altar. It was a room well used and appreciated, and a musk hung in the air. Valette found herself walking quickly to the altar, where a large circular basin sat in front a statue of Almir, his clean-shaven face gazing downward.

"What else did you mislead me on?" Valette asked.

"I apologize for falsifying my past. It is true I fought in Akara's war as you did. However, I only found worship of Almir there. He did not Choose me. Through his teachings did my soul heal from the atrocities I committed. This chapel needs a cleansing rite," Otto said, taking a seat in one of the pews. "I've meant to do so for some time. You may find some benefit to it."

Valette nodded and removed the glove from her left hand, picking up a dagger from the altar before her. The clean steel of the blade glinted. She cut her palm from the thumb to the fifth digit. Closing the hand into a fist, she held it out over the basin.

Blood dripped down and splattered onto the copper, filling her nostrils with a metallic scent. She was reminded of battle, defending the innocent and frightened, and killing Maer. When she opened her eyes, a small pool of red had formed.

"Bless this place, Might of the Light, Defender of a Thousand Sons. Let not this place fall to Starlight, and hold these souls in your strong arms. Heal their wounds as you grant me the grace to heal my own." Valette tapped the channel, and light filled her palm as she finished the ritual. When she unclenched her fist, the cut was perfectly healed.

She wiped the dagger on her tunic and placed it back on the altar. When she turned, her vision flooded with light. Buildings of amber light grew around her, as if summoned by her ritual. Where they stopped, she couldn't tell.

Figures of light formed around her, all bowed in reverence. Valette wasn't standing anymore but seated on a massive throne, her arms gripping the sides as if it were the most important thing in her life.

Time seemed to slow for her, every moment stretching into an eternity, then flowed against her as if she was standing in a river of it. Her mind became vast, and she felt Aerlia. The mountains of Kaladan standing firm and tall. The Maka-maka trees of Tarha waving in the wind. The desert sand of Algantha being blown across a sandstone wall. The waters of the Crystal Sea splashing against an unfamiliar coast. She stood among the spires of Aoxia, then in the grain fields of Granthea. Her body seemed to hang high above Aerlia, staring down at it as if it were a globe sitting on a desk.

Then she felt it. A presence wormed through her thoughts, as if there were another creature in her skull. Unlike Almir's presence, she could sense whatever it was squirming.

"*Oh. And who is this?*" it asked. It was trilling and soft.

*What?* Valette thought.

"*Curious, how did this one join us? They are not bound to her,*" another voice said, this one booming and commanding. "*We ought to remove her from our mind.*"

"*No. She could be my host,*" the first answered.

"*Fool, this one has not the power to conduct you to divinity,*" the second snarled.

Valette felt her brow knit when she noticed the large amber sun in the sky. These creatures were talking about taking control of gods.

*"Of course we are. How else does one consume power? Should we be like the lesser ones, who feed on Chosen?"* the first voice asked.

*"You saw how our host's angels bowed before us? So shall all of the servants of your gods. It is inevitable, little one,"* the booming one said.

*How? How is that possible?* Valette thought.

*"We consume all,"* the booming presence said again. *"There is no end to our hunger. Our thirst for revenge against the divine shall never sate. Your time is short, or we shall consume you as we have this one."*

*"Even now, the Zal'Kerathan brings us more into your world, Aerlia,"* the other voice said.

*"Indeed. A useful pawn, Death always is. On every world, Death calls us. We come to end the suffering. Get in our path again, and you will know your share of it,"* the booming presence added.

Valette blinked, and she found herself on a mattress in a dark room. Moonlight glinted off the blade she'd stolen from Ryn's paladin. It was close to midnight, yet Otto was sitting in a chair near the bed she lay in, concern etched onto his face.

"Are you alright?" he asked.

Valette sat, rubbing her head, which felt like it had split in two. "Aye, I had a strange vision. I know not what it means or how it happened," she said.

"You've been out cold since the rite. Many of our remaining parishioners began to doubt you were Almir's Chosen. Almir's light, I've not heard of any vision during a such a simple ritual," Otto muttered. The sounds in the room seemed to dampen, if that was possible. He looked at her with earnestness in his eyes. "Tell me everything."

Valette did. She described the vision in as much detail as she could. When she finished, Otto had a strange look on his face.

"You must find this Zal'Kerathan. I could not hazard a guess as to the creatures you spoke with, but they sound dangerous. If she is aiding them in any way, even unintentionally, then we must prevent her."

"And what of Akara? What of Ryn?" Valette asked. This vision would not make her forget the atrocities she'd seen.

"Inconsequential. Or related. You were in the mind of a god, don't you see? You can't rule out it being Akara, or not. This could lead you to her," Otto said.

Valette frowned and crossed her arms. It felt too easy to make that movement without armor on. If Otto had been one of her superiors, she'd be compelled to do as he said. As a priest of Almir, his advice was little more than a suggestion.

*What do you suggest, Almir? Have you been listening?*

"*Aye*," he said, allowing a lengthy pause. "*I believe Otto may be correct. When you had the vision, I couldn't reach you. It was as if you'd died. The first scene you described sounded like Akara's realm. I too believe you should seek out this Zal'Kerathan. See if you can find out if she is aiding these creatures intentionally.*"

*Aye*, Valette agreed. Mayhap they are the reason she killed Senator Plithy. She felt giddy—she might be able to exact judgment on this assassin after all. It was the way it had to be. Valette knew in her bones it was the right course of action.

"Very well. Almir agrees," she said. "I have no idea where to begin with that."

"Well, you're on your way to starting. The rioters erected a barricade outside the Solar Dominion while you were out. Akaran paladins appear to be subverting it and killing Halga's Chosen throughout the city. We thought they were going to assist us, but they are clearly not concerned with the rebels. If this Zal'Kerathan is working with whatever this is in Akara's mind, then they might lead you to her."

"Gods, how much time did I miss?" Valette asked. As she stood, she took the stolen blade from the corner.

# Chapter Thirty-One

# THE PEARL

Eversburg's streets were empty save for decaying corpses and abandoned barricades, which made navigating the city's interior difficult. Sophia was astonished by the amount of blood the revolutionaries had spilled and how many of their own citizenry the paladins had killed in such short a time. The way Katri described it, the first days of the Revolution had been defined by lines that shifted up and down Noon. Now, the line was thoroughly entrenched in the Dawn district, making the lower districts safe from the war, but not from opportunistic bandits and looters.

Sophia stood outside the doors to The Pearl for the first time in weeks. It was conveniently close to Mal'Evir's clinic and had to be her first stop of the evening. The bar was built into a row of houses and businesses that resided on the north end of the Noon district. The doors and windows were barricaded with scorched and battered wooden planks.

Her sister's face flashed through her mind again, concern clearly etched on her brow. Even when Ilara spoke of leaving the city, there was a tiredness to it. She knew she couldn't escape the ramifications of the past few days.

Sophia took a deep breath and forced herself to the door. She knew she might not see anything but the red sound waves of battle. Balan continued to deny her use of them and refused to explain why. So, she needed help, and she hoped she could find it here.

Raising her closed fist, she swung it repeatedly at an exposed portion of the door. Shortly, a large-sounding voice echoed from inside. "Go away! Nothing left here but scared folk, and I won't let you hurt them."

"Glenda, it's Sophia," she shouted.

"Soph?" Glenda said. "Come around back, sweetie. No easy way to dig out the door."

The alleyway was littered with people who'd spent the last moments of their lives out in the chaos of the streets. Paladins and civilians both lined the walls. The stench of the corpses was akin to the smell of rotting steak and caused Sophia to gag.

Glenda propped the back door open as Sophia arrived. Her long shirt was pulled up to cover her mouth, revealing her barrel-shaped belly. Sophia wrapped her arms around the short, broad-shouldered woman. Glenda's curly hair smelled like rotten fish, and her chest was damp with sweat.

Despite everything, the familiarity soothed Sophia, until Glenda's burly arms wrapped her ribcage into a vise. "Glenda, I think you're crushing me," she squeaked.

"Oh, I know, sweetie," Glenda said as she released the embrace. "I'm just so glad to see my favorite singer. I was worried about you with the riots, like they'd take another joy from the world. Heard you were picked up by the pals a few weeks back. Come now, you must be starving. We have plenty of soup."

"Tempting," Sophia said, her words followed by a rumble from her stomach. Glenda's chicken soup was legendary, and it would beat the porridge Mal'Evir served in his clinic. "How did you shelter the riot?"

Glenda turned a nob and spoke a command word, and her oven roared to life with magical fire. She hefted a large steel pot from a nearby counter onto the stove.

"About as well as it gets. Still ongoing, last we heard. They rolled through Noon this afternoon. Terrible thing to hear all the death outside the door. Men screamed their last a hundred feet from us. Never thought we'd see so much death. Marty's upstairs. Took an arrow to the chest. He's fine, I hope. Bed rest is all we can give him now, though. His heart's still beating, and it don't look infected, thank the Pantheon."

"Was he in the riot?" Sophia asked, as she knew the tavern owner wasn't known to hold his own in any bar fight. The man would rather scramble for a closed room than face down an upset patron.

"Marty? No. Arrow flew in through one of the gaps in the windows. We were huddled in the upstairs apartments, hoping it would all blow over without looters. What has this world come to?" Glenda trailed off as she stared into the pot, not seeming to see it. "Where have you been hunkering down?" she asked.

"My sister has a friend on the other side of Noon. Very well-enforced town home. One of those prepared types. They took us in when the riot got bloody," Sophia said. She'd rehearsed this the whole way over. It was important that Mal'Evir not sound suspicious. She didn't need Glenda sending anyone to check on her.

Glenda ladled a healthy amount of soup into a wooden bowl and slid it in front of Sophia. The vapors of chicken broth wafted into her nostrils, and she nearly passed out. It was the most delicious thing she'd smelled in a month.

"Where were you when it happened? We were on the balcony watching the parade when the bomb went off. Could almost bloody see Tezza's face," Glenda said.

"I was closer than I wanted to be," Sophia told her.

"Alright. Be honest. I know you didn't come here for my hugs and soup."

Sophia nodded, suspecting that Glenda would see through her soon enough. No one would brave such dangerous streets just to check up on an old friend.

"I need to borrow Bleeder," she said.

"What for?"

"Ilara's worried about the kid of one of her friends. He's in the guard. Best scenario is that he hasn't been able to get home. Worse would be . . . Well, I'd like Bleeder's extra muscle for the trip."

"Aye. Bleeder's in the bar, though he's been drinking himself to oblivion most every day. I'll go fetch him for you." Glenda ambled from the kitchen through a large wooden door. Sophia heard her shouting Bleeder's name, followed by several bangs and the shattering of glass.

Moments later, the large, square-faced man burst through the same door. He moved to ladle some of the soup for himself. "'Phia," he said.

Sophia's heart sunk a little when she noticed new scars on his arms, which hadn't been there when she'd seen him last just outside her apartment. "Bleeder. Good to see you again," she said.

He was The Pearl's bouncer, and part of his compensation allowed him to live rent free in  the apartment above the bar. Glenda said their employees had always been late before she'd begun offering that stipend. Still, Sophia rarely saw Bleeder leave the place. He'd been one of the toughs for Jonas's gang when they first arrived in Eversburg. Sophia didn't normally say more than a dozen words to the man. He'd owed her a life debt, and now that it had been settled, she wasn't sure he'd help her.

"Who's the kid?" Bleeder grunted.

Sophia relayed everything her sister had told her. Son of a guardsman, likely didn't have anyone now. "We're just to check in, make sure his dad made it home safe," she said.

"And what if he didn't?" Bleeder asked.

"We'll have to get him off the street. I think he'd be safest here in The Pearl," Sophia said.

"Glenda agree to that?"

"She won't turn him away."

"Aye, you're right about that. Won't be bad—streets have been quiet the last few nights."

She waited for the man to finish slurping his soup, then he stumbled back to the barroom. Sophia rinsed and cleaned the bowls with a waiting bucket of water. The last thing she wanted to do was put more strain on Glenda. Bleeder returned wearing a tight-fitting set of leather armor. He was carrying a large mace that looked like nothing more than a stick with a spiked ball shoved on one end and an old metal shield that looked like it had been subject to many beatings.

The pair nodded to one another and departed using the same door Sophia had entered through. Bleeder was a man of few words, and Sophia was familiar with that. He grunted, and they walked out into the night.

The winter air nipped at their faces. Sophia hoped that doing this at night meant there was no chance they'd get caught up in any battles between the Revolution and the Paladins.

The silence between them ate at her. The last time she'd seen Bleeder, she'd absolved him of his life debt to her and Ilara. She wasn't sure if what she'd aske of him was overstepping the bounds.

"Not seen the shield before. Looks old, though," she said after a few minutes.

"Bought it when I came from the Southern Territories. Figured I'd need it after—"

"After Ilara and I saved your ass?" Sophia interrupted.

"Aye. I thought a big man with two hands on a mace would be more intimidating. A shield implies that you expect to be hit," he said.

"Hmm. Perhaps, there was a time in this city when that wasn't necessary. Those first years felt like heaven. I do remember the road here was busy."

"Aye, war does that. Empire went around and conscripted every sword-wielding maniac from the Crystal Sea to the Aerlian Strait. Paid them a dragon's hoard of gold and turned them all on the lizards. When they leave the war, they all come to Eversburg and try to sell those swords again. It's the only skill they have. Most of them don't find the work. Makes for a dangerous place," Bleeder said.

"I'm surprised you didn't want to fight in the war."

"Seen enough friends die. Thought the city would be different. Turns out that men like me only have one use."

Sophia was satisfied that Bleeder wasn't going to turn on her. They traveled on in silence. The moon shone above them like the watchful eye of a predator.

Every street in the Noon district looked like some kind of horrid battlefield, with dead strewn about for all to see. Occasionally, Sophia saw the dark spot of a shadow milling about—people, no more than vultures, picking the corpses clean of their valuables.

"Gods, there are so many," she muttered.

Bleeder grunted as they trudged onward.

Sophia's life in Eversburg had never been lush, but she'd never truly wanted for anything. Not like these revolutionaries, so discontented because of a lack of food and work. Would she stoop to killing a man if she felt her freedom was at stake? Was her freedom at stake? She thought about the beets she'd bought, her last purchase before the paladins arrested her. It had been all she could afford.

Bleeder stopped suddenly, and Sophia ran into his back, which felt like walking into a brick wall. Two figures were standing in the street ahead of them—a man and a woman. Each held a blade the length of Sophia's arm at their side. Their faces were set in a way that mirrored a paladin's. Terror bubbled in Sophia's stomach. She'd hoped Bleeder's presence would dissuade any bandits.

"Well, look what we have here, sister," the man said. He pointed the tip of his sword toward them. "A little dove out for a walk with her bodyguard, no doubt. Seeing the sights of our fair city?"

"Look, now. We don't want any trouble. Just like you, we have friends to check on," Bleeder said, and held his shield and mace up in a fighting position.

The man laughed, an empty hollow sound. "No. All my friends are dead. Killed by pals and left in the street for all to see. All except my sister, who is just so skilled at opening veins.

Now, we're taking what is rightfully ours. You'll pay our toll, or you'll pay Death's toll."

Sophia felt her breath catch in her throat. More figures hung at the edge of her vision, barely visible in the low light of the moon. She counted a half dozen, at least.

"We have nothing to pay you," Bleeder growled, settling back with his weapon held out defensively.

"The big man thinks he can fight all of us!" the man said with another mocking laugh. Moonlight caught his face, and Sophia realized that he was barely more than a boy. Guard armor hung lazily over his thin chest. He and his sister took several steps closer, stopping just out of Bleeder's reach.

Bleeder howled as he swung his mace in the man's direction, though it missed entirely. In moments, several thugs rushed forward and surrounded the larger man. Swords crashed against his shield and armor. Sophia saw them come back coated in blood. Bleeder's weapon and shield clattered to the stone street as he fell to the ground. The mob began kicking him as if he were a downed animal. Red sound waves engulfed her, that tempting, haunting melody of a life being taken.

Sophia's mind raced back to the Librarian's death. All she had done was watch as Markus commanded the Aoxian to kill him. The warm blood covered her face again, hands stained with blood she could have kept from spilling. Her mouth began to form words, but she barely thought them.

Feelings tempered,

Flee before me, cretins,

Your body altered,

See yourselves beaten,

And risen new.

New waves sprang from Sophia's song, wrapping around the melody of the dying man. She reached her hand into the wave and pulled forth the spell. The haunting melody left her lips when the face of the man who'd stopped them twisted and contorted. He froze, limbs held awkwardly in the air. Soon, the rest of the thugs were in similar stances. She felt her mind meld with theirs as it had with Plume and Bucket, and she forced upon them the idea of their flesh rotting. One of their cohorts fell over and rose again in undeath. She felt fear cascade through their minds.

"Oh, gods. Adias. Run! Run!" one of the men shouted, and dropped his weapon. He fled into a nearby alley way. Another looked at his arms and screamed, trying to wipe away the perceived rot.

The sister of the man who'd first spoken to them drove her blade into the neck of a thug. They tried to fight her off but couldn't. She dropped another man before fleeing down an alley herself.

The group dispersed as quickly as it had formed. The original speaker was left standing over Bleeder, his eyes wide, and Bleeder stared at him incredulously. He was holding a club up, frozen in the motion of bringing it down. Sophia felt the connection between their minds waver, as if she couldn't keep ahold of him.

"Sophia, what the bloody hells happened?" Bleeder asked as he held his hand to his side. Blood flowed around the palm, and Sophia assumed it was a deeper wound.

"Get up and away quick, Bleeder. He's resisting the vision, and I can't hold him long."

"What the fuck, 'Phia?" he asked again as he scrambled to pick up his mace. He stood, raised it, and cracked it against the man's head. The bandit fell to the ground with a thud, blood oozing from the impact area.

Bleeder fell back to the ground. Angling his back against a building, he tore a part of his trousers off. "How didn't I know you were Chosen? This kid bleeding Chosen too?" He asked as he wrapped the cloth around his torso. Blood quickly dampened the wounded area.

"Maybe. I don't know," Sophia replied as Bleeder spat at the ground. She could hear stones rattling. Sickened, Sophia realized it was the sound of teeth.

"Anyone at the bar know?"

"No. Not about me or the kid."

"We'll keep it that way. I owe you that much. Thought I was going to meet the Dead Lady today. Still might," Bleeder grunted.

"Glad we have an understanding," Sophia said. "I never asked—what happened to Jonas's gang? And how did you know the pals would be after me?"

"Jonas needed to get back at Thorn. He figured the two of you were related somehow and tipped off the pals. Thorn learned about that while you were locked up. I assumed Ilara is Thorn, though I could never tell through the cha'ak."

"Aye. She went after Jonas again, didn't she? While I was arrested?" Sophia couldn't believe her sister's need for blood. She didn't know how to feel. Instead of looking for a way to free Sophia from the mistake Ilara herself had made, her foolish sister had gone to take vengeance first.

"Aye, she did. Your sister has an angry streak. She nearly died filling this one. But she did kill him. The whole damned Syndicate knows that Thorn delivered Jonas to her Dark Lady. Markus tipped me, or I might have fallen to her blade."

"Horrible." Sophia shook her head. She had no love for Jonas or the Gray Syndicate. In fact, she felt sure that Aerlia was better without Jonas in it. So she wasn't sure why she felt so bad about it.

They sat next to each other in silence while Bleeder cleared his throat a few times and kept pressure on his wound until it stopped bleeding. The man he had killed stared between the two of them lifelessly.

The man Sophia had killed.

# Chapter Thirty-Two

# STRANGE VISITORS

Ilara was playing Kick the Dragon with Sophia and some of the boys from their town. Their short, stubby limbs moved awkwardly, as if they were learning to use them for the first time. Sophia's golden hair shone in the sun and made her look as beautiful as her laugh sounded. Ilara knew why the boys were playing with them and secretly hoped Sophia wouldn't pick one. None of them were worthy of her.

Ilara's foot connected with the scaled ball, and she felt the spines pierce her boot and bite her skin. It flew over the heads of the defending team and bounced off a tree at the edge of the field. The defenders scrambled after it, giving Ilara enough time to collect the leather mats and pull them to her team's side of the field.

No, that wasn't right. Kick the Dragon required her to stab each of the boys for the way they looked at Sophia.

Ilara's brow furrowed. That was still wrong.

She waved her hand through the thick grass and found she was able to dismiss it as easily as her daggers. A dream.

Days had passed slowly between bouts of Mal's treatment and sleep. She only had dreams like this while she was undergoing treatment. She was sitting in the now grassless meadow, watching the boys of her past chase after the spiky ball. Sophia giggled as she watched them fall over themselves to be the first to catch it. It had been a time of innocence, before Zal'Keratha. Before all the killing.

The field faded until it was barely a memory. A small light was hanging over Ilara, illuminating a small room. Black robes lined the walls, hoods up and facing away from her, draped over the shoulders of some dozen of the faithful. A single man sat on the floor in front of her. She hadn't asked for him, but here he was. His hood down, he stared at her intensely with emerald eyes. She knew the man well. Her master, Uto.

The cloaks slowly turned to her, hands and arms covered in decaying flesh, and each drew down their hood. They weren't Zal'Keratha's faithful. They were corpses.

Ilara recognized some of them. A portly woman who'd taught at the orphanage—she'd died for poisoning the children's food. A middle-aged man who ran an inn, whose son had tried to rape Sophia. The man's son next.

His sister after. They weren't all supposed to die, only the son. But Ilara had been sloppy back then.

More of them turned around, standing silently. Judging her. Each was like a corpse given life again. They moaned softly as they regarded Ilara.

She tried to feel guilty for killing them.

Most had meant nothing to her, all ordained by Zal'Keratha to die. A baker's son who extorted gold from the neighbors. A guard who whipped his subordinates. A mayor who killed his servants.

Ilara gasped as the final pair turned to her—a man with a glass eye standing next to a much shorter woman. She was plump, with a kind face that was half-rotted away, leaving one of her cheeks and half her jaw bare.

Ilara leaned to her and stretched out her arm. "Mother!"

The man next to her took a step forward and caught Ilara's neck in one of his hands. His gaze bored into her, the reflection of her face shining in his dead eye.

"Father," she grunted. Every other kill she'd want to feel guilty over, but with this one, all she felt was rage. His fingers tightened around her neck. His steely eyes burned red.

Ilara gasped as she opened her eyes. Hard wooden planks were under her back. There was blanket wrapped around her, pinching her arms and legs. Untangling herself, she pushed up to a sitting position. Tears fell from her eyes as she sat in the dark room. She thanked the powers that be she was alone—or at least she thought she was.

As her eyes adjusted to the darkness, she saw a familiar shadow sitting in the corner. She knew him before he stood. His hair was long and ragged, and he wore black leather armor. A shiver passed across her as he sat back in front of her, his emerald eyes staring back at her.

"Uto," she whispered. He wasn't a dream this time. His flesh was as real as her own.

"You can speak freely. No one can hear us in the clinic. I shouldn't have to remind you of that."

Ilara nodded. Uto's gift from Zal'Keratha was noise suppression. He could create zones of silence so that no sound could move into or out of his influence. At first, it had been a small zone around himself, but as he grew more powerful, he'd extended it to include others.

"I could not forget our Lady's gifts, master," Ilara said. She hadn't apprenticed in years, but the mentality came back to her in an instant. Uto had taught her nearly everything about killing and fighting.

"Indeed. She woke me to tell of your difficult opponent," he said.

"Aye. A Chosen of Ameri blocks my path. Zal'Keratha has tasked me with defeating him, and I know not how."

"You doubt your abilities?"

Ilara fumbled the rest of her blankets back onto the cot. "Odds are not good. We could use your skill as a Reaper," she said.

Uto immediately shook his head. "This is not my purpose. While much hangs in the balance, I was forbidden to offer you assistance outside of advice. Times are different now. When you were a fledgling Chosen, our mistress could allow me to walk the lands of men to train you in our ways. Now, all of her magic goes to you. I'm only here because she deems you unable to use your abilities. Because you have doubts. Zal'Keratha is worried you will fail this trial."

"Zal'Keratha cannot see the outcome of my struggle. How should I not doubt?"

"Yet she believes this is the correct course. We knew the altar was here when I was her Chosen, and we did not push for it. Only when you took my mantle did she wish for this. Your goddess believes you can accomplish this," Uto said, his face rigid.

Ilara fell silent. Did Zal'Keratha really believe she could achieve this impossible task? She seemed more insistent and impatient than this calculating goddess Uto was portraying. "I suppose she thinks I can," Ilara said.

"Then why do you worry?" Uto asked.

Ilara shook her head. She needed to be honest with him. His presence wouldn't do her any good if she wasn't. "Our Lady risks everything for the sake of this war. She doesn't see the cost of what she asks."

"You fear you will lose that which you fight for. But, if you do not fight, you will lose it anyway," Uto said.

"Aye. Even now, trapped in this clinic, I cannot protect everyone. Sophia could be dead, Theo made a martyr for his father's cause." Ilara wiped a tear from her eye. "Not to mention all who perish around us while I'm on this godsdamned cot."

"The dead do not provide for the living." Uto rasped the mantra that he'd drilled into Ilara's head. "If Zal'Keratha would sacrifice everything, you must be willing to do the same. Have you not yet learned? Death is not the end."

"That's easy for a dead man to say," Ilara scoffed.

"Perhaps." Uto chuckled. "If our mistress deems it necessary that I come from the grave again on your behalf, I'll make your stay in Death's domain all the more uncomfortable."

Ilara smirked and leaned forward to grab ahold of the man's cold hand. His skin felt brittle, as if he might fall apart at any moment. "I do miss our time together, Uto. I think of it often. What advice can you give me about this Scholar, Markus?"

"In my lifetime, I sparred with a single Scholar of Ameri. A fine woman, this Chosen was, and closer to the gods than many. She described to me once how the Sight functioned. It is not all-knowing, as you may think it is. There are ways to stretch it thin. More Scholars looking into it makes it weaker, so they see fewer paths. In addition, a Scholar can see no futures in which they are not involved or cannot conceive of. The more outlandish your scheme, the more likely they won't be prepared for it."

Ilara thought, but only for a moment. Markus had killed most of the Scholars in Ameri's Library, which would strengthen his Sight. That meant they had to find a guaranteed path to his death.

"I can work with that," she said with a frown. She knew the black metal worked well against Chosen. She could use it to block Markus's Sight. Zal'Keratha would hate that plan, however. "There is much Zal'Keratha does not tell me."

"This concerns you? That a goddess has secrets?" Uto asked.

"Aye. How can I trust her if she does not fully trust in me? How can I handle opponents she understands, yet I do not?"

"There will always be something she does not tell you. What she does not say protects us from whatever truth she hides. You ought not concern yourself with such things. Do what our goddess commands and you will have your victory against all who have ever wronged you."

Ilara cocked her head, catching sight of the spear. It was propped against the wall, tip sunken into the stone as it cut through it. Following Zal'Keratha's commands would mean leaving the powerful weapon behind.

"If that is all the help you are offering, then I dismiss you back to your rest."

"Very well," Uto said, and sat up straight. Dust formed at his fingers, and his eye dropped from his skull. The flesh fell from his face, and his hair fell strand by strand. His body slowly turned into a small pile of dust on the floor as he disappeared. Moments later, there was no evidence he'd been there at all. His absence left Ilara feeling empty.

She ambled from the room, using the spear as a crutch, driving the point into the stone floor. She limped up a set of stairs to a balcony overlooking one of the streets of Noon. Chek'Va's golden scales twinkled in the evening light. The moon was high in the sky, and cold winter air brushed her warm cheeks.

Chek'Va's green eyes looked over her as she leaned on the banister. "Restless evening?" he asked.

"Most are. Dangerous for you to be out here, no? Your kind would have been murdered for showing their scales in the open air of Eversburg a week ago," Ilara responded in his language.

"The paladins have their hands full with the riots. It's nice to breathe clean air."

"Aye to that. How is Aox?"

Chek'Va's limbs stiffened at the mention of the god's name. "He is recovering. I understand we have Zal'Keratha to thank."

Ilara nodded. "She sustained many wounds from her battle with Ameri's Chosen. We can't rely upon her for the fight to come."

He scratched his chin and looked down on the empty street. "What has Aerlia come to, that gods do battle with mortals? Aox has ordered me to see your goddess on the throne for the kindness she has done him. Though I'm not confident Death should rule in these times."

"Zal'Keratha would see Aox restored to the Pantheon if she ascends. It is not the ascension Aox truly desires, but you would see a new Aoxia if that happens. Many more Aox-ians would be full Chosen," Ilara said.

"Truth. These events make me feel confident your goddess foresaw the movements of Ameri. How could Zal'Keratha know?"

"She would not say," Ilara answered. "I believe that Markus overplayed his hand. Zal'Keratha doesn't need the Sight to read people. She never trusted anyone, and when I said that Markus was joining me, I think she put together the clues."

"Aye. Yet now he is the only one that knows where the altar is. I'd wager my tail that it is within that accursed Solar Dominion, as they call that palace. Or is it a temple?" Chek'Va said.

"Both, I think. Where else does a deity rule from but a temple? Has Aox told you why they are shedding so much blood?" Ilara asked.

"Aye. I don't know if I believe the stories of monsters between worlds. He called them creatures of the void. You do not believe that Akara means to summon them, do you?"

"I don't know. Part of me does wonder if Akara meant for the rebellion to occur. Zal'Keratha said that blood calls out to them as if they were sharks." Ilara paused to look at the stars. "Zal'Keratha took me to a world that was dead, destroyed by those creatures. I wonder how vast that distance is between us that they have yet to find us here."

"Perhaps we are the lone world they have not feasted on. Our divines' stories cannot be proven, but we have not the right to question."

"Perhaps." Ilara frowned. What else could she say? She couldn't cast doubt on her goddess while such a fervent follower was standing right next to her.

They sat in silence for a long while. Ilara contemplated the endless worlds that could ever have been and that would ever be. The weight of their future seemed to hold her mouth shut. The enormity of what they might do in the coming days. How much it would impact things to come.

"Are you willing to give everything that we might succeed?" she asked.

"I would give my life," Chek'Va answered after a long pause.

"You have the makings of a martyr. I have a task for you before we go back to the Solar Dominion."

"Speak it."

"Capture one of Akara's paladins. I don't care how, but I'd prefer alive. Akara did something to her Chosen, and we need to know what. They should have beaten the peasants back by now. We need to know why they haven't," Ilara said.

"It will be done," the lizard told her.

The pair turned their gazes to the street below, mesmerized by the stillness.

# Chapter Thirty-Three

# TRAILS

VALETTE FOUND THAT THE Dusk district had been spared the worst effects of the riot. Not surprising, since it had started at its northern edge. The district was still as run-down as the last time she'd been here.

She was wearing a warm coat and cape that Otto had generously left her before disappearing several days ago, she assumed to serve with the remainder of the guard. Valette kept the jeweled sword strapped to her hip and tucked under the cape. She couldn't have bandits spying it and trying to help themselves to it. Although she secretly hoped she'd see a gang try it—she could use a good fight.

Based on her last conversation with Otto, she'd decided to start tracking the paladins circumventing the rioters' barricades. That turned out to be easy. They'd left a trail of bodies and burnt homes in their wake. What Valette was planning to do when she found these paladins irked her. She didn't like the idea of killing Akara's Chosen, even if she'd killed Maer.

Maer's death felt different to her. It had been a sporadic act of self-defense, but this was planned. She'd try not to kill them as she tailed them back to Thorn, but she knew that she'd probably need to to get the information from them.

As she strode down the empty street, a figure of white light appeared in front of her, stepping forward as if from the rays of sunlight itself. His gleaming armor glinted. It covered every part of him, leaving none of his divine skin exposed. Valette wondered if he even needed it now.

"*Your mind is troubled,*" Almir said.

"How are you not troubled? An ally you've trusted for a hundred years has betrayed you. How can you just shrug that off?" Valette asked aloud. When he appeared before her, it was always easier for her to simply speak.

"*I do not do so easily, but I do not let my thoughts on the matter impede my duty. You should not either,*" he answered.

"What do you consider your duty now? It feels like we're here to keep Zal'Keratha and Akara from killing each other. If Akara is even alive," Valette added.

*"Aye. You didn't mention that you felt her presence. I concerned myself with Akara's integrity, but what you relayed causes me even more concern."*

"Tezza spoke of the declining power of Akara's paladins during her time in the Aoxian war. Do you think it's possible that those voices I heard were somehow draining her power?"

*"Perhaps, or Akara used it all herself. She moves her Eye liberally, and it takes the strength of many gods to change its pattern,"* Almir answered.

Screams echoed down the street, and Valette saw a group of silver-clad paladins dragging a bare-chested woman into the street, blood covering her dress. Valette dashed forward with a hand on the sword under her cloak. Almir dissipated as she ran, content to watch from on high.

One of the paladins noticed her, and commanded the rest to stop. Three of the paladins were coated in armor with few gaps, while one had a bow slung over his shoulder. Still, all their eyes glowed red with Akara's power.

The paladin in front smiled through a gap in her helmet. The metal face mask that should have protected her was raised to her forehead, revealing her angular chin. Valette swallowed back the bile inching up her throat. Best to get this done with quickly.

"Come to join in the fun, soldier?" the paladin asked.

"Knight commander's orders to see what you bleeding idiots were doing. I expect a full report," Valette said, putting commanding inflections into her speech. She hoped that none of these paladins had seen her in the Tribunal. She looked a lot different without the armor, and she was sure the hood of her cape obscured her face. She pointed her sword at the closest paladin. "Name and rank."

"Sergent Tyla, ma'am," the woman answered, and raised her hand in salute. "I leave Chosen Hal, Gaban, and Rile is the archer over there. Who's your commanding officer? You don't look like a Chosen."

"Why aren't you quelling the rebellion?" Valette asked, ignoring the question.

The woman on the ground whimpered again. Valette tried to hide the look of distaste on her face.

"There is no reason to. Her Sword will put them in line. Her command was to cleanse the city of Chosen, which we have nearly done, starting with every Amerite in the Solar Dominion. The peasants have not a Chosen in their ranks. Clearing out the Crafters now. This bitch is the last of Halga's Chosen we could find," Tyla answered.

Valette's eyes widened. If what the paladin was saying was true, it meant that nearly every Amerite in the Akaran Empire had been killed over the last day, which meant that every Amerite in the world had been killed. Not surprising, given what Wren said on the statue and in the Tribunal. She wondered if Markus had died as Yila had.

"And what do you have to do with the Zal'Kerathan?" Valette asked.

The paladins paused, and the archer, Rile, pulled back his bow. "I know nothing of a Zal'Kerathan," he said.

Tyla was still standing in salute. Valette put the tip of her blade against the woman's neck. "Lie to me again and I will run her through." They deserved it. She knew they did, but she needed more answers.

"I speak truths, as all Akarans," Rile said with a smirk. "A captain of Akara's Chosen would know such a fact."

Valette had a moment to think before he released his arrow. It hurtled at her face, and she moved a moment later as it grazed her cheek. She shoved forward with her blade, and the archer nocked another arrow. Valette's blade pierced Tyla's neck, exploding out the other side. Rile lined up another shot and fired.

Halga's Chosen screamed as a gold-scaled Aoxian landed in the middle of the street. He launched a strike at one of the paladins. Metal screeched against metal as the man was cleaved in half. Blood covered the Aoxian's scales.

"Trabema lucin," Valette said, and a beam of light shot from her blade, cutting through the arrow and searing a hole in the archer's leg. He dropped to one knee. Valette pulled her blade back, coating the front of her fur-lined tunic with Tyla's blood.

Rile shot another arrow that caught Valette's shoulder, exploding the bone in pain. He then turned his bow on the Aoxian, who had just cut through another paladin.

Valette's eyes found the half-naked woman on the ground. She was holding her hands in front of her and had been spattered with a good portion of Tyla's blood. "No, please. Mercy," she begged.

Valette's mouth twisted into a grimace as she grabbed the woman under her shoulder. Her eyes went wide as Valette dragged her to her feet. The Aoxian's blade came down, separating the Rile's head from his body.

"Run," Valette commanded.

The Halgan stumbled over herself as she dashed to a nearby building. Valette followed and found an entryway with blood-covered sigils of Halga adorning the floors and walls. Bodies had been piled against the walls, swept aside by paladins, most likely. The Halgans all had defensive wounds, and many had died with swords in their hands.

Vomit surged from Valette's mouth and onto the cold stone, steam rising from her stomach juices. She'd been like those paladins just a few short months ago. When she'd served, all she'd done was take orders unquestioningly. If they deserved death, she knew she did as well.

The Halgan was now struggling with the large stone doors. Her chestnut skin was turning blue from the chill. Valette pulled the arrow from her shoulder and immediately channeled her healing tract to seal the wound. Pulling more magic from the tract, she strengthened her arms with fighting spirit and pulled the doors closed.

The Halgan dropped back in a huff. "You are a Chosen of Almir, aren't you?" she asked.

"Aye," Valette replied, pausing for a moment to look over the woman. "This door won't hold the Aoxian for more than a moment."

The woman produced a flame in her hand and held it close to her chest. Calluses coated her fingers, marking her as a Chosen of the crafter god. "Thank you for saving me," she said. "I'm sure I wouldn't have survived without your bravery. You may call me Helen."

"Tell me what happened to this guild," Valette said. Halgans lived together in large guild halls. They fed off each other's creativity, which allowed them to create incredible pieces of work. Sometimes, it led them to innovate fantastic pieces like Valette's armor or the relatively new stove.

"Many died." Helen shivered, as if the memory chilled her soul. "We thought we were safe from the riot when paladins came to our door. Halga hadn't yet been dismissed from the Pantheon. Our Guildmaster welcomed them in with open arms, only to find a blade in his chest. I was the last because I hid in an unlit kiln. I heard them when—when—" Her words caught in her throat.

"Helen, I'm sorry." Valette noticed the woman tremble again. "Let's get you into something warmer. Is there anything we could use here?"

Helen nodded. "Maybe. We can light one of the kilns for warmth. We may even have a set of armor on the rack that would fit you, if you're planning to fight that Aoxian."

Valette shook her head, bending over to pull a helmet from one of the dead men on the floor. "The fire will attract him. Aoxians have a sense for those things."

As if on cue, the stone door shook. "Go find a place to hide," Valette hissed as it shuddered again.

Helen shuffled back and out of Valette's view. A snarl came from the other side of the door in that devilish language. Valette recognized the word for Akaran. Her grip tightened on her blade as she prepared to spill lizardkin blood.

# Chapter Thirty-Four

# THEO

"Posh neighborhood," Bleeder grunted as they scanned the row of houses that lined the edge of the Noon district. The homes here all butted up against one another, which left little room for alleyways and side streets. Broken windows and burned buildings made it impossible to tell how much these people had flaunted their wealth before the riot. Many of these people had been frequent patrons of Sofia's shows.

"You ever live in Dusk?" she asked.

Bleeder shook his head. "No, I've lived in The Pearl the whole time I've been in Eversburg. Lived in plenty of places like Dusk, though. Sad people, living sad lives. Getting by with the prick in the house means self-medicating on anything ye can get your hands on." He gave a long sigh and crossed his arms. "Been there. Done plenty of that."

"I think this is it," Sophia said as she pointed to one of the buildings. It was burned out and abandoned. Looters had picked it clean, like every other house on the street, then torched it.

"Doesn't look like the kid is here," Bleeder said.

"Odd." Sophia glanced up and down the street. "Don't you think it's strange that this is the only house on this street that caught fire? They're so close together that it should have spread through the whole row."

Bleeder shrugged. "Maybe the rioters have a fire brigade. They live here, same as the rest of us."

"I doubt it. And who would stop long enough to put out a fire in the middle of a riot? Much less when you know paladins might be here at any moment."

Sophia curiosity got the better of her, and she walked to the front door. Despite everything, it was still on its hinges, with broken glass on the ground in front of it. That was another oddity—for broken glass to be outside a home if looters had been breaking in.

Sophia rapped her knuckles on the door. "Theo, Ilara sent us," she shouted.

A gasp came from inside the door, followed by the quick thumps of a child's footsteps. "Who are you?" his small, quiet voice said from inside.

Sophia looked through the broken window. She should be able to see him. "Ilara's sister, Sophia."

"I've heard it was people like you who started all this," Theo said.

Sophia looked to Bleeder. "Your father might be in a lot of trouble. Ilara said he'd want us to check on you. He might not be coming back for a long time."

The door creaked open. The boy's face was covered in soot. Thin and ragged, he swayed like he hadn't eaten in days. His eyes darted by her toward Bleeder and the street. He couldn't have been older than ten. His eyes took on a far-off stare before they landed on Sophia's. Like Ilara's, they were black, as if the pupil had taken over the iris. Sophia felt like they might suck her in.

"You mean he's dead. My father can't be dead," Theo said, and tears began streaming down his face.

"I know, and you must be tired. You can let the illusion go now," Sophia told him.

He reached out his arms to her. Behind him, the burned house staggered and faded, replaced with a home that could have fit anywhere in Eversburg, and was remarkably undamaged. The boy had worked some illusionary magic on it.

Sophia grabbed Theo in the warmest hug she could muster. He felt small, almost breakable. She'd always wanted kids, and to nurture them like flowers. Ilara had never struck her as the motherly type. Why was she so concerned about this kid?

"Make it a lie," Theo said. "Make it a lie that he's dead." He burst into sobs, burying his face in Sophia's chest. He began gasping uncontrollably as tears streamed from his eyes.

"We don't know that he's dead. But we're going to find him, together." Sophia gripped the boy tighter and ran her fingers through his hair. A rhyme came to her, so she spoke:

Hush, little child,

Let it out,

The darkness is wild

Without doubt.

Hold firm your faith,

Honor us,

Us who were scathed,

The calming truss.

Waves of sound formed in Sophia's words. They danced playfully around the pair as if to soothe the crying boy. Sophia didn't need to reach into them to make the magic work on Theo.

She felt his gasps slow until he was breathing normally. She pulled him away from her. His eyes closed, and he was mouthing words so quickly she couldn't tell what they were.

A moment later, he opened his eyes and looked at Sophia. "You have power, too," he said.

"Aye, I am Chosen. My sister didn't say you were."

"She wouldn't. Father said she couldn't find out. So I pretended I wasn't around her. Around everyone, really."

Sophia nodded. "Who Chose you?"

"Ytria," Theo said, almost whispering. The god of darkness. Sophia hadn't heard any stories of Ytria giving his Chosen power over illusions.

"Before we find your father, can you tell us a safe place we can take you? Where is your mother?" Sophia asked.

"I don't know. I've never had a mother." Theo gripped her tighter. "Father had to leave during the riot. He told me to stay here and keep hiding the house. "

"It was a clever trick," Sophia muttered.

"You can save him, right? From all the rioters?"

"Of course." Her mind whirred with all the possibilities the boy presented. "Which way did he go?"

Theo pulled himself from Sophia and turned north to point up the street, toward Akara's massive statue by the Solar Dominion. "North," he muttered.

Sophia nodded and turned to Bleeder. "Take the child, I'll—"

"I'll need the bracelet," Theo said, and scrambled back into the house. He reappeared a moment later, holding a black felt band that he slipped over his wrist. It didn't adhere to his skin as Sophia's had, but dangled there loosely.

"You ought not to wear that. It's dangerous." Sophia's hand flitted to her neck where the burn marks from her encounter with the band were still healing..

"Why? It makes the skull mask go away.."

"What man?"

"The man with the skull mask. He has antlers like a fendeer and eyes like black marbles. Father said that he'll hurt me if I don't wear my circle. I just can't make things change like the house. The man gets mad at father a lot," Theo said.

Sophia nodded. The description matched what the stories said about Ytria. He had always been known as the god of darkness—the antithesis of Akara. Sophia wondered, not for the first time, if he was more than that.

"You know not to activate your tracts while you have it on?" Sophia asked.

"I do." Theo nodded.

"Fine, but be ready to pull it off if we need you to." She stood and turned back to Bleeder.

"What do we do with him, then?" Bleeder asked.

"The Pearl, as planned. You must take him alone, though. I have to go back to Ilara."

Theo's hand wormed its way into Sophia's, and he linked his fingers with hers. "I'm going with you. I want to see Ilara, too," he said.

Sophia got down on one knee to bring herself to the boy's eye level. "Ilara and I still have dangerous business to attend to. You'll be safer with Bleeder here. He looks scary, but he is a good man."

Theo nodded, and Sophia stood again. "Bleeder, you must give me your oath. Give your oath that you'll not say a word to anyone about the boy being Chosen or whom he worships."

Bleeder's eyes widened. "I wouldn't dare. The Ancestor wouldn't abide by such a thing." He'd already given his word, but the oath was binding. To demand more was sacrilege.

"Your oath, Bleeder. The oath of your tribe, or I'll trek back to The Pearl myself and get Glenda to force it from you," Sophia said.

"Bloody hells," Bleeder muttered, reaching deep into one of his pockets. He produced a copper tube as long as his forefinger and twice as thick. He held it up and revealed runic etchings that ran along the sides. The top rim had been worn down by years of his finger running across it.

"I swear." The runes glowed with a faint blue light as he spoke. "I swear on all that is holy and on my vow as a descendent of the high seas and shores that none shall know this boy's heart, nor will any harm come upon him, by blood or spirit."

As he finished, the rod ceased glowing, and in response, a slight glow illuminated Bleeder's eyelids, then faded as quickly as it had begun. "I am bound by this oath," he said. He looked back at Sophia. "The Ancestor would regard me as a disappointment. Nearly killed by street thugs, then bullied by a woman the size of a twig. How did you learn of my ancestry?"

"Balan has many stories. He shares them. When I learned of the Vani, I began to understand you needed to satisfy your blood oath to Ilara and me. I would hear your tale, that I may transcribe it to song, if you see fit."

"It may do me some good to share it, though we have not the time. Suffice it to say, I am the lone survivor of my people here in the city of my mortal enemy. Although these old bones couldn't do anything against that wicked goddess that rules here even if I them wanted to."

"You don't believe anyone else made it out of your home? The great knights of the sea were known for their hardiness," Sophia said.

"Unfortunately, I was in Chrys at the time, on a trading caravan. My people did not travel extensively. Even I was naught but a caravan guard. I thought I was making my way from tradition. That loss is what I miss, now. No, I know Akara slaughtered them all."

"I'm sorry. It seems all paladins do is take," Sophia said.

"Aye." Bleeder turned to look at the entrance. Theo was sheepishly sitting in the doorway, a sack hanging from his back that was as long as he was. "Time for us to be going then." Bleeder stood as the boy did.

Sophia walked with them back to The Pearl. No trouble came to them, and Glenda was happy to see the boy. Sophia wished she could have stayed with them, but she knew Ilara would come looking for her sooner or later.

It was time to get some bleeding answers.

***

As Sophia walked into Mal'Evir's office, the stench of incense attacked her nose. The doctor was lounging on a large cushioned chair. His red and gold scales reflected in the lantern light. He glanced up from the book spread across his lap, eyes bulging when he saw her tear-stained face. She hadn't bothered cleaning up on the walk back to the clinic. Everything seemed insignificant to her now.

"Tell me what happened," he said. There was no malice in his words. He seemed to know that this was not the time to prescribe or analyze.

"I killed a man today. A full human being with thoughts, feelings, and family. I had no choice. Kill him or he would kill my friend. But I—I—" Sophia felt the tears welling up again. If she kept talking, they would come. She wished she could have found another way. There must have been a way not to kill him.

"Oh, child." Mal'Evir motioned to the chair across from him and closed the book in his lap. He regarded her with sorrow in his eyes as he stroked his chin with two of his fingers.

Sophia feared his judgment. She'd never killed before, and felt it a stain on her. In the Cavern of Souls, it was said that Zal'Keratha weighed the actions a person had committed in their life. If the good outweighed the evil, they were sent to serve a divinity of their choice so that they might further their cause in Aerlia. The best ascended to be gods. The evildoers found eternal torment at Zal'Keratha's hand, a chore she derived much pleasure from.

"It never fails to amaze me," Mal'Evir said, "how much a kill weighs on a person. Even your sister, as much as she hides it, is burdened by the weight of the lives she's taken. I serve criminals. Each bears that burden in different ways. Some find comfort in those they've killed having earned it. Whatever that means. Others know that they did what they had to, as you say. Still others find that a bottle dulls the pain.

"I cannot speak to what is right for you. Maybe there isn't a right way for you to hold the pain of that man's life in you. I do not believe that anyone deserves to die, myself. But I do trust that when a person like you kills, there is often no other way to solve the situation."

"I— No," Sophia said. Tears streamed down her face again. "There had to have been another way. That man didn't need to die. If only I could control these powers better. If only there had been a way to convince him to leave us alone."

Mal'Evir crossed his legs and gently placed his arms on the sides of the chair. "Dear, the only way not to kill in this world is to stay as far away from it as you can. I don't know where you would go, but Eversburg has been, and always will be, a place where people kill. Some say that this riot is a reason, others say it's a war, or see how to benefit from ill-gotten gains. You find a way to live with it—or not."

Sophia nodded and took a moment to calm herself.

"You may take your time and recover here. I am always willing to lend a listening ear, should you find the need for it," Mal'Evir said.

"I have another question." Sophia took a deep breath. "Is there any way to find out who gave birth to a certain person? I have an idea, but I need to know for sure."

"Now that is an interesting question."

# CHAPTER THIRTY-FIVE

# NEGOTIATION

ILARA FROWNED AS THE COLD wind snapped at her face. She had spent too many days in that decrepit clinic. She leaned on the butt of her spear, and the tip sank deeper into the cobblestone street. Using it as a crutch slowed her and Katri down, but it was necessary to get Ilara moving, which they both needed.

They'd decided—well, Katri had decided—that she needed to take Ilara on the errand she'd been given. Ilara had reluctantly agreed, if only to get out of the clinic. Mal'Evir acquiesced only because the treatment had finished and he'd given Ilara a clean bill of health. Parts of her chest were still black from infection. He'd assured her they weren't dangerous.

Initially, Ilara had been excited about leaving the clinic and seeing what had become of Eversburg. Now, as she watched the corpse of her friend sway in the winter wind, she was far less certain this was a good idea. It'd taken them hours to find it—Ilara had assumed he'd be among the dead littering the street, not one of the ones hung from the barricade. His neck was broken and his face slack.

Truth be told, Gavin had been one of the few men she'd bothered to know well. He was an honorable man, friendly. A good father to Theo, as far as she could tell. It was an injustice that he now hung there, dangling by his neck, for serving a goddess who didn't care about him. The violence Ilara saw before her didn't account for the complexities of the man.

"And yet, you leave me with my own mistakes. Perhaps this is the cruelty of your final act," she muttered. At least she didn't have to worry about him asking about Theo anymore. She just had to worry about Theo.

Sophia will want to take care of him. I hope.

Katri and Ilara were standing next to the makeshift gallows just outside the encampment the rioters had made. They'd set it up once they'd pushed the paladins into the Solar Dominion. Ilara assumed these were the prisoners that the rebels didn't have the food to feed.

Here, the glorious rebellion stalled, entrenched around the Dominion like an occupying force. Both paladins and rioters had constructed barricades on either side of the gate in front of Akara's statue. The gate itself hung lopsided, with a large crater underneath it. There was an empty space, fifty feet wide, between the two makeshift war camps. Corpses littered the stone street, too muddied and rotten to determine which cause they had fought for.

"Devastating," Katri said.

"Indeed," Ilara agreed. "You sure this Desmond will help us?"

Katri shrugged. "Maybe. If anything, I will threaten him for leaving me behind. I was surprised he made it out of that mission alive."

Whether or not the man would help them was up in the air, which was why Ilara had agreed to come along. It was so out of the ordinary for her that she wasn't sure Markus would think of it. She could only hope that he didn't know about Katri's affiliations to these rioters, who thought themselves a Resistance to Akara. In addition, it was something to do to stave off the feeling of being useless. And they hadn't been stabbed for entering the encampment.

"Well, how do we find this man?" Ilara asked.

"Start asking about, I suppose," Katri said, signaling one of the rebels.

They marched over to a stocky young guard. He looked like he hadn't slept in days. His plate armor looked crisp and shiny, like it had been forged a week ago. The boy couldn't have been two decades old.

"Kid, we need to get to the leader of this whole outfit. Where can we find him?" Katri asked.

The guard looked at them incredulously. "Who?" His eyes shot from Katri to Ilara several times.

Ilara pulled the hood of her cloak lower. Her cha'ak hung loosely from her neck.

"Desmond is the man. Are you deaf, or am I speaking Aoxian?" Katri asked.

"I, uh—" The guard scratched the side of his helmet. "I don't know who that is but, uh, all the commanders are in the large tent toward the center of camp. He would be there if he's a big tent type."

"He's the sort of person who would be in the big tent?" Ilara asked.

The kid's head whipped toward her. "Well, that's where me orders come from."

"I guess that'll be our first stop then." Katri smiled. She and Ilara walked past the young man, who looked bewildered. Every person they passed seemed to be a similar age, not much older than Theo, truth be told. And all of them were armed with black metal weapons. Ilara was curious to know why they hadn't breached the Solar Dominion yet.

"These rioters seem too well armed for a pop-up rebellion," she muttered.

Katri nodded. "Aye. Makes one think this may have been planned rather than the work of a group of opportunistic rioters. Has to be a thousand fighters in here."

Finding what their way was simple. They walked toward the center of the encampment and toward a tent that wasn't tall, but as wide as a dozen of the other ones put together. The tents were all stained—if not by dirt, then by blood. Everyone they saw was carrying a weapon. Many of them leered at Ilara and Katri as they passed. A cripple and an unarmed woman likely looked like easy pickings after the hell these people had gone through.

Banners waved outside the tent, showing a pair of crossed swords on a red back drop. The flags caught the wind better than the bodies that hung outside the camp, and they whipped furiously as the darkened skies threatened a winter storm.

They spotted two men in ornate red armor that Ilara recognized as Akaran paladin plate. Both were holding six-foot-long spears that were standard issue in the Akaran military. One raised a hand in a halting gesture, then raised an eyebrow as he scanned the women in front of him.

"Desmond," Ilara said with authority. "I must speak with him."

"And who are you, ma'am?" the guard asked.

"A friend and old baggage," Katri chimed in. "Not to mention that we're Chosen. We have a proposition from the Fallen gods."

"The Fallen gods?" he asked, clearly confused.

"That's what we're calling those newly outside the Pantheon. Desmond will understand," Katri said.

The two guards looked at each other. "Wait here. Don't let these two out of your sight," one of them said, and disappeared into the tent.

Ilara wondered what the implications of this rebellion were. She needed Markus off his footing, a future too obscure for him to See. He'd mentioned that they'd been planning this revolt. Did he know Katri had a connection to these people? Were they playing into his hands by having this meeting?

"Fallen gods? Really?" Ilara asked.

"Makes it sound more official."

The guard reappeared a moment later. "Come with me," he said.

Katri and Ilara were escorted into the tent. Large hallways made of curtains and tarps joined together several different rooms. Laughter came from one side, while screams of the injured and dying came from the other. The guard led them to a room that Ilara was certain was the center of the complex.

There were people sitting around the edge of the space. All of them were wearing the dresses and garments of in-fashion nobles—people whose families had known the comings and goings of the city for longer than Akara had ruled here.

A curly-haired man with a dark complexion and a rough, untrimmed beard was standing with his hands resting on a large table , inspecting a crudely drawn map of the temple. When he noticed them come in, he smiled a wide smile that didn't reach his eyes. This was the man who had organized these people, the one Katri called Desmond. The man who'd killed Gavin, even if indirectly.

Ilara gripped her spear, fighting the urge to throw it through Desmond's chest.

"Katri!" he exclaimed. "I see you made it out of that gods-damned dung—"

"No thanks to you," Katri interrupted.

"Ha, and as quick of a tongue as I recall. No hard feelings, I trust? You wouldn't be here if so," he said.

Katri snarled. "I'd say we still have some—"

"And," he continued, unabated, "I see you've brought a friend." His left eye flashed, and a rune appeared on his pupil. "Quite a dangerous one, too. I understand the paladins are looking for you. You stole something quite valuable to them."

"Clearly," Ilara said.

The man had a seeing eye. It was a rare invention of specialized Crafters, and it could tell if someone was lying. Few knew the formula, and even fewer had the skills to make it. Desmond had likely stolen it from some paranoid lord who'd paid a small fortune to obtain it.

Katri's face had turned red, and her frown had deepened. She was not one to hold a grudge, but there was palpable tension between these two.

"And what on Aerlia can a man like myself do for the both of you? Or did you decide to interrupt our war council for a catch up?" Desmond asked.

Katri crossed her pale arms. "You owe me a favor. You would have been broken in a that dungeon, and I took the fall for you. I brought this rebellion as far as you did."

"Aye, you did," he said, then walked around the table and glanced toward the edge of the room. Guards in paladin armor stepped back through the entrance. They had steel strapped to their waists. "Surely, Katri, you know that I'm most grateful for your contributions to my great Revolution," he continued, seeming not to notice the armed men. He clearly didn't want his visitors to pay attention to the guards.

"I think there is a way we can assist one another," Katri said as she uncrossed her arms and paced around the tent. Her eyes didn't leave Desmond's face, like a wolf sizing up her prey.

"I didn't come here hoping you would assist a woman you left for dead. I brought a proposition that would benefit you."

Desmond's smile disappeared. "What are you suggesting?"

"We need you to attack the Dominion in two days. If you draw enough of the pals out, we can portal in and kill whoever remains in their leadership. With no head, your Revolution will have no opposition," Katri said.

"That," Desmond said, smacking his lips, "does not sound like sound military strategy. Is that the best you have, Beas—"

"The hell it's not. You've been stuck out here since day one of your revolt." Katri's face turned a shade red.

"Indeed. I expect we'll be camped outside the Dominion until summer, though only until Tezza crawls from the hole she's crawled into. She and her paladins will have starved for months. I will not sacrifice more of my people in a foolish assault against whatever demon repels us on each assault. The first dozen of those left us with half our numbers. And watching the pigs starve after getting fat off our backs sounds like a delightful time."

"What about the Imperial Army?" Ilara huffed.

"You mean the ones we've killed? Slaughtered like the scoundrels they are for enforcing the rules of Akara? They, who lived—"

"No, not the city guard," Ilara said. "The ones in the south who've been fighting the bleeding Aoxians. The ones that have certainly been notified that there's an insurrection going on. Those hundred thousand strong that are no doubt marching back to the city this very instant. Did you think Akara would let her capital, her holy city, fall into disarray and not stop fighting lizards for a few months to quell it?"

The color drained from Desmond's face as the nobles in the tent began to whisper. His joyful visage faltered for a moment as panic set in. "How could they have possibly gotten word to a group so far away? It's preposterous."

"Gods." Ilara groaned.

"They have Amerites in the Dominion who have means of communicating across vast distances," Katri explained, then pointed to her head. "With their brains."

"Aye," Ilara agreed. "The powerful ones can communicate across continents."

"And we saw most of those Amerites thrown from Akara's Sword," Desmond said.

"I know at least one survived," Ilara growled as pain flared in her chest. "If he's been caught by the Akarans, he's been forced to communicate."

"If," Desmond echoed. "If he was, I've been assured that they have no way of communicating."

"Who made those assurances?" Ilara asked.

"That would be me," said a figure as he entered through the curtained door. Ilara recognized the graying mustache as the tap of a cane hit the ground.

A black blazer was draped over Gray's shoulders, sleeves hanging loose by his sides. A black felt cap sat on his head, hiding his balding scalp. He smirked as he glanced over at Ilara. She understood the purpose of the guards. They'd have to speak carefully not to be caught in this one's trap.

"Gray," she growled. Katri's eyes flicked to her, then back to the man.

"Sir Fenwald," Desmond said. "I'm glad you're here. You should hear the proposal of these Chosen."

"I am aware of their proposition. These two and their band have been within my network for some time. How is Mal'Evir, Ilara? Or should I call you Thorn, for old times' sake?"

"Only if you want to scream like your son did," Ilara hissed as she formed a dagger in her hand. She leaned heavily on her spear, still stuck in the ground like a crutch.

Gray held his hand up, making her pause. "As I told you in our last meeting, Jonas deserved his death. Whether or not you agree with the guild's decision to support him over you is not my problem. But that is well and truly behind us now—you've seen to that."

Ilara nodded. Gray didn't call the Syndicate by name, which meant Desmond didn't know who his true sponsors were. She didn't know what Gray wanted out of this Revolution, but it couldn't be good.

"Explain your plan in detail. I will decide its merit based on what your idea is worth, not the death of my son," Gray said, pulling up a chair next to the table Desmond had been leaning on.

"It is simple," Katri said. "We have an Aoxian that knows portal magic. He's been inside the Dominion, so he can get us close to Tezza's throne. What we can't deal with is the number of paladins around her. Should your forces attack just before we do, it will draw most of them out. This would expose Tezza and allow us to kill her and turn on the paladins. Without her leadership, they will flounder," Katri said.

"Aye, but they'll still be paladins. And Akara will appoint a new Voice immediately, elevating another to the station, likely before you can kill all the paladins," Gray said.

Ilara shook her head. "You're right. We have to go further."

"How much further?" Katri asked.

"We have to kill Akara," Ilara said.

"And you have a way to do that?" Desmond asked.

"I do," Ilara said, gripping her spear.

"And you expect us to trust you to do the impossible?" Gray asked. "A god has not died since that bastard of the sea, Vanis."

"No, Fenwald, this could be it." The woman, one of the nobles seated around the sides of the room, stood as she spoke. She was dark-skinned and had her hair swept back into a long, thick braid. "We have argued for days whether it would be possible for us to attack the Solar Dominion. Some among us have settled back into fear and hope that our Revolution can survive without doing so. But I tell you, that bitch must die."

"There must be a different way, Lady Pendrossa," Desmond said. "I—"

"No." Pendrossa stamped her foot. "There is no other way. We have tried for years to deal with Akara and her clergy peacefully. When that damned goddess's armies marched upon my city, we did not resist. We laid down our bows and swords in favor of her divine authority.

"Yet, as her Eye stretched further southward and the days grew longer, our crops died of the heat. Our homes caught fire. Our children died of starvation. No. If our Revolution means to survive, we must act, and act fast. With each day we give the paladins to lick their wounds, we give them the opportunity to survive this. Akara would not show us such grace. I support these Chosen and believe we should accept their offer of assistance," Pendrossa said.

Desmond looked over at Gray. "I must say I agree with the lady. We cannot continue to twiddle our thumbs."

Gray nodded solemnly, then glanced back to Ilara. "It seems I am outvoted. I may, however, impose a stipulation. I would like this sister you speak of to join our camp and fight with us on that day. She will need to be here tomorrow night in order to begin the assault the next morning."

"I concur with this," Lady Pendrossa said as she returned to her seat.

"Very well," Ilara said. "Sophia is not a fighter. I would appreciate it if she is kept from the front line."

"We will do our best," Desmond told her.

Ilara stormed from the room, smacking the tip of her spear into the ground with each step. She was halfway through the camp before Katri caught back up with her.

"That went better than expected," Katri said.

"I don't trust any of them," Ilara muttered as they strode through an opening in the southern barricade. "I might just take Sophia and Theo out of this godsdamned city and let the gods sort out their own squabble."

Katri frowned. "You really don't give her enough credit."

"Lady Pendrossa? Pretty difficult to, since I just met the wom—"

"No, your godsdamned sister," Katri said.

Ilara stopped and turned to her. The woman's face was red, and her fists were balls at her sides.

"She is much stronger than you believe she is. You left her for years wondering if you'd died or abandoned her like everyone else in her life. She is utterly dependent on you for any and all familial ties, and you're too selfish to even try to mean anything to her. Not to mention that you wouldn't even let her solve her own problems. You put her in a glass bottle and refused to let her out. How can she prove herself to you if you never let her think for herself?"

"I left her alone for five bloody years," Ilara shot back.

"You disappeared for years without telling her where you were. You could've been dead for all she knew. For all I knew," Katri said, running a finger under her eye.

Ilara brushed one of her dark hairs away from her face. "I didn't think you'd care."

"We were partners under Jonas for years, Ilara. That must count for something. The most I've heard about you since was what Sophia told me while we were in the bloody dungeon. And I didn't even know it was you," Katri said as she held Ilara's gaze.

"We were criminals. I thought you'd want to leave that behind when you left. You left me," Ilara said. The words hung in the air like a cloud of gas, making it harder to breathe.

Katri shook her head. "I couldn't believe that you of all people wanted to keep killing for the Syndicate after everything you said about death and the finality of it."

Ilara saw Katri now for what she was and not for the mask she'd worn when they worked together. She should have seen it sooner. Katri had always been vulnerable around her, even when they worked with Jonas. That had to mean something.

Ilara felt her shoulders slump.

Katri brushed past her with finality. "We should be getting back."

# Chapter Thirty-Six

# LOSS

VALETTE SIZED UP THE gold-scaled Aoxian. He was holding a massive sword that would have been heavy enough to crack her armor if she'd still been wearing it. His leather armor was decorated with feathers and intricate stitching that looked like it had been torn and mended many times—scars of past battles. She had only a moment to analyze him before he launched his first attack at her.

Almir's shield formed on her arm before she had time to give it thought. She parried the lizard's blow. If he had swung with his full strength, he would have knocked her to the side. Valette continued blocking with her shield. Each blow grew harder, but it was clear to her that this Aoxian was not trying to kill her.

An idea struck her, and she took a step back, bringing her sword up to her face so that the hilt was near her nose with the steel extending upward. The Aoxian froze, recognizing the formal challenge of an honor duel. He brought his weapon into a pose that mirrored her own.

"Valette, Almir," she said. The purpose was to inform her opponent of her name and the god she served. Aoxians lived in many kingdoms with varied languages. A formal duel was structured so that the warriors would know who was striking whom. Valette was the challenger. It was this Aoxian's right to decide whether to accept or deny the duel.

"Chek'Va, Aox. Ich."

She nodded in response. The first to draw blood would win the duel, and the loser would submit to their will. Slavery was a common punishment. In Valette's case, she was going to kill this lizard.

The Aoxian snarled at her in his slithering language. He took a step back and moved the handle of his blade to his face, settling back into a stance that reminded her of a coiled snake. His movements were precise, like a seasoned veteran's.

Valette had fought many Aoxians during her service and had seen their insides more often than not. She'd never battled one alone, though. They were weak at the ankles and backs of their knees, where they had fewer scales. They were excellent hand-to-hand combatants, as they knew by instinct where their scales would protect them, having worn them since they'd hatched. Seeing which side this one favored could give her an idea where his scales were already weak.

Her biggest disadvantage was being unarmored. One mistake and she would lose the duel.

The Aoxian brought his scaly hand to his mouth, the second and fifth fingers extended, and breathed out. Fire formed between his fingers and billowed over Valette's shield. She dove from the flames before they could singe her face.

She recovered and readied her sword. Steel sliced through the billows of flame as she forced the Aoxian to step back. He slapped the flat of her blade with his palm and launched a haphazard swing at her head.

Letting her momentum take her, Valette continued forward and dipped below the blade's arch. As she did, she drew the sword back and slashed at the Aoxian's leg, aiming for one of their weak points. He turned so he could pick his leg up and move it from her reach.

He stood now where she had been a moment before, his next strike aimed toward her unarmored torso. Valette formed a buckler on her forearm and deflected the attack.

Their battle continued like this for several minutes. Whenever Valette was able to create space, the Aoxian drew close with his long strides and reach. The likelihood that she would be able to create the space she needed became thinner and thinner as she tired. The clang of their swords and scales rang against the walls of the rows of abandoned houses and shops.

At that moment, Valette thought she'd be locked in this stalemate until one of them fell over from exhaustion. This Aoxian was one of the finest swordsmen she'd fought since Almir had trained her.

She saw her opportunity when she noticed the lizard failing to fully extend one of his arms—a potential weakness. After he made another downward slash, Valette dodged and twisted swiftly, clipping his forearm. Golds scales clinked to the ground, ringing like a pile of gali. It hadn't been weak before, but it was now.

In an instant, the Aoxian took a step back and launched himself toward her, angling a steep diagonal slash. She stepped back to dodge it. He was too close for another strike, so she ducked under and aimed her sword at his side. A claw caught her cloak and dug into her back. She felt her feet leave the ground as he dragged her down. She could feel the blood warm her skin where he'd struck her.

She'd lost.

Then and there, she made the decision that she wasn't going to die here. At least she'd take him with her, even if it meant breaking Aoxian traditions. Valette thrust her sword up with the swiftness Almir's spirit gave her to pierce the forearm she'd already wounded. Instinctively, the lizard dropped her as her spirit ran out. She hit the ground and her knees gave way.

Aoxian blood covered the stones.

Valette struggled to her feet, exhausted, when her opponent's blade came down again. Working on the memory of years of practice, Valette raised her sword to block it. Her weapon was cleaved in two by the flaming blade.

She screamed as it cut into her shoulder. She could barely hear the sound of breaking bones. The Aoxian raised his sword again, blood dripping from it. She should be dead.

She should be—

***

Valette's eyes creaked open, and she almost believed that she was in Zal'Keratha's domain, land of the dead. She was lying on her side across a wall made of plaster. Red paint covered it, as if it had been dumped lazily over the structure in a half-hearted attempt make it look more inviting. It made her think of blood running from open veins.

A moldy aroma overcame her and caused her to gag. Her arms were bound in front of her, and chills ran up her spine as she realized she'd been stripped of the cloak Otto had given her. In place of it, she was wearing a threadbare tunic suitable for a prisoner.

*Gods, that must be what happened. I'm a prisoner in this place.*

Her shoulder and back throbbed with pain. The memory of the fight washed over her in an instant. Heat rose to her cheeks as she contemplated the consequences. She should be counting her blessings that the gold-scaled lizard hadn't killed her, but all she could do was seethe. Honor required him to kill her the moment his claws hit her. The fact she that she was alive was an insult. The Aoxians sword had dug deep, and she likely wouldn't have use of her arm until she healed it with Almir's magic.

Valette shifted to a sitting position and moved her leg, which erupted with fiery pain. It was certainly broken below the knee. She'd never let a wound go without healing it, but she couldn't do so with her current restraints.

One of her fathers, Father Mikan, had insisted she enroll in a field hospital on her Decision Day so many, many years ago. He'd argued she had an eye for healing and knew the Akaran army would nurture that.

Right now, sitting in a dank dungeon, she didn't know why she hadn't listened to him. The infantry was tough, and she'd seen too many of her comrades die.

She wished she could see both her fathers again, Mikan and Halen. Two lovers in Almir's church. They'd raised her since her birth mother died and her birth father perished. But Mikan was dead and gone now, and Halen had been a wreck of a man since.

Not that Valette could blame him. She'd been away from her sons so long she couldn't remember their faces some days. Almir's orders were more important than whatever family she'd been raising.

She regretted, in that moment, every choice that had taken her away from them. She could have had a life in Chrys, a nice home and a garden where she scolded her children for playing too roughly. She could have been a field doctor who saved lives instead of ending them. Then, she could have retired to live out her days treating broken bones and mild flus.

It was a path she could no longer take. Instead, all she did was kill. The thought had never occurred to her when Almir called her to the fronts to kill Aoxians. Akara needed them, and Valette was grateful to be needed. She'd hoped to become Chosen when she left Chrys, and it had worked. She'd never questioned it when she led soldiers into Aoxian towns and villages. She brought peace predicated by the sword. It never mattered what crime they had to commit to get that job done. Their cause was just, so their actions must be too.

Valette had turned a blind eye to it then, but she knew what her soldiers had done when they were behind enemy lines. Tears formed in her eyes when she thought about the Crafter the paladins had tormented. The woman would have been another victim. The sins Valette's soldiers had committed stained her hands, even if she didn't want to think about it. Thinking about it was acknowledging the blood that covered her.

The homes they'd burned, the people they'd killed, had nowhere to rest but in Valette's mind. Did that Aoxian know what she'd done to his people? Was this his justice? Was that why he hadn't killed her—so that he could commit every crime she'd ever committed back unto her?

The door across from her creaked open. A blue-scaled Aoxian wearing a white tunic stepped into the room. "Oh, my dear. What on Aerlia are we going to do with you?" he said, in a manner that was far too prim and proper.

"Unbind me or kill me," Valette said.

The lizard chortled. "My stars, you are a funny one. I am merely the doctor."

"I could heal it myself. I have no need for whatever primitive treatment you've put me in."

"You think I hatched yesterday? With the way Chek'Va looked after your little bout, you're lucky I don't have you in chains, though it sounds as if you're lucky to be alive at all. These bindings should be enough." The Aoxian tapped at the black felt bonds around Valette's forearms.

She was familiar with the bonds that severed a Chosen from their god, which now restrained her. "Indeed," she said.

The lizard started fussing with the bindings on her shoulder with the tender care of a physician. He would endeavor to better her so that they could break her down again.

He undid the wrapping to show a dry green paste covering the wound. As he brushed Valette's shoulder, she saw a clean break in the skin where the sword had split it. New flesh had already begun to grow.

"You should know, for the sake of honor, Chek'Va did not spare you out of some kind of moral code. That one has turned his back on much of our tradition," the doctor explained.

He talked on as he placed a clay mortar on the floor next to her. It contained a green sludge, and Valette smelled the mildew on it as he started to work it with a small pestle.

"Truly, what is one more to a crowded house?" he asked himself as he worked. It came out in such a way that Valette felt as if she was intruding on his thoughts.

"Oh, gods, where are my manners. Mal'Evir, at your service. Physician extraordinaire, at least for you fleshies. Patching up Chek'Va was the first time I've cleaned a wound on a scaled body since before I left Aoxia. I nearly forgot how. Clench your fist, please."

Valette did her best to flex them through the pain. She was surprised she could move her fingers. "Valette," she grunted as his claws grazed her leg. "Chosen of Almir."

"Almir, the first paladin. Knight of the poor, defender of the meek. An honorable deity. Chek'Va will be somewhat disappointed. He was seeking an Akaran."

Valette blinked slowly. The Aoxian had been hoping to pick up one of the paladins she'd killed. That did not bode well for her chances of getting out of this place alive. Still, the way Mal'Evir spoke of Almir gave her hope. There was something there she could work with.

"Where am I?" she asked.

"Nowhere I'm willing to say. I would hate if you escaped and brought your paladin chums back here. Even if they aren't doing so well against the rioters," Mal'Evir said. He applied the poultice to her skin.

Valette grimaced as it burned in the wound. "The paladins are losing?"

It made no sense if they had Al-Kaise on their side. The powers of a literal angel would devastate mortal soldiers. So why were they holding out?

The image of Tezza's skull splitting from the tentacle of light sent a shudder through Valette.

"A bit of a surprise all around," Mal'Evir said as he began wrapping her leg again. "As it happens, there is little to be done for them, it seems. Not that it changes my position much."

He tied the bandage to trap the poultice against her skin. Her mind flicked back to the way the rioters had fought, attacking in waves and stripping the soldiers of their armor.

"They were certainly too coordinated for a mere mob," Valette said, then looked back to Mal'Evir, who was cleaning his mortar and pestle. "If you are mending my wounds, does that mean I still won't be killed by those you work for?"

The lizard let out another quick chortle. "Heavens, no. No one in this clinic has enough ability to kill anyone I don't want them to. And you, in particular, will be under my explicit protection." He stood. The entirety of his height loomed over her. "I believe Thorn will wish a word with you when she returns, however."

The criminal's name stunned Valette's ears. She'd somehow accomplished her goal, despite losing battle after battle.

"Very well, Aoxian," she said. "I look forward to meeting the Zal'Kerathan who has doomed us all."

# CHAPTER THIRTY-SEVEN

# RAGE AND MEMORY

THE CLINIC WALLS CREAKED UNDER THE force of the wind. Sophia could hear Mal'Evir chattering cheerily down the hall while the doctor healed Chek'Va's wounds. Though she couldn't understand the language, she could sense the passionate nostalgia of speaking of a place far away settle into their conversation. She assumed they were speaking of Aoxia and longed to know what they were saying.

Sophia had always wanted to see the land, but with Akara's war the way it was, she'd never had the chance. At least where her memories began, she'd never had the chance.

She couldn't remember her early life. When she asked, Ilara was always vague about what their parents had been like. Perhaps they were spies in Aoxia, or smugglers bringing in fine Aoxian wines.

It was a fantasy. Sophia had the distinct feeling that her parents had been nothing more than meager farmers or crafts-people. The fact that Ilara would never elaborate on their background made it that much harder for Sophia to ask her what she had to. Gavin might not have seen the resemblance in Theo, but Sophia knew it too well. Ilara wouldn't keep another secret from her, and Sophia would be damned if she let her sister ruin that boy's life.

Mal'Evir poked his head into their room, his scales shimmering in the light. "Your sister has arrived," he said, then gently closed the door again.

Sophia huffed as she ambled off her cot and down the hall. She found Ilara lying upon Mal'Evir's examination table again, runes gently glowing as the doctor continued her treatment.

"—you're all but healed. Once we stop these treatments, you should have most of your strength back. You'll never be as strong as you were, as the curse will always sap some of your strength," Mal'Evir said as Sophia entered.

"That means I won't need a crutch?" Ilara asked.

"Likely as soon as tomorrow," he replied, then they both turned to Sophia. "And all of you can leave my clinic for safer horizons."

"Cheers to that," Sophia said. "Whomever your household god is, you've done them quite proud."

"Aye," Mal'Evir grumbled, stepping out of the exam room.

Sophia met Ilara's eyes once the two were left alone. Ilara buttoned her tunic and pulled her cloak back to her shoulders. "How is Theo?" she asked.

"He's at The Pearl. Safe," Sophia said.

"Is that possible in this city?"

"He's as safe as he can be," she clarified. "Did you find his father?"

"Aye, Gavin died a hero for a shit goddess," Ilara said.

"And is his mother trying to do the same?"

Ilara paused a moment, then stood from the table and pulled her spear from the wall. "I wouldn't know."

"Trollshit. You can't believe I wouldn't know as soon as I saw him," Sophia said.

"The hell do you mean?" Ilara moved to leave the room.

"How is he related to us?" Sophia asked. "The kid has your eyes and my face."

Ilara paused, hand on the doorknob. "He's my son. I had him a year after we stopped speaking. Gavin is his father, but he was so drunk the night we . . . And, I had Markus wipe his memory. Suffice it to say, he never knew Theo was mine."

"I know it isn't my business. Is his birth the reason you cut contact from me? How could you keep the fact that you were godsdamned pregnant from your sister? How dare you? I don't know. I guess I expected you to tell me, considering we have no other family. How could you let that boy grow up knowing only one of his parents? The cruelty of leaving Gavin all the duties of a parent is beyond what I would have attributed to you. You fucking knew him. You watched him struggle. I can't imagine what he must have gone through," Sophia said.

"My life is not one that is conducive to being a mother. Theo would have been in constant danger due to the nature of my work. Not to mention Zal'Keratha. You should have seen how our mother struggled with our ass of a father. You wouldn't have wanted our parents for family. Be glad you don't remember them," Ilara huffed.

"And how would I know that?" Sophia asked loudly. "You've kept them all from me as if I'm some porcelain doll who would break at the mention of them. I don't have memories of them, so I don't grieve them. And it seems like you never did."

"I keep telling you, it's of no consequence. It's good that they're gone," Ilara said. "It's good that I—"

"What, Ilara? What? I promise you I can handle whatever truth you're hiding from me. I survived that forsaken dungeon, and came out better for it. I can handle it. Or are you forgetting who saved who in the Solar Dominion?"

"I am continually reminded." Ilara put a hand on her rib. "I'm grateful for what you did there. But I can't tell you our past. I can't relive what happened."

"So it will still hang between us? For how long? When can I learn the truth?"

"I don't know if I'll ever be prepared." Ilara crossed her arms and cast her eyes to the side. Her shoulders drooped as the silence continued, and Ilara's brow furroughed. "Damn it. Katri was right—you should know. Come with me. I need to tell you everything about this new Revolution."

***

Mal'Evir's study was cluttered with books as well as small bronze statues of a kind Sophia recalled had been all the rage with collectors several years ago. A strange spice she couldn't place lingered in the air. Some mix between cardamom and sandalwood.

Ilara sat across from Sophia holding a large copper bowl etched with runes similar to those on the exam room table. It was the size of a mixing bowl and filled to the brim with dark, briny water.

"I trust you know what you're doing with my memory bowl," Mal'Evir said. "It was expensive, more so than anything else in this room, and the Crafter that made it is likely dead."

"I know, Mal," Ilara said, shaking her head.

She placed her hands in the bowl with her palms breaking the surface. As she did, the runes etched into it illuminated, lighting the water with their soft azure glow. Ilara moved her hands to the sides of the bowl, and an image formed in the middle. A young, portly woman was knitting, seated in a wooden chair in the corner of a room. A pot hung in the fireplace next to her.

This wasn't the first time Sophia had seen through a memory bowl. It was a favorite way for street performers to show dense, imaginary worlds. They'd been outlawed by the Akaran clergy years ago, with the reasoning that they inspired laziness in the citizenry.

In this case, the images in the bowl would be from Ilara's perspective. It was her memory.

The runes flickered again and made the sounds of crackling fire. A memory came back to Sophia: this woman sitting calmly while flames danced playfully across her face. This was her mother.

The woman grew smaller, and the bowl revealed a girl playing with a wooden horse on the ground while Ilara bent over a chopping block and silently cut carrots.

"Fairy . . . woods . . . secret meeting," the girl's voice rang through the runes. The words were unclear, as if Ilara remembered only parts of them.

The clip-clop of a horse's hooves and the squeal of wagon wheels caused their mother to stiffen in her chair. She knit more intentionally, and Ilara stared down at the carrots, chopping quicker. The girl next to her—a young version herself, Sophia assumed—continued to play with her horse, oblivious to the danger the other two sensed.

As the front door swung open and cracked against the wall, a man Sophia didn't recognize walked in. He was burly, with an axe swung over his shoulder and a long, graying beard on his face. He scowled through one good eye and a glass eye.

Young Sophia continued to play with her toy and to speak of whatever fairy she was telling Ilara about. Sophia wished she could reach through the memory and get her to be quiet.

She stopped abruptly at the sharp sound of flesh impacting flesh. Ilara moved to see the side of her mother's head, her cheek red.

"You would let her prattle on about childish stories?" the man bellowed clearly through the runes. He spoke hoarsely, as if he'd been shouting for hours. "She'll never be married if she doesn't grow up and help with the chores. She'll soon be as old as you were when I took you. Godsdamned seamstress of a woman."

It was clear to Sophia now why Ilara refused to think of their father. This was the type of man he had been. He was saying she'd would never be useful.

"The girl is only a decade old. I'll let her be a child as long as she can," her mother said.

"If you won't teach her a lesson, I'll show you all," her father muttered. In an instant, he grabbed Sophia's wrist. The two were out the front door before Ilara had time to react. She was knocked to the side a moment later as their mother pushed by her.

Ilara ran out the door after her mother, snow settling on the hillside. A decrepit farm spanned out to her right, and an old horse was still tied to the wagon her father had rolled up in.

Sophia's cries echoed through the runes. The little girl's heels kicked into the ground as she tried to slow her father's advance. He had her by the hair now and was pulling her behind him. Sophia felt her scalp ache watching it, as if remembering the pain.

Her father dragged her toward the top of a hill, where a well seemed to wait for them. Their mother yelled for him to stop again, her dress balled up in one hand and her ladle in the other. When she caught up to them, the metal ladle hit the man's head, sending a sharp sound across the field. Ilara's feet thudded on the ground as she ran toward them. Her pounding heart echoed through the runes, as if it were the only sound she could hear.

Sophia gasped as her father's backhand connected with her mother's neck. It moved with such force that his whole body shook when it connected. The sound of bones cracking echoed from the bowl. The woman fell limply to the ground as he turned back toward the well.

"No!" young Sophia screamed.

Ilara neared her mother as their father hauled Sophia up over the well. "Mother," she said, kneeling next to the woman. She didn't move. Ilara's small hands shook her mother's shoulders, and her head lolled back unnaturally. A stifled sob came from Ilara as she looked back to her father, still holding Sophia over the well by her arm.

"No! No!" Sophia screamed, in the shrill way only children can. The woods behind the well extended into an eerie darkness. She was holding her father's thick wrist with one hand and trying to reach her feet to the sides of the well.

A smile etched across the man's face, as if he had suddenly been possessed by a demon. "Learn from this, Ilara, or you will be next."

He let go and wrenched his hand down. Sophia screamed as her grip slipped and she disappeared beneath the lip of the well. She was cut off by a bang, then a splash. He peeked over the side, then ambled slowly down the hill, passing Ilara and his wife.

Ilara rushed to the well. Darkness stared back at her. She whipped back to her father, who was near the bottom of the hill now.

"I hope you remembered to put the carrots in the stew, girl," he said back.

Ilara's head shook, and she turned back to the well, as if hoping that Sophia would crawl back up, as if she could find a handhold.

"Soph," she shouted, and it echoed back to her. Tears flowed freely down her cheeks, and she was sobbing loudly. Sophia didn't know why, but she understood this feeling. Ilara was alone. Alone, she would have to put up with her father. Alone, she would live out the rest of her years. No one to reminisce with or to suffer the bad times with.

"That's horrible," Sophia said quietly as she stared into the bowl.

Ilara nodded, and the vision in the water flickered.

Young Ilara stood and ran past the well into the woods. "Help me!" she shouted several times as trees quickly passed her. She stumbled forward until she fell to her knees.

"I don't understand," Sophia said. "I can't be dead."

"Keep watching," Ilara grumbled.

Young Ilara's cries echoed through the clinic for several minutes. The child emitted such visceral sobbing, like a fox caught in a trap, but when Sophia looked at her sister's face, it was not only stone cold—it was pale as a ghost's.

The child's vision in the bowl lifted from the forest floor and leveled at a small, winged creature, shaped like a human with pointed horns and ears, that slowly approached. Its wings were leathery like a bat's, and it flapped them to bob up and down in the air. Its skin was stretched tightly over its face, like a piece for fabric stretched over a seamstress's hands, as if it were a mask. Its tunic was caked with mud, but there was an echo of the color it may have once had.

It landed on a nearby branch and grinned mischievously. "You've come to the woods of my lady. Zal'Keratha has seen your plight and sent me to aid you."

"My sister," Ilara said between sobs. "She's stuck at the bottom of our well. You must help."

"What is your sister's name?" the pixie asked.

"Sophia B-B-Blackwood," Ilara said.

The creature's pupils dilated until they took up the entirety of its eyes. Its head flitted around quickly, seeming to be seeing things Sophia couldn't. As it turned back to the girl, it grinned at Ilara, revealing a toothy smile.

"Your sister is dead, girl," it snarled.

"No. No, no, no, no, no," Ilara sobbed. "It's all my fault. Please, can you do anything for her? Zal'Keratha is merciful."

"Girl, you know the gods can do many things if you pay the price," the pixie snarled.

"I will give anything," Ilara said.

The pixie cackled. "Good." He gestured toward the ground, where some of the soft moss parted. A knife handle appeared, blade buried in the soil.

"Take it, girl. Pledge your soul to be Chosen of my lady, Zal'Keratha. Seal your pledge with the blood of your father. Do this tonight, and you'll see your sister in the morning."

Ilara's small hands pulled the knife from the ground to reveal its curved edge. Her tear-stained reflection stared back from the blade, then she looked to the pixie. "I-I-I have to kill father? I can't. It's impossible. He's too strong," she stammered. "He already killed Mother."

"I'm sorry." The pixie flew closer to Ilara's face and took her chin in his hand. "I thought you said you'd do anything for your sister's life. Say it again, girl."

"I would do anything, a-a-anything," she stuttered, then began to sob again.

"Best toughen up, then. If you want to kill him, you best get creative."

Ilara stood again and ran from the pixie, blade in one hand.

Now, she looked up from the bowl and made eye contact with Sophia. Tears stained her face, and new ones rolled down her cheeks. "I didn't know then if I could or not. I didn't know if I could even try," she said.

"Were you able to?" Sophia asked quietly.

"I will show you." Ilara focused on the bowl again.

Her younger self was standing outside the door to the home. Her father's incessant cursing over vegetables and burnt soup could be heard through it. Ilara's hand tensed on the dagger before tucking it into her clothes. She opened the door to see him bent over the fireplace, tending to the boiling pot.

"Your bitch of a mother burnt the soup," he said as he turned to her. "Can you believe that? I wish you hadn't made me kill them, Ilara. I told you more than once to get that sister of yours in shape."

"Sorry, Father," Ilara said.

"If you expect to be a good Blackwood, you'd best shape up."

"Yes, Father."

The girl's demeanor had changed. She bent over and helped the man dole out dinner and save what he could from the merciless fire. They ate silently, until he ordered her to her room. The worst thing was that he seemed so godsdamned certain that his lesson had been effective.

Once in her bed, Ilara waited, eyes open, and stared at one spot on the ceiling for longer than Sophia was comfortable with.

Their father wailed in the next room. Thumps pounded against the walls, and the breaking of glass sounded from the runes. Sophia knew the sounds of drunken men who were trying to throw their lives away. It reeked of loneliness and fear.

Ilara rose from bed when the moon was near the horizon. Faint light from Akara's Eye softly lit the sky with the approaching dawn. Her father had long since stopped making noise. As she left her room, she could see the mess the drunk's rampage had caused. Glass littered the house, and her mother's chair had been shattered to bits. A table was upturned, and ashes from the fireplace had been spilled out.

Her father lay in the middle of it all, passed out in front of the hearth. There was a stein next to him, and his drool seeped onto the floor.

Ilara glanced down at the dagger in her hand as she strode up to the man. She moved before Sophia was prepared for her to. A red line appeared on his throat where the sharp blade passed over it, and blood seeped across the skin.

It wasn't deep enough to kill. Worse yet, her father's eyes creaked open as Ilara was midway through the cut.

He caught Ilara's forearm. The vision in the bowl became a whir of chaos as she tumbled and was thrown into a wall. A sickening crack came from her arm as she hit the floor. Their father stood, holding a hand to his neck, and staggered toward Ilara. Blood oozed through his fingers as she crawled in pain on the ground.

She fumbled for the dagger, which she'd dropped when she'd been thrown. Her father took another grueling step toward her, murderous intent in his eyes.

The blade, surrounded by a purple aura, seemed to fly through the air and land in Ilara's open palm. Not questioning this, she brought it out in front of her. Her father, set on his wicked intent, fell toward her with his arms outstretched. The dagger buried itself up to the hilt in his lower ribcage with the momentum of his fall.

Surprised, he pushed away and fell to the side as his hands clutched the new wound. He was on his back next to Ilara and gurgled loudly as his throat began filling with blood. She quickly got up and straddled his chest with the dagger gripped in both hands.

Grunting through the pain of her broken arm, Ilara raised the dagger above her head and drove it into her father's chest again. The blade bounced messily between the bones. His bloody fingers grabbed at Ilara, but their slickness kept him from finding purchase on her arm.

It didn't stop her from stabbing him again.

And again.

And again.

Sophia lost count of the number of times the blood-soaked child stabbed her father. When Ilara was done, the man didn't move again. The child, now realizing what she'd done, screamed and kicked herself into a corner. She left the dagger near the man as she wept, hugging her knees to her.

This tale wasn't about Sophia at all. This was Ilara's birth.

Sophia stared soullessly at the bowl as the light in it faded and the runes dimmed. Ilara sat back in her chair. Her face was covered with tears and sweat. The silence between them was uncomfortable.

"Why can't I recall them?" Sophia asked.

"Zal'Keratha said that the dead she sends back are still subject to the physical ailments they had in life. I think that means you hit your head on the well. You would have lost those memories even if you'd survived."

"Am I—" The words caught in Sophia's throat. "I'm not a corpse, am I?"

"No. I don't understand the magic, but you are here as you. Body restored and soul returned from the other side," Ilara said.

"But I was there? With the gods? In the Cavern of Souls?"

"You were."

Sophia covered her gaping mouth with her hand. "Should I even be alive, Ilara?"

Ilara's gaze stiffened, and she shifted in her seat. "I think you should be. As far as I'm concerned, I traded a bastard's life for my loving sister's. And I would do it a thousand times over."

"You sound a little like he did, at the end," Sophia said.

Ilara's eyes shifted to the floor. "Maybe I do deal with life as flippantly as he did. The older I get, the more of him I see in me. That's why I couldn't raise Theo. I couldn't be—I couldn't do what he—" She stopped and buried her face in her hands.

"No, stop thinking like that. You aren't him. You'd never do what he did," Sophia said, taking Ilara's shoulders and pulling her into an embrace.

"You don't know that, Soph. I've done horrible things to stay alive. Zal'Keratha demands so much. I could never keep Theo from that. I—I couldn't even keep you from that." Ilara sobbed.

"I wish you'd never had to make that choice. If I could go back and do it all differently—"

"No. No, you were a child. That is not your fault." Ilara was more resolute as she put her hands back in her lap. "Father paid for his crime. We're lucky that he did. So much evil goes unpunished."

Sophia let that hang in the air as Ilara buried her face in her sister's neck. "Well. What do we do now?" Sophia asked.

"Try to make the world a better place." Ilara broke the embrace and wiped her eyes.

"I agree. That starts with making sure Akara pays for her crimes."

"I know. Look. We met with Katri's friend, Desmond. Those rioters think they are the head of some glorious revolution. They agreed to the assault, though. And they'd like you in their camp during it as a guarantee we won't attack them."

"No, that's trollshit," Sophia said.

"Both Katri and I think it's a good idea. You can be there to make sure they go through with their part of the bargain. Gray is there, and I think he might fuck with our plans."

Sophia crossed her arms. She may have saved Theo, but it still felt like Ilara was doing her best to keep her from the gods. She understood why now, but it still made her feel like a child being coddled.

"I do need to know everything the Librarian told you about the altar, though," Ilara told her.

"He gave me some strange vision. I've been puzzling about it for a while. I think it's going to require the sacrifice of two Chosen."

"Alright, then. Go through it, in detail," Ilara said.

# Chapter Thirty-Eight

# PRISONER

Ilara could still feel the curse on her chest. Even though Mal'Evir had given her the last of his treatment, she felt drained. Katri and Chek'Va looked back at her incredulously. She'd just told them that two Chosen needed to die so that Ilara could kill Akara. The air was heavy with indecision as they stood in the bunk room Mal'Evir had given them when they'd arrived weeks ago.

Katri crossed her arms. "You can't be serious. None of us should have to die for this."

"I would gladly give my life for the glory of a new Aoxia," Chek'Va snarled in his native tongue.

Ilara waved her hand through the air. "None of us should have to die—if the plan goes right."

"Then who in the bloody hells would we be killing?" Katri demanded.

"Markus, for one. He should already be near the altar. I think he's waiting to sacrifice several of us," Sophia said.

"And the second?" Katri was frowned as Ilara translated Sophia's sentence for Chek'Va. He still didn't have a good grasp on the language, despite practicing with Mal'Evir for several weeks.

"We have another paladin here. She's not Akaran, but Mal'Evir says she's Almiran." Ilara turned back to Katri..

"So we're sacrificing someone outside of all this? Almir's been cast from the Pantheon, too."

"He may be now, but his Chosen have done as much as the Akarans in establishing Akara's Empire. There is no hesitation in my mind," Ilara said.

Katri shook her head. "I'm still not so sure. Chek'Va said he saw her attack Akara's paladins before he fought her himself. I think we should speak with her, and try to bring her to our side. She may have more concrete information on where the tower is other than that it's 'the tallest tower of the Dominion.' They're so close together that we might choose the wrong one."

"We can ask her that," Ilara agreed. "But I know this Almiran. She's the one who had Sophia captured, who defended Senator Plithy—a godsdamned killer in his own right."

"There's more to it." Sophia met Ilara's gaze, and she saw a firmness in her sister's expression. "Chosen Valette defended me from an Akaran while I was in their captivity, one who'd gone insane and thought he was Akara's Voice. I would be dead if not for her. She is honorable."

Ilara let out a long, drawn-out sigh. Why couldn't this just be easy? "Fine. I'm still not above putting her in manacles and dragging her to the Solar Dominion without all of you." She huffed, then moved to leave the room.

Katri caught her by the shoulder. "Give this one a chance. If she did one act of good, she might be capable of others."

Ilara nodded curtly, then left with her black metal spear in hand.

As she rounded the corner, she saw Mal'Evir pacing nervously outside of their prisoner's room. His face scales bunched up in a concerned look when he saw Ilara. He looked from her to the weapon she was holding.

"Gods, you aren't going to kill her, are you?" he asked.

"Not if she cooperates," Ilara said. The urge had built in her without her noticing it. She needed this kill. This Almiran deserved to die more than any of the others. "Open the door, Mal."

His back stiffened. He held the large iron key to his chest. "You must give me your word that you won't kill her."

"What do you care? You're a Syndicate doctor. Every-one you've ever treated has done something awful to get here, then went on to do something awful after you patched them up."

"That may be, but it doesn't change the fact that I wish for this one not to die. Give me your word, Zal'Kerathan," he said.

"Fine, sure. I won't kill her." Ilara's grip tightened around the spear. She wouldn't if she could help it.

"Thank you," Mal'Evir said as he slid the key into the lock.

He opened the door, and Ilara saw the woman. Valette was sitting against the wall, her blonde hair covered in blood and dirt. One of her hands was badly burned, and one of her shoulders was still bandaged. Even without her armor, she cut a burly figure, as if she could break Ilara's bones with her bare hands.

Ilara made eye contact, and Valette smiled. "Here to settle the debt, Zal'Kerathan?" she asked.

"Maybe," Ilara said, then heard a scoff from Mal'Evir. "No, I guess I'm not."

"Then what could you possibly want from me? Have you not aided in Eversburg's destruction enough?"

Ilara laughed. "My sister is convinced you're a good per-son. Despite the number of his people I'm sure you've killed, even Chek'Va is convinced of your honor, and you actually tried to kill him. What am I missing?"

"Your sister, Sophia. I gave her clemency during a time in her life when she could find none. I tried to honor the Aoxian code in my duel with Chek'Va, and failed. I was disappointed to find myself awake. The doctor is a caring creature. I'm sure he'd see to it that every egg in his clutch survived if he could," Valette answered.

Ilara sneered. This woman was the reason Sophia had been in that accursed palace. "And why did you come here? Why did you leave the safety of the Solar Dominion?"

"The Solar Dominion was not safe for me. I saw my only salvation get torn apart by Akara's power. And, I had to go looking for you."

"To right your god's honor? To have justice restored for that murderer I killed?" Ilara asked.

Valette fell silent, a confused look on her face.

"Almir says that he is a god of honor and justice," Ilara continued. "I might believe that if his justice wasn't so often misplaced."

"He is justice. His ways are justice. You aid the enemy in ways," Valette hissed.

"No!" Ilara slammed the butt of her spear against the ground. "If that were so, you would commend me for Plithy's death. You judge without the whole picture."

"You serve the forces of evil. Death clambers for the Pantheon that life may end. If Plithy had been evil, he would have gone to trial and been judged in the court of the land," Valette snarled.

"No. Those you serve are the true evil," Ilara said. "Akara has slain thousands and will slay thousands more, all innocent."

"I don't believe Akara controls the Pantheon. Not anymore. Whatever those things are, you serve them. You and your goddess put them there, whether you realize it or not. I came here to find out why. To find out how that might be possible."

"You speak lies," Ilara snarled. "Explain yourself."

Valette took a deep breath. She seemed like a cracked pot holding too much water. Terror spread across her face, as if it were something that she had veiled until that moment. She told Ilara of her strange vision of seeing the goddess's eyes. Of the extra voices she'd heard and how Zal'Keratha's ploy fit into their plans. It did almost make it seem like the goddess was working with them.

Ilara's grip tightened on her spear. She needed Zal'Keratha's input. Calmly, she placed the weapon on one end of the room, far from Valette's reach, then walked to the other side. She felt a wave pass over her mind as her connection reestablished with Zal'Keratha.

*What do you know of this?* Ilara asked her goddess.

*"I have not assisted any other against Akara. If what this Valette says is true, the goddess may be compromised. It is all the more imperative that you ascend on the altar. It must be done forthwith,"* Zal'Keratha said through their connection.

*Tell me the whole truth, now,* Ilara said.

*"They are likely the creatures I told you of. The Qel'm. They must have infiltrated the Pantheon—they are clever creatures. We must be done with these politics you insist are so important. I'm offering you godhood, Ilara. If you ascend and slay Akara, you will be the one to take her power, and I will be queen of the Pantheon. But we must take that power now."*

Ilara strode back over to the spear and picked it up, shutting Zal'Keratha out of her head. She knew then what she had to do, and she relished it. "Aye, I hear you. These politics are what will make this plan work," she said to herself.

"I take it to mean that she didn't admit to it, then?" Valette asked.

"You will assume nothing," Ilara responded. "I haven't aided these creatures you speak of. Whether or not Zal'Keratha has is another thing. She claims to hate them, but speaks of them with such reverence." She turned to Valette. "Do you know of Akara's altar?"

"I have not seen it," Valette said.

"An altar of naked and nude bodies?"

"That? I have seen that."

"And you could lead us to it, if need be?" Ilara asked.

"Aye, I could. What are you intending?"

"To kill Akara and everything in her head," Ilara growled. "I will speak with my fellows and decide what to do with you."

She stepped out of the room and walked down the hall.

*"I want to speak with her. If you can, find a way to send this Chosen to me,"* Zal'Keratha said as Ilara sat down on her cot.

She rejoiced slightly. At least this would calm the panic rising in her mind.

# Chapter Thirty-Nine

# CAVERN OF SOULS

There was a finality to the silence that engulfed Valette when Ilara closed the door to her cell. She wondered how many men and women had been caged here before. Was she the last in a long line of prisoners, or was this a repurposed clinic room? She suspected these were the last walls she would ever see. There was a comfort to it that she hadn't expected.

"Gods," she grumbled, and stood up. There were no chains keeping her to the floor, but her arms were still bound in front of her with the black velvet bands.

She heard shouting from an adjacent room, but she couldn't tell what they were saying. She knew they were deciding what to do with her. Ilara could kill her now. It was the sane thing to do. It's what Valette would do if the positions were reversed, but Plithy's corpse still accused Valette in her mind.

Escape likely wasn't an option. There was no channeling magic with these bands on—she'd seen the effects of them too many times. The door to her cell was sufficiently locked and made of thick wood. She wondered how many times she'd need to kick it before it broke.

Probably too many.

She turned her attention back to the bands. The thick black fabric pinned her forearms together and prevented most movements of her arms. They were tied near her elbows in a complicated knot that she was certain only a sailor could replicate. If she could twist her spine down, she might be able to pierce them with her teeth.

It was this awkward contortionist pose she was in when the lock to her cell door clinked. When she looked up, Mal'Evir nearly fell into the room, carrying a long parcel under one of his arms, which could only be holding a sword.

Valette froze, unsure what the doctor's intentions were with such a deadly weapon. She didn't think he'd knew how to use one effectively, but she was certain any Aoxian could launch a hunk of metal at her head and kill her.

He dropped it at her feet opened it. "The other patients in my clinic are going to kill you," he said.

"Come to do the job for them?" Pain throbbed in Valette's broken leg. "I can barely move about this room."

Mal'Evir pulled a dagger from his waist. She recoiled instinctively as he brought it toward her, covering her chest and face with her arms. She hoped that the bands would block his strikes, at least for a while.

"*Valette!*"

She felt the tension in her arms release as the bands fell away. Her tracts of magic seemed to fill in response to her connection to Almir being restored.

Valette stared, bewildered, from Mal'Evir to the sword at her feet. It was sheathed in a cracked leather scabbard that looked like it was as old as she was.

He picked it up and held it out to her, revealing a large diamond inlaid in the hilt. "For the Chosen of my god," he said, speaking as an Almiran worshiper. "Use it to defend yourself and Almir's devoted."

Wordlessly, Valette took the weapon and marveled at how light it was. The sword was nearly as long as she was tall, but felt like she was wielding one half its size. She pulled it from its sheath to check the sharpness and found that the steel was tainted blue, with waves etched into the flat of the blade. None of the markings gave any indication they'd been etched by hand. A soft blue glow began emanating up from the handle, as if reacting to her touch.

"It was crafted many years ago by a Chosen of Halga. It was a gift for a dear friend of mine, who never had the chance to receive it. I hope you will do her memory justice." Mal'Evir swallowed hard and looked away.

Valette smiled. "A fine sword that befits a warrior." If it had been forged by a Crafter, she wouldn't have to worry about it dulling or rusting. It would cut as finely as the day it was made. Still, she couldn't do much in her condition.

Gently, she slid the sword back into its sheath. "What makes you think I won't run you through?" she asked, her hands beginning to glow a soft white. She grimaced as the wound healed and the bones in her collar and arm knit back together. These were the most painful injuries to mend.

"You won't, Chosen. I have worshiped Almir for all my life. He was my household god when I lived in Aoxia. My partner and I met in one of his temples. At times, I let him overtake my soul above that of my lord Aox, Serpent be praised. Needless to say, I know his parables well. I have lived my life in emulation of the Good Physician," Mal'Evir said as he sat cross-legged on the floor beside her.

"I know the one. Heal the evil that the evildoer might repent their ways," Valette said. It was an odd parable, as it seemed to contradict others. The story centered around a doctor who would heal the wicked to redeem their souls. "It is an admirable goal."

"I mean no rush, Chosen, but my absence will be noted soon. Is it possible that you could hurry along this mending of yours?" Mal'Evir glanced nervously at the closed door.

"There's no rushing a cure, even a magical one," Valette said calmly, moving on to her calf. Chek'Va had done a thorough job in breaking it. "Tell me what the plan is."

"Chek'Va stands at the door. He has promised not to harm us but has sworn to see Ilara's mission to fruition—an oath he took for Aox, to see the Lady of Death on the throne."

"But where are we going?" Valette asked as she mended the bones in her ankle. It healed nicely, but drained all the magic from her tract. She'd have to be careful until it was refreshed tomorrow.

"I will go south. I request your company out of the city, but no farther. Our knight has promised to guide me to the land of my forebearers. It is the only safe place for my kind, even though Akara has ensured that much of it is unsafe."

Valette nodded as she stood, sword in hand. Almost too late, she noticed the glint of steel of a dagger being hurled in her direction. She flinched and knocked it to the side. The door was open, Ilara's vicious form standing in the frame as she formed another pair of daggers in her palms.

"Seems we won't be out of here without a fight," Valette said, drawing her weapon from its sheath.

Ilara looked from Valette to Mal'Evir. "What is going on?"

"The good doctor says you intend to kill me," Valette said.

"And you would defend Plithy again, if he were brought back from death?" Ilara asked.

"I stand by my actions, just as you stand by the goddess who aids my enemy," Valette growled.

Ilara positioned herself to block Valette's escape. "It is decided then."

Valette mirrored Ilara's stance, pulling her blade back so that she could strike if Ilara got close.

She couldn't move forward into the cramped hallway, as she wouldn't be able to swing the large sword freely, which was what Ilara wanted.

Ilara must have known this as well. She strode forward confidently into the reach of Valette's weapon. Valette released her strike, aiming at the smaller woman's center of mass. The blade was light, which allowed her to swing it faster than her opponent was expecting.

Still, Ilara ducked under it and rushed into range to strike with her daggers. Valette redirected her sword quickly. It responded well to her intentions, as if it could read her mind, and parried Ilara's attack.

As metal met metal, the momentum of Valette's sword knocked the daggers from Ilara's hands. She put her hand out to form new ones, but a spear appeared instead. The black metal tip made Valette think of the dagger Maer had used against her. She knew the danger it posed.

Ilara took one step back, then disappeared as she had when they'd first fought in the inn. Back then, Valette had panicked. She wouldn't do so here. Quickly, she forced Mal'Evir into a corner, her back to him, and waited. The blue-scaled lizard was the only leverage Ilara could take from her. Valette just had to be sure neither of them was hit by that spear.

Valette heard footsteps padding softly from her left. Without knowing how Ilara would thrust her spear, Valette took several steps forward and hurled her weight into the sword. It was a hard and fast swing that she felt catch as pain erupted from her leg.

Ilara became visible again, and Valette would have rejoiced in seeing her sword buried in Ilara's side, had it not been for the spear stuck in her own leg. She felt a draining sensation coming from the wound, grasping the spear as she lost all feeling in the limb. She toppled to the ground and pulled it out, staring in horror as the blood on the tip seemed to be sucked into the stone.

"Gods damn it, I just fixed this leg," she muttered, trying to hold her hands to the open wound.

As she glanced up, she saw a familiar form standing between her and Ilara before the light faded from her vision.

*** 

When Valette opened her eyes, she was standing, surrounded by jagged stone walls. It was a natural cave of some kind, lit by candles that sat on an altar carved from the stone floor. The striking figure of Zal'Keratha stood behind the altar. Her massive horns were illuminated by the flickering light, the shadows of them dancing on the wall behind her.

"Almiran," she said coolly as she placed her hands on the corners of the altar. Carved runes began to glow a dull magenta, fueled by the goddess's energy.

Valette grimaced as she looked around. "This is—"

"The Cavern of Souls, where each soul meets their due judgment. The place that Almir imprisoned me more than a century ago," Zal'Keratha said.

"So I've died?"

"Close to it, yes." A wicked grin flashed across the goddess's face. "A trick by my Chosen. One I've denied her to use."

"That spear," Valette said. The wound had been deep, but not deep enough to outright kill her. She had planned to use what was left of her healing spell to stitch it up enough for Mal'Evir to escape.

"Yes. It is the spear of our enemy, the one I showed you in your vision."

"You showed me Akara's mind? But you are the one aiding them."

"Of course not. Showing you the vision was necessary to turn you further from Akara. These creatures believe my Chosen furthers their ends. This is by design. You met one by the name of Al-Kaise—one of them given form. The Qel'm."

"So you understand that Akara is not the enemy?"

"Aye."

"What are these Qel'm?"

"Creatures of a power opposite the gods. One could call them demons or devils, though they would chafe at the words. Once, they were mortals of another world, ruled by distant gods. Gods that they found ways to consume. They feast upon the power of the divine but have no way of generating it themselves," Zal'Keratha said.

As she spoke, she waved her pale blue hand through the flames of a candle. Her skin changed to a rosy pink each time, then faded back to blue.

"So they fed on Akara," Valette said, and felt herself grow ill. Could spirits grow ill? Was that what she was now?

"Indeed. I have no idea how long they have been on Aerlia. We banished them once, and will do so again," Zal'Keratha said.

"If they have Akara, then they must have the power of the Pantheon. The gods will be doomed. None of our armies could stand against Al-Kaise," Valette said.

"True, but as evidenced by Eversburg's revolution, the Qel'm do not know yet how to use it. They hesitate to let Al-Kaise leave the Dominion. Not only that, but they were unable to maintain Akara's Chosen, as each became weaker than the last. They know little of carving tracts in mortals," Zal'Keratha said, grinning. "We have time, but it grows short."

"I can do nothing now," Valette said.

The goddess smiled again. Her mouth was full of pointed teeth. "I can send you back, Chosen, but there are certain assurances that I require."

# Chapter Forty

# FORSAKEN

"*I hope you understand the risk,*" Balan said as Sophia walked into Valette's cell.

She gasped as she saw Valette's large blade slam into Ilara and the spear slice into Valette. The sword clanged to the ground as Valette grabbed at her leg, toppling over before Ilara did as well. Blood was everywhere.

Ilara leaned against the wall, staggering to her feet as Valette lay on the ground. She was forming another dagger in her free hand. Sophia had only a moment.

"No," she shouted as she moved to the space between the two women. "I will not let you kill this one, sister."

Ilara looked blearily between Sophia and Valette.

Mal'Evir shuffled past Sophia and began tending to Valette's wound. He muttered worriedly and gasped at the injury. From what she could tell, it was likely fatal.

"She will kill us all, Soph," Ilara gasped as she held her side. Blood seeped through the cut in her armor. "Her loyalty is still with the Akarans. She has not renounced them. She cannot see any others as good or just. Leaving her alive is a liability. Step aside while she is still weak!"

"I can't. She saved me from evil. Today I will do the same," Sophia said.

"You doubt me?" Ilara asked. Sophia saw bloodred rage in her eyes. There was a need in them that Sophia couldn't place.

"No," Valette said from behind her. Faint white light glowed from her hand as she stood again.

Ilara formed another set of blades but stumbled down, her face turning white. She'd lost a lot of blood.

"You will not fight, this one, my Chosen," Valette said, but it wasn't her. Valette's eyes glowed a soft purple, and she held herself with her shoulders flung back and fingers steepled in front of her stomach.

"My lady?" Ilara asked.

"Yes," Zal'Keratha said through Valette. "You succeeded in sending this Chosen to meet me. She'll be back momentarily. Valette and Almir have agreed to help us find Akara's altar. She believes she knows where it might be."

"And if we send her back to you?" Ilara growled.

Zal'Keratha shook Valette's head and picked up the black metal spear. "Then I'll be finding myself a new Chosen. You'll do as I command, Ilara. And you'll be doing it without this." She waved her hand, and the spear disappeared. "I warned you this was a method of the Qel'm to manifest in our world, and you did not listen. Further attempts to use these weapons will cause me to Forsake you."

She turned to Sophia. Katri and Chek'Va entered the room, eyes widening when they saw Valette's new form.

"Chosen of Shyll, you will be taking charge of this group by my command. Get my Chosen to Akara's altar and activate it by any means necessary," Zal'Keratha said.

"Aye." Katri closed her eyes for a moment. When she opened them, the green flecks in her irises shone brighter. "Shyll agrees that you shall be queen."

"Good," Zal'Keratha said, then turned back to Ilara, who had fallen back to the floor. She was holding her hand against the gash in her armor. Zal'Keratha put Valette's hand on top of hers. White light channeled through it, and the wound healed.

"You know that you are beholden to me. If this goes wrong at all, you know what I'll take from you," Zal'Keratha hissed.

Ilara's eyes flicked to Sophia, then back to the goddess. "Aye. I know. I won't disappoint you again."

"Good." Zal'Keratha turned back to the group. Valette's eyes dimmed and returned to their blue, yet they now had a small purple ring around the outside of the iris.

Valette gasped and nearly stumbled forward. "Gods," she said. "I take it she told you, then?"

"Aye," Sophia said. "We have a lot of work to do still. The Revolution attacks the Dominion at daybreak."

***

Sophia shut the door to the clinic room. She never intended to see this place again. Once this was over, Eversburg as a whole seemed like it would be a shit place to be. Every path away from the city had a brighter horizon than the dawn that kept her here.

She'd still miss the velvet drapes of The Pearl, and how each audience hung on her every word. She'd miss the sunrise running across the main road of the Noon district and the cool sea breeze.

Katri appeared at the far end of the clinic's hallway. Her stride was confident, and the embrace she pulled Sophia into was warmly calming.

"Is this going to work?" Sophia asked as they broke apart.

"If Ilara cooperates, it will," Katri said.

"She will. Though I think she blames Zal'Keratha for her own trauma, in a way."

"Aye, Mal told me she dumped your past on you." Katri looked at Sophia with a softness in her green eyes. "Do you want to talk about it before the fighting starts again?"

"I don't, not right now anyway. I still have to process it all, I think. I do appreciate the offer, but in a way, it's like it isn't all about me. I'm glad to know what happened, and that alone brings me a peace like I've never known. I'm more worried about Ilara. She's carried that pain for her entire life. In many ways, it has made her a fool."

"Now isn't the time to feel bad for her. She almost risked everything for this weird vengeance on Valette," Katri said.

"Aye, she did. But Valette acted the same way. You are going to have your hands full dealing with those two. You sure you don't need me?"

"I'll be fine, aye." The lower city drawl meandered into Katri's speech like an afternoon walk. "Unlike Ilara, I've spent time among people, and I know how they think. In many ways, this Revolution was inevitable, and I'm happy to play my part in it. But— Well, just in case I don't get a chance."

Her hand swept behind Sophia's head and pulled her face to her own. She locked Sophia into a kiss, her plump lips filling Sophia with lust. She felt her face redden as she wrapped her arms around Katri's wiry torso and allowed herself to kiss her back.

"We'll . . . need to follow that up later. What made you change your mind?" Sophia said as she moved away.

"Hope." Katri winked, and as Sophia walked away, both women giggled like teenagers. It was so rare to find someone like Katri that Sophia couldn't help but feel swept off her feet.

The sun colored the sky an amber red as dusk made its way across the horizon. Sophia found her way quickly through the battle-scarred streets. There were notably fewer corpses than the day before, as if the city were cleaning herself—ridding herself of the dead to make her arteries clear so that the living might make use of the life still in her veins.

Sophia paused when she reached The Pearl. She weighed whether to take Bleeder with her. She imagined him inside, eating soup and chatting idly with Theo. The thought of his near unconscious body being beaten by bandits turned her against it. Better for her to go alone than endanger the lives of others. It would be good for her, she thought.

Moonlight was shining quietly on the city by the time she arrived at the Revolutionaries' camp. The air around it was oddly quiet. No owls hooted or horse hooves clomped, as if the city were at a turning point. Sophia's future would be decided today, and it would be playing its casual music until it had been settled.

Or Balan was warning her that this day would be more dangerous than she realized. The city didn't care who won the coming conflict. It would be here no matter what happened. All that would change was the song sung, and the survivors would decide what that sounded like.

# CHAPTER FORTY-ONE

# WATCH

Valette knew the importance of what they were doing but hated the tedium of it. From the balcony, they could see the Solar Dominion and the revolutionary camp settled in next to it. The statue of Akara and her sword loomed over it like a menacing omen.

They were to watch for when the battle began and let the group know. The plan would continue as discussed. Valette had suggested Zal'Keratha put Katri in charge. It seemed like the Shyllan would be a neutral third party between the Chosen. So far, it had worked.

Ilara had huffed but agreed quickly once Zal'Keratha and Sophia left. She'd even taken the first watch over the camp with Katri. Mal'Evir took the next one with Valette.

She was just surprised he was still here.

Now, Mal'Evir clucked his tongue and crossed his arms, a small parcel held out in front of him.

"Where will you go?" Valette asked. She wanted to break the tension. She knew from her days in the army that keeping these watches could make a soldier irritable if they had bad company.

"South, as I said before. I suspect any Aoxian would be killed on sight no matter what happens here in Eversburg. Aoxia will be safe, I think. The journey will be long. I can't convince you to escort me from the city?" he asked.

She shook her head. "Larger things are happening that I must tend to. When this is over, perhaps I'll visit you in Aoxia. I'd like to know how Almir is worshiped among the lizards."

She could already feel the hunger itching at the sides of her mind. Zal'Keratha had warned her this would be the case, but Valette still hadn't been prepared for it. Images of stabbing the Aoxian through the skull flashed through her mind. She could almost bathe in the blood.

"Not lizards," Mal'Evir snapped.

"I mean no offense," Valette said quickly.

Mal'Evir smirked. "Most Aoxians do not know the difficulty of living with humans in Eversburg. You assign endearments in your language that Aoxians do not. The change can be jarring, but we do prefer not to be called lesser beings. But truth be told, I will be happier with these walls at my back.

My reasons for leaving are many. Even if it weren't for what the Akarans have done to my people, my family, I believe I would still go. This is no place to raise my clutch," he said, hugging his parcel.

"I'm surprised," Valette said. "You've done a fine job at hiding them."

Mal'Evir side-eyed her, then continued. "Aye. They've lain dormant in their eggs for many years, out of the sight of the Syndicate. My partner and I made them so long ago. They are all I have left of her. Do you know of Aoxian mating rituals?" he asked, turning back to Valette.

"I wouldn't know even the simplest details about how Aoxians mate."

"Oh, no, no." Mal'Evir tutted under his breath. "Not the process—that is none too different from humans. The ritual we take when we choose a mate is unique. We choose for life. My people are born with a single color of scales, but as you can see, I have this lovely streak of gold through my red, while our Chek'Va does not. When we Aoxians bond, the color of our mate becomes part of our hide, a manifestation of our love for one another."

"That is beautiful."

"And all the more heartbreaking when it is cut short." Mal'Evir gently brushed his claw along his cheek.

"Every day I look in the mirror and see my Shel'Ta's scales staring back at me. They accuse me of being unable to save her. Of being a coward."

"How did it happen?" Valette asked.

"I was attending to clients when she was taken. Eversburg's priests sang for the blood of my people. I knew this. I could have been there." He spat out the last words like they were a rebuke against someone standing in front of him.

While counseling had never been her strong suit, Valette felt she should try. She felt she needed to say something, anything, to ease his wounded heart. "Losing a loved one is the most difficult. It's not the same, but I know that pain. I have been away from my Antony for nearly a half year. This was my choice, to serve Almir, and I knew I would make sacrifices. I have a fear in the back of my head that the next letter I receive from Chrys will be from my father, informing me of Antony's death, or of my children's. Above all, I worry my choice lessens their view of me. That I wasn't there during their hard times. Even more, I worry they think me the coward I feel I am for not being with them. I'm sure you had a good reason to be away from Shel'Ta. I'm sure she would forgive you."

Mal'Evir crossed his arms. "You are right that she wouldn't want me flogging myself. I miss her so and would give years of my life to be with her once more."

"And yet here you are, carrying the memory of her," Valette said.

"Indeed. I feel regret at the choices I made. Do you think you will be the same? When life ends, will you feel sadness at killing Akara rather than spending your time with your Antony?"

"Perhaps, though I feel that I cannot dwell on those thoughts. If I do not do this, who would? Would my children be well off in the world Akara is cultivating?"

"I suppose not. The bliss of the ignorant. But do you suppose those gods you fight for truly care about us? Will this new world they create be better than Akara's?"

"Are you always this philosophical?" Valette asked.

"Not normally. I find myself growing nostalgic for the place of my birth."

"Why did you come to Eversburg?" Valette felt the need to keep the night from growing silent.

"Like many who fled Aoxia, I desired to free myself from the influence of the god of my homeland," Mal'Evir said.

Valette arched her eyebrows in surprise. "Aox provided some of his power for all his people. Why would you turn from a god like that?"

"Aox oftentimes felt like a parent who tried too hard to be in their children's lives. He gives, but he also expects much in return. I wanted to escape that influence. I cast away the magics he gave me in favor of Crafter-built contraptions. I turned away from his worship to one I felt better aligned with my ideals. I may have lost his power and become Forsaken, but I was free to live a life of my own. I thought there was no price I'd be unwilling to pay for that." Mal'Evir clasped his parcel tighter. "I suppose that there was."

"You couldn't have known," Valette said. She saw a row of lights ignite in the gate of the Solar Dominion. Was this a routine patrol checking on the revolutionaries or something more?

"We should have." Mal'Evir shook his head. "Like so many others, we rushed headlong into a situation that turned against us overnight. It makes me glad that you're bringing this fight to Akara. Perhaps you will right some of her wrongs."

"So you do think the gods have our interests in mind?" Valette asked.

"No, I— What is that?" Mal'Evir asked as a figure shining in bright red light emerged from the doors of the Solar Dominion.

Valette knew it could mean only one thing. Al-Kaise has come out to the fight.

## CHAPTER FORTY-TWO

# AN END BEGINS

"YOU'LL HAVE NOTHING TO do with the battle?" Desmond asked.

Sophia nodded. She found this man to be earnest, but he loved the sound of his own voice. He wanted her to fight, but he didn't seem to know how to ask her.

"She's told us she won't," Sir Fenwald said. This was the man with the gray mustache. Ilara had warned her about him.

"I am a Balanite. We are not normally trained in any combat or spells that harm," Sophia explained. "I'm much more worried I'd get in the way of your soldiers."

And I don't want to kill anyone again.

Fenwald grinned. "Perhaps we can strap you with a drum and call you our drummer girl."

"Aye, maybe. How loud can you make that lute on your back?" Desmond asked.

"Loud enough to fill a bar," Sophia said. "What are you thinking?"

"It may be good to play a song for morale when the time comes. We've camped longer than we've fought at this point, and my people are restless. A small ditty could help us prepare for the fight, more than all this training Fenwald is always on about," Desmond said.

"I could try?"

Loud bells began to ring from the Solar Dominion. They splintered the air like shattering glass. Desmond's eyes widened in panic.

"To arms," yelled someone outside the tent.

"Table it," Fenwald said, drawing a black metal rapier from his cane. Desmond unsheathed one as well. Sophia's eyes widened at Zal'Keratha's warning. These were vessels of the Qel'm.

They all rushed from the tent to see paladins and revolutionaries fighting in the area between their barricades and the Solar Dominion. There was a wall of people holding shields against the paladins, whose eyes and mouths all emanated a bright red light.

Bones crunched. Steel flashed. Men and women let out death cries. All of it formed a brutal hymn of death and struggle.

Above them hovered Priestess Tezza, as Valette had warned. From her back arched wings made of red light, and in her hand she held a similarly glowing sword. She swept it in front of her, and it swiped down to the battle lines. The tip dragged like a whip, and it passed through the formation of Revolutionaries on the field. They fell over dead.

Akaran paladins surged forward, knocking over and stomping past the bodies. Desmond and Fenwald both disappeared amid the chaos. Sophia assumed they had run to help their men. Another line formed in the gaps of the barricades.

A line of archers fired from inside the camp, their arrows slamming into the line of their attackers. Sophia didn't see any of the paladins fall, though they began emitting more light. She suddenly felt very unsafe.

"*The time is now. You must cast the battle hymn!*" Balan said. He was uncharacteristically urgent and drove her to pull the lute from her back. As she strummed, she pulled the spells to amplify the sound waves so that they might travel farther.

Red waves reverberated back to her. "*Who are you, Balanite?*" There was a viciousness to the words that unsettled Sophia. Their suddenness caused her to miss the spell as the waves of sound rocketed past her.

Paladins slammed into the waiting battle line, and the metallic crash of steel reached her ears again. Explosions shook the ground, throwing those fighting to the side. They were only a hundred feet away from where Sophia stood. She willed herself to strum again, and another sound wave flew out. When it came back, she slid her fingers into it. A tingling sensation washed over her, and she couldn't contain it.

Green light burst from her chest, and tendrils of power sought the fighters near her. She felt their minds, some panicked and terrified, while others were resolved to win or die trying. Each was a warrior who hadn't gotten to a line for one reason or another.

Their thoughts melded through the power of the spell, becoming one. They fell in around her, a small shield wall against the coming onslaught. Sophia strummed again, and the green light coated their weapons. She felt the power in it. The light thrummed in the air like beautiful background noise.

As Akara's paladins broke the line, Sophia felt the panic around her, yet there was a calm inside her that battled against it. She shifted her fingers down the lute and strummed a discordant melody.

The soldiers in her control struck forward like a spear.

# CHAPTER FORTY-THREE

# RYN

A LIBRARY OF BOOKS extended up around Ilara. The multicolored volumes in Mal'Evir's study seemed to grow redder with each passing moment. Her fingers twitched nervously as Katri seemed to study every pore on her face.

"What is going on with you, Ilara?" Katri's expression seemed to soften for a moment before hardening again.

Was this the way she was, or was the need to kill overpowering Ilara's perception? Valette's blood had spilled, yet she itched to kill so badly. It had never been this way before.

"It is so unlike you to act so rashly," Katri continued. "You were a cold, calculating killer when we worked together. You'd never fight someone in the open like that."

"A closely guarded secret of my goddess's children. Akaran's develop red eyes, Balanites gain perfect pitch, and—"

"And Amerites gain an expanded mind," Katri finished. "The known effects of being Chosen by these gods."

"Aye. Zal'Keratha gives a boon that requires an offering, or the bloodlust gets to be too much. Cooped up in this clinic, I hadn't spilled blood in a long time," Ilara said.

"How often do you need to kill?"

"Every few days now." Ilara cast her eyes to the floor. "At first, it was only once a year at the most, before I lost control like I have now. It steadily got more and more frequent."

"Good news for you, there's going to be a lot of paladins to kill soon," Katri said. "Why didn't Zal'Keratha kill you? She seemed pissed that you tried to kill a Chosen for a tribute she requires."

"She told me to kill Valette. I think she's looking for a reason to Forsake me, honestly. Zal'Keratha still needs me as her Chosen. Nothing more. I need to get to the altar and send her to Akara. From there, I'll take the place of the goddess of light while Zal'Keratha becomes queen of the gods. Then she'll be done with me. It's all she wants," Ilara spat.

Katri folded her hands in front of her and rested her forehead against them. Her nails were long like claws and sharpened to points.

"Is that what you want?" she asked.

"No," Ilara said without hesitation. It wasn't what she wanted. She didn't want to kill, and she didn't want to play these games anymore. She was tired.

"Then why? Becoming Zal'Keratha's Forsaken seems like a fine choice given how much you don't want what she's offering."

"She said once that the perfect Chosen is one that owes her something. It keeps us in line as much as it keeps her interests valid. I feel—I know—that if I betray Zal'Keratha she will take the life she's given to Sophia. Keeping Sophia alive keeps me in line. I walked away from her all those years ago, hoping that I could disassociate. If she didn't mean anything to me anymore, then I could leave Zal'Keratha, become Forsaken, and finally live my own life."

"But you couldn't do that," Katri said.

"No, I—"

The door to the study burst open. Valette scanned the room, taking in everything from Chek'Va lounging in the corner to Ilara's tear-filled eyes. Katri stood and looked at her expectantly.

"The paladins have attacked. We have to move, now!"

***

Ilara stepped from the portal Chek'Va had hurriedly created and into a large cathedral. Moonlight shone through stained glass windows, creating slants of colored beams that stretched ominously.

Chek'Va was behind her. He stepped through and collapsed. He'd warned them that creating a portal alone was draining on the caster.

A man was standing at one end of the cathedral, wearing plate that hummed with a similar energy as Valette's sword. Ilara recognized it as the armor Valette had worn during their first encounter. This was Knight Commander Ryn.

Behind him, corpses adorned the wall, hung using spears and swords, like hunting trophies. Some were bald while others had thick, stocky figures, brutal sacrifices to Akara made so that their energy might rejoin the Pantheon.

Ryn's expression turned into a wicked smile, and his eyes glowed with a fury Ilara couldn't know. "Almiran, Aoxian, Zal'Kerathan, and Shyllan," he listed as he pointed to each of them. "How many of your pitiful gods does it take to match the power of the radiant queen?"

"Ryn," Valette growled. "How many of Ameri's children did you kill? How many Chosen in this city died?"

"All of them. Except you," Ryn snarled. He held his hand outstretched, and a flaming sword appeared in his hand. The Flaming Sword of Latinyth—Akara's Sword. The very one depicted in the giant statue outside the Dominion. A shield of red light took shape in his other hand, as if he were building it out of light.

"The power of their feeble gods feeds the Pantheon, returning their power to Akara to make her all the more powerful, that she might send her power down to me."

"Seems he's missed a few," Ilara growled, and created daggers in her hands. Ryn didn't have a black metal blade, only Akara's Sword.

"He's going to try to rectify that," Valette hissed. "I'll fight him head-on. Mal'Evir's sword should withstand the heat. You and Katri flank and try to wound him."

"Aye," Ilara said, running her hand over her forehead. She disappeared and stalked around the side while Katri transformed into her lupine form and moved around the opposite side.

Ilara felt her pulse throb in her head. It ached. It needed. This Akaran was filled with so much blood that could spill right out of him. A single dagger thrust to his thigh to bring him to his knees, then another in his throat.

It would be so easy.

She shook her head and crouched as she silently approached Ryn from behind. He shouted something, then Valette met his blade. Her exposed face grimaced as Ryn wound up for another strike. Valette had told them earlier that this man hadn't been a Chosen until a few days ago, yet he moved in a way that accentuated Akara's boons.

Still, he was leaving room for Ilara to slip a knife into the back of his armor. It would be so easy that she almost moved to do it. She could sate her bloodlust here and now if she offered this Akaran Chosen as a sacrifice to her Lady of Death.

It would be too easy.

Ilara paused. Katri might sense Ryn's weakness and kill him as easily as Ilara could. Perhaps this was the time to rid herself of a different thorn. Zal'Keratha trusted Valette, but Ilara didn't have to. She could just as easily slip her knife into the Almiran's back.

She held back and weighed the option as she unsheathed the dagger at her side. Sophia hadn't felt her lift the black blade from her dress. She watched as Valette deflected Ryn's latest attack and made a strike at his chest. She expected it to fail. She wasn't trying to kill him.

"Almir," Ryn huffed as he corrected his stance. "He was Akara's greatest disappointment. Did he ever tell you that?"

"We do not speak of Almir," Valette said.

"A pity. Akara told me that she'd groomed him to be her successor. On that day, a hundred years ago, when they banished Zal'Keratha to her own domain, he was to take Akara's place. Yet he was too cowardly to take her power. Instead, he carved out his own religion, made his own power. He became a lesser god with his own followers. He was only ever anything because Akara let him onto the Pantheon."

"And now she rules alone," Valette hissed.

"Aye. She consolidated the power of Ameri, Halga, and Shyll into a single entity. She has the power to torch this world. In her mercy, she lets us live. Slay me, and you may learn her wrath." He lunged forward. His flaming sword moved at incredible speed.

Ilara cursed herself and threw a newly formed dagger to knock his blade to the side. She hated to admit it, but she still needed Valette, so she tucked the black metal knife back in her belt. The Almiran still hadn't told them where the damn altar was. It now sounded like they'd need to be quick about getting to it.

She launched forward and formed another set of daggers in her hands, aiming her strikes at Ryn's leg. He swept his sword toward her and smacked her with the flat of the blade. Katri lunged from the opposite side, using the window of opportunity to get in close.

Ryn hopped backward to allow Katri's claws to dig into the marble wall he'd been standing in front of. He raised a gauntleted fist and slammed it into her face. Teeth clattered to the floor as he broke her jaw.

Valette screamed and swung the runic sword at Ryn's back. Ilara darted forward as silently as she could. Ryn met Valette's blade with his, steel clashing as her weapon was knocked wide. Her guard was down, and she was vulnerable for a second, but so was he.

Ilara slammed a dagger through the gaps in Ryn's armor, feeling it slice into the flesh of his shoulder. He grunted and dropped his sword. His elbow flew at her instinctively and collided with her nose, knocking her away from him.

Katri filled the space between Ilara and Ryn and growled, while Valette recovered and raised her blade again. Ryn caught it as she brought it down. His gauntlet cracked, and the blade dug into it. Blood spilled out the sides as the sword tore through his hand.

He laughed, the hollow sound echoing in the empty cathedral. Valette tried to pull her blade back, but it was stuck. Ryn reformed Akara's Sword in his opposite hand.

"I will die this day, but I will take Almir's Chosen, the last Shyllan, and a Zal'Kerathan with me!"

Katri pounced forward. He sliced the blade across her chest, and Ilara heard the squelch of metal meeting flesh. Katri fell to the side with the sword embedded in her chest, and the momentum slid her body across the marble floor. She was still breathing, but weakly. Ryn's weapon dissipated as he called another to him.

Rage and bloodlust filled Ilara. Ryn was vulnerable for a moment as his blade reformed. She lunged at him and summoned Zal'Keratha's daggers, and his eyes widened as her invisibility fell away.

She drove the daggers into his neck, drawing his blood for a sacrifice to her Dark Lady. Pulling her blades back, she slammed them into him again. It felt exactly like her first kill. The hot, sweaty, sweet sensation of blood covering her hands. Ryn breathed heavily as life left his body. He slumped to the side, and the room turned red.

Ilara met Valette's eyes as Chek'Va returned. Valette let go of Mal'Evir's blade and rushed to Katri. Akara's Sword disappeared as Ryn died, while Katri slowly morphed back from her wolf form. A deep cut ran from her shoulder to torso. Usually, wounds didn't pass between forms, but Akara's Sword had cut so deep that it wounded her human body.

Valette immediately held out a hand immersed in white light while Ilara rushed to a nearby window. She peered out to see Akara's Eye rising above the horizon. It moved fast across the sky—faster than it should have.

Ilara met Valette's purple-ringed eyes as she returned to the others. The gash across Katri's chest was now healed, the skin pink. She still looked weak. The stone around her was coated with a layer of her blood.

"We'll have to be careful. I'm out of healing," Valette mumbled.

"Ryn wasn't lying. Akara looks to be retaliating directly," Ilara said. Through the windows, she could see the Eye rising in the same place it normally set. It was well on its way here.

"Not good," Katri whispered, her eyes creaking open.

"We have to go on without her," Valette said. "The wound is gone, but I can't return her strength."

"I will carry her," Chek'Va said. Ilara nodded as he picked Katri up from the ground. "My supply of Aox's magic is gone as well, and I've not recovered from my fight with the Almiran. This will be how I can help."

"We need you to defend the doors from retreating Akarans," Ilara said.

Chek'Va looked at Ryn's corpse. "The plan was to use Ryn and Markus as sacrifices to the altar. You need me now."

Ilara's eyes widened when she realized what he was suggesting. She relayed the information to Valette, who nodded her head solemnly.

"He's not wrong," she said, and her eyes darted to the window.

# CHAPTER FORTY-FOUR

# MARKUS

"We must get to the altar quickly," Valette shouted as Ilara and Chek'Va hurried up the stairs behind her. From the top of the tower, she could see Akara's Eye with clarity. It was moving across the sky with frightening urgency.

Valette was no stranger to Akara moving her Eye. It was a common battle tactic of the Akaran clergy. When the seasons of your enemy were unexpectedly disrupted by the presence of Akara's Eye, crops starved. It was an effective way to break an enemy's supply lines. Usually a city sieged like this would surrender in days, rather than engage in an extended campaign.

With the one city that didn't, Akara had rained fire from the heavens.

Valette knew what option Akara's dark passengers would choose. Zal'Keratha had said they didn't yet know how to use all of the powers Akara had bestowed on them. They had clearly experimented successfully with Ryn, and it worried Valette that they might soon figure it out.

Glancing down, she could see Al-Kaise's assault on the small encampment outside the Dominion. They were clearly overwhelmed.

"Sophia," Ilara said. She'd crept up next to Valette and placed a hand on the tall glass window. Valette made eye contact with her for the first time since they'd killed Ryn. Ilara's dark eyes were filled with worry. "They don't have much time."

"Through here," Valette said, and walked quickly to the large oak door that led to the room where the Syl had taken place. A memory of Tezza flashed through her mind. This was where they'd met that night several weeks ago. When they'd made plans as if they'd have a tomorrow. They hadn't known Tezza wouldn't live another day.

Valette shook her head as she muscled the door open. Now was not the time to think like this.

*"Your will is strong."*

As they strode inside, Valette could almost hear the echoes of laughter as she stared across the large circular mattress.

"This matches Sophia's vision," Ilara said as she took in the naked statues on the walls. "I'd never have imagined that Akara would allow a place like this."

"She wouldn't. Tezza was foggy on the details, but this place was built long before Akara had anything to do with it," Valette said.

"Sophia said there was a trap door in the center of the room." Ilara began moving the mattress from its stone dais.

Valette ran her hands along the stone carvings. Each of the statues had empty eye sockets, as if gems had fallen from them.

"I never asked how you knew this place existed," Ilara said as Katri and Chek'Va entered the room. The gold-scaled Aoxian panted loudly, setting Katri on her feet. She leaned against the wall to let him rest.

"Almir was worried. I came to Eversburg, not to seek out the lone Zal'Kerathan, but to learn more about Akara's clergy here. Almir believed that they were sabotaging Akara's rule as queen. I never expected the effort to be led by the Voice, nor that Almir would want to side with her," Valette said.

"Or the cause for Akara's change, no doubt," Ilara said.

Valette noticed one of the statues still had one of its eyes. "No, I couldn't have predicted that," she said as she walked over to it. She rubbed the jade gemstone, which seemed loose in the socket.

"There is a trapdoor here. I don't see a way to open it, though," Ilara said just as Valette pressed on the jade eye.

A loud click came from the center of the room, and a ring seemed to slide out of the trapdoor. Ilara muscled up a large, square stone from beneath where the mattress had been.

"Where do you hide your most shameful secrets?" she asked.

"I don't think 'under the bed' really qualifies in this situation," Katri groaned.

"I was going to say 'in a place you don't want to acknowledge,'" Ilara said, her hand on the sheath at her waist. "The two of you should wait here. He's definitely down there."

"Zal'Keratha was clear we couldn't trust the two of you alone. We're coming," Katri said.

Ilara looked to Valette, who shrugged. "I agree. We need Chek'Va to come down," she said, and approached the trapdoor. A set of deep spiral stairs greeted her, with walls close enough that it would be impossible to enter while wearing armor.

Valette wished they'd had time for her to rip her armor off Ryn. Or to pry free the sword stuck in his gauntlet. She felt vulnerable without plate on her back or a weapon in her hand. She was going to need to pull out her new talents.

Chek'Va held up his hand, and a small flame grew in his palm and flickered there. It provided enough light for Valette to find her footing.

The stone stairs were ancient, though they still had sharp edges, as if unweathered by thousands of steps over thousands of years. They all descended in silence, past where Valette guessed the cathedral lay, lower than the Tribunal hall, and lower than the main entrance of the Solar Dominion. Valette was certain that all that surrounded them was earth.

After many minutes of walking, they reached the bottom. A doorless entryway greeted them, which opened into a much larger room containing a big table with three chairs around it, emerging from the floor as if carved from the stone. Two of the chairs had rivulets that ran from the arms into the floor. Similar grooves covered the table, seemingly forming runes that overlapped in a dizzying pattern.

"The Altar of Akara," Valette whispered as the group fanned out around it.

"The Altar of Ascension," Ilara said.

A voice rang out from behind the chair farthest from the entrance. "I hope it is obvious how this will work." Markus stepped from the shadows and placed his hands on the shoulders of the stone chair in front of him.

His head had grown noticeably since Valette last saw him, and he had a large black dot in the center of his forehead. As he stepped further into Chek'Va's light, Valette realized that it was made up of hundreds of small eye tattoos packed tightly together.

"Three Chosen sit together. Two get their arms slit, and the third ascends. The others—"

"Bleed to death," Valette said.

Markus nodded gravely. "Which is why I'm so glad you brought me more than enough Chosen to work with."

"I think you'll find this will work much differently than you think," Valette said, bringing her hands up to frame her face like a boxer. She cut a burly frame, but this seemed ridiculous. Best not to show her hand to soon.

Markus barked a laugh. "Chosen Bilaut, you know as well as I that Akara suffers a mortal affliction. If one of us doesn't deal with her soon, we'll find that Aerlia will change drastically. I would much rather leave Almir's Chosen alive. You were, after all, such a useful pawn."

Valette moved when Ilara did. Ilara formed daggers, while a purple blade etched itself into Valette's grip.

Markus was faster. His hands flew out in front of him, and a faint beam of blue light snaked through the air toward Valette like lighting. Her mind exploded with searing pain. It was like her head had filled with so much water that it was exploding from her eyes and ears. She crumpled to the ground when she realized blood was running down her face.

Ilara fell as well, hands holding her head.

Markus marched forward as Chek'Va snarled. Valette heard another set of thumps as the Aoxian, then Katri, fell. The seconds stretched to hours as the pain in her head flared.

There had to be something she could do. During the moments she could open her eyes, she saw Markus put Katri and Chek'Va into two of the stone chairs. Valette fought the pain as she shakily put her palm to the ground and pushed herself up. In an effort that felt Pantheonic, she raised her hand toward Markus.

He looked over a moment too late.

"Trabema lucin!" she yelled.

A beam of light connected with his shoulder. He grunted, and the pain in Valette's mind subsided. He aimed another spell at her, but she tapped into a new tract. A glowing purple sword created itself in her hand. As Markus fired his spell, she deflected the lightning with the blade. It collided against the wall with a spark.

Ilara pounced toward him like a panther. She had a dagger in her hand—a dagger made of black metal.

Valette was on her feet as Markus shot another spell and blasted her in the chest. She suddenly felt weak, like she was fighting off exhaustion. Stumbling, she caught herself on the chair Katri was tied to.

In one swift move, Ilara stabbed Markus through the chest.

# Chapter Forty-Five

# DEATH

The battlefield brightened as Akara's Eye hung overhead. Sophia scanned the battlefield, intense rays of sunlight baking her skin. Revolutionaries were brandishing black metal weapons against leagues of Akara's Chosen, and both sides were suffering heavy losses. Akara's Chosen were toppling as the blades drank their blood, and revolutionaries were pulling away barely wounded.

Sophia's battalion of soldiers smashed into the line of paladins like drunk tomcats. She felt their minds, melded with hers, felt the power of Balan coursing over their weapons, and felt the surety of their hearts as they killed more paladins.

They ripped at each other's lines. Swords and spears shoved into men as if they were living pincushions, so much so that the ground under them became coated with blood and gore. Sophia tried not to think about it, as if she did, she'd surely vomit.

*Try not to think about the lives ended today. This is right. We have to. Kill or be killed.*

*"I warned you of this spell's cost,"* Balan said. There was true sorrow to his tone, as if the god were crying.

Through it all, Sophia continued to strum her lute, though the tune had turned from a confident march to a soft ballad without her realizing it.

These paladins were power incarnate. They held Akara's essence in their souls, and her light shone through the cracks in their skin, each wound letting out more and more of that red glow. To kill one required multiple mortal blows.

And killing her soldiers only required one. Still, they managed to neutralize the first line of paladins, who were still steadily streaming into the Revolution's camp. When one of the fighters Sophia was controlling died, she felt the blow. Each death ripped her soul to shreds.

She moved them cautiously, seeking an engagement that would test their mettle but not end them. There were other pockets of resistance around the camp, solely centered around Lord Fenwald and Desmond.

With renewed vigor, Sophia strummed aggressively, and her soldiers shot forward, tearing into a new group of paladins that stood between her and Desmond. That was when she noticed Tezza's body hanging over her small mass of troops. Her wings of light arched out from cracks that rippled across her back, and she was brandishing coils of light in her hand.

Al-Kaise. Angel of the Qel'm, masquerading as Akara's Sword.

"I shall take great pleasure in consuming your life, Balanite, for the queen of light rules these lands," Al-Kaise rasped.

"I know what you are, demon," Sophia said through gritted teeth. Al-Kaise's frown deepened.

Sophia strummed her lute, and a different melody played. Her hands seem to work on their own as she operated the instrument by pure instinct. When the sound waves came back to her, she reached into them and pulled a soft-green-glowing shield above the line of soldiers in front of her.

Al-Kaise swept forward with her whip a moment later. It cracked against the magical barrier. Sophia gasped as the whip disintegrated. The angel hissed in response, and the soldiers Sophia hadn't enthralled gave a weak-hearted cheer.

Sophia's song became more violent. She directed the waves at Al-Kaise and activated each as it came back. There had to be a way to influence her. Sophia was sure that was the way to win this battle.

The next spell she activated was the one she needed. Sophia felt the resistance of Al-Kaise's mind as Sophia tried to connect to the angel's mind. Then, it felt like she was overfull, like a barrel holding too much water. Her brain prickled as she pushed through the flaming pain in her skull.

Relief.

All Sophia's thoughts, feelings, and fears melded together, and she dissipated. She was left with a calm that came from a life filled with meditation and soft pleasures. One where her songs were sung across the land.

She was old, at the end of her years. She rocked in that same rocking chair her mother had sat in. No longer was it broken into pieces. Sophia held a half-knit stocking in her frail hand. It would take her a few more hours to finish, then Baphim would have warm feet.

*No.* She frowned. This wasn't her life. This was an illusion her spell must have reflected. When she opened her eyes, she saw herself from above. Her soldiers' eyes had the empty look of death as they lay on the ground.

Al-Kaise's wicked whip was in her hands, and a jagged smile crossed her face. The battlefield faded. Sophia heard a distant scream.

"A worm has crawled into my head," Al-Kaise said.

Or had Sophia said that? Her spell hadn't reflected—it was different than she'd anticipated. Her being was intertwined with Al-Kaise's in a way that was intimate, yet deadly. Sophia's body lay exposed while she was here in Al-Kaise's head. But she might be able to influence this demon in some way.

She also knew she could lose herself if Al-Kaise took over again. Sophia's mind wrapped around the goddess's like the embrace of a wrestler, but Al-Kaise gripped back.

Sophia blinked, and when she opened her eyes, they'd untangled, and she was looking from her own eyes back at Al-Kaise's cracked skin. Light writhed from the open wounds on Al-Kaise's arms and torso. They were standing on a plain of white, facing each other with no weapons in hand.

"You've brought us from Eversburg," Sophia said. Panic rose in her, which she was quick to quiet.

"Merely a sanctuary of the mind. You learn to create them when you've lived in seclusion for a thousand years," Al-Kaise said, twirling a finger through what was left of Tezza's hair.

"I've killed countless Chosen across hundreds of stars. None have forced me here. I wonder how powerful this god of yours is, or was it your will that caused him to succeed? In the end, it matters not. He cannot reach you in this place, and I merely need to keep you here while my heavenly host cuts down the rest of your allies."

"Balan could elect another Chosen," Sophia snarled. Desmond would make a good candidate.

"Hardly. He still has all his power nestled in you, or have you forgotten he's no longer in the Pantheon? No lone god has enough power for more than one Chosen. You know these rules. And the power in you is what I will consume. That will leave Balan powerless," Al-Kaise hissed.

The angel took one step toward her, and Sophia panicked. She threw her arms forward, and a raucous melody blared from behind her, as if a thousand voices were singing in symp hony—a melody that created sound waves, even here in the mind of this foreign creature. The waves rippled off Al-Kaise's form and flowed around her, as if she was unaffected by them.

"Who were they? Those who cried out?" Sophia asked.

"The ghosts of the forgotten," Al-Kaise said. "The gods I have consumed, and the Chosen I have devoured. An echo of them will live in me always. The ones you and your tyrant of a god will join when this is all over."

Her flaming eyes burned at Sophia. The angel attempted another step, and Sophia felt the music around her again. It empowered her, and she shoved Al-Kaise back once more.

Sophia heard the song sung by those lost souls. It was familiar, yet it felt ancient, like it had been sung in ages long past in a language Sophia would never know. Consonants danced into vowels and back again, as if the music was woven into speech.

"Fah sah tir a villi," Sophia sang with them, picking a phrase they kept repeating.

Al-Kaise's eyes drooped as she fell to a knee. "What have you done?" Her words sloshed together as if she were drunk.

Sophia smiled to herself, not knowing what Balan had done to give these soft-spoken sounds such power, but grateful just the same.

"No!" Al-Kaise yelled. Her hands balled into fists, and she punched her chest three times in quick succession. A blast sounded in the empty cavern of her mind, and a shock wave erupted from her.

Sophia was knocked to the ground. She gasped. The song still rang out in her head, and she searched each verse for some usable melody. These creatures were telling her something in these strange tongues. She just had to find the right structure. The song looped and layered, which made it harder and harder to understand.

Al-Kaise was on her feet and began to approach Sophia. Her whip was forming in her hand.

"Fera . . . Gipu," Sophia muttered.

"Maybe it would be better to consume your soul now. Make the rest of this so much easier. Al-Haide always tells me I play with my food too much," Al-Kaise growled. "Yet you seem to have been reduced to a mumbling lunatic in the presence of the pure divine. It is such a shame that manifesting ourselves like this requires so much of their power to maintain."

"Flippa . . . santori . . . ra'isti," Sophia said, with more confidence. It was closer, but not right. Al-Kaise was directly over her now. Her whip moved as if it had a mind of its own. The tip curled around Sophia's neck.

"You should see yourself now, grasping for power that you could never understand. Pitiful." Al-Kaise's face contorted into a sneer. The whip tightened, as if trying to cut the words from Sophia's throat.

"Tieru bi fa'isti," Sophia gasped. The song stopped, leaving deafening silence.

The sky above her seemed to break in two. Al-Kaise turned her head up as the wings disappeared from her body. The light from her skin winked out, and she crumpled to the ground. Purple mist seeped through the crack in the sky and settled to the ground.

"No. It cannot be. She cannot be here," Al-Kaise cried.

Sophia kicked herself from Al-Kaise as the whip released its hold. She glanced back to where the mist coalesced into a singular form. It looked like a demon with horns, but Sophia would have recognized Zal'Keratha anywhere.

"Al-Kaise. Sister," the goddess said as she raised a hand to the woman who now kneeled at her feet as if before a queen. "How far have you fallen? Your sanctuary was broken by a mortal."

"I ought to kill you for all you did to me. For all you did to our Qel," Al-Kaise snarled. Sophia thought she saw tears running down the angel's cheeks.

"Oh? You believe Qel treated you better than I? You both always had such an issue with authority. You were a useless Chosen. You twisted the powers I gave you, raising the dead as you did." Zal'Keratha shook her head. "Disgraceful."

Amber light began to flow from Al-Kaise to Zal'Keratha. Al-Kaise shuddered and gasped as the energy intensified and strengthened. She shriveled as she aged, then, mercifully, fell into dust.

Zal'Keratha's eyes flicked to Sophia, who still lay on the ground. "Oh, dear. It looks as if we'll be seeing each other quite soon."

Sophia's eyes stitched together when she felt a stabbing pain in her chest. She clutched at it, or tried to. Her hand rammed into an invisible metal bar that stemmed from the point of pain. It was hard to breathe.

Sophia's vision dimmed, and when she opened her eyes again, she could do so for only a moment.

A thin black metal sword was sticking out of her chest, belonging to Sir Fenwald.

"Apologies. You were but a debt I had to collect. I hope you understand."

# Chapter Forty-Six

# QEL'M

Ilara's dagger pierced Markus's arm, passing through him like it was passing through air. Blood ran up the black metal, every inch of it covering the blade and handle.

He launched himself back, which pulled the weapon from Ilara's hand. He seemed to fade slightly, as if he were getting thinner, and screamed a hollow scream. The dagger's clump of blood and metal flattened, and the black metal flowed over his skin. Markus held his hands in front of his face as he was slowly covered in it.

Ilara took a step back, shocked.

"What have you done?" Valette asked.

Chek'Va struggled against his restraints on the chair. "You play with powers you don't understand. You've put our duty in jeopardy," he hissed.

"Zal'Keratha kept something about the metal from us," Ilara said as her hand formed another dagger. She felt the magic flow from the tracts in her arms, but they didn't empty. The tracts shrunk. "I-I-I didn't know. I thought the only way we could succeed was with this."

Markus fell, covered in thick black slime. His arms cracked and lengthened, followed by his legs and torso. He sobbed and cried in agony as each limb broke and reformed.

The ooze dripped off his face, revealing eyes and a mouth that were sewn shut with the black material. A single, bulging eye was open on his forehead. It was dark as night, with a fleshy pink iris that darted from Ilara to Valette and regarded them with hunger. The creature's arms pulled the rest of the ooze down from its neck, and when it stood, it towered over them.

Its facial features were a distortion of Markus's, elongated as if the face had been stretched by a rolling pin. Terror welled up in Ilara as it stared at her. There was new emptiness in her that she couldn't place.

"*World: Aerlia. Form: Chosen Scholar First Ascension. Gods Assimilated: One,*" the creature said in Ilara's head. It forced its way in like an unwanted guest, sending a twinge of pain across her temple.

Valette's hand darted to her head as if she had heard the creature too.

"*You have called us, Forsaken of Death. You fed us the power of an Ascended Chosen of whose memories I know. I fed also upon a Chosen of Honor and a Chosen of Light, though neither were consumed entirely. One is here now, the other I killed before consumption.*"

"What?" Ilara asked.

"*I am Kal'Teth, Forsaken. I offer power. Power that comes at great price.*" The voice rasped, as if straining for each word.

"You are mistaken. I am Chosen, not Forsaken. You were a knife, and now you have Markus's body? I don't understand. What do you want?" Ilara coiled back and raised her daggers. She wasn't sure who this was, but she knew that anything that lived could die.

Its red eye flicked back to Valette. "*The will of the gods is fickle. They give and take. You have lost favor. My master knows the will of the gods. He rebelled and created his own power. Power you may drink of as well, as I said, at great price.*"

Ilara shook her head. If Zal'Keratha had Forsaken her, she wasn't aware of it. There'd barely been a warning, but it didn't matter right now. Questions about her status as Chosen could wait.

"There is no power outside of the gods. Who is this Qel? Why were you in a dagger?" Ilara asked.

"*The dagger was a vessel for my inert form. Manifesting life outside its intended time takes much power—power you saw fit to provide. Qel was Chosen once, as were you and I. He fought against the gods. You have much more to learn, more questions to ask.*

*"Fear not. We will meet once more, and I will answer them. I pray you learn to ask the right ones. Until then, I have duties to attend to for the coming coronation."*

The creature began to fall apart, like a statue made of ash, its laughter echoing in Ilara's head until it had faded entirely. A blade cut through its foggy form. Valette was standing on the other side of where it had been, hands clenched around that purple sword. A sword given by Zal'Keratha.

Ilara understood then. Her tracts, all half-empty, would never be refilled again. Ryn had been her final offering to Zal'Keratha.

Valette's purple-rimmed eyes were like daggers. "What the hells, Ilara? You've altered the plan a second time."

Before Ilara could respond, Valette lunged forward again. She stabbed toward Ilara's chest. Ilara formed a dagger and knocked the sword to the side. If she was Forsaken, her daggers were limited, and would only last until the magic from Zal'Keratha ran out. She had maybe a dozen left. She didn't have time to wonder where Valette had gotten the blade before it swung at her again.

Still, Valette was slow. The fight with Ryn and Markus had drained her strength. Ilara felt it too—her movements were tired, but she just needed to be quicker than her opponent.

Valette expertly dodged Ilara's riposte, and a second later, a small version of Almir's shield collided with her face. She hit the stone floor with a grunt, and one of her daggers clanged away and immediately disappeared. Warm blood seeped from her nose. Ilara struggled up and found the point of Valette's blade in her face. She blinked and waited for Valette to run her through.

Instead, Katri's large, furry hand landed on Valette's shoulder. Her human face looked back at her. In the rush, she'd changed only her hands into paws to escape Markus's bonds.

"Explain yourself, Ilara," Katri said. Her face was hard and unforgiving.

"I didn't know that would happen, if that's what you're asking. Zal'Keratha has been secretive about these weapons, but I knew they countered Chosen powers. I thought we might need them against Ryn or Markus. It turns out I was right. Markus was illusory. His body wasn't actually here. Our weapons would have passed through him. The black metal didn't."

Valette relaxed visibly and nodded. She dismissed the sword she was holding and put her hands on her hips. "Zal'Keratha predicted as much. She insisted that she wouldn't give you the strength to overcome this obstacle. The blade was the power she offered."

Ilara nodded slowly.

"She insists that you're out of line," said Katri. "She's screaming in all of our heads that you summoned a Qel'm to Aerlia intentionally. She's offering an angelic ascension if we kill you."

Forsaken. Ilara had never in her life thought that the word would apply to her. It stung in a way she wasn't prepared for.

She glanced down at the dagger clutched in her hand, her bruised and bloodied face reflecting in the metal. Blood smeared her mouth like gory lipstick.

"Fine," Ilara said. "If you have to kill me, then make it quick. I don't want to live in this world of gods anymore."

Valette shook her head. "Zal'Keratha does not force our hand. And, as I see it, we still need you to complete the ritual. You cannot ascend any longer. That has been my duty."

"What do you mean?" Katri asked.

"Zal'Keratha Chose me when she sent me back. I will be ascending to Akara's domain. With Markus's death, if that's what we'd call it, I'll need either of you to be sacrifices along with Chek'Va. We don't have time to trek back to the battlefield and try to pull one of Akara's other Chosen. Akara's Eye is probably already above us."

The silence hung between them as Katri met Ilara's eyes. It should be her. It should be Ilara who went. But there was something that drew her back to the world. She wanted to live for Sophia, now that she could finally be free. But she knew Katri would want the same thing.

"I'll go," Katri said, her mouth forming a line. She turned and quickly stalked back to the ritual seat.

"Katri, I don't think you should do that." Ilara sprang from the floor and placed a hand on her shoulder. "I can still go in your place. Is my sister not worth living for?"

"Of course she is," Katri said, shaking her head. "Sophia is like the light that reflects off a still summer pond. She is everything that makes this world good. I must make Aerlia safe, and if that means we kill a god, then we kill a god.

"You can't do this, Ilara. You finally have what you want. We both know you're too selfish for this. Take your sister and your son somewhere safe, away from Zal'Keratha and the worries of this life. My life was over when Akara killed my tribe. I have nothing but Sophia. And she deserves someone better."

Ilara grabbed Katri's shoulders and pulled her close. "So you're sure of this? I'm going to miss you. Gods know I'm not looking forward to cutting into you."

"I'm sorry," Katri said, pulling away. "I'll need you to hold the knife. I can't cut myself. Believe me, I've tried."

"Can we trust you with that, Ilara?" Valette asked.

"You're asking me to kill the only ally who hasn't tried to stab me in the back," Ilara said.

"I know. If things were different, we wouldn't have to. I'm contracted to get Zal'Keratha to the throne. It was the only way I could come back," Valette said.

Ilara shrugged. "No one asked you to do that."

"Aye, but I had to. You put me in that position, swayed by Zal'Keratha or not. I have kids, and a duty to them and Almir. One that I cannot forsake as you did."

Ilara cringed at the slight. Perhaps it was fair. Perhaps it wasn't. Then again, she had killed Valette. Zal'Keratha may have asked her to, but any sane person would have told her to shove it.

"Killing people was the one thing I couldn't bleeding fuck up. I might as well make sure that these two go out well. You seem earnest, at least. You'd make a better goddess than I would. Don't trust her completely," Ilara said, as resolutely as she could.

"Good. I have no choice but to trust you, as much as I hate to now. There's no time to track down another. Know that if you fail this, Zal'Keratha will kill you and Sophia, as well as a boy named Theo." She paused as if waiting for a reaction, then turned for the only chair that  wasn't occupied.

Katri's hands bent and cracked until they were back in their human form.

Ilara composed herself and followed Valette. She didn't look at Ilara as she approached.

Valette pointed to one side of the table. It was covered in runes, but they were separated into several sections. "You'll need to read these after you complete the sacrifices." She indicated a set that were clear instructions, while others were detailed history. "We have to start now. Everything is prepared."

Ilara placed her hand on the altar and felt its age through the weathered stone. She didn't know when it had last been gazed upon by mortal eyes. A hundred years ago? A thousand? She realized Valette was waiting for a response when she asked another question.

"Why did you give into the temptation of the metal? Surely you felt how it affected the Chosen bond."

"I did. I was glad to have Zal'Keratha out of my head. Not to mention, it was a solution to a problem I didn't need to rely on her for."

"It is odd, then, that Zal'Keratha trusted you. Surely she knew your feelings," Valette said.

"It doesn't matter. I think she knew I never trusted the gods as much as someone like you. It is easy to trust when you've had an easy life," Ilara said.

"I never thought I had an easy life," Valette scoffed. "Though I suppose none of us had a choice in the gods we served."

"I'm seeing more and more that we always had a choice," Ilara said. There was a sadness in her that ached. She moved slowly around the altar, as if drawing out the process. She let out another breath. "If you think you can't trust me, know I do what I do for Katri and Chek'Va. That is all."

Valette nodded and began to speak a set of incantations in front of her. The runes on the altar came to life with a dull red light, and a piece of stone popped out from the edge of the table. Valette drew it forth and held it out to Ilara. It was a small, curved obsidian blade.

"It has begun. Don't do anything that would cause Zal'Keratha to smite you," Valette said as Ilara took the ritual blade.

Ilara walked to Chek'Va, who had secured his straps. She placed the dagger against his arm, aimed at one of his veins. His expression was stony as he faced death.

"You've been a trustworthy ally these last few weeks," Ilara said as she readied herself.

"Get on with it, Forsaken. Take my life as you have so many others. Let us not pretend it was anything more than a beneficial partnership."

"Aye, then," Ilara said. She cut his forearms from elbow to wrist. He did little more than wince. She placed her hands over his eyes as she spoke. "Rest in Death, warrior of the true Aoxia." It was the last sentence of a lengthy poem sung at the funeral of each Aoxian who died in defense of their kingdom.

Chek'Va smiled, as if he were seeing the fields of his homeland. His blood flowed freely into the grooves cut into the stone arm of the chair. His gaze was far-off, and his smile faded.

Katri shifted in her chair as Ilara took up the same position by her. Ilara hesitated. None of this felt right.

"I wouldn't want anyone else to see my last moments," Katri said, as if sensing her thoughts.

Ilara took that as a sign and made the cuts. Katri gasped, and the blood began to run down her arms.

"I didn't expect it to hurt so much," she said, tears forming in her eyes. "Too late for regrets. Tell Sophia I'm sorry."

Ilara pressed her lips to Katri's forehead. Her friend's breaths grew shorter and shorter. Bleeding out took longer than many other deaths. It wouldn't have been the one Ilara would have chosen for either of these Chosen.

Their blood now covered the altar, transported in rivulets through the grooves carved in the chair arms into the runes that lined the table. Each rune filled to the point of overflowing.

Ilara chanted the ones that Valette had indicated. The words were weighty with power and the runes filled with blood as she spoke them. The blood of her friends.

A dull red hue filled the room as the altar glowed brighter. Rings of blood beneath each chair lit up, casting a similar glow on the faces of the sacrifices. Valette's chair took on the color that dominated the altar as another scarlet circle lit under her. Ilara heard her say something, but a hum filled the room and drowned out any and all sounds.

The ring of light became stronger and stronger, until it was fully opaque, completely obscuring them all.

# Chapter Forty-Seven

# LATINYTH

AMBER LIGHT FILLED VALETTE'S vision as the chair beneath her disappeared. Her body felt light, as if she were in a state of in-between—not quite where she'd been, but not where she was going.

When her eyes creaked open, she was standing on a golden disk hovering over the clouds. Almir stood stoically next to her, his hands planted on his armored hips. He was wearing an off-white tabard over his silver armor. His holy symbol of a fist haloed by a half disk was embroidered in large swooping lines across his chest.

Standing on a separate disc, Valette recognized Zal'Keratha, who adjusted her rumpled skirt as wind swooshed by them. The discs were taking them high up into the blue sky toward a larger golden disk.

"Valette," Zal'Keratha said as she eyed Almir. He hadn't moved his gaze from Zal'Keratha for several minutes. "How are you feeling?"

"Bloated, like I ate too much and need to hurl," Valette answered.

"I imagine so." Almir's words sounded muffled through the faceplate of his armor. "You are the only mortal to be Chosen by two gods at the same time."

"I didn't know that was possible."

"Yes. If only such a thing weren't necessary," Zal'Keratha said. "This was the only way to make sure I could see my sister. You feel ill because our energies are combining to fill your tracts at twice the usual rate. Casting will lessen the effect."

"And how did you know Ilara would summon this thing?" Almir asked.

Valette called forth her blade and shield, let them fall away, and did so again. It relieved the pain in her chest and arms marginally. She chanced a glance upward as they passed through a cloud, wiping away the condensation that built up on her face. A gigantic golden disk seemed to hang high in the air. It was so large that it blotted out the sun above it.

"Please, Almir. I've watched Ilara for the entirety of her life. I knew she would disobey my orders. And one does not disobey a god without consequences," Zal'Keratha said.

"And why trust her in the first place?" Almir asked. "Not to mention that you could have given her the sword you gave Valette."

"She hadn't directly disobeyed me up to that point. One does not punish an act that hasn't yet occurred."

"What is this place?" Valette asked, looking down over the side of the disk. Through the clouds, she could see ruined buildings covering the ground below. She didn't see an end to them. It was like a city that had no boundary.

Zal'Keratha peered over the edge as well. "Latinyth. Akara's home. The place where she lived as a child and where she chose to rule from when she became a goddess. It was untouched by Qel. This place was ruined by Akara's people."

"Qel was what Ilara created?" Valette asked.

Almir hummed.

"No. What Ilara created was of Qel. They call themselves the Qel'm," Zal'Keratha said.

"You said before that one inhabited Tezza—that was Al-Kaise—but Ilara manifested one from a black metal dagger. How is that possible?" Valette asked.

"The Qel'm feed on divine magics. Al-Kaise consumed Akara's magic to enter Aerlia from Latinyth. The one Ilara created was dormant. It awakened when she fed it enough magic."

A sun the color of blood shone high above them as their disks merged with the gigantic one, like drops of water joining a larger body. The golden disk stretched out for miles, an empty plane of endless nothing.

"And here is Aerlia's Pantheon," Zal'Keratha said. "The magic of all the gods, gathered into this massive disk."

"A massive waste is what it ended up being," Almir said.

"Yes," Zal'Keratha said, nodding slightly. "It hampered all the gods to the point where they couldn't resist Akara's reign. Our goal lies to the center of this place."

No clouds hung above them. There would be no reprieve from that massive red sun, which seemed to take up the entire sky. Heat pulsed from it, and Valette began sweating in moments.

"Whoever's Eye that is hasn't lost any power," she huffed.

The fullness in her chest was making her more and more uncomfortable. Without thinking, she called forth Almir's shield and sighed in relief as the magic left her body. She held it over her, but the opaque shield offered little in terms of shade. She dismissed it and summoned another.

"No god rules this star," Zal'Keratha said as she began to stride forward. Valette and Almir fell in behind her. "As with most places in this universe, this place has been cleansed of gods. It seems there are fewer and fewer of us as each millennium passes."

Almir hummed again.

"What will we do if she is dead?" Valette asked. It felt wrong to say Akara's name now.

"She is. Otherwise, you will kill her. I will mourn, then prepare," Zal'Keratha said.

Valette didn't bother to ask anything further. The gods said what they meant, and that was enough. With Zal'Keratha especially, everything she said seemed like a performance. Whatever her true intentions were, they would not be evident from her words.

Despite her efforts, Valette had to stop the group several times to catch her breath. Oppressive as the heat was, Zal'Keratha set a wicked pace. Both of the divinities seemed unaffected by their surroundings.

It occurred to Valette that she'd never before been around a divinity as much as she had been on this trip, despite being Chosen. Almir usually chose quick, quiet moments in which to show himself. Never had he manifested for as long as the hours it took them to reach their destination.

Valette was in the midst of wondering if Ilara was plagued by Zal'Keratha constantly when she saw it—a speck on the horizon, which she would have attributed to a mirage if Zal'Keratha hadn't pointed it out.

Akara's throne.

They were still far away when the stench hit Valette. A wave of nausea poured over her, and she couldn't help but wretch as it overpowered her senses. It was like a dozen crates of rotten fruit had been left in a ship's hold for three voyages past their destination.

"It would be better for you both to wait here," Zal'Keratha said.

"No," Valette and Almir said in unison.

"I must finish my duty," Almir added with firmness.

"And I mine." Valette gave him a nod. The tightness in her chest had returned. She let the purple straight sword fill her hand. She didn't need to speak words, but simply willed it into existence.

The goddess nodded, and the two drew closer to Akara's throne. The stench was coming in waves now, and grew stronger the closer they came. Valette found ways to power through it.

Thoughts of her family worked best. Without prompting, she saw them dead, wicked Aoxian arrows riddling their bodies. The death of her husband came next—his handsome face dismembered by Akara's faithful as he was accused of being a revolutionary. Her children, being stoned by those same revolutionaries for being raised among the faithful.

Valette tried to divert her mind, but she saw them die again, and again, as she walked forward. Were these visions of the future or merely visions given to her by creatures who saw their own death in her stride?

When the throne came into view, Valette immediately wished she could blot the image from her mind. Akara's helm rested on a body that was pruned and slumped to one side. The throne itself was made of a textured black material, and her hands were splayed across the arms. Her fingers tapped furiously at the buttons raised there.

Her skin was unnaturally pale, and her jaw was slack. A crack in her visor allowed Valette to see her eyes dart to Zal'Keratha as she approached. Her mouth began to open and close erratically.

"H-h-hel—" Akara rasped.

*Gods. She is alive!*

"Creature of Qel," Zal'Keratha said.

*"Another divine being for my control, for the will of All. Do you, Mistress of Death, wish for our power?"* the voice rasped,

like the Qel'm in the altar room had. *"Two is too much for Us. Generating Another."*

"Use the blade, Valette," Zal'Keratha said.

Valette glanced at her hand. She didn't remember summoning Zal'Keratha's blade, but it was there nonetheless. The smooth metal felt like it weighed nothing.

"Do it, woman. Or do you deny the will of the gods?" Zal'Keratha asked.

Tentatively, Valette stepped toward Akara. Wheezed, panic breaths choked through the goddess's mouth as Valette brought the sword to her throat. There was strained panic in her eyes as Valette pressed it to her collar bone.

No blood came as the sword pressed back. Akara let out a chilling howl, her mouth opening wider than it should have. Valette pressed the blade in until it struck the stone chair, then fell back. Akara struggled against it. The weapon jostled uncomfortably and threatened to loose the creature on the band of gods and mortal.

At that moment, a scythe appeared in Zal'Keratha's hand, and she decapitated the goddess. Almir gasped as her head fell to the ground. Zal'Keratha bent down and picked it up.

"Bloody hells, she was alive!" Almir hissed.

Zal'Keratha dropped her scythe, which fractured into a thousand jagged  pieces that quickly disappeared. A dagger formed in her hand, and she immediately drove it into Akara's skull.

Screeching filled Valette's mind as Zal'Keratha used the blade to pull out a slug the size of Akara's head. Its flesh was segmented, and it writhed against Zal'Keratha's grasp. The point of her dagger had pierced its side.

With the expertise of a surgeon, Zal'Keratha sliced it open to spill a dark sludge from its body onto the Pantheon's golden surface. It sat there a moment before searing off, like a shameful stain. Zal'Keratha looked at Valette's shocked face.

"Bloody hell," Valette said, backing away instinctively.

"There was no saving her." Zal'Keratha dropped the remains of the head to the side. She strode forward and pushed Akara's corpse out of the throne. It slumped forward awkwardly, more black blood seeping from the stump of the neck.

Zal'Keratha sat on the now vacant throne and began tapping furiously on the armrests. She glanced once more at Almir. He sank to one knee and bowed his head. Valette remained standing.

"You wish to ascend to Akara's place?" Zal'Keratha asked.

"As I should have a century ago. Aerlia needs a god of light to smite her enemies. It no longer needs a god of honor," Almir said.

Zal'Keratha nodded, and with a flick of her hand, the surface of the Pantheon below him warped and jumped upward. It covered every inch of him in light, and he seeped into the ground.

"What the fuck?" Valette asked.

"He will emerge greater than he entered. You will find that you are no longer his Chosen," Zal'Keratha said.

"What? I thought I would become a god."

Zal'Keratha shrugged as she went back to plucking at the controls. "No god of Aerlia determines who becomes a god or not. I promised that to Ilara, just as Akara promised that to Almir. Neither of us had the power to do so. Akara just got lucky that Almir was ready. Now, your god of honor and justice will cease to guard the tenet of honor on Aerlia. He will be reborn the god of sunlight and justice. Therefore, your contract with him as his Chosen has been broken," Zal'Keratha said, pursing her lips.

Valette moved close enough to the throne to see that the arm was covered in little raised buttons and several flashing red lights. There was script on the interface that she couldn't read.

"Worth noting," Zal'Keratha continued. "Our deal is over as well. You shall cease to be my Chosen when you return to Aerlia."

"So I will be Forsaken?" Valette asked.

"Hardly. Forsaken are forbidden from seeking another deity. Another may Choose you, though I will make sure that the magic in your tracts is continually renewed. The ones we forged will remain, as will Almir's," Zal'Keratha said.

Valette crossed her arms. "Gods give nothing for free."

Zal'Keratha smiled. "Indeed not. Truthfully, a god has not given up a Chosen since before Akara introduced permanent Chosen a thousand years ago. I find myself loathe to see you go, but I believe, more so than ever before, that you should be free to choose. You may work outside the gods if you wish, but I would desire for you to be my Chosen."

"The first of many, as Akara had?" Valette asked.

Zal'Keratha pressed a button, and the disk lurched, which threw Valette to the ground. A loud, churning noise began to thump below her and grew steadily louder. It caused the whole of the plane to shake and vibrate. The red sun above blurred and faded as the sky darkened.

The dark of night cloaked them now, lit only by new stars. The Pantheon beneath Valette glowed a soft purple to match the change in the sky. She didn't know how she knew, but she was in a different place.

"No," Zal'Keratha finally answered. "I will Choose several, to be sure. The power of the Pantheon must return to the gods of Aerlia. We all must gather Chosen to defend our world from the Qel'm. All those I can convince, at least. I will retain some of the Pantheon's power to maintain my place as queen, but I will not rule from fear. They fear Death enough as it is."

Valette furrowed her brow as she sat upon the Pantheon. It was cool to the touch now, and she suppressed a shiver as she stood. Being the Chosen of the queen was tempting. She knew that she would have plenty of power, but there would be just as much responsibility.

Then she thought about her children. She hadn't seen or heard from them in a half year. How much more would she miss if she accepted this offer?

But, she'd always have magic in her tracts. Did that power mean she had certain responsibilities to Aerlia? To eradicate those creatures and the countless black metal pieces they inhabited?

"You do not need to agree now," Zal'Keratha said, as if sensing Valette's hesitation. "Know that it is an open invitation."

"Aye. I must think on it," Valette said.

"I will send you back to your world now. Know that I will be forever grateful to both you and Almir."

Wisps of purple energy sprang from the Pantheon and latched on to Valette's palm. Valette grabbed them with clutched fists as they pulled her down into the suddenly soft ground. She was surrounded by that lavender essence, which smelled strongly of flowers.

When it faded, Valette was in a room similar to the one she'd left Aerlia in, a circular stone altar in front of her and a short stone staircase beyond that. Sunlight shone through a doorway at the top of the stairs.

Neatly stacked next to her was a set of armor. She recognized it as her own when she spied the broken gauntlet from her fight with Ryn. She wondered briefly how Zal'Keratha had returned it, as she'd last seen it being worn by the knight commander.

Valette sat next to that armor until the sunlight faded to darkness. By the time she stood, she'd come to a decision. She needed to go see Antony.

# Chapter Forty-Eight

# DEFIANCE

# EPILOGUE

Kal'Teth waited on a scorched marble balcony as he watched the building burn across the city. Mortals were strange beings. The city's embers had hardly died before they set it on fire again. It was likely a symbol he couldn't understand. He could barely remember the life he'd lived on his forgotten home world. It never bothered him that he couldn't remember.

Eversburg would survive. Like a phoenix reborn, it would become something different, but of the same form. Cities were like that. Get enough people together, and they would control at least the surrounding area—sometimes a continent. Only in such a horrible place would people decide that they could rule over others simply because they had a larger stick.

He held his hand out and gazed down at his elongated fingers. What a pitiful resemblance to the form he'd once had. These humans were so small. The last world they'd consumed had held creatures of much longer proportions. His movements in this body were stunted in comparison, as if he was constantly moving farther than he felt he had to. Such were the consequences of transposition.

"When is the last time you were alive?"

Pulled from his thoughts, Kal'Teth turned to see the woman they called Theyda. Her red cloak, stained with blood and soot, hung limply over her shoulders. Her bald head shone in the light of the Eye in the sky.

*"I have always been alive. A pleasant form you have brought me, however. I understand your mistress worked very hard for this meeting,"* Kal'Teth said. *"Not to understate the work that you did, as well."*

"Indeed, I did. The fates are fickle creatures. They endeavored just as much to keep you from seeing the light of our Eye," Theyda said. She leaned against the railing of the balcony to take in the same sight Kal'Teth was looking at.

*"As they would. This power of Ameri's is unlike anything else. I feel it is less useful than she gives it credit for. Though I find these visions are somewhat random. It must take one such as yourself much time to interpret them."*

Theyda laughed. "It is not as difficult as it seems. Once you start to see the branches, it comes quite easily."

*"So it will,"* Kal'Teth said. *"My last form had such great strength that I could keep the earth from quaking. Mountains*

*were built and destroyed at my whim. This will take more skill to master, I think.*"

"You must know the what Ameri wants."

"*Knowledge and power, I would surmise. That is what they all want when they bring us here. Though I have not processed as to what end.*"

"Ameri would like to rule," Theyda told him.

"*She could have had the throne of the Pantheon with Markus's ploy. She did not accept that,*" Kal'Teth said.

"Aerlia is a start, yet she has grander designs."

"*Qel will require an offering for his services.*"

"And he will have it." Theyda produced a small amber crystal and held it out.

Kal'Teth took it with his elongated fingers. "*You have more of these?*"

"Many."

"*Then, this will be the start of a beautiful partnership.*"

www.ingramcontent.com/pod-product-compliance
Lightning Source LLC
Chambersburg PA
CBHW061030310726
48969CB00004B/899